RACHEL

AMETHYSTS
& ALCHEMY

© 2024 Lightning Conjurer Books, LLC

All rights reserved. No portion of this book may be reproduced in any form without permission from the author, except for the use of brief quotations in a book review.

This is a work of fiction. Names, characters, businesses, places, events, locales, and incidents are either the products of the author's imagination or used in a fictitious manner. Any resemblance to actual persons, living or dead, or actual events is purely coincidental.

ASIN: B0D7KKBC7T
ISBN: 9798328534154

Obligatory Disclaimer: The fictional stunts written in this fictional book were performed by fictional characters living in a fictional world. In other words, DO NOT EAT ROCKS. Seriously. Your tummy, teeth, and health insurance will thank you.

Also, don't ever, ever, *ever* go exploring in abandoned mines, especially by yourself. There are approximately 1,001 ways to die in them, none of which are painless or pleasant.

Lastly, and most importantly, no pigs were harmed in the plotting of this book.

Other Works by Rachel Rener:

The Gilded Blood Series
I. Inked
II. Jinxed
III. Linked
IV. Synced

The Lightning Conjurer Series
I. The Awakening
II. The Enlightening
III. The Christening
IV. The Reckoning

The Bone Whisperer Chronicles
I. The Girl Who Talks to Ashes
II. The Boy Who Lurks in Shadows

Amethysts & Alchemy

The Little Morsel

The Pilfered Quill

The Precipice of Sin
(As part of the *From the Shadows* Anthology)

Autographed Books Available At
www.RachelRener.com

Table of Contents

Foreword 8
Chapter 1 11
Chapter 2 19
Chapter 3 30
Chapter 4 39
Chapter 5 53
Chapter 6 64
Chapter 7 77
Chapter 8 89
Chapter 9 102
Chapter 10 119
Chapter 11 136
Chapter 12 152
Chapter 13 165
Chapter 14 179
Chapter 15 192
Chapter 16 203
Chapter 17 213
Chapter 18 223
Chapter 19 234
Chapter 20 245
Chapter 21 254
Chapter 22 266
Chapter 23 276
Chapter 24 290
Chapter 25 304
Chapter 26 325

Real-Life Photos 347
Mineral Classifications 348
The Gilded Blood Series 352
The Lightning Conjurer Series 353
The Little Morsel 355
The Pilfered Quill 356
Acknowledgements 358
About the Author 359

This book is for anyone who has ever been called weird, annoying, or a "know-it-all." Your weirdness is always welcome here.

—RR

Foreword

I used to eat rocks as a child.

Pebbles, gravel, and even small river stones held a strange and inexplicable allure over me. I would lie awake at night, thinking about all the minerals buried in the ground, just waiting to be unearthed – dozens and dozens of complex flavors I couldn't even begin to imagine. Wherever my parents took me, and regardless of how fiercely they reprimanded me, I would put rocks in my mouth. The pediatrician diagnosed me with pica, a mental health disorder in which a person compulsively eats non-food items. They tried to medicate me, but it didn't work. They tried intensive therapy to no avail. My parents tried every trick in the book, ranging from begging to bribery, followed by increasingly severe punishments that had little effect on me. I couldn't stop. My dentist bills, I'm frequently reminded, were through the roof. In fact, by the age of seventeen, my parents had to sell one of their two cars in order to afford a full set of dental implants to replace the teeth I'd ruined with what my therapist described as "massively disordered eating compulsions resulting from unverified childhood traumas."

Because of that, I rarely smile.

It wouldn't be until much later that I would understand that the all-consuming, insatiable cravings that spurred me to eat a variety of rocks and minerals weren't just a simple matter of pica, but an innate yearning for the powerful "essence" contained within those rocks and minerals. The purer the mineral, and the clearer the crystal, the more potent its essence; tourmaline for speed, celestine for strength, augite for powerful laxative effect that can only be assuaged by the smallest pinch of biotite lest you want to be intestinally backed up for a week.

I had to learn that the hard way.

Not just about gastrointestinal-interfering minerals, but all of the effects of every mineral on the planet – all 5,500 of them. In my twenty-eight years, I've cataloged the effects of 1,396 minerals, ranging from super-hearing to magnesis to uncontrollable flatulence. Some of the effects are minimal, others are extraordinary, and I find that the more toxic an element – arsenopyrite, for example – the more potent its effect. The arbitrary "value" of a mineral, on the other hand, means nothing; most diamonds, for example, are rarely worth swallowing, unless you can get your hands on the black ones, which are commonly sold as drill bits by ignorant troglodytes who know nothing of innate value.

But, as I'm often told, I digress.

While I'd prefer to tell you my unique story from the time of conception, I'm reminded that most people only care about the big picture – the hook, so to speak. So I've been advised to begin this tale not with an in-depth catalog of all the minerals I've tried and tested over the years, but with something exciting and adventurous, preferably filled with lots of danger and steamy romance. And so, with as minimal detail as possible, I'll begin my story a mere fourteen months ago, with something exciting and dangerous, though admittedly lacking in lurid sexual exploits…at the beginning, at least.

Chapter 1

As I dangled from my rope, clutching the fraying nylon for dear life while the light of my lantern flickered weakly from the bottom of the forty-foot mineshaft I'd inadvertently fallen into, it occurred to me that this was not the most ideal situation. It was just after midnight, and the first time I'd checked out this particular abandoned mine, known for its copper deposits and "worthless" gangue minerals like galena and pyrite – both highly effective at enhancing knowledge absorption and memory retrieval, respectively. The husband of one of my favorite clients was suffering from late-stage Alzheimer's, and his wife had prepaid a pretty penny for one of my patented "Memory Serums." Unfortunately, that meant traipsing to the top of Mt. Glines in the middle of the night and breaking through the metal bars that were meant to prevent trespassers (like me) from tumbling down one of its washed-out shafts (which I had).

Muttering curses I'd learned while working alongside foulmouthed sailors and fisherman at the docks, I strained to reach into my toolbelt of potions and elixirs while clutching the distressed rope with my other hand. The absurd maneuver brought back flashbulb memories of high school P.E. class, when I could barely hoist myself up three feet of rope, let alone thirty. Shoving the unpleasant memory aside, I used my "teeth" to pull out the cork stopper, then took a large swig of the ice-blue liquid swirling inside the vial, grimacing as I did. That swallow alone was worth at least two thousand dollars, and I wouldn't be able to replenish it anytime soon, given my dwindling celestine stores.

Still, as I glanced several stories below, where the dim light of my lantern had just flickered, then died, I was grateful for the sudden burst of strength that fueled my aching muscles, giving me the boost I needed to hoist myself back up and over the remainder of the rocky ledge that hadn't just crumbled beneath my feet. I rolled over onto my back, working to catch my breath after what might have been a neck-breaking fall – or something worse. As I lay there, splayed out on the damp ground like a washed-up starfish, something warm and wet pressed against my cheek, emitting a series of reproachful snuffles as it did.

"I'm fine, I'm fine." I sighed, pushing away the worrying snout of Topie, my ten-year old spotted Juliana pig. "What are you doing here, anyway? You're supposed to be waiting in the truck."

He let out another expletive-laced string of snuffs and snorts.

"Yeah, well, I'm not dead, am I?" I grunted, sitting in an upright position. "You, on the other hand, would have been a pig-shaped splatter at the bottom of that mineshaft if I'd let you come with me." My stomach did a small flip as the two of us peered over the cliff that had sent me tumbling to what could have been my violent death. "Good thing I remembered to bring my paracord this time."

Topie grunted in agreement.

I straightened my glasses and adjusted my headlamp, switching the light from dim red to bright white. The glare of its reflection against the nearby glistening rock wall made me instinctively avert my eyes, but when I peered back down the caved-in borehole, the concentrated beam allowed me to make out a small tunnel at the bottom of the shaft, as well as the rusted ladder that led into it.

"C'mon, boy," I muttered, scooping Topie into my left arm and clutching him against my vest. Any other time, I wouldn't have taken that risk, but the effects of the celestine wouldn't wear off for a few hours, making his stocky thirty-five pounds feel like a tenth of that. "Just don't fall," I added, "because I'm not fishing you out of some muddy abyss if you do."

Topie buried his nose under the crook of my arm with a muffled squeal.

After double-checking the carabiner and the metal climbing piton I'd wedged into a tight rock seam a few minutes earlier, I wiped the grime from my fingerless leather gloves, looped the rope through my harness, then took a swig of a milky white calcite solution to temporarily bolster my otherwise-brittle bones. I'd already shattered both my ankles falling into a mineshaft once before and didn't want to have to use the last of my special morganite and cinnabar slurry to heal myself from a fall that could have easily been avoided in the first place.

Besides, the high levels of mercury in cinnabar always gave me a tummy ache.

Muttering a small prayer to a god I didn't believe in, I gathered the nylon rope in my right hand and rappelled down the crumbling rock wall, pushing off every few yards while chunks of red stone clattered against the ground far below. Topie did his best not to wriggle, though he did jump every time my boots made impact with the wall.

I couldn't help but chuckle. When I was young, my parents – both big fans of idioms – would often tell me that they'd only let me do certain things "when pigs fly." It wasn't until I was twenty years old that I realized it was simply their way of saying, "Not a chance in heck, Delaney."

Well, Mom and Dad, looks like some pigs do *fly.*

Once I'd rappelled to a "safe" height of about fifteen feet, I took a deep breath and jumped, muttering a silent thanks to my bone-fortifying calcite potion as I landed in a graceful superhero pose. Topie, on the other hand, let out a shrill squeal and all but leapt out of my hands the moment my boots made contact with the ground, shooting me what appeared to be an irritable look over his shoulder.

"You're the one who wanted to come down here," I pointed out. "Before you go scampering off, hold on a sec." I unslung my utility bag from my shoulder and fished out a second headlamp. "We can't have you falling into any dark abysses." Kneeling to the ground, I strapped the headlamp around his head, allowing his floppy ears to hang over the elastic strap. "There. Perfect."

He let out a grateful snuffle, then trotted over to the narrow tunnel just ahead, his little light bouncing gaily against the walls.

"Don't forget Item Seventeen on our Mine Safety Checklist!" I called after him. "Leave a mark at every fork to prevent disorientation!"

"Reee!" he reassured me.

After dusting myself off and gathering more slack from my rope – I'd gotten lost in one too many underground labyrinths prior to the instatement of MSC-17 to go exploring without a line to lead me back – I followed Topie into the dripping tunnel, adjusting the output of my headlamp to compensate for the low ceiling. Just as I'd hoped, telltale clusters of brassy pyrite and metallic galena were scattered across the ore vein that snaked through the sedimentary rock. The mine's previous workers might not have considered these to be valuable minerals, but I certainly did.

If only they knew.

Chuckling to myself, I removed the fine chisel from my toolbelt and began carefully chipping at the rock matrix. The gleaming pyrite was cupriferous, meaning it contained copper and was therefore not pure, so the effects wouldn't be as potent. Still, cupriferous was better than nothing. On the other hand, the galena crystals had formed in perfect hexoctahedral clusters, making them prime specimens.

Once I'd collected enough material in the emptied and sanitized ibuprofen bottles I'd brought from the pharmacy, I broke off a tiny piece of pyrite and placed it on my tongue, letting out a quiet hum of contentment. Pyrite has a sweet, nutty flavor – almost like butterscotch toffee – that's made all the sweeter by the pleasant, long-forgotten memories that burst to life when you ingest it. In this case, the memory that flashed behind my eyelids was of the first time I'd ever met Topie. Our nearest neighbor, Paul – a small-time farmer who owned a creamery two miles away from my parents' house – had come by to tell my dad about his sow's surprise litter, which had come too late in the season and included the "tiniest little piglet you ever saw in your life."

"What are you gonna do with it?" I asked, looking up from the pile of pebbles I'd been sifting through and cataloging on the front porch.

"I'ma put the little feller out of its misery, 'course, since its momma won't even bother feeding it," Paul replied, scratching at the thinning wisps of hair sticking out from underneath his baseball cap. "I'm just waitin' 'til the morning in case the sow decides to off it herself an' save me the trouble."

"You're going to kill a helpless animal just because it was born too small?" I demanded, clambering to my feet.

Paul stared me down, his eyebrow arching in either ridicule, annoyance, or amusement – I couldn't be sure. "Aw, come now, Laney. Just 'cause *you* were born small don't mean you gotta take it personally. Pigs are born to be food and nothin' else. I'm doin' the little feller a favor before it starves to death in the cold."

"My name is *De*laney, not Laney," I muttered, crossing my arms.

"Be nice," my father reprimanded me.

"How is correcting my own name not being nice?" I retorted, which for some reason made my father knuckle his forehead in what looked like irritation.

Later that night, I waited until both of my parents had fallen asleep and hopped on my bicycle to ride two miles down the dirt road in the dark. After leaning my bike against the fence, I quietly climbed into the pen of snoozing pigs and snatched up the littlest piggy, which had been relegated to the far side of the pen and was so cold I had to keep him under my shirt just to warm him up. I named him Topaz – our shared birthstone – and hid him in my closet for the next two months, hand-feeding him goat's milk until he was big enough to eat scraps of solid food on his own. By then, I'd graduated from twelfth grade. The moment I'd collected my hat and diploma from the Podunk high school I'd been forced to attend, I grabbed my belongings and my pig and left, having already secured a job at a fishery in Camden. My parents weren't happy I'd left, or so they'd repeatedly told me. But they didn't seem particularly happy when I was at home either. So I chalked it up to a personal problem on their part and went about living my life exactly as I pleased, tasting every rock I came across without anyone berating me for it.

"Those were the days, eh Topie?" I turned in his direction. "Gutting fish and exploring mines while getting through pharmacology school?"

He was too busy pawing at the muddy ground to answer.

I knelt beside him. "What's that you've got there?" I asked, letting out a sharp gasp when I saw a glass-clear quartz crystal poking out of the rust-colored muck. "Topie, you brilliant little rock hound, you! Look at that scepter!" I was practically drooling as I withdrew my trowel from my toolbelt and carefully began unearthing it from the gash vein[1] embedded in the schist. "Regular quartz is no better than Dayquil as a cold remedy, but a transparent crystal like *this*? Oh man, there's not a

---

[1] A fissure containing veinstone, the commercially "valueless" material in which ore is found.

rhinovirus in the universe that could stand up against it!" After a few minutes of meticulous digging, I was able to extract the quartz crystal from the clay. Working to contain my excited squeal, I turned it over in my hand; there was nary a scratch nor a defect on it.

"Oh, Topes, I could kiss you!" I exclaimed, drawing him in for a tight squeeze.

He let out a sound somewhere between a contented grunt and an uncomfortable wheeze.

"C'mon, boy." I stood up, clutching my pig in one hand and my prized antiviral remedy in the other. "We've got potions to brew!"

Chapter 2

My boots splashed in one of the many puddles that had gathered between the uneven cobblestones in the back-alley street that housed my home and my shop – both one and the same. It was early, far too early for the throng of summer tourists that inundated Old Port – the historic district of Portland, Maine – to be up and about. The sun had barely risen over the quaint red-brick buildings and the crawling green ivy that adorned them, and the cobblestone streets hadn't yet been trampled by the horrid combination of Birkenstocks and calf-high socks seasonal tourists frequently sported.

For once, I actually stopped to admire the lavender-pink sky, where a flock of seagulls soared lazily above the collection of white sails that bobbed in the harbor, and breathed in the salty, briny scent of the ocean that had been carried in by the early morning rainstorm. Old Port was beautiful. Or rather, it *would* have been beautiful if it hadn't been for the caravan of buses that dumped hundreds of Californians at the harbor, putting a damper on what was otherwise a postcard-worthy town. My pharmacy was strategically located in one of the off-the-beaten-track alleyways that lay between the waterfront and downtown Fore Street, so I managed to avoid the very worst of high-tourist season inside my tiny, unmarked shop. I didn't need the casual acetaminophen-seeking patron, anyway; my regulars knew where to find me.

After unlocking the front entrance, I stepped inside the shop, letting the door swing shut behind me. The bell clanged against the glass loudly, making me wince. How I hated that dang bell, especially when I was deep in the throes of concentration and it clamored for my attention. But I hated being caught off guard by customers far more than the noise of the bell. At least I still had a few hours before it would be clanging at me again.

Giddy with excitement, I hung my leather jacket on the hook and traded my muddy climbing boots for clean slip-on sneakers that never needed to be laced or unlaced – a huge waste of time, if you ask me. Topie ran straight to his bed behind the front desk while I made a beeline for my lab in the back of the shop, clutching my backpack full of newfound treasures in two reverent hands. After setting it on the stainless steel countertop, I went to grab my favorite white lab coat, hesitating when I noticed the layer of dirt and grime that coated my arms. I wrestled with myself for a moment, waging an internal battle of whether I *really* needed to take the time to stop and clean myself up before begrudgingly deciding that I probably ought to. Huffing impatiently, I reached up and pulled on the cord that hung from the ceiling, exposing the extendable ladder that led directly to my loft upstairs, then darted up the rungs two at a time.

My "bedroom" was nothing special – just a couple hundred square feet of space with a mattress that lay directly on the floor, a reading light, a dresser, a tiny closet, and an entire wall devoted to my alphabetically-sorted textbooks, most of which were either mineral- or medicine-related, with the occasional travel book thrown in. Travel and minerals were two of the five primary reasons I tolerated the noise and the crowds of Portland; there were nearly eight hundred mines in Maine alone, with most of the major roads to said mines passing through the city. Plus, the Portland International Jetport, where I stored my Bonanza A36TC in one of the private hangars, was less than fifteen minutes away. When a mine was too far to reach via a small plane with limited fuel capacity, I could always take an international flight wherever I needed to go, loath as I was to fly commercially.

  I yanked off my black tank top, now riddled with holes and dirt, then shimmied out of my leather pants, which had survived my fall unscathed, just as they'd been designed to do. After tossing the shirt in the overflowing hamper and carefully refolding and placing the pants at the bottom of the drawer that I'd specifically designated for worn-but-not-torn leather gear, I threw on a pair of khaki shorts and my favorite t-shirt featuring a cluster of amethysts and the caption, "Of quartz I love geology!" I had five duplicates of that shirt, which was perfectly soft, not stiff or starchy, and had roomy sleeve holes that didn't bunch under my armpits. (In the grand scheme of things, armpit-bunching sleeves aren't as bad as tight socks but they're at least twice as bad as damp flip-flops.)

  Dirty clothes swapped for clean, I hurriedly made my way back to the ladder, stopping short yet again when I caught my reflection in the closet mirror. Frozen with one foot hovering in the air, I studied my reflection for a long moment, inwardly debating whether I *really* needed to worry about hygiene when there were potions to be made, then let out an irritable groan. Muttering to myself about the many inconveniences of the human body, I darted into my tiny bathroom, barely larger than a lavatory on a Boeing 737, and tore a brush through my tangled bob of chestnut-brown hair – which I maintained at just below chin-length to minimize the inconveniences of having to manage it – then splashed soapy water on my face to rid it of its grimy sheen. After brushing my teeth, fastidiously counting to one hundred as I did, I hurriedly put on some under-eye concealer, Chapstick, and black mascara so my regular customers would be less inclined to tell me how "tired" I looked, which must have been some sort of socially-acceptable show of sympathy on their part but always left me feeling annoyed.

What was wrong with looking tired?

Ablutions finally finished, I lunged for the ladder, skipping the last three rungs as I hopped to the ground, snapped on a pair of nitrile gloves, and unzipped my scuffed-up backpack. After reverently unwrapping the protective strips of bubble wrap from my brand-new transparent quartz scepter, I rinsed off the crystal with a strong vinegar solution, patted it dry with a microfiber cloth, and hurriedly took it over to my magnifying-glass. I couldn't help letting out an excited squeak as I switched on the built-in LED light to examine it. Scepters are second-generation crystal tips that grow on top of another quartz crystal, and in this case, the primary scepter was one of the most immaculate specimens I – or rather, Topie – had ever found.

"Topes, you really outdid yourself this time!" I shouted toward the front of the store.

He let out a somnolent grunt.

Once my imaging and extensive cataloging was done, I quickly got to work on processing the quartz's essence into a powerful antiviral potion. Another person might refer to the process as "magic," but that's because most people are [insert socially-acceptable euphemism for "obtuse"]. Being the devout scientist I was, there was no room in my lexicon for such careless hokum. I preferred the self-coined term "parascientific" – i.e., science-adjacent. While *thus far* unexplainable by our current laws of science, there existed, I was all but certain, a simple, elegant, and scientific explanation for my one-of-a-kind abilities. It just hadn't been discovered yet.

Where was I? Oh, right. Potions.

Most of the tinctures I made for my own consumption were simple, yet highly potent – i.e., a straightforward solution of pure, ground-up minerals preserved in a lipid suspension. The tonics I brewed for my customers, on the other hand, were far less simple, and only a fraction as potent. Since most normal humans are unable to safely consume rock fragments and hazardous minerals, let alone metabolize and make use of their intended properties, I had to take all sorts of tedious extra steps when preparing potions for commercial use. To begin with, I only used relatively non-lethal minerals: silver, calcite, and diamond, for example, as opposed to highly toxic minerals like cinnabar, orpiment, and arsenopyrite (which gives even me a slight tummy ache). Then, after grinding the specimens into a fine powder, I would manually extract the essence from the specimen via a highly-complex process that I've been told is too convoluted and uninteresting to explain in detail.

Long story short: the tonics in my personal collection were full-strength and often poisonous to other humans, while my customer's potions contained baby doses of essence and were relatively free of toxins like lead and mercury.[2]

Anyway, given the quality of this quartz crystal, I couldn't bear to pulverize the entire thing into dust, so I instead broke off chips from the smaller crystals and ground those into a fine quartz powder, preserving the main crystal for my personal collection. After that, I further triturated the microcrystals with a proprietary slurry of chemicals to safely extract the parascientific property, which would need to be suspended in an inert lipid solution for several days before I could—

D-I-I-I-ING!

The ungodly clang nearly made me drop the vial I'd been filling with a dropper of painstakingly-measured liquid. My head snapped up in frustration. After gingerly setting the vial back in its stand, I yanked off my gloves and prescription goggles and leapt from my chair, storming toward the front of the shop.

"Can't you read the store hours?" I snarled at the intruder, surprised to find bright morning sunlight streaming through the window.

"Er…" he started, glancing at the clock above the register, which read 9:17 a.m.

I blinked at the numbers in surprise. Had I really been working for three and a half hours? As if in response, my stomach let out a hollow grumble, reminding me of the hot pocket I'd accidentally left in the lab microwave two hours before.

---

[2] Which is more than can be said for, say, chocolate and sushi, which are known for containing not-so-insignificant levels of lead and mercury, respectively.

Sighing, I turned back to the man. "What do you want?"

"Er…" he stammered again, seemingly flustered. "I need to speak to the pharmacist."

"You're speaking to her," I replied, folding my arms across my white jacket, the breast pocket of which read *Delaney Stone, Pharm. D.*

The man grimaced, his discomfort evident even to me. "What I mean is, I'm looking for the owner of the pharmacy."

My eyes narrowed as I blithely gestured toward the sign on the front window, which from our position inside the shop read *ʏɿɒɔɘʜɈoqA ɘnoɈƧ*, but would have clearly spelled *Stone Apothecary* had he even bothered to glance at it upon entering the building. "You found her."

Middle-aged and round in the middle, the man took a step back, his beady eyes darting from side to side as though he were about to confess a crime. "Oh, well, um…" His sharp laugh was as awkward as it was abrupt, making me wince. "Boy, I guess I wasn't expecting to find an attractive young lady running the joint." The man's gaze lingered uncomfortably on the t-shirt and shorts I was wearing beneath my lab coat. "You don't even look old enough to be a pharmacist. What are you – twenty-six? Twenty-seven?"

I bit the side of my cheek to keep myself from making a snide remark about *his* age and appearance. As a matter of fact, I was turning twenty-nine in five and a half months, which I was tempted to tell him for the sake of ensuring his information was correct while simultaneously reminding myself that disclosing personal details is one way of indicating that you are romantically interested in a person, which I most certainly was not.

Still, it bothered me that he was operating under an inaccurate assumption about my age. I wondered if there was a way to correct him without—

"I'm here for Viagra," the man blurted out, his cheeks turning several shades of crimson.

"Hmm?" I started. "Oh. I don't carry Viagra."

The man's eyes bulged. "B-But my friend – er, my coworker, that is – told me that you have the 'good stuff.'" He pitched his voice lower. "I assume that means the stuff from, uh, south of the border? That doesn't necessarily require a prescription?"

I stared at him, saying nothing, which for some reason always seemed to make the most aggravating of people chatter more, not less.

"It's just that my girlfriend is much younger than me," he barreled on, scratching at his wispy comb-over. "But I can't ask my family doctor for the script because my wife might—" He stopped abruptly, his owl-like eyes widening even farther. "Er. What I mean is—"

Ew.

Before he could further incriminate himself, I held up a hand. "I don't deal in illegal prescription drugs. What your coworker was likely referencing are my special holistic blends, which aren't FDA-approved but highly potent. I assume he told you the prices for those are significantly higher than commercial pharmaceuticals, and I don't accept insurance?"

The man nodded weakly.

"Good." I swiveled on my sneaker and made my way for the display cabinet tucked behind the front desk, unlocking and sliding open the glass panel to reveal six LED-illuminated glass shelves that had been meticulously lined with hundreds of tiny glass bottles, all arranged in alphabetical order by mineral name. The top three shelves were part of my own personal collection, while the bottom three were for customers. After snatching a pastel-green liquid from the bottom shelf and re-locking the cabinet, I turned back to the man, who had approached the other side of the register and was wringing his hands.

"As I said," I repeated, setting the vial in front of him, "I don't carry Viagra. But I do carry a proprietary 'PGO' emulsion – short for 'prasiolite, gypsum, and olivine' – that acts as a powerful libido-booster. Plus, it has a vasodilation effect so potent, it makes Viagra look like candy in comparison. Of course"—I chuckled to myself, remembering a rather humorous anecdote from a few years back—"to counter the effects of gypsum's twelve-hour erections, you need to add the smallest pinch of olivine, just enough to tamp the erectile effects without nullifying them completely. That's why…" I trailed off as I finally looked up and found what appeared to be bewilderment – or possibly disdain – etched on the man's face.

Right. I pressed my lips together. *No one actually cares about the how, just the 'how much.'*

He glanced over his shoulder at the sign on the window, then turned back to me, his face hardening. "I was told you were a pharmacist, not some snake-oil peddler."

"I am a pharmacist," I replied, feeling my cheeks flush. "And I can assure you, I'm not 'peddling' any such thing." I plucked the PGO emulsion from the counter, curling my fingers around it defensively. "You're welcome to go back to your family doctor and ask for a script, though I can't imagine what your wife would think if she ever found out."

"I'll take it, I'll take it!" he blustered, pawing at the vial in my clenched hand.

"Fine." I set it down with a demure *clink*. "That'll be three-hundred even."

"Three hundred…dollars?"

"Well, it certainly wouldn't be in rupees."

The man gawked between the vial and me, the vertical crease between his brows growing deeper and deeper, before angrily shoving his hand in his pocket, withdrawing a weathered wallet, and slamming a wad of cash on the counter. "Take it!" he snarled. "But I swear, if this stuff doesn't work, you'll be hearing from my lawyer!"

With that, he snatched the bottle, spun on his heel, and made his way for the door.

"Sir, there's one more thing—" I started.

Waving a dismissive hand in the air – at least, I was fairly certain it wasn't in farewell – he bolted out the front door, letting it slam behind him.

I flinched at the sound of the clanging bell, then released the breath I'd been holding, muttering, "Guess you'll just have to sort out the dosing for yourself." I couldn't help but snicker at an image of his much younger girlfriend screaming at his thricely-engorged testes, which they would almost certainly become if he took even a millimeter more than the prescribed one-half dropperful.

"Ah, well," I shrugged to myself, making my way once again for my lab in the back of the shop. "At least now I can get back to—"

The bell on the door sounded.

"Oh, what is it now?" I snarled, whirling around to find not a pudgy, penny-pinching philanderer, but a much younger, trimmer, and conventionally-attractive man standing in the doorway – if one was into muscular builds, wavy dark hair, and piercing blue eyes. Which *I* most certainly wasn't, particularly when all of those attributes belonged to the man I hated most in the entire world: My sworn archnemesis, Heath Spencer.

Chapter 3

"You!" I breathed, the tips of my ears growing hot.

"Me," Heath agreed, taking a step inside the store. "It's been a while, hasn't it?"

I crossed my arms over my lab jacket. "Far too short a time, if you ask me."

His grin wavered. "Ouch."

I didn't care if I hurt his feelings. With his hokey, overpriced rock[3] shop located just down the road, the gimmicky New Age nonsense he spouted about healing crystals and chakras, and the casual way he went about collecting minerals not for utilization but for "aesthetics," Heath Spencer spat in the face of everything I held most dear – hard science, sound data, and the unrelenting pursuit of knowledge. If the rarest element in the universe, unlisted on the periodic table itself, were to be discovered in our backyard, Heath's first question

---

[3] Here, "rock" is obviously used disparagingly, since minerals are not equivalent to rocks. A rock is an aggregate of one or more minerals and may also include organic remains and/or mineraloids.

wouldn't be about any sort of scientific implication, but rather about the mineral's artificial value. Then, he'd probably find some way to weasel into the extraction site and scoop up every last nugget to mark for sale in his stupid rock shop, forcing actual scientists like me to go through the residual, used scraps of minerals floating around on eBay. By the time a mineral makes it to eBay, for the record, it retains almost none of its original essence; the more grubby hands a crystal passes through, the more essence it loses. That's why idiots like Heath think that certain stones have "healing properties" – I mean, they *do*, obviously. But in the hands of amateurs and lay people, the effect is a slow trickle compared to the gushing torrent I'm able to extract from them.

Heath's store – which he didn't even establish himself, but rather inherited from his late father the previous year – represented a waste of proportions so epic, the very sight of his face made me want to hurl something at it.

"So, how have you been, Laney?" he asked, leaning his shoulder against the doorframe.

I clenched my fists. "For the tenth time, *Heath*, it's *De*laney."

He held up his hands in some sort of pseudo-apologetic gesture. "For the eleventh time, *Delaney*, you have my apologies."

"That doesn't even make sense!"

His lips pressed into a barely-contained smirk. "What doesn't make sense?"

Oh, how I hated that smug voice, his haughty swagger, the aggravating way he insisted on referring to me by a nickname I absolutely loathed as though he *enjoyed* getting a rise out of me! Through tightly gritted teeth, I forced out, "Why would you have apologized eleven times if I've only corrected you ten times?"

"Has it only been ten times?" He pressed his finger to his lips. "Honestly, it feels like so much more than that."

I rolled my eyes. "Many."

"Sorry?"

I opened my mouth to inform him that "much" is used to describe non-countable nouns like juice, happiness, and patience, while "many" is used to describe things that can be counted, like airplanes, rocks, and minerals, when a high-pitched, exuberant shriek announced the scampering arrival of a certain treacherous pig.

"Topie, don't—!" I started, but the little swine was already making a beeline straight for my archnemesis's open arms.

"Reeeeeee!" he squealed as he leapt into Heath's embrace like a soldier's wife greeting her husband after war. At the force of it, the stupid pig nearly fell on the ground – along with Topie.

"Hey, buddy!" Heath grinned as he crouched beside *my* emotional support animal, scratching Boar-edict Arnold right on his exposed pork belly. "I brought you your favorite – truffles!"

Topie let out another, much louder, squeal of delight.

"Traitor," I muttered.

Heath looked up at me with twinkling, obnoxiously-blue eyes.

I shifted uncomfortably. Didn't the man ever blink?

"I found an entire host of mycorrhizal fungi just outside the Tonglushan Mine – you know, where they just made that new blue chalcopyrite discovery."

My jaw tumbled open. "*You* were at the Tonglushan Mine?" I gasped. "But…*how?* That mine is supposed to be closed to the public!"

"Well, it helps to be fluent in Mandarin." He grinned as he stood, dusting off his designer slacks. "It also helps to have a ten-year unrestricted visa and a close relationship with the Hubei Province's governor's son. I'd be more than happy to arrange a visit for you – *if* there's any chalcopyrite left after a handful of big-name mineral collectors came in and cleaned out the entire pocket," he added, making my hands clench into fists. "I mean, have you seen this stuff?" He reached into his vest pocket and, to my simultaneous dismay and delight, pulled out a perfectly-spherical, grape-sized chunk of iridescent, cobalt-blue chalcopyrite that glittered dazzlingly in the morning sunlight.

My feet moved before my brain gave them permission to. Snatching the specimen from Heath's hand, I retrieved a pair of soft cotton gloves and a loupe from the pocket of my lab coat and examined the druzy submetallic microcrystals, salivating at the sight of them. Honestly, it took everything I had not to pop the chalcopyrite in my mouth right then and there. "These haven't been artificially-colored or heat-treated in any way?" I demanded, turning the smooth ball over in my palm. The crystals shifted from blue to purple as I did, making my breath catch. "I mean, I had heard this find was superb. But this…this is—"

"Magnificent, I know," Heath interjected softly.

I looked up from my loupe, surprised to find he was standing just a few inches away from me, inspecting the chalcopyrite above my left shoulder. He was so close, I could smell his aftershave.

My cheeks flushed as I angrily jerked away from him. "Well…good for you!" I snapped, attempting to thrust the stone back in his hands. "How nice of you to come all this way just to brag!"

Instead of snatching his prized mineral back, as I most certainly would have done, he took a step *backward*, holding up his hands as though proclaiming his own innocence. "I didn't stop by to brag about the chalcopyrite, Laney. I came to give it to you."

I opened my mouth to snarl a retort, then closed it again. "You…what?"

"I brought back more than enough specimens to stock my shop, and I know how badly you wanted to see this mine. I still feel terrible that the Chinese embassy shot down your visa request. That's part of the reason why I came here. Next week I'm heading back to Hubei, then hopping over to the Fujian Province to take a look at the new Tanzanite fluorite discovery there—"

"There's no such thing as 'tanzanite' fluorite," I interjected. "That's a misnomer."

"Okay, fine, tanzanite-*colored* fluorite—"

"Wrong again!" I snapped, tearing off my gloves. "Tanzanite, or *blue zoisite*, as it's actually called, is naturally grass-green or brown. It's the artificial heat treatment and irradiation that gives it that phony indigo color." *And robs it of its essence completely,* I added in silent condemnation. "Anyway, as a so-called 'rock' purveyor, you of all people should be calling these specimens by their actual monikers, not the garbage descriptions you find on eBay. 'Tanzanite fluorite!'" I scoffed, rolling my eyes. "It's offensive to anyone who actually cares about mineralogy."

Heath's eyes widened, then narrowed, as he regarded the nearby shelves of acetaminophen, calamine lotion, and simethicone – for all of the people who stumbled in the pharmacy complaining of 'acute appendicitis' when all they needed was some Gas-X. When he turned back to me, his left eyebrow was arched in either amusement or derision. I couldn't be sure what he was thinking, but I had to assume it was something along the lines of, *You're even less of a geologist than I am, lady.*

After a heavy moment of silence, he took a deep breath and exhaled slowly. "Look, all I'm *trying* to say is I could help you get a Chinese visa. I have contacts here in Portland who could make that happen in seventy-two hours. You could even accompany me there next week…if you wanted to."

My breath caught and held, unchecked excitement flaring in my chest at the prospect of finally seeing – and tasting – actual Chinese mineral specimens I previously could only drool over while browsing the online archives of Mindat.org for hours at a time…

And then a wave of dejection and humiliation yanked me right back down to reality.

I had dealt with men like Heath all of my life – extremely good-looking, self-centered, arrogant jerks who pretended to be kind to my face while secretly ridiculing me behind my back – like James Ostrowski, who'd asked me out during our last year of pharmacology school. Brilliant as he was, I'd fallen for him hard, like a new favorite hobby. Instead of daydreaming about rocks and minerals or studying for the NAPLEX,[4] James alone occupied my every thought. I was utterly infatuated –

---

[4] North American Pharmacist Licensure Examination

clinically addicted, even – in a thrilling, all-consuming way I'd never thought possible. Meanwhile, James had secretly been calling me "Mrs. Roboto" around his friends because of the way he claimed I spoke. He and his buddies had even made bets about the types of noises I would make during certain activities in the bedroom. I only found out because my lab partner had overheard them making fun of me from one of the men's toilet stalls and tipped me off. By then, James and I had been sleeping together for four weeks, with him apparently telling his friends every lurid detail of our encounters. I was told intimate photos had also been involved.

It took me the better part of the year to get past the heartbreak and humiliation, and even then, the experience still loitered in the back of my mind as a warning. From that moment on, I had diamond skin, and nothing – and no one – would ever penetrate it ever again.

"So?" Heath hedged. "What do you think?"

"I don't need your help or anyone else's," I retorted, shoving the stone back toward his hand, but he merely took another step backward, that insufferable, antagonizing smirk on his face growing wider and more intolerable by the second.

"That chalcopyrite is yours whether you want it or not." He grinned again, stopping once more to scratch Topie's exposed belly before making his way for the exit. "Come by the shop sometime, would you? In addition to the chalcopyrite, I also managed to snag some of those strawberry-red fluorite specimens from the Huanggang Mine in Inner Mongolia just before they tapped it dry. They're remarkable. Gemmy, great color saturation, razor-sharp crystals – you'd love them."

The edges of my vision went white with rage. Once, I'd dropped everything to make a mad rush to Mont Blanc, France, where a new pocket of extremely rare, pale pink fluorite had just been discovered. But the effort had been in vain because a horde of greedy mineral collectors – some of the most serious and affluent in the world – had already swept in and cleared out the entire pocket. That was one of the main reasons I'd decided to get a private pilot's license the following spring, so I didn't have to rely on the stupid commercial airlines and their stupid flight delays and cancellations. The ability to fly my own plane had made the "getting there" part infinitely easier, but it didn't help with certain countries' visa requirements, something I had no way of solving unless I could find a mineral essence that somehow facilitated world peace – an unlikely feat, to be sure.

Anyway, all of that is to say I'd never even been able to get my hands on *pink* fluorite, let alone red! Meanwhile, this ignorant, hokum-spouting, New Age *hack* had managed to pilfer the very last of those mouthwatering Inner Mongolian fluorite octahedrons that I'd been poring over for *months*. And for what? To mark them up 1200% from what he'd paid for them so he could then turn around and sell them to some Colorado tourist who didn't know the difference between a red beryl and a ruby?

My teeth ground together so hard, pain zinged through my molars. *Stupid Heath, with his stupid overpriced rock shop and his stupid rich and powerful contacts all over the stupid globe!* It wasn't fair that spoiled, well-connected people like him were granted unrestricted access to remote places with exotic minerals I'd never have the chance to see – like the emeralds hidden deep in the Hindu Kush Mountains of Afghanistan or the tantalum deposits found in the Majahayan region of Somalia… My eye twitched. *Or the Inner Mongolian octahedral red fluorite that should have been mine!* What if the essence from that fluorite regrew severed limbs or cured childhood leukemia? More importantly, how would I ever be able to finish my growing-but-*far*-from complete catalog of data if I wasn't able to get my hands on *every* single mineral in the world? Every glaring hole in my data felt like a hole in my head. I ran my hands through my hair, exhaling sharply through my nose.

"Laney?" Heath asked – repeated, rather, since he'd apparently been talking to me for the last minute or so. "You okay?"

"I will be once you leave!" I snapped.

"All right!" He held up his hands. "I'm going."

And yet he took his sweet time as he casually sidled toward the exit, stopping to give Topie one last scratch between his ears. Topie promptly rolled over onto his back, inviting Heath to indulge him in a vigorous, two-handed belly-scratching operation.

"Who's a good boy?" Heath cooed.

Topie's coiled tail thumped against the tile in bliss.

Eventually, I couldn't take it anymore and blurted out, "I really do hate you, you know!"

Heath stood. I half-expected him to shout something back at me, but for some reason, his idiotic smile only softened, making him appear almost sad. "I know," he said, pushing the door open. "Talk soon, Laney."

"No, we won't!" I shouted, but the door had already jingled shut behind him.

Chapter 4

I watched through the glass as Heath strode with his hands shoved deep in his suit pockets to the other end of the alley, where his awful gem and mineral shop stood, full of overpriced amethyst baubles and citrine trinkets that made absolutely no difference to the world or to me. He paused outside the entrance of his shop as though he might turn around, then quickly ducked inside without giving me or my pharmacy so much as a second glance – which for some reason made me even angrier.

When I was sure that walking dirt clod wasn't coming back, I hurriedly popped the chalcopyrite ball in my mouth, letting out a euphoric moan the moment the dense weight of it sank against my tongue. I'd tasted regular pyrite, sure, but I'd never tasted anything like *this*. I sucked on the marble-shaped stone like a candy jawbreaker, savoring the crisp, fruity taste – a tangy cross between stewed blackberries and plum sauce – as I waited for the mineral's supernatural effect to manifest. A few moments went by, but nothing happened. I puckered my cheeks, attempting to pull the essence from the mineral.

Still…nothing.

"I don't understand," I mumbled. Frowning, I turned to Topie. "Do you see anything different about me?"

He shook his head grumpily, still cross that I'd kicked his favorite truffle supplier out of the shop.

Pointedly ignoring him, I spat the chalcopyrite ball into the palm of my hand. "Is this stuff inert?" I wondered aloud, once more pulling out my loupe to inspect it. "Maybe it was touched by too many—"

The alarm on my watch went off, making me jump.

I stuffed the chalcopyrite in my shorts pocket with a harrumph, irritated once again at the interruption. At least *this* was a relatively pleasant one, unlike stupid Heath Spencer and his stupid defective Chinese mineral.

Shrugging out of my lab coat, I slung it over the chair behind the front desk and retreated to the back of my shop, making my way to the towering stack of shipping boxes in the far corner that I'd packed, labeled, and stacked the day before. They were part of my special mail order program, where folks could fax me their requests, pay over the phone, and then receive my proprietary parascientific potion blends anywhere in the world. I even had a client at the McMurdo Research Station in Antarctica who happily paid four figures for a weak ruby potion that had kept her warm for the duration of her six-month placement there. Not that she knew she was drinking ruby essence, since the tonic was cleverly packaged as a simple metabolic-stimulating vasodilator.

After placing all but one package in the back alley for the mailman to pick up later that morning, I stuffed the remaining package and a stapled white paper bag into a messenger bag and strode into the front of the shop, where Topie was by the front door, resting his chin on crossed hooves and moping.

"Are you going to be grumpy with me all day or would you like to go see Mrs. Lautner?" I groused as I flipped the sign on the door from OPEN to CLOSED.

The dour expression on his face didn't change, but his tail thumped to life.

"All right then. Let's call a truce and get out of here."

He made an amenable snort as he stretched out his hooves and arched his back like a cat.

"Such an arduous life," I muttered to myself while I knelt to strap on his red Emotional Support vest, even though he'd been anything *but* emotionally supportive that day.

After adjusting my prescription sunglasses and noise-canceling headphones, I took a deep breath, opened the door and locked it behind us, then began my long trek down the busy street – thankfully in the opposite direction from Heath's chintzy-yet-bustling rock shop. Unlike earlier that morning, when all was still and serene in downtown Portland, the cobblestones were now completely inundated with ankle socks, Birkenstock sandals, and white yipping dogs, who gawked at Topie with wide eyes as he merrily trotted past them. I kept my head down as we wove through the teeming street, which was packed with little kids clutching dripping ice cream cones, amateur musicians playing for spare change, and tourists aggressively jerking their index fingers at various sights as they meandered and caroused – one such finger narrowly missing my left eye as I ducked beneath it.

I let out a sigh of relief as we darted into FedEx a few minutes later, which was mercifully quiet inside. Removing one ear of my headphones as we approached the woman at the register, I mentally rehearsed what I was going to say in response to the imminent bout of small talk.

"Good morning!" she chimed predictably. "Oh, what a cute little piggy you have!"

"Good morning," I answered, working to keep my voice properly inflected.

"How are you doing today?"

Cranky, overstimulated, and wishing I were back home in my lab. "Fine," I replied, withdrawing the cardboard box from my bag and gingerly setting it on the counter. "How are you?"

"Fine, thanks!" she smiled at me, displaying a set of perfectly white, natural teeth. "What can I do for you?"

"I need to send this to Saudi Arabia – quickest shipping possible." I fished a piece of paper from my bag and handed it to her. "Here's the address. Also, I need to purchase insurance for the contents."

"Okay." She started typing the address on her keyboard. "What's the declared value of the package?"

"Forty-thousand dollars."

"Oh!" Her eyebrows arched. "Unfortunately, the maximum we insure is two thousand dollars, unless you have the High-Value—"

"I have it."

"Oh. So, you're shipping…jewelry?" she guessed.

"Medicine." An extra-strength PGO emulsion for a sexually-prolific and inordinately-monied Saudi prince, to be precise, but she didn't need to know that. She just needed to see the applicable forms and credentials required by the DEA and Federal law, all of which I brandished for her review.

She skimmed through the paperwork, her eyes growing ever wider as she did. "I...I'd better get a manager."

The bell on the front door clanged, making me wince, as another customer strode in with an oversized box and stood uncomfortably close behind me while tapping their foot on the tile. Meanwhile, cold air from the vent directly above me was blowing in my face, the fluorescent lights embedded in the ceiling were buzzing like mosquitoes, and I was suddenly hyper-aware of my sneakers constricting around my feet.

I took a deep breath, reminding myself that it was sexually-prolific Saudi princes and U.S. congressmen who had indirectly paid for my Bonanza A36TC, then flashed the woman a strained, tight-lipped smile that hopefully hid my teeth and my growing discomfort. "Take your time."

She certainly did take her time; I left the shop thirty minutes later and several thousand dollars poorer. Luckily, my Saudi customer had paid more than enough to cover the cost of shipping and insurance. To him, money was no object, so long as he could maintain a certain "lifestyle" well into his forties.

As Topie and I once more braved the busy street, I straightened my sunglasses and turned up the volume on my headphones to distract myself from the throng of people jostling me from every direction. Luckily, Mrs. Lautner's house was located in a much quieter neighborhood, about ten blocks away from downtown. I sucked on my blue chalcopyrite ball like a jawbreaker as Topie and I left behind the furor of Fore Street to stroll along the tree-lined cobblestone and red-brick homes of West End, breathing in the sweet smell of lilacs – one of only a few floral scents I actually liked.

When we arrived at the front door of Mrs. Lautner's red-brick row house, which was trimmed with pink petunias and purple clematis vines, I was actually humming cheerfully to myself. After spitting out the stone and replacing it in my pocket, I pressed the doorbell with my knuckle and waited for one of my favorite customers to answer the door.

But it wasn't Mrs. Lautner who appeared a few moments later. It was a young, gruff-looking woman wearing a badge that denoted her as home healthcare nurse. "Yes?" she barked, brushing wisps of brown hair from her eyes and straightening the stethoscope around her neck.

A lump appeared in my throat. Nurses in residential homes were never a good sign. "Um, is Mrs. Lautner here? I have the medicine she ordered for her husband."

She rolled her eyes. "We have all the medicine we need, thank you. The last thing Mr. Lautner needs right now are useless homeopathic oils and herbs." She said the last part with enough disdain that even *I* heard it in her tone.

Topie let out a low growl.

I did the same. "These aren't—"

"Is that Delaney?" Mrs. Lautner called, shuffling in her slippers toward the doorway. "Oh, hello dear! Come in, come in!" She ushered me inside, then turned to the woman. "I've got this, Mariana, thank you!"

"If you say so." Mariana turned to go but didn't actually leave. She just positioned herself beside the nearby spiral staircase, crossing her arms over her chest like a stone sentinel.

"Welcome, dear!" Mrs. Lautner said, her eyes crinkling with a wide smile as I awkwardly stepped inside the foyer.

"The pig, too?" Mariana glared at Topie as he scampered inside.

"Of course he's welcome!" Mrs. Lautner knelt down to pat him on the head. "I just put cookies in the oven. Would the two of you like one? They're oatmeal chocolate chip, your favorite!"

"Reeeee!"

The corner of my mouth quirked up. "That sounds delicious, thank…" My words trailed off as my eyes settled on her chest, where a glowing, grapefruit-sized black spot simmered just beneath her coral-pink sweater like boiling ink.

I rubbed my eyes furiously, but the angry stain didn't go away. "What is *that?*"

"What is what?" Her wide-eyed gaze followed mine to the area left of her sternum, then back to me, her eyes narrowing with confusion. She couldn't see what I was seeing.

"I…" I faltered, reaching my hand toward the swirling black vortex embedded in Mrs. Lautner's chest, realization sinking in my stomach like a heavy brick.

The chalcopyrite hadn't been inert after all.

She took a reflexive step backward, her eyes widening. "What is it? Is there something on my shirt?"

Without answering, I walked up to the nurse, seized her stethoscope without asking – eliciting an outraged gasp from the woman – then returned to Mrs. Lautner. I was by no means a doctor, but I knew enough to get by. "Would you mind?" I asked, motioning for her to turn around.

"I—er…" she started, her eyes darting to Mariana, who was emitting a strangled sound from her throat – incredulity, perhaps.

Ignoring her, I looked Mrs. Lautner in the eye. "Please?"

Puzzled as she may have been, she obediently turned her back to me.

I gently pressed the stethoscope above the churning black spot, which I could see from this angle as well – as though it were oozing out of both sides of her. "Take a deep breath," I instructed. "Then exhale slowly."

She did as she was told. The inhale sounded relatively normal, but the exhale was accompanied by a high-pitched whistling that reverberated through my earpiece, along with a paper-bag crackle that turned my insides to cold slush. "Mrs. Lautner…" I started, lowering my stethoscope. "You—"

"I know," she interjected, turning back around to face me. "It's stage three, but I've already told the doctor I've no interest in chemo. What I'd like to know is how *you* figured it out just by looking at me!"

She blinked, waiting for an answer, but I didn't even try to muster up a response. I just stared at the malignant darkness lurking in her chest, my eyes stinging with anger. It wasn't fair. Mrs. Lautner was quiet, kind, and generous – one of the few people in the world that I would have done just about anything for. But what could I possibly do for *this?*

"There must be something," I muttered, more to myself than to her. Quickly, my mind flipped through the various tonics and potions I kept locked behind the counter of my shop. *Dolomite for detoxification, quartz for rhinoviruses, selenite for bacterial strains...* I ticked the vials off in my head from memory, knowing full well that none of them had anticarcinogenic properties.

If such a mineral existed, I hadn't discovered it yet.

"May I have my stethoscope back, please?" Mariana demanded, her words polite but her tone anything but.

I absentmindedly placed it in her grasping, outstretched hand. "There's got to be something that works for cancer," I muttered, pacing in front of the door.

Upon hearing the "C" word, Topie let out a startled snort. He circled around Mrs. Lautner's stockings, rubbing his snout on her shin – whether to comfort her or himself, I wasn't sure.

"I'm okay, little friend," she said, reaching down to pet the top of his head. "Don't fret."

"Hello?" a frail voice filtered in from another room. "Is anyone out there? Where am I?"

I turned my head toward the sound. There was a set of double glass doors that separated us from the living room, where Mr. Lautner had been propped up in front of the TV in a borrowed hospital bed as his dementia continued to progress beyond the scope of what modern medicine could treat.

"Hello?" he called again.

"Coming, Mr. Lautner!" Mariana shouted back, giving me one last dirty look as she turned to go.

My eyes lingered on Mr. Lautner's yellowed skin and sunken eyes, the lump in my throat growing larger. His haggard appearance reminded me of my old friend Norm, who had also had a glazed expression and jaundiced pallor just before he died. But I'd been too distracted to notice his failing health. And then he was gone. Before I'd even had time to process the loss, his son, Heath, had arrived to take over his mineral store. Now, his son was a constant reminder of the friend I'd lost.

No. I blinked back stinging tears. *The friend I'd failed to save.*

The doors shut behind Mariana, startling me from my reverie while eliciting a long sigh from Mrs. Lautner. "I didn't want to ask you outright because I was afraid the answer would be no. But based on your reaction, it seems not even magic can cure cancer. Is…" She swallowed. "Is that right?"

Magic. I winced at the misnomer but chose not to correct her this time. While none of my other clients knew the truth about my "special" remedies, Mrs. Lautner was so gentle and understanding, I'd recently found myself telling her more and more about me, including many of the things I'd hidden from everyone else. Apart from Topie, she had become my closest confidante since Norm's passing.

My shoulders slumped as I shook my head. "No 'magic' that I've discovered…not yet, at least."

At that, her eyes seemed to brighten. "Well, that means there's hope then! But that's not important right now. What *is* important is that I get Mr. Lautner back in tip-top shape. I can't bear the thought of him having to go into a home when I'm gone." I couldn't help wincing at her casual use of "when," though she hardly batted an eye. "Is his tonic ready?"

Nodding mechanically, I reached into my bag and retrieved her order – a thousand-dollar galena and pyrite blend I'd labeled with instructions earlier that morning, along with a clear vial of dolomite to help with unwanted side effects. "Make sure Mr. Lautner takes this on a full stomach," I intoned, my inflection flat and my words rote. "One full dropper every forty-eight hours, or as often as once a day if he metabolizes it too quickly. It should last you a full month, but I've gathered more than enough ingredients to make more just in case it doesn't."

"Are you okay, dear?" Mrs. Lautner asked as she took the vial from me, a look of what I presumed to be concern etched on her face.

"Mm-hmm." I ducked my head, using that opportunity to search for the pen I'd lost in my bag the week before. "I'm fine."

She was quiet for a long moment before asking, "How much do I owe you?"

I popped my head back up, recovered pen in hand. "Nothing."

Mrs. Lautner frowned, making me wonder if I'd offended her. "But I thought the fifty dollars I gave you last week was only for the first installment—"

"You don't owe me anything," I reiterated, taking a step backward. "Just tell Mr. Lautner to get better soon – which he will, if you follow the directions and make sure not to let him eat any foods or supplements containing zinc for two hours before or after taking his tonic. Oh, and make sure he takes a full dropper of the dolomite tincture every evening. This new memory tonic is stronger than usual and might upset his stomach." I kept walking backward as I talked, until the heels of my sneakers hit the threshold.

A wide smile spread across Mrs. Lautner's face as she pressed her palm to the black spot on her chest. "You really are an angel, Delaney. Thank you."

"It's nothing, really," I mumbled, glancing at the doorknob over my shoulder. "I…I wish I could do more."

As I went to open the door, she stopped me, taking my hand in hers. I flinched, nearly pulling away, but managed to stop myself at the last moment.

"We all die, sweetheart," she told me, the smile on her face unwavering. "What's important is how we live our lives in the meantime." She squeezed my hand. "Thank you so much again – for everything." Dabbing at the corner of her eye with the sleeve of her dress, she started to walk toward the kitchen. "Now let me get you those cookies."

"Mrs. Lautner—" I started.

She stopped, glancing at me over her shoulder. "Yes, dear?"

"I-I'm sorry, I don't have time for cookies." Topie shot me a disapproving look, which I ignored. "I just remembered I have somewhere to be. But, um, in the meantime…" I faltered, then cleared my throat roughly. Having no idea what to say in that moment, I resorted to hollow clichés. "Please take care of yourself."

Smiling, she nodded. "You as well, Delaney. I hope to see you soon."

I nodded, tightly gripping Topie's leash in my hand as I turned and ran out the door. As I hurried down the Lautners' petunia-lined walkway, I glanced over my shoulder. Mrs. Lautner was still watching me from the doorway, smiling and waving as though she didn't have mere months to live. After casting her a feeble wave, I picked up speed, until I was all but running down the sidewalk. When her house had disappeared from sight, I collapsed against a tree, too breathless and lightheaded to keep standing.

Topie's leash slipped through my trembling fingers as I sank to the ground. The world felt like it was spinning around me. I pressed my forehead against my knees and started rocking back and forth, fighting against the emotions that were bubbling up in my chest.

I'm not sure how much time passed, whether it was just a few seconds or several minutes, but it wasn't until Topie's wet snout pushed against my elbow that I started, my eyes darting from him to the chalcopyrite I was clutching in a white-knuckled fist.

"I'm fine," I reassured him, working to convince myself of the same. "Really."

Propping his chin on my knees, he peered up at me with an incredulous expression but was polite enough not to argue.

I averted my gaze and cleared my throat, working to channel my residual emotions into something useful: Logic. "I think it's time you and I took a trip," I told him, retrieving the field notebook from my bag. Cheered by the distraction, but still shaken, I began hurriedly jotting down notes with far less detail than usual:

Mineral Name	Region	Color	Effect
Chalcopyrite	Tonglushan Mine, Hebei, China	Conjoined clusters of 1cm spheres; Navy blue, iridesces purple/gold	Shows location of cancerous growths in body(???)

"There are so many incurable illnesses in the world, and so many minerals we haven't found yet," I muttered, thumbing through my notes, the vast majority of which were marred with infuriating question marks. "The chalcopyrite showed me where the cancer was in her body. And since minerals with similar essences tend to cluster together, it's possible we might find something else that can help her in or around Tonglushan." I rolled the chalcopyrite between my finger and thumb. "I mean, it's worth a shot, right?"

I looked up from my notebook as Topie peered up at me from the grass, his head cocked quizzically.

"I have no idea," I answered. "But I'm not giving up until I find what I'm looking for, even if it means having to ask…" I grimaced, unable to bring myself to say his name, then heaved a defeated sigh. "Even if I have to ask *him* for help."

Chapter 5

It had been a very long time since I'd set foot in Heath's shop, and upon entering, I immediately remembered why. It was as though he'd somehow discovered every single pet peeve and annoyance of mine and set them all to full blast, like a medieval torture chamber custom-tailored for me. The moment the door swung open, a cloud of incense hit me square in the face, so pungent my eyes started tearing, while a high-pitched whine emanated from a Tibetan bowl some grubby-faced child was fiddling with. Worse still, a suffocating crowd of tourists milled about the place, fussing over dusty and disorganized shelves of once-powerful stones that had since been carved and polished and artificially irradiated, obliterating them of all traces of essence and leaving only worthless trinkets behind.

In every possible sense of the word, Heath's rock shop was my own personal hell – and standing in the very center of the chaos and commotion was the devil himself, smiling widely at two college-aged girls who were fawning over some sort of rose-quartz pendant that would supposedly put an end to all their relationship woes.

"May I use your restroom?" one of the girls asked, gesturing to the wooden door behind the front desk. My hands became cold and clammy at the sight of it.

"Oh, uh, that's not a bathroom," Heath quickly replied. Indeed, it had once been his father's office, where Norm and I used to sit and chat about minerals for hours.

Now, the door was permanently locked.

That was it for me. I spun on my heels to escape the same way I'd entered, but Topie was watching me from outside the window, his hooves and snout pressed against the fogging glass in reproach. He was right, of course. I couldn't give up on Mrs. Lautner so easily; I *had* to find a way to get to China, even if it meant putting up with Heath and his nightmare-inducing rock shop.

With a deep, incense-infused breath that threatened to send me into a coughing fit, I straightened my back, squared my shoulders, and started making my way for Heath…only to be distracted by the display of strawberry-colored Inner Mongolian fluorite that appeared in my peripheral vision. With a ninety-degree about-face, I shoved through the dense crowd until I found myself nose-to-crystal with some of the most incredible minerals I'd ever seen in my life. Heath hadn't been wrong; these Inner Mongolian fluorite octahedrons were gemmy, lustrous, and had crystal edges so sharp, they looked like carved glass pyramids resting atop inverted byssolite bases. Beside them were several more of the chalcopyrite balls Heath had been bragging about, except *these* pieces had multiple interconnected spheres that resembled glittering, bonded bunches of blue grapes. My eyes widened as they roved across the remarkable shelf of rare minerals, only to bulge in disbelief upon seeing the water-clear fluorite octahedrons resting on lustrous magnetite matrices. The only thing rarer than red fluorite is colorless fluorite, and these were about as transparent as they come. I almost couldn't believe he'd mined all of these incredibly rare minerals from the same remote region of the world.

I *had* to see those mines for myself, no matter what.

Those Chinese minerals had me salivating so badly I had to clasp my hands behind my back to keep them from snatching the fluorites right off the shelf and shoving them in my mouth like a proverbial kid in a candy store. Eating strange rocks in front of strange people was a no-no for several reasons – most notably because I couldn't be sure what effect the new mineral would have on me. Would I light up like a bioluminescent jellyfish? Grow extra limbs like an octopus? Form my own electromagnetic field and accidentally cook everyone around me like hotdogs in a microwave? It was a bad idea, to say the least…

And yet, something about these stones was so tantalizing, my normally unflappable self-control was slipping. After a quick glance to make sure no one was in my immediate vicinity, I covertly popped one of the red fluorite octahedrons in my mouth, germs be damned – I had an antibacterial selenite tonic back at the shop, anyway.

The instant the crystal touched my tongue, it was as if someone had found the master volume switch for the entire store and cranked it all the way up to level ten. Instead of thirty voices casually chattering among themselves, it suddenly sounded like they were all shouting at the top of their lungs right inside my head.

"Wow, this is so expensive!"
"Shit! Did I leave my cell phone at the restaurant?"
"Ugh, these panties are giving me such a wedgie!"
"I really should have put on deodorant today."

"Augh!" I clapped my hands against my ears and staggered backward, nearly knocking over a skinny blond child as I did.

His eyes were as wide as half-dollars as he peered up at me. *"Did she really just put a rock in her mouth?"* he asked, though his own mouth didn't appear to move alongside the question.

I gaped at him wordlessly. *Did I just hear this kid speak telepathically?*

"This lady is kind of weird," the kid thought, his eyes darting around for a safe adult.

"Oh, for Pete's sake." I scrubbed a hand down my face, forgetting I was wearing mascara.

"Laney?" A voice called, barely audible over the telepathic cacophony of voices. "Laney! It *is* you!" Heath appeared at the kid's side, an absurdly wide smile painted across his face. "And here you said you'd rather fall down a mineshaft than ever come by the shop!"

I froze, partially because I'd just shoved a chunk of his highest-priced inventory in my mouth, and also because the torrent of voices flooding my brain made me want to claw my ears off and die rather than engage in polite conversation with my archnemesis.

"Uncle Heath, do you know this lady?" the boy asked, his lips actually moving this time.

Heath answered in the affirmative, though I couldn't make out his exact words. I was too busy staring at his nephew's pale white skin and the glowing black veins that pulsed underneath. A loud roar filled my ears at the sight, drowning out the sounds of both internal and external chatter. I reached a trembling hand toward him, which caused him to take an uneasy step toward his uncle.

Leukemia? I wondered, dread pitting in my stomach at the thought. The kid couldn't have been older than ten. *No...* I shook my head slowly. *It's iron-related... Blood-poisoning, maybe?* Except that didn't feel right either. *Could it be...hemochromatosis?* As soon as the thought formed, an inexplicable yet satisfying tingle warmed me from the inside out. *Okay, yes. Definitely hemochromatosis.* The residual chalcopyrite essence lingering in my tissues made me absolutely certain – which meant its essence revealed multiple types of diseases in the body, not just cancer.

I have to go update my notes, I thought, my eyes flitting to the exit.

"Earth to Laney?" Heath waved a hand in front of my face. "Do you copy?"

"She can't talk, Uncle Heath!" The little boy flashed me an antagonizing grin. "She's got fluorite in her mouth!"

I shot him a sharp glare before attempting to smooth my expression into one resembling innocence and bewilderment. The problem was, I didn't even know how to recognize those expressions on other people's faces, let alone convincingly plaster one on myself.

"Very funny, Chess." Heath clapped a hand on the little boy's shoulder. "But really, Laney, what brings you in? Inner Mongolian fluorite, I presume?" He turned toward the shelf and gently took one of the larger octahedrons, from which four smaller octahedrons had been growing, to flaunt in my face. That's when I noticed the price tag stuck to the bottom: $3,400. I was pilfering four-digit's worth of merchandise in my mouth, which had gone dry and was no longer working properly.

My ears, however, were working a little too well.

"No one would notice if I just took this one tiny rock without paying."

"Damn. Now that *is a nice ass."*

"Toilet paper, ketchup, iodized salt, tampons…"

I rubbed my temples, which did nothing to rid the sound of people's innermost thoughts from my head.

The corners of Heath's grin wavered. "Seriously, Laney, is everything okay?"

I didn't know what to do, so I did the first thing that crossed my mind: I feigned a loud sneeze – which made Heath and his tattletale nephew jump in surprise – forcefully expelling the fluorite into my cupped hands. The internal chatter died down almost instantly but didn't fade completely. That's the problem with salivary glands – they start digesting food (and rocks) even before you swallow them.

"I think that guy over there is stealing from you," I said, pointing to the teenager whose inner thoughts had tipped me off, and who was now rushing out the front door with his hands buried deep in his pockets.

While Heath and his nephew turned in the direction of my pointing finger, I hastily replaced the fluorite on the shelf, sighing in relief.

Instead of chasing the thief out the door, Heath just watched him leave, his shoulders rising and falling in a sigh. "Yes, that happens several times a day, I'm sure."

"Aren't you going to do something about it?" I demanded. "People shouldn't steal."

He shrugged, further irritating me. "If I chased down every person who stole a glass bead or tumbled rock, I'd be running laps around this city."

"But—" I started, then bit my tongue. I wasn't dealing with a reasonable human being. I was dealing with a psychopath – which made my forthcoming request all the more difficult.

Heath turned to his nephew, whose veins were still faintly glowing black. "Hey, Chess, would you mind seeing if those two ladies near the ammonite fossils need any help?"

"Yessir!" Chess saluted his uncle, before turning back to me, eyes twinkling. "Just make sure your friend Laney doesn't eat any more of your rocks!"

"It's *De*laney!" I shouted after him as he sprinted away. "And I didn't eat any rocks!"

It wasn't a lie. By definition, "eating" involves swallowing. And fluorite isn't a rock, it's a mineral.

I turned back to Heath, who was eyeing me with an odd expression. Instead of looking away, I deliberately focused my attention on the center of his forehead, making it seem like I was looking into his eyes without actually having to meet his unnerving stare. "So... You let your nine-year-old nephew help with customers?" I asked, folding my arms over my chest.

"Ten, actually." He flashed me a half-smile. "Besides, the kid's a walking encyclopedia, just like his grandpa. He probably knows as much about minerals as you do."

Doubtful, I thought, then blurted out, "He has hemochromatosis."

I've never been particularly good at small talk.

"Sorry?" Heath blinked.

"It's a toxic build-up of iron in the blood," I explained. "It causes fatigue, headaches, weight loss, and pain in the joints, among other unfavorable symptoms. Have his parents take him to the doctor for a blood test."

"How the hell does she know that?" Heath's internal thought whispered faintly between my ears, though outwardly he just continued to stare at me as though the fluorite had made me grow horns.

I self-consciously reached up and checked the top of my head, just to be sure it hadn't. *Phew.* "Anyway." I cleared my throat awkwardly. "It's easily treatable. I actually have a tonic that would work well for it, though he should see his doctor first to be sure."

"He's been complaining about all of those things for months…" Heath muttered, running a hand through his dark hair. His eyes trailed to where Chess was animatedly talking to two ladies about the difference between ammolites and ammonites. One of the women had a faintly-glowing black spot swirling right where her pancreas would be. Diabetes – yet another disease for which I hadn't yet found a cure.

The muffled thoughts of its inhabitants settling to a dull roar, I glanced around the room, taken aback by the number of black ailments that simmered like ink spots throughout the crowd. Every black blemish was another punch to the gut – a reminder of all the diseases I hadn't yet found the corresponding mineral to cure. So many antidotes out in the world, just waiting for me to find them. And yet, here I was wasting time in some inconsequential shop of worthless rocks. Sure, the red fluorite Heath had just mined still had some of its impressively powerful essence, but that would soon be run down, thanks to all the grubby hands that diminished its potency with every casual, ignorant touch.

I sighed loudly.

Heath turned back to me, his eyes boring into mine with a kind of intensity that made me squirm in my spot. "Thank you," he whispered ardently. "I'll be sure to tell my sister what you said."

"It's nothing." I dropped my gaze to the ground. "Um, so…I actually came here to ask you"—I cleared my throat again, hating myself for what I was about to do—"if you wouldn't mind, um…helping me get that Chinese visa." I muttered that last part as quickly and quietly as possible, as if mumbling might somehow lessen the humiliation of the request.

"Jesus. How can someone so infuriating be so goddamned attractive?"

My head jerked up in surprise. Had that thought come from *Heath?*

No, I shook my head, pushing the ridiculous notion from my mind. *Of course it didn't. He's not even looking at me.* Indeed, the man had turned his attention to his phone, apparently bored with the conversation.

"Well, fine then—" I started, my cheeks burning alongside my flaring temper. "Don't both—"

"Done," he interjected, stuffing his phone back in his pocket.

I gaped at him in disbelief. *That's all it took? A text message?* I'd been trying for the better part of a *year* to get an appointment at the Chinese consulate, only for my visa to get denied – twice!

"I'll take you there myself tomorrow morning."

"But the embassy is in D.C. How—"

"We're not going to the embassy, we're staying right here in Old Port. Just be sure to bring your passport and two other forms of identification…" He faltered, as though searching for the right words. "Um, just don't ask too many questions, okay? My guy will take your info and get you a bona-fide visa within seventy-two hours. It just might not be…*entirely* by the book." He winced and I distinctly heard him inwardly mutter, *"Here we go,"* as if I were some rigid stickler that lost it every time a rule was bent or circumnavigated in the slightest way… Which, okay, maybe I was. But rules without enforcement are just guidelines, and what's the point of that?

I opened my mouth to fire off a snappish retort along those lines, surprising myself when I instead blurted out, "I'll have you know I broke into a private mine just last night."

Heath's eyes grew unreasonably round, as though he were impressed. "You did?"

For some reason, my already-elevated heart rate grew even faster, bringing me perilously close to hyperventilating. "Yes. Um. Here's my number." I thrust a business card in his direction. "Just let me know what time we're meeting tomorrow."

With that, I spun around on my heel and made my way for the exit, too flustered by the chaos of his store to remember to say "thank you." As I ran past Heath's nephew, however, I *did* remember that he would soon be getting bad news.

I skidded to a grudging stop, even as my overagitated parasympathetic nervous system beseeched me to keep running. When I was a child, anytime my pediatrician gave me bad news – usually about my GI tract – he'd slip me a Werther's caramel from his pocket and pat me on the head. As a healthcare professional, I too had a non-negotiable social nicety to uphold. Grinding my teeth together, I dug around my messenger bag until I found one of the stale Werther's caramels I kept on me just for the occasion and handed it to Chess.

"There, there," I said awkwardly, patting him on the head while he stared up at me with what appeared to be a look of bewilderment "You'll be okay."

"Delaney?" Heath called, hurriedly making his way toward me through the crowd.

Without wasting another second, I spun away from Chess and pushed open the door, fleeing from the shop's acrid smells and errant thoughts and awful, clanging racket. As I did, one unspoken thought rose high above the others, following me outside even after I'd let the door slam behind me: *"And here I thought that woman couldn't surprise me any more than she already has."*

Chapter 6

I closed up shop early that day, using the extra time to properly jot down my new mineral notes. It had been reckless, popping those specimens into my mouth without any inkling of their effects – and in public, no less. In my salivating frenzy, I'd sucked most of the essence out of the chalcopyrite, leaving just barely enough for a weak disease-detecting potion. And I had nothing left of the red fluorite, of course, since I'd left it behind in Heath's shop. I could have bought the entire shelf from him and made one heck of a telepathy tonic, something that would have saved me a tremendous amount of effort during face-to-face interactions; instead of wasting time trying to translate my customers' subtle cues, nonsensical euphemisms, fake compliments, and useless observations about the weather, I'd have been able to read their minds and get straight to the point. But that would involve forking over thousands of dollars to the man I despised most in the world, and that was never going to happen. Ever.

It's better this way, I reassured myself as I brushed my teeth late that evening. *Being subjected to other peoples' internal monologues all day long would be* way *more exhausting than listening to the stuff they bother to speak out loud.* I spat into the sink, flossed judiciously, then dabbed the sides of my mouth with a towel. Topie was already waiting for me at the foot of my mattress, curled up with his beloved Piglet stuffie in front of a tablet that was streaming his favorite movie, *Charlotte's Web.*

"Don't eat all the popcorn!" I reminded him.

He let out a muffled snort.

I poked my head out of the bathroom, rolling my eyes at the sight of his entire snout buried in the popcorn bucket. "What a pig," I muttered as I pulled on the oversized "rock-paper-scissors-lizard-Spock" t-shirt I always slept in.

Hurriedly tiptoeing across the cold hardwood floor, I flicked off the ceiling light and slipped under the comforter. After sticking my cold feet under Topie's belly to warm them – eliciting a disparaging *oink* as I did – I flicked on my mattress-side reading lamp and flipped open the cover of the textbook I was rereading for the third time: *5,001 Minerals: The Rockhound's Guide to What, Where, and How to Find Them.*

"Did you know most fluorite glows under a UV lamp?" I asked Topie. "It's usually from impurities like yttrium and europium, but there are some UV-fluorescent minerals out there, like hyalite, that glow because of trace amounts of uranium. Isn't that cool?" I glanced at him over the top of the textbook. He was too engrossed by his movie to spare me a glance, but he did flick his coiled tail as if to say, "That's nice."

"I wonder what would happen if I ate uranium?" I wondered aloud. "Other poisonous minerals don't seem to affect me, and it does seem like the rarer and more lethal they are, the more powerful their essence."

Topie made a polite-yet-disinterested grunt.

I chuckled to myself. "Of course, even if the radiation poisoning didn't kill me, I'm pretty sure a gram of uranium would have something like a billion calories." I sat bolt upright. "Wait. Is that right? No, that can't be accurate…can it?"

I reached for my "smart phone," which was about ten years out of date and therefore, perhaps, a "not-so-smart" phone. No matter though, since I only used it to browse Mindat.org or to make my annual obligatory phone call to my parents on their respective birthdays.

"Okay, so if a calorie is 4.184 joules and a watt is one joule per second," I muttered, punching numbers into the phone's calculator, "that means a kilowatt-hour is 860420.65 calories. So that would mean that one gram of uranium-235, when undergoing complete nuclear fission, would emit a little under a hundred billion joules—or about twenty billion calories." Barking out a laugh, I slapped my hand on my thigh, making Topie jump. "That's amazing! Topie, can you believe that? Twenty *billion* calories? That's like four million Thanksgiving dinners!"

He flashed me a dirty look before turning back to Wilbur and Charlotte.

"You know, there's probably a man out there who would appreciate a self-sufficient woman with a deep knowledge of math and medicine and minerals," I muttered, scooching farther under the covers to continue reading. "And I bet he'd *love* to hear how many calories are in various radioactive metals."

Topie made a noise akin to a scoff.

"Oh, what do you know?" I grumbled, stifling a yawn. "I'm going to bed. Don't stay up too late. I've got an alarm set for seven a.m. since Heath is coming by early." For some reason, my stomach did a little flip at the notion.

Come by my shop sometime, would you? Heath's words whispered against my ears. *Those strawberry-red fluorite specimens are remarkable. Gemmy, great color saturation, razor-sharp crystals – you'd love them.*

I shoved a pillow over my face in an attempt to smother his words – after all, what did *he* know about what I loved? But his twinkling blue eyes lingered in the darkness, making me squirm from the intensity of their gaze. Ten minutes passed, and then twenty, but sleep continued to elude me.

Finally, I reached for the bottle beside my bed and retrieved not one but two fast-acting melatonin gummies, which should have knocked me out within minutes. And yet my heart continued racing like a propeller and I had no idea why. A full hour passed. Soon Topie's tablet had gone dark and his soft snores took the place of silence. Desperate for some shut-eye, I reached for my emergency-use-only sleeping aid – a glass vial of swirling, opalescent moonstone, and took a large swig. Sleep evaded me for only a few more minutes, as my eyelids had grown too heavy for anything else.

But not even the heavy, unyielding fog of melatonin and moonstone was enough to keep Heath from invading my dreams.

My eyes burst open, finding nothing but darkness, thanks to my heavy blackout curtains. My nightshirt clung to my torso from night sweats, while my legs had become tangled in a knot of sheets. Worst of all – my hand was halfway down the elastic band of my panties, where a hot flush had spread between my legs. I jerked my hand away with a gasp, my breasts rising and falling in quick, shallow breaths as I sat bolt upright in bed.

Heath hadn't just been *in* my dreams. He'd been…

Oh God.

I rubbed my eyes furiously, trying to scrub the searing images from my mind, but they had imprinted themselves there as though by a hot branding iron.

The phone beside my bed rang, and my hand instinctively went to answer it.

"Hello?" I mumbled, pressing my hand against my eyes.

"Laney?"

"Heath!" I practically screeched, reflexively flinging the phone away. It bounced off Topie's rump with a *thud*, sending him flying off the bed with a startled squeal.

"Laney, are you there?" Heath's muffled voice sounded from the opposite end of the mattress. *"I've been knocking for the last five minutes."*

I let out a vicious sailor's curse as I lunged forward to fumble for the phone. "I'm coming, I'm coming!"

Without offering any further explanation, I skidded out of bed, yanking off my nightshirt as I did, and began frantically rummaging through my clean shirt drawer until I found a pale pink tee that read *'Rock 'n' Roll'* and featured several spinning agate slices. After yanking it over my head, I threw on a pair of fitted jeans and then pulled on my socks one at a time as I hopped toward the bathroom on one foot. Morning ablutions done in record time, I snatched my Portland Sea Dogs baseball cap from its hook on the wall to hide my bed-head and all but leapt down the ladder.

"Ree?" Topie stuck his snout through the square-shaped hole.

"No time for breakfast!" I snapped. "We'll get something on the way."

With a huff, he turned around and reached out a chubby hind leg, clumsily searching for the rung.

A rap sounded on the front window, where Heath was giving me a pointed look and tapping on his watch.

"I'm coming!" I hollered, only for a hot flush to promptly fill my cheeks. "Ugh!" Scrubbing a hand down my burning face, I whirled back to Topie, who was still struggling down the top rung. "Topie, let's go!" I reached forward and plucked him from the ladder, momentarily forgetting that he was nearly a third of my body weight. "I—*auugh!*" Teetering from his heft, I stumbled backward and tripped over the stool behind the register, sending us both plummeting to the ground.

I landed on my back with a hard *"oof!"* that knocked the wind out of me, while Topie landed safely on top of me, forcing the rest of the air out of my lungs.

"Laney!" I heard Heath shout. *"Are you okay?"*

Having a hog sitting on my chest made it hard to answer, so I just lay there wheezing for a good long moment, white feathering at my vision while the rest of the world pitched and heaved like a fishing boat on rough waters. I squeezed my eyes shut to try to make the room stop spinning, but that only seemed to make it worse.

Topie must have hoisted himself off me to unlock the front door, because when I opened my eyes again, it wasn't a hairy wet snout that was inches from my face, but the visage of an implausibly-attractive man with wide eyes the color of London blue topaz. A hot flush crept all the way down my breasts, which were standing firmly at attention from the memory of the last time Heath was leaning this close to my face – just this morning, in my dreams.

My mortifying, R-rated, sexually-explicit dreams.

"Laney?" Heath asked, kneeling beside me. "Are you okay? Should I call an ambulance?"

"No!" I yelped, lurching upright. The motion nearly made me vomit.

"You've got quite the goose-egg on the back of your head." Heath bit his lip, which for some reason sent a hot jolt of electricity straight between my legs.

"I'm fine!" I snarled. "Just—help me up." I started to offer him my hand, faltered, then quickly pulled it away. "Actually, on second thought…" I pulled a key ring from my pocket and dropped it in his palm. "Open that cabinet over there and look for an olive green vial labeled 'Aventurine' on the top shelf."

Heath flashed me a puzzled look but did as he was told, returning a moment later with a glittering vial of green liquid. "What's this for?"

Ignoring him, I took the vial from him, removed the cork with my teeth, and took a large swig. A relieved sigh burst through my lips as the powerful anti-inflammatory properties of aventurine kicked in, making the swelling from the concussion I'd just given myself all but disappear. Heath extended a hand as I struggled to my feet, but I pointedly ignored it.

He inspected the back of my head, exhaling softly. "I could have sworn you just had a huge bump on the back of your head."

"I'm fine," I interrupted, self-consciously brushing the dust from my rump before replacing my baseball cap firmly on my head. "Let's go."

After shimmying between Heath and the register to make my narrow escape, I located Topie, who was busy scarfing up the truffles Heath had dropped for him on the way in.

"Traitor," I muttered to him as I strapped on his vest.

Heath jogged to catch up to me as I swung the door open and stepped outside. "Well?" I demanded, shooting a murderous look at the world's worst emotional support animal. "Are you coming or not?"

Topie hurriedly licked the crumbs from the floor before gaily trotting outside. I closed and locked the door behind us, double-checking that the sign was set to CLOSED. It was Sunday, but some entitled tourist would no doubt bang on the door regardless, demanding a bandage for his Birkenstock-inflicted blister or an ankle brace for a cobblestone-induced sprain.

"Where are we going?" I asked Heath.

Heath gestured in the direction of the harbor. "Do you have your IDs? Also, I forgot to mention Jonah charges a few hundred bucks for expedited services, but I can cover that if you—"

"I'm good, thanks," I answered. "I figured it wouldn't be cheap."

He nodded, his blue eyes once again darting to the back of my head as we strolled through the empty cobblestone street. "That liquid you took…did it really have aventurine in it? I mean, that stuff's pretty toxic, isn't it?"

"It's just labeled that way because of the color," I replied, a lie I'd practiced many times in the mirror for this very reason. "It's an anti-inflammatory tonic."

"That you made yourself?"

"Er…yes." I avoided his probing gaze, looking straight ahead as we walked. It was barely seven thirty in the morning, and while the sun had risen long ago, most of Old Port had not. "How far of a walk is it?"

"He's just right around the block," Heath replied, pointing toward Fore Street. "Tucked in the middle of a narrow alleyway, kind of like you and your pharmacy. Seems like you rely more on regulars than tourists, eh?"

I didn't answer. I was still trying to clear the last sleepy vestiges of melatonin and moonstone out of my system and would have rather walked straight off the pier than make small talk at that very moment. Besides, what did Heath care whether my customers were regulars or not?

"I just always thought it was…interesting that you seem to have a lot of regular folks who come from pretty far out of the area," Heath continued. "I only know because some of them end up popping their heads in my shop…" He trailed off, most likely because I was staring straight ahead, trying to get as much direct sunlight into my retinas as possible.

Topie gave my hand a firm nudge.

"Yes," I replied mechanically.

Heath didn't try to make small talk after that, and we made it to his "guy's" office within ten gloriously silent minutes. The only problem was the guy wasn't there.

"Hey, Jonah, open up!" Heath yelled. He banged on the barred glass, letting out a groan when he saw the yellow sticky note that had been taped to the door:

> HEATH, I'LL BE IN BY 8:30.
> THANKS AND SORRY!!
> -JONAH

I arched an eyebrow in Heath's direction.

"He specifically told me to get here before eight," he muttered, knuckling his forehead. "Umm…" He looked around, his eyes settling on a café at the end of the alley. "I suppose we could grab some coffee to kill time." Glancing down at Topie, he added, "Finding a table outside would probably be best."

I scoffed. I had far better things to do on a Sunday morning than waste my time sitting at a coffee shop with a man I didn't even like. As I glared up at him to say so, my gaze settled on the aesthetically-pleasing profile of his face, which was softly illuminated by the glinting sunlight that danced off the rolling waves of the harbor. A fresh jolt of electricity shot straight through my lower abdomen, settling between my thighs, where it buzzed like a live wire.

Bewildered, I stopped in my tracks. *Maybe I shouldn't have mixed moonstone and aventurine in the same twelve-hour period.* I mean, that had to be the cause of whatever physiological phenomenon was happening to my body… *Right?* I gulped. Except the strange buzzing between my legs had started *before* I took the aventurine tonic. Which meant…

"You okay?" Heath's voice punctured my reverie.

"Yeah," I replied, my voice cracking from the lie. I needed to flush the poorly-interacting minerals out of my system and *fast*. "Coffee sounds great. Er, drinking it, that is."

He raised an eyebrow. "As opposed to mainlining it?"

"I just meant that the act of drinking coffee would be great," I clarified, "not the part about drinking it with *you*."

Heath's mouth pressed into a tight line. "Has anyone ever told you that you're extremely direct?"

"Yes." I nodded. "Being direct saves time."

He opened his mouth as if to argue, then closed it again, perhaps to reflect on the wisdom of my words. In the moment of silence that ensued, I found myself scrutinizing the fine details of his face, trying to make sense of the inexplicable effect he was having on my body. His hair was dark, well-combed, and suitably thick, which indicated health and virility – not that I should have cared, since I had no interest in bearing children. His eyes were a striking blue, which was an admittedly intriguing combination; dark hair tends to be a dominant trait while blue eyes are recessive. His brows were nicely shaped, and his lips were full and well-moisturized, optimal for kissing.

Wait…what? I blinked, forcing my eyes to settle somewhere else. His chin? No. It had a small cleft, which was actually quite attractive given the angular shape of his jaw. His chest? *No!* I winced. Not when the top two buttons of his shirt were undone, displaying a hint of dark chest hair resting atop well-defined pectoral muscles. Yet another thing I couldn't help but find appealing, even as I furiously reminded myself that the human sum of all those attractive parts was utterly loathsome.

What's wrong *with me?* I chewed on the inside of my cheek, mentally ticking off my symptoms: Clammy hands, flushed skin, increased heart rate, tingling genitals... And then it hit me.

Prasiolite.

He must have given me the wrong vial, I realized, cool relief flooding my overheated, malfunctioning body. It made perfect sense. The vials of prasiolite and aventurine were both similar shades of green – but one was an anti-inflammatory while the other was a powerful libido-enhancer. I palmed my forehead in frustration. *How could I have been so stupid, trusting him to follow one simple instruction?!*

"Laney, did you hear me?" Heath asked.

My head whipped in his direction. "Huh?"

"I said, there's a great coffee shop just around the block. Do you want to go there, or did you have another place in mind?"

I stifled a groan. How had a simple business errand turned into a prolonged, lust-filled coffee date? Biting my lip, I glanced over my shoulder, seriously considering bolting all the way back to the pharmacy. But then Mrs. Lautner and the awful black disease swirling in her chest popped into my mind. I *had* to see those minerals, if not for my own sake, then for hers. I ground my teeth together. *Stupid cancer. Stupid prasiolite. Stupid Heath and his stupid pheromones.*

Heath raised an eyebrow at me.

I clenched and unclenched my fists, sighing. "No."

"No?"

I couldn't bring myself to meet his piercing gaze. "No, as in, I don't know any other coffee shops. So..." I gulped, praying it wasn't audible. "Let's just hurry up and get this over with."

Chapter 7

When we arrived at the coffee shop, Heath offered to go inside and place our orders while I waited outside with Topie. Several sets of tables and chairs faced the Portland Pier, where a dozen tugs, island ferries, water taxis, excursion boats, and yachts bobbed on calm, navy blue water. Farther out in the harbor, an oil tanker drifted by, with a cruise ship puncturing the line of the horizon. I chose the table farthest away from the other patrons, though that didn't stop a rogue seagull from landing atop a nearby umbrella and loudly squawking at me for handouts.

I sighed heavily, rubbing my temples.

Heath appeared a few minutes later, balancing two drinks in his hand. "I got you this, too," he said, pulling a wrapped sandwich from his suit pocket.

"Thanks," I mumbled as he set down the food and iced coffee in front of me. My stomach growled hungrily as I unwrapped the sandwich – a poppyseed bagel with egg, cheese, and—I sighed—bacon. Grimacing at the grease and the texture, I began peeling off the meat with my fingertips.

Heath's eyes darted from our sandwiches to Topie, doubling in size. "Oh God." He pressed a hand to his mouth. "I didn't even think about the bac—"

"Shh!" I interjected as I covertly wrapped the meat in the sandwich paper to hide it. "And anyway, he doesn't know B-A-C-O-N comes from P-I-G-S."

Topie cocked his head at me, his beady eyes squinting suspiciously.

"Why are you spelling in front of the P-I-G?" Heath asked.

"Because he doesn't know how to spell."

"But he understands English?"

"He understands me."

Heath blinked, then shook his head slowly. "You really are…something."

I frowned. Nonsensical statements like that were the reason the world needed more telepathy tonics…which reminded me. "So, you're going back to China next week?" I asked, taking a small bite of my bacon-excised sandwich. Topie pawed at my leg, so I tossed him a chunk of bagel and egg. "What brings you back there so soon?"

Heath shifted in his seat as though he'd just sat in a puddle of water. "Oh, well, I ran out of time during this last trip, so I divided it into two visits to get everything I needed sorted out."

"Why not just have your contacts ship you the minerals once they've been mined?" I took a sip of coffee. "Isn't that what most resellers do?"

The corner of Heath's mouth twitched. "You know, I don't just buy rocks to resell them. I have…other business dealings I attend to, many of which are on-site." He took a sip of coffee – or rather, a large swig – then fell silent.

"Business dealings?" I echoed.

He took a deep breath and let it out slowly, like I sometimes did when I was trying not to say the things I actually wanted to say to people – e.g., "go away, I'm busy," "the sound of your chewing makes me want to punch you," and "none of your damned business," to name a few. I frowned. Was there something he was thinking that he didn't want to say?

"Let's just say, some of the things hidden in those mines are more precious than minerals."

I scoffed. "What could be more precious than minerals?"

Heath didn't answer, which made me doubly suspect that maybe he wasn't as much of an open book as I'd always assumed, which actually made me want to know more about him – purely for curiosity's sake, of course.

"So, what sparked your interest in minerals?" Heath asked. "Because, as I understand it, yours is more of a direct interest in geology rather than a collector's itch. Seems unusual for a pharmacist."

"Not really," I retorted. "Albert Brun was a pharmacist-slash-vulcanologist-slash-mineralogist. Alfred Lacroix, too. And André Laugier—"

"Okay, okay – I stand corrected," Heath interjected, running a hand through his hair. "That said, I'm still curious to know."

"Know what?"

He rubbed the bridge of his nose like I sometimes did when dealing with an infuriating customer. Which made no sense since there were no infuriating customers in the vicinity. "What spurred your interest in minerals?"

"Oh." I took a large bite of my sandwich, stalling for time. Even if I couldn't tell him about my special parascientific interest, he'd broached a subject I could have gladly talked about for hours, even with a clod like him. But the moment I opened my mouth, excitement buzzing in my veins at the prospect of discussing my most favorite topic on the planet, James Ostrowski's face took the place of Heath's.

Hel-lo, my name is Mis-sus Ro-bot-o, he had mocked me in that awful robotic voice, stiffly moving his arms like an animatronic.

The memory made the bite of food I'd just swallowed settle in my stomach like a stone. "I just like them," I muttered, eyeing my half-eaten sandwich that I'd suddenly lost my appetite for.

"I see," Heath responded, his voice tinged with what sounded like disappointment, but was probably derision.

Dipping my head so the brim of my hat would hide the blush creeping into my cheeks, I tossed Topie the remainder of my breakfast then quickly excused myself to the bathroom. Once I'd made sure no one else was in the stalls, I retrieved my dental kit from my purse and began vigorously brushing and flossing my teeth. All the while, the snickers of another boy I'd had a crush on – Ricky Klostreich – scraped between my ears like two coarse pieces of sandpaper.

"Did you see Delaney's teeth?" he'd hooted to the other boys while pointing straight at me. *"They're so nasty, she looks like Shrek!"*

The ogre moniker haunted me until the age of seventeen, when the bullying had grown so unbearable I eventually refused to go to school. After nearly two weeks of missed classes, my parents finally relented, selling one of the two family cars so I could get veneers, followed by a full set of dental implants. But even with a brand-new smile, the name-calling never really stopped; it only shifted to my other "undesirable" traits: my chubbiness, my acne, and my unbrushed hair – to name a few – plus the fact that I refused to wear anything but brown Crocs because the feel of socks and sneakers squeezing my toes together made me want to chop my feet off.

After high school, when Topie and I moved out of that awful farm town as fast as we possibly could, I worked and scrimped and saved until I could afford an expensive skin care regimen and a stylishly short haircut from an actual hairstylist, rather than my mother's dull kitchen shears. And while my weight never really bothered me, loading and unloading fishing boats for nine hours a day on the docks made me lean out enough that the men I worked with often "complimented" my looks, though I could never fully be sure they weren't making fun of me behind my back like James Ostrowski and Ricky Klostreich used to do.

I spat into the sink, rinsed my mouth out twice, and made a toothy grimace at myself to make sure there was nothing stuck between my teeth. Then, with a heavy sigh, I trudged back outside, where Heath was giving Topie yet another vigorous belly scratch.

Swallowing tightly, I made my way back over to them. "Can we go yet?"

Topie shot me a dirty look the moment the scratches halted, but Heath just smiled. "I thought maybe you'd gotten lost on the way to the bathrooms."

"How could I get lost when there's a big sign that says Restroom?" I sniped, rolling my eyes.

He frowned. "It was just a joke, Laney."

"Stop calling me Laney!" I exploded, making both him and Topie jump. "It's *De*laney, okay? Not Shrek, not Missus Roboto, not Laney – just *Delaney!*"

Without sticking around to hear what would most likely have been a nasty retort, I stomped off, gritting my teeth so violently I heard my dentist's voice in my head admonishing me about chipping the porcelain.

Heath's "guy," Jonah – a surprisingly young man with a round, pock-marked face and shifty eyes – was cagey yet mercifully uncommunicative. He merely asked me a few questions about my criminal history – though he apparently wasn't interested in the number of mines and private quarries I'd trespassed on – then took my passport, which immediately made my fingers itch to have it back.

"That'll be six-hundred even," Jonah said, holding out his hand expectantly.

I blinked at him. "Six hundred…dollars?"

Heath cleared his throat. "I was hoping you'd give La—er, *De*laney the same friends and family discount you offered me."

"But we're not friends or family," I told him pointedly.

For some reason, that made Jonah laugh. "Fine. Five hundred then."

Puzzled, but in no mood to pay the extra hundred dollars, I handed him a stack of bills, which he scrupulously counted before pocketing.

"I'll have your visa back to you by Thursday," he told me after stuffing my passport and a wad of paperwork into a manilla envelope.

"Doesn't it normally take two to four wee—"

"Thursday," he repeated gruffly.

I opened my mouth to ask more questions, but Heath put a hand on my arm and tightened his eyes – the universal gesture for "stop talking," or so I'd been told on numerous occasions. I clamped my mouth shut, my eyes anxiously darting back to the envelope. What if he lost my passport and I couldn't travel for the next six to eight weeks?

"Thanks, Jonah," Heath called over his shoulder as he nudged me toward the door. "I'll be back on Tuesday for the, uh…other thing."

I darted a questioning look at him, but he just shook his head, further aggravating me. I hated not knowing things, even when those "things" admittedly had nothing to do with me.

Outside, Topie was sunning himself on the cobblestones, soaking up rays and the attention of several dozen passersby.

"Oh my God, he's so precious!" A college-aged woman with bottle-blonde hair was enthusing as she crouched beside him. "Is he your pet?" she asked Heath, gazing up at him with a perfect smile and eyes the color of polished emerald.

"Oh, uh, no… He's my, uh…friend's," he answered, glancing at me out of the corner of his eye.

"We're not friends," I corrected him.

Heath's expression tightened.

The woman stood up, dusting off her knees. She was wearing impossibly short shorts, had a heavy spray tan, and possessed a self-assuredness I could never dream of having. "Well, if she's not interested, maybe *I* could be your friend?" she purred up at Heath, who took a step backward.

Vivid memories of my prior R-rated dreams came back to me at that exact moment, pummeling my mind with crystal-clear images of Heath lowering his naked, sweat-glistening body between my legs, his hand gently cupping my breast, his full, soft lips parting to brush against mine…

I staggered backward as a deep, hot flush crept into my cheeks and between my thighs, the sheer, unexpected intensity of my arousal knocking the breath from my lungs.

"Th-Thanks for your help," I all but gasped, not bothering to wait for Heath's response as I fled for the safety of my shop.

"La—er, Delaney, wait!" he called, but I had already bolted ten steps in the opposite direction.

I dug my fingernails into my palms, trying to distract myself from the gushing torrent of erogenous images flooding my brain.

Damned Prasiolite! Damned Heath!

"Delaney, please – wait!" he called breathlessly, jogging until he fell into step beside me. "I don't understand. What have I done to offend you?"

I stopped, hugging myself to keep from trembling. My mind was racing through the entire catalog of things Heath had done to "offend" me in the past eighteen months, like taking a perfectly good mineral boutique, which was owned by one of the few people I genuinely liked and respected in the entire world, and turning it into an incense-burning, tourist-teeming, hokum-spewing rock shop. Or hoarding exotic and precious minerals from around the world, robbing them of essence while peddling them off as overpriced "healing crystals." Not to mention his boastful, obnoxious swagger and how he reminded me of every boy I'd ever loved – every boy who'd ever hurt me.

But for once, I didn't say any of that.

"Nothing!" I lied, reminding myself that honesty only ever got me in trouble.

"Then why can't we be friends?" he asked softly. "I like you."

I whirled on him, breathing heavily. "You don't know anything about me!"

"Because you don't tell me anything about you—"

"Because we're not friends!"

Topie trotted between us, cocking his head back and forth as we argued, his tail drooping lower with every angry repartee.

Heath crossed his arms. "Well, that's some circular logic you've got there."

"Says the most illogical man I've ever met!" I flung my arms up in the air. "Look, thank you for your time today and for…for *helping* me," I forced myself to say the words. "But please don't mistake that as an invitation to be friends. That's never going to happen."

Heath's face fell, then hardened. "So…I take it we're not heading to China together next week, even though we'll be going to the exact same place at the exact same time?"

"Please!" I snorted. "I literally bought myself a plane so I wouldn't have to travel with anyone else, *especially* people like you—"

"People like *me*?" Heath balked.

"—and that's precisely how I'll be getting there. So…goodbye!" I shouted, flustered, flooded, and on the verge of tears for reasons completely unbeknownst to me.

Without another word, I turned on my heel and ran back to my shop, not bothering to see if Topie was following.

"Go on, boy," Heath said from somewhere behind me. "She needs you more than I do."

I don't need him or anyone else, I reminded myself, even as my hand reached into my pocket to clench the chalcopyrite ball Heath had given me the day before.

I flung the door to my shop open and slammed it behind me, retreating into the safety of the shadows behind the counter. Slumping against the locked cabinet of potions, I pulled my knees to my chest. The part of my brain that constantly thirsted for knowledge begged me to see whether Heath had indeed given me the libido-bolstering prasiolite potion instead of the aventurine. But another, much louder part of my brain, the part that was too frightened of the answer, overrode it. For the first time in recent memory, I couldn't bring myself to face the facts… The *truth.*

Topie slunk through the back door of the shop five minutes later, only to find me rocking behind the register, my forehead pressed to my knees. Without so much as an admonishing grunt, he wedged his snout in the small triangle of space between my face and my thighs.

"I'm sorry," I whispered. "I don't mean to be an awful person. I just…can't help it sometimes."

He let out a reassuring snuffle.

I reached forward and pulled him into a tight hug, burying my face against his neck. "I really do love you," I murmured, the words feeling strange and foreign on my tongue. "Even if I'm an idiot and have no idea how to show it."

Emitting a noise that sounded oddly similar to a chuckle, Topie nuzzled against me, imbuing me with steadiness and warmth. After a few minutes, when my breathing had slowed and my tears had subsided, I scrubbed a hand across my face, got to my feet, and made my way to the lab in the back of my shop. There was no time for irrationality and silly emotions.

My minerals were calling.

Sketchy as Jonah may have been, he hand-delivered my passport – along with a brand-new Chinese visa that had been adhered to one of its dwindling unmarked pages – first thing Thursday morning, as promised. Part of me wanted to know if he'd spoken to Heath, as we hadn't said a single word to each other since my middle-of-the-street meltdown four days earlier, but I couldn't bring myself to ask. During my lunch break that day, I convinced myself to brave the harrowing smells and sounds of Heath's shop to offer him an apology – not because I cared about his feelings, but because it was the right thing to do. To my dismay, the lights were out and the sign had been flipped to CLOSED.

No matter, I reassured myself later that evening as I packed my bags for my upcoming trip. *It's better this way.*

After all, I'd spent the entirety of my life cataloging not just minerals, but *all* things, people included: pleasant vs. unpleasant, good vs. bad, safe vs. unsafe. Rudimentary as the system may have been, it was efficient, allowing me to better predict and understand an otherwise complex and daunting world. It also provided security; "once bitten, twice shy" had become my life's motto. The steamed broccoli I was forced to eat as a child was bitter and mushy and always triggered a gag reflex; therefore, as an adult, I made sure to avoid all cooked green vegetables without exception. It was the same with people. Elderly women with crinkled eyes and blue-tinted hair – like Mrs. Lautner – were always kind and understanding, while attractive, conceited men like Ricky, James, and Heath were to be avoided no matter what.

Then why can't we be friends? I like you.

I shook my head roughly, banishing the words from my mind. A "friend" was someone you could be your authentic, true self around. Someone who would always be there for you and never hurt your feelings. Someone with whom you could share all of your secrets without fear of them abandoning you – someone like Topie. Enemies were the opposite, and I staunchly eschewed them alongside steamed vegetables, Dalmatians, and tourists from Boston. It was the people who fell in between "friend" and "enemy" that always left me bewildered. Better to shove them in one of two simple categories instead, with enemies being the easiest to avoid. It was a reliable system that, once implemented, had never served me wrong.

"Why fix something that isn't broken?" I wondered aloud as I stuffed a Chinese dictionary into my bag.

It was sound logic, to be sure. And sound logic was *always* the way to go.

Chapter 8

Early Friday morning, well before sunrise, Topie and I trotted down the cobblestone street behind the pharmacy with our bags in hand: me with two suitcases – one full of clothes and the other empty, for rocks – and him with a makeshift backpack with his tablet, water, snacks, and favorite Piglet stuffie. There was never any room to park my pickup truck in the narrow alleyway, so I'd rented out a downtown garage parking space several streets over – expensive, but convenient. Stifling a yawn, I opened the back door for Topie, loaded our stuff in the truck bed – sans Piglet, which Topie was using as a pillow in the backseat – then slumped into the driver's seat, still rubbing the sleep from my eyes. At least I wouldn't have to drive far; Portland International Jetport was less than fifteen minutes away without traffic.

After scanning my badge at General Aviation, the security gate swung open, granting me access. My private hangar was on the far end of the tarmac, where the first rays of sun were just starting to peek above the jagged black silhouette of storage buildings and parked airliners.

I parked the truck just outside our hangar and got out, letting Topie sneak in a few more minutes of sleep. He was always cranky in the mornings.

With a grunt, I unlocked and slid open the double hangar doors. The garish fluorescent lights flickered to life, which would have made me wince in any other circumstance, but seeing my beautiful red and white Bonanza A36TC brought a huge smile to my face. I did a quick but thorough walkaround as part of my preflight checklist, first inspecting the flight control surfaces to make sure they moved freely. Next, I checked for visible leaks and potential problems around the outside of the aircraft, then carefully examined the fuel tank for any signs of water, which can freeze mid-flight and stall the engine. I eyed my tip tanks wistfully. I'd spent a pretty penny on those, which allowed my plane to carry extra fuel for longer trips. But even crossing the Atlantic was out of the question, let alone flying all the way to China; I'd need to spend a few million more dollars for a private jet that had the capacity to do that.

So long as I have a long line of adulterous old men asking for prasiolite tonics, I might be able to save up enough money for a Bombardier Challenger by next summer. I started to chuckle to myself, then winced. Even though I never did check to see if Heath had accidentally given me the light green, libido-boosting prasiolite potion instead of the slightly-darker-green, anti-inflammatory aventurine tonic, I was all but certain he had. After all, it was the *only* logical explanation for the bizarre physiological response I'd experienced in his presence. Heat filled my cheeks at the humiliating memory of me inadvertently lusting all over him – a memory that I quickly shoved to the farthest recesses of my mind in order to focus my full attention on the rest of my preflight checklist, where it was needed.

After climbing up on the stepladder next to the left wing and unscrewing the fuel filler cap, I checked the wing and tip tank fuel levels, which were as full as I'd left them after my Herkimer diamond hunting expedition in the Adirondacks the week before last. With my exterior preflight checklist complete, I hopped off the wing, removed the wheel chocks, and attached a motorized tug to the front wheel to pull the plane from the hangar and onto the tarmac. Then, with Topie still snoring in the back seat, I parked my truck in the hangar, loaded our luggage into the back of the plane – making sure to keep the weight balanced – then set about the hardest task of all: waking up the pig.

"Rise and shine, Topes." I patted him on his spotted rump. "It's time to fly."

He let out an irritated grunt.

"Topie, c'mon!" I groaned, glancing at my watch. "We've gotta be at JFK in two hours."

He flicked his tail dismissively.

I sighed. "If you get up right now, I'll let you ride in the front of the plane."

He opened one sleepy eye, and then the other, then slowly rose on his hooves to stretch like a lazy feline.

"Atta boy," I said, coaxing him out of the truck.

Pickup truck safely parked and hangar closed and secured, I hoisted Topie into the co-pilot seat of the cockpit, helped him strap on his UV-protective goggles and headset, then did the same for myself in the pilot's seat, my heart thrumming excitedly. Apart from minerals, there was nothing in the world I loved more than flying.

"Help me with the preflight checklist?"

After releasing a big yawn, Topie took the clipboard and laminated checklist in his teeth and passed it to me.

"All right." I scanned the list. "Seatbelts"—I checked his, then mine—"secured. Now for the passenger briefing." I turned to Topie. "We're heading southwest to JFK airport at a cruising speed of one hundred and ninety-five miles per hour at seven thousand feet. Shouldn't take any longer than ninety minutes. If we run into any issues, there are parachutes in the back. Any questions?"

He shook his head.

"Passenger briefing, complete," I muttered, crossing it off with my dry erase marker. "Charts, circuit breakers, beacon – check, check, check. Avionics, brakes, fuel valve... Topie, flip that switch for me," I said, pointing to the nav lights. "All right, check."

Pale orange light from the climbing sunrise slowly illuminated the dashboard steam gauges as I continued marking off my list with Topie's assistance. Newer models of this plane had a glass cockpit with big fancy digital display screens, but I preferred my vintage dials and instruments to a fully-electronic interface because technology, as far as I was concerned, was untrustworthy. Besides, I liked my plane exactly as she was.

Once Topie and I had finished the preflight checklist, I stuck my head out the window and called, "Clear!" to make sure no one was stupid enough to be hanging around my propeller, then switched on the Master Battery, fired up the avionics, and started up the engine. The prop roared to life, making both the cabin and my insides vibrate with anticipation. "Here we go!" I grinned at Topie, then switched my radio to ground control. "PWM Ground, this is November-two-one-niner-Charlie at hangar twelve, requesting permission to taxi to the active, over."

The headset crackled. *"November-two-one-niner-Charlie, top of the morning to you – we haven't even had our first cup of coffee yet. Go ahead and taxi to runway thirty via taxiway Alpha-two-Charlie-one-Delta. Wind one-twenty at ten, altimeter three-zero-one-zero."*

"Copy that." I gently pushed in the throttle lever, pressing on the rudder pedals to follow the taxiway signs to the runway. Once there, I switched my headset to tower frequency. "Portland tower, this is November-two-one-niner-Charlie at runway thirty, requesting permission for takeoff."

"Is that you, Delaney?!" a familiar voice hooted.

"Hey, Frank!" I waved up at the tower.

"Where're you headed today, missy?"

"Oh, you know, just taking a quick trip to Beijing."

"Beijing?!" Frank hollered. *"You do know you can't fly to China in a Bonanza, right?"*

I rolled my eyes. "I'm catching a commercial flight from JFK. Permission for takeoff, runway thirty?"

"Affirmative. November-two-one-niner-Charlie, you are cleared for takeoff."

After setting the takeoff flaps and trim and punching in the mixture, I grabbed the throttle knob and turned to Topie with a wide grin. "You ready?"

He nodded at me, clenching his emotional support stuffie between his teeth as I pushed the throttle knob in.

"Here we go!"

The plane shot forward with full power, building speed and momentum as we sailed down the runway. Just as the sun made its official appearance, lighting up the morning sky in bands of orange and gold and blue, I pulled back on the yoke, sending our stomachs plunging. The plane went soaring into the sky, leaving the tower, the airfield, and the rest of the sleeping world behind.

"Woo-hoo!" I cheered, forgetting my headset was still set to tower control.

Frank's laughter erupted in my ears. *"Godspeed, Lady of the Skies!"*

"And her trusty flying pig." I grinned at Topie as we soared higher into the clouds, chasing the adventure that lay before us.

Unfortunately, the "adventure" that lay *directly* ahead was JFK Airport, where I had to pay an exorbitant fee just to land on their runway and then another equally-exorbitant fee to store my plane in one of their rental hangars. Combined with the cost of our business-class tickets, this trip was already well into the quintuple digits.

"Those Chinese minerals better be worth it, eh, Topie?" I said to him as we trotted toward security, carry-on bags in tow. "The next time someone balks at the price of one of my potions, I'll show them the travel receipts."

He made a petulant snort, extra grumpy that he was forced to be on a leash indoors.

"It's just until we get on the plane," I said, glancing at the security line, where only a smattering of passengers were milling about, stifling yawns and rubbing at glassy eyes.

My shoulders sagged with relief. Traveling the world was one of my absolute favorite things; traveling through commercial airports, however, was near the very bottom of my list, just one entry above root canals. To help combat the stress of glaring fluorescent lights, ultra-high ceilings, teeming crowds, and blaring PA announcements, I donned dark sunglasses, my Sea Dogs baseball cap, and noise-canceling headphones. Unfortunately, my travel companion made the teeming crowds part of the debacle that much worse.

"Mama, look!" a shrill voice cried. "It's a piggy!"

Before the little girl could duck under the ropes to accost us, I tightened my grip on Topie's leash and hurried over to the special PreCheck queue. I paid an annual subscription for the privilege, which was well worth it if it meant I got to skip past the horde of amateur yokels who acted like they'd never seen a pig before and *still* didn't know they had to separate their liquids from their solids.

Of course, it doesn't help that TSA views deodorant as a solid while the EU defines it as a liquid, I thought, crinkling my nose. *Which is absurd, since a solid, by definition, is the state in which matter maintains a fixed volume and shape – e.g., stick deodorant – whereas a liquid—*

"Next!" A sharp voice punctured my molecular reverie.

Grumbling, I approached the TSA agent, my passport, boarding pass, and TSA PreCheck Number at the ready. When she didn't immediately take them from my hand, I removed my sunglasses and arched an eyebrow at her expectedly. To my annoyance, she wasn't looking at me, but gaping at Topie as though he'd sprouted a second head.

"Uh…" she started.

I removed one ear of my headphones. "He's my emotional support pig and both the airport and airline have already okayed it," I told her, impatience creeping into my voice. "Where's Murat? He'll tell you."

"Uh… Murat…?" she called over her shoulder.

A tired-looking man with a salt-and-pepper mustache came over a moment later. "I've got this, Kendall," he said, stifling a yawn. "Why don't you go ahead and take your break?"

She nodded wordlessly as she stood, still gawking at Topie and me like we were Martians.

"So"—Murat smiled congenially as he took Kendall's seat behind the glass and accepted my travel documents—"where are you headed today, Miss Stone?"

"Beijing," I answered, my heart skipping a beat when he started thumbing through my passport, lingering for an extra moment on the visa I'd procured through what were very likely illicit means. My hand went to my pocket, anxiously worrying the chalcopyrite ball Heath had given me. Not that I'd brought it with me for that reason, of course – I'd just forgotten to take it out of my pocket.

Murat's head snapped up, making me take a step backward. But instead of calling airport security, he merely said, "Sounds exciting," as he handed me my documents. "Safe travels." He reached down to pet Topie, but the pig was having none of it as he yanked me toward the metal detector.

"Sorry – he's not a fan of the harness," I called to Murat over my shoulder, stumbling as the leash-jerking intensified. "Topie, stop tugging! We still have to put our bags through the X-ray machine!"

He sat down hard on the floor, impatiently gripping Piglet in his mouth as I unstrapped his backpack and unhooked his harness.

"You need to give me that too," I reminded him, wrestling the stuffie from his mouth. "For all they know, you might be using him to smuggle truffles through security." I snickered at my own joke, though Topie apparently didn't find it very funny. "Go on," I sighed, nudging him toward the metal detector.

He hurriedly scampered through it, then parked himself at the far end of the conveyor belt, anxiously waiting for Piglet.

With an unhappy sigh, I removed my own comfort items – headphones, sunglasses, and weighted jacket – then approached the metal detector. At the TSA agent's gesture, I stepped through.

Beep beep beep!

I winced.

"Did you forget to remove a watch, or maybe a necklace?" the TSA agent asked.

"I don't wear necklaces."

"Try again," he suggested, motioning me back through.

I sighed, then again did as I was instructed.

Beep beep beep!

The man's frown deepened. "Would you mind standing to the side over here so Kendall can pat you down?"

I shook my head and obediently held out my arms, having been subjected to this same discomfiting ordeal on numerous occasions.

"Hello again," Kendall chirped, tugging on a pair of Nitrile gloves. "Any idea what might be setting off the alarm? A barrette, maybe?"

Nope, just the heavy metal build-up in my blood from all the rocks and minerals I ingest, I thought ruefully, though I bit my tongue. It was never a good idea, as I'd more than once learned, to tell strangers about my rock-eating habit.

Kendall patted me down several times with a look of consternation on her face, while I gritted my teeth from the unwanted physical contact. "I don't feel anything that could be setting it off…" She glanced up at the metal detector, doubt creasing her face.

"I have a copper IUD," I told her truthfully, knowing full well that wouldn't set off a metal detector on its own.

"Ah…that explains it," she replied blithely. "Well, then, you and Mr. Piggy have a good flight!"

I forced a tight-lipped smile before running over to collect our belongings.

The rest of our arduous trek through the airport was no better, and when we finally slumped into our seats nearly an hour later, I let out a long sigh of relief. "Have I mentioned I hate flying commercial airlines?" I muttered to Topie, which garnered a hearty snort of agreement. "Thank goodness it's a direct flight to Beijing."

Unfortunately, my relief was short-lived. A shrill screech sounded from the row behind me, where a teenage boy wearing noise-canceling headphones similar to mine had begun screaming and flailing his arms and legs.

"Can't you shut him up?" the boy's father hissed at his wife from his solo seat across the aisle.

"His headphones are dead!" she shot back, turning her overflowing carry-on bag upside down to empty the contents into her lap. "I don't know where the charging cord is!"

"What do you mean you don't know where it is?! This is a sixteen hour flight!"

"Richard, I had to pack his bag and my bag *and* yours this morning, so please forgive me if I forgot one damn thing—"

"Here," I turned around in my seat, thrusting my own spare charging cord in the boy's direction. "This should help."

His screaming stopped abruptly as he regarded the USB-C cable he was now clutching between two hands, his red rimmed eyes darting up to meet mine for the briefest moment.

"I know the feeling," I said, casting him a small smile. Then, before his harried, wide-eyed mother could start talking to me, I replaced my own headphones over my ears and abruptly turned back around in my seat. "And you said three charging cables was too many," I muttered to Topie.

He didn't respond; he was too busy nosing through his backpack, trying to sort through his assortment of toys and in-flight entertainment.

With a pang of envy, I helped Topie with his sleep mask and headphones, then covered him with his special Winnie-the-Pooh weighted blanket. The lucky swine would sleep through the majority of that sixteen-and-a-half-hour flight, while I fidgeted uncomfortably and counted down the literal minutes – all nine-hundred and ninety-five of them – until our arrival the following day. At least I had a Mandarin textbook to help me pass the time. I took it out and buried my nose in it, familiarizing myself with the basic Hanzi shapes.

"What can I get you to drink?" A flight attendant asked me some time later, after the rest of the plane had boarded. She didn't ask anything about the pig-sized pile of blankets beside me, most likely assuming it was a small child.

I paused the Chinese-language mineral podcast I'd been listening to, then glanced down at the section I'd been studying – *Dining Out in Beijing* – to make sure I pronounced the tones for "tomato juice" and "extra napkins" perfectly. *"Wǒ xiǎng yào xīhóngzhī hé bǔ xí cānjīn."*

"Dāngrán—ehh?!" Her eyes widened. *"Nǐ huì shuō zhōngwén ma?* How long have you been studying Chinese?"

"About thirty-five minutes," I replied, flipping the page to the food and beverage glossary.

Her jaw dropped. "Did you say thirty-five *minutes*?"

"Yes. By the way, in case there's any problem during the flight, would you please let the captain know I'm a trained pilot?"

"Sure thing…" She gave me a funny look before turning to get me the tomato juice I'd asked for.

"Oh, and don't forget the, uh"—I glanced down at the glossary of my book to double-check my pronunciation of "napkins"—"*duō yī diǎn cānjīn*. My pig is potty-trained, but his aim isn't very good – hence the extra napkins."

"*Ai ya*," she muttered, rubbing the bridge of her nose as she turned away. *"Zhè bān hěn cháng, hào fán."*

"What does that mean?" I called after her.

For whatever reason, she didn't reply.

"Ma'am?" I tried again.

Still no answer.

Scowling, I put my headphones back on and returned to my studies. At least I still had sixteen hours and thirty minutes to figure out what she'd said…

Chapter 9

…which, it turns out, wasn't very nice.[5]

That same flight attendant and I flashed one another wary side-eyes as Topie and I squeezed past her to disembark, him bright-eyed and springy-tailed and me frumpy-looking and disheveled.

"Stop trying to run off," I groused, tugging on his leash. "Folks in this country don't have the same ideas about pigs being cute and cuddly pets as they do in America."

Indeed, all of the other passengers were openly staring at us, with one old lady muttering something about *gū lǎo ròu* – sweet and sour pork – under her breath.

I shot her a dirty look.

Topie, meanwhile, was blissfully ignoring me, all four of his legs scampering furiously on the slick tiles as we neared the end of the jetway.

"Stop! Remember what happened in Frankfurt?" I hissed. "They nearly turned you into Wiener schnitzel!"

---

[5] Something about how this was going to be a very long, annoying flight.

At that, he slowed a little.

"And anyway—" My mouth abruptly snapped shut as we stepped inside the colossal terminal of Daxing International Airport. Even Topie skittered to a stunned halt.

I'd read up on Beijing's new, state-of-the-art airport well before we'd even left Portland: boasting the world's largest airport terminal, Daxing spans seven-and-half million square feet – the equivalent of ninety-eight soccer fields. Including the runways and annexes, the entire complex – which cost $11 billion to build – covers eighteen square miles and can handle three-hundred takeoffs and landings an *hour*. But none of that prepared me for the sheer enormity of the terminal we'd just stepped inside – and by "terminal" I mean the singular, massive star-shaped structure that housed five concourses and spanned an entire kilometer from end to end. Glaring white tiles, paint, and lights screamed at me from floor to ceiling, which was easily a hundred feet high. Worst of all, there must have been thousands – no, *tens* of thousands – of people teeming about, many of whom were shoving past us to make their connections.

I dropped my bags on the ground, my body immobilized from head to toe. The building itself spun wildly around me, its pulsating lights bleaching the edges of my vision and the throbbing roar of the crowd cutting right through my noise-canceling headphones. My breaths were coming fast and shallow by that point, the resulting presyncope[6] making me drop to a crouch. I squeezed my eyes shut and folded my arms over my head to help smother my overwrought senses, but it didn't help.

---

[6] Near-fainting

It's unclear whether a few seconds or a few minutes had passed with me kneeling on the floor of the airport in full-on panic attack mode, but two things eventually roused me from my stupefied state: one, the feeling of Topie shoving something smooth and cool in my hand – a swirling purple amethyst potion that I'd brewed the day before to help with travel anxiety – and two, the young man in a crisp black suit and matching chauffeur cap who appeared beside me, waving a sign that read MISS DELANEY STONE in my face.

I slapped the sign away before upending the amethyst potion into my mouth. The cool liquid slid down my throat, ironing out the roughest edges of my nerves as it did. My tunnel vision slowly feathered back to normal, while my heart rate slowed back down to around a hundred BPM – still elevated, but not tachycardic.

"Miss Stone, you okay?"

Heat blossomed in my cheeks when I looked up at the man, who was staring down at me as though I were a child having a tantrum.

"I-I was just tying my shoelace!" I sputtered, leaping to my feet. My eyes narrowed. "Why is my name on your sign?"

"I am Zhang Li, your driver for the day," he said with a small bow. "You can call me Li!"

"I never requested a driver!"

"I'm with private tour company Mr. Spencer hired to accompany you to Tonglushan Mine."

"Wait… *Heath* Spencer?" I demanded.

He nodded.

My mouth dropped open. "Why would he do that?"

Li, who was shifting his weight as though he had a pebble stuck in one of his polished black shoes, rubbed the back of his neck with a white-gloved hand. "Ah, well, you would not be able enter the country without tour guide, Miss Stone, because of stressed relationship between American and Chinese governments."

I gaped at him, an embarrassed flush further heating my cheeks. I should have known that, of course. It wasn't like me to just show up in a country without understanding what regional travel requirements and advisories were in place. But I'd been so excited to finally be able to come here, I'd just…overlooked it.

Damnit. I blinked away the tears forming in my eyes. *What is the matter with me lately?*

I was so embarrassed and furious with myself, I nearly turned around and walked back onto the plane, Chinese minerals be damned. But that would have gotten back to Heath, and I didn't need him making fun of me any more than he probably already was.

Besides—I sighed—*Mrs. Lautner needs me.*

"Miss Stone?" Li asked, glancing between Topie and me. "Should I call Mr. Heath, or—"

"No!" After sucking down a deep, steadying breath, I let out a slow exhale. "Don't do that. Just, uh…" I scrubbed a hand down my face with a defeated groan. "Just show us to the car, please."

Li gave me a small bow. "Of course, Miss Stone. But first, I escort you through customs and help you retrieve your bags."

I nodded dumbly, keeping my head down as Li led me through the bustling terminal. It took nearly an hour just to get through customs, with Topie causing more of a fuss than either of us had anticipated. Even though I explained over and over in both English and severely-stunted Chinese that he was a certified emotional support animal, not "livestock," they made him go through an entire quarantine inspection – a rather hands-on experience he was *not* happy about.

"That was rough, I'm sorry," I clucked, handing Topie *his* emotional support piggy when the process was through. "At least the visa worked out okay," I added in a whisper, casting Li a sideways glance.

Topie let out an irritable snort as he snatched Piglet from my hand, clearly unimpressed with China thus far.

After stopping for a quick bathroom break, where I brushed my teeth and Topie and I both splashed water on our faces to freshen up, Li motioned us toward the exit. The doors slid open, sending a blast of warm, muggy air that made me stumble backward. Topie stopped halfway through the door, looking over his shoulder as though trying to decide if the air conditioning was worth another potential run-in with handsy Chinese Customs Officers.

"June is very hot time in China," Li said, shepherding us toward the large SUV that had just pulled directly in front of us. Its windows were tinted so dark, there was no color difference between them and the vehicle's black paint, save for the metallic flecks that were embedded in the latter. "Would you like water?" he asked, offering me an ice-cold bottle from the built-in cooler wedged between two creamy white leather seats.

"No," I answered automatically, then thought better of it. "Actually, yes, please."

Li handed me the bottle as I stepped inside, then reached for Topie's leash.

My hand tightened around it. "The pig stays with me."

His eyes bulged. "On leather seats? Wouldn't trunk be better place for—"

"The pig stays with me," I repeated levelly.

Li sighed, gently closed the door behind the two of us, then traded places with the driver who had pulled the car up to the loading zone. The valet gave me a low bow from outside my window before hopping inside a *second* SUV that had appeared behind us.

As we pulled away from the terminal, I leaned forward with the intention of asking Li if two cars were *really* necessary, but there was a pane of privacy glass separating the backseat from the driver. "Seems excessive," I muttered. With an incredulous shake of my head, I turned to Topie. He was gazing at my water bottle and licking his lips. "Oh, right. Sorry." I rooted around the cooler, which was filled with both still and sparkling water, Tsingtao beer, and a bottle of champagne, and handed Topie a bottle of water that he happily upended in three swigs. I followed suit, only now remembering that I hadn't had any liquids in the last few hours.

"Okay, time to get situated…" I murmured, pulling out my China travel book and flipping it open to the fold-out map. Now that I was properly hydrated and out of that awful building, my thoughts were finally beginning to unscramble. "Right, so, both the airport and Tonglushan Mine are in the Hebei Province," I told Topie, "which is this small area in the northeast." I tapped the page. "It's bigger than it looks, but it shouldn't be more than a few hours' drive from here. We can have Li drop us off at a hotel that's close to the mine. The Hebei province is heavily urbanized, so it shouldn't be hard to find a place to stay."

Topie nodded as he inspected the map, which he couldn't read but pretended to anyway.

I regarded the fancy console embedded in the door on my left, which had several different switches and buttons, then pressed the one labeled "玻" – the Hanzi symbol for "glass." The window separating the back seat from the front rolled down.

"Excuse me, uh…Li?"

He glanced at me in the rearview mirror. "Yes, Miss Stone?"

"How long of a drive is it to the Tonglushan Mine? And at which hotel will you be dropping us off?"

I watched Li's eyes grow wide. "Miss Stone, Tonglushan Mine is twelve-hundred kilometers away. I am driving you to Mr. Spencer's private jet."

"Heath's private what?" I demanded, panic seizing me by the windpipe as I once more regarded the map spread across my lap. "But Tonglushan is supposed to be right here in the Hebei Province—"

"*Hu*bei Province," Li corrected me.

"It's pronounced 'Hubei'?" I asked, puzzled.

He shook his head. "No, no. Daxing Airport in *Hebei* Province. Tonglushan Mine in *Hubei* Province." After stopping at an intersection with a red sign that had the Hanzi symbol for "S<small>TOP</small>," he turned all the way around in his seat to point at a large area on my map halfway across the country. "Ancient copper mine *here*, in *Hu*bei Province."

My jaw tumbled open. I brought the map up to my nose, gaping at it in disbelief. "But… But…"

"Now we drive to FBO hangar, where Mr. Spencer waiting for us." He stepped on the accelerator, making me jerk backward in my seat.

"Where Mr. Spencer is *what?*" I yelped, knocking into Topie.

"Mr. Spencer waiting right over there," Li said, pointing to the other side of the barbed wire security fence we were driving alongside, where a gorgeous, sparkling, seventy-eight-million-dollar Gulfstream G650 was sitting out on the tarmac.

"Where?" I frowned, craning my neck to get a better view. "Is his jet behind the Gulfstream?"

"Gulfstream *is* Mr. Spencer jet," Li replied, glancing at me in the rearview mirror.

I was too stunned to muster a reply, my shock only growing as we entered the FBO – "fixed-base operator," a.k.a. the private plane sector of the airport. Pressing my hands and nose against the window, I stared open-mouthed and unblinking at the unbelievable sight of one of the fastest, swankiest private jets in the history of aviation. I'd never even seen a Gulfstream in person; they were typically reserved for A-list actors and corporate billionaires.

"That *can't* belong to Heath. Do you think Li was joking?" I whispered to Topie, who merely shrugged. To him, a plane was a plane—unlike truffles, all 140 species of which he could identify with a single sniff.

Anyway, as it turns out, Li was not joking. After brandishing his security clearance at the armed guards standing by the gate, Li drove us right up to the jet, parked alongside it, then got out of the car and opened the door for me. I stepped onto the hot tarmac while he retrieved my luggage, my jaw dangling open as my feet shuffled toward this divine masterpiece of aviation. In the sun-beating heat of mid-afternoon, it almost looked like a shimmering mirage. I gazed up at it in reverence and disbelief, joy swelling in my chest – until the passenger door unfolded vertically like a Lamborghini door, revealing the last person I wanted to see at that particular moment – or ever, really.

"Need a lift?" Heath called down to me.

My stomach lurched at the sight of him, as though I were flying a small plane that had unexpectedly hit a patch of rough air. "I…" I started, licking my lips to put moisture back in my parched mouth. "Um…"

"Reeeeeeee!" Topie squealed, his leash tearing from my outstretched hand as he bolted toward Heath at full-speed.

"Good to see you too, buddy!" Heath grinned, slapping his thighs like he was beckoning a golden retriever. "Want some truffles? I've got the good stuff."

"REEEEEEE!" Topie's hind legs kicked up in excitement.

"Maybe I *should* have let that old lady turn him into sweet and sour pork," I muttered under my breath as I trudged toward the Gulfstream, my excitement at the prospect of near-Mach speeds severely dampened by my dismay at having to share the experience with Heath, of all people. I reached into my pocket to finger my chalcopyrite worry stone, momentarily forgetting who had given it to me.

"Pardon me, Miss Stone." Li appeared at my side, huffing as he carried two suitcases and a backpack on each shoulder.

I started. "Oh, Li, you don't have to carry those. Here, let me—" I reached for my suitcase.

He veered out of my reach. "Sorry, Miss Stone. Mr. Spencer paying me, not you."

Sighing, I rummaged around my jacket pocket for cash. "At least let me tip you."

When Li saw me extending a ten-dollar bill in his direction, he barked out a laugh. "Miss Stone, I get paid many times that for one hour work. Put money back in pocket, *shǎ guā!*"

I blinked in surprise. "Did you just call me a melon?"

Li didn't hear me; he was already marching up the carpeted steps of the jet, stopping first to bow to Heath, who flashed me another toothy smile as I approached. As much as I wanted to know what "shǎ guā" meant, I set the question aside – for the moment, at least. I had far more important questions, all of which required immediate answers.

"What *is* all this?" I demanded, gesturing between the SUV and the jet. "Since when do mineral collectors fly around in eighty-million-dollar jets?"

Heath shrugged one shoulder. "I don't own it – I'm just borrowing it from a friend."

My eyes bulged. "*Borrowing* it? From who? Xi Jinping?"[7]

"Of course not!" He flashed me a wink as he motioned me inside the jet. "It belongs to Jingping's nephew."

Instead of stepping inside, I stopped just below Heath, forehead-to-chin with his obnoxiously-chiseled jaw, and crossed my arms. "That's not funny!"

"I'm not joking."

"But—"

"C'mon," he interjected, glancing at his watch. "We've got to get back to the mine before sunset."

"We?!" Blustering, I followed him into the ritzy passenger area, which looked like something out of a

---

[7] The current President of China.

James Bond movie. Plush carpet lined the entire floor, bordered by polished wood trim. Four creamy-white leather seats, as wide and cushioned as La-Z-Boy recliners, were arranged around two polished wood tables, one of which had an abalone-shell checkerboard built into it. Behind the four seats was a flip-up flatscreen TV and a long leather couch, which ran along the entire right side of the main cabin. Topie, who had already made himself at home, was lounging across it, basking beneath the sunny rays of a large oval window.

Heath appeared behind me. "The G650 is more than just pretty to look at. She's broken more than a hundred world records for speed and can fly over 7,365 statute miles nonstop, at cruising speeds of 650 miles per hour. She can even fly around the world in just over—"

"Forty-one hours." I turned around to face him, crossing my arms. "I know."

He arched an eyebrow. "You do?"

"Of course I do! I'm a pilot."

Heath burst out laughing, which made the edges of my vision turn crimson with rage.

Blinking away angry tears, I plopped down in the nearest seat, fastened the belt across my lap, and hugged my knees against my chest. Gently rocking back and forth, I stared at the sprawling airport outside the window, calmed by the sight of dozens of planes taking off. Every time one soared into the sky, I named the model under my breath.

737 Boeing Max 9... Airbus A380... Boeing 747-400...

Heath lowered himself into the chair in front of me. From my periphery, it looked as though he were frowning.

"When do we take off?" I asked levelly, not looking in his direction.

"I don't understand..."

"You don't understand what time we take off?" I balked, my eyes glued to the Cessna Citation Longitude that was turning onto the adjacent runway.

"No." He sighed in what I assumed was exasperation. "I don't understand why I make you so angry all the time."

"And I don't understand why you're helping me!" I snapped, finally turning to look in his direction. "I mean, what's the point of bringing me all this way just to make fun of me? It's not like you can't do that back in Portland."

"Make fun of you?" The creases in Heath's face softened. "Wait...about being a pilot? Honestly, Laney, I thought you were joking."

"Why would I joke about being a pilot?" I asked, waving away the flight attendant who had just come over to offer us two glasses of champagne.

Heath barked out a laugh. "Because you're already a pharmacist and an expert mineralogist! How could there possibly be enough hours in the day for you to have learned how to become a pilot as well? I mean, you're not even thirty yet – unless you're some sort of vampire who's actually hundreds of years old?" He waggled his eyebrows, ostensibly to let me know he was joking.

"Oh." My rocking stilled as I considered his words. "So...you weren't making fun of me, then?"

His eyebrows drew together. "Of course not. Why on Earth would I make fun of you?"

I leaned back in my seat. James had said the same thing when I'd confronted him about the terrible things he'd said about me to his friends. The memory, painful as it was, had been preserved in my mind in perfect, crystal-clear detail, all the way down to his outfit: cargo shorts and a peach-colored Polo shirt, despite the growing chill in the air and rain clouds looming above us. *"Is it true?"* I'd demanded, rocking back and forth on my heels as I hugged my body, unable to meet his eyes. *"Of course not."* He'd scoffed. *"Why the hell would I make fun of you?"* As James said those words to me, I distinctly remembered his Adam's apple bobbing up and down while he loosened the top button of his collar, as though it had suddenly gotten too tight.

I studied Heath for a long moment, my gaze lingering on his Adam's apple, which had already been exposed by the unbuttoned collar of his white dress shirt. Though it wasn't bobbing, the sight of it sent an unexpected jolt of electricity between my thighs, as though I still had prasiolite in my system – which I didn't. This time, I was sure of that.

My eyes cautiously flitted to his, which were watching me intently.

The knot in his throat bobbed.

A lie? I wondered, biting my lip. *Or something else?*

"I'm so sorry to interrupt." The flight attendant appeared again, bowing her head. "But the captain has advised that we'll be taking off in just a few minutes. Would either of you like anything to drink before then?"

"We're fine, Meng." Heath smiled up at her, which annoyed me for some reason. "*Xièxiè.*"

"*Bù kèqì.*" She smiled back, then took her seat in the back, beside Li.

"Li's coming with us?" I asked, glad to have an excuse to break the awkward silence simmering between us.

"Yes. He's my dedicated driver for the week."

Frowning, I looked out the window, where a second SUV had arrived. The same valet from before stepped out of the passenger side seat of that vehicle and into the driver's seat of the car Li had left parked on the tarmac. A few moments later, both cars drove away.

Heath leaned forward in his seat. "Laney—"

"*De*laney," I interrupted, gesturing out the window. "This is all so wasteful."

"What is?" His eyes landed on the shrinking cars. "Oh, that. I agree, but it's standard security precautions, most of which come from the Chinese government. Now, do you mean to tell me that you really weren't kidding before? You're actually a pilot?"

"Yes!" Irritation spiking, I kept my gaze steadily aimed outside the window. "Why do you keep asking me the same question over and over?"

"Because I'm floored by how incredible you are."

I started, caught off guard by the compliment.

"Do you want to fly the plane?" Heath asked, his eyes twinkling as though he were still teasing me. "I can ask Yǔxuān to let you in the cockpit—"

"Impossible," I interjected, waving away the suggestion. "My private pilot's license doesn't have a multi-engine rating or even a type rating for this kind of aircraft. I guess your knowledge of airplanes rivals your knowledge of minerals – rudimentary."

"Oof," Heath muttered, rubbing at the crease between his eyebrows. "Are you this mean to everyone, or am I just lucky?"

"Lucky?" I asked, puzzled. "Oh. You were being sarcastic." I sighed. "Sorry. I suppose that was unkind. I just don't have a lot of respect or patience for ignorant people."

"How is the apology somehow worse than the offense?" Heath muttered.

I opened my mouth to answer, but the engines had just started, drawing my attention back outside. "Knowledge is everything," I said absentmindedly, craning my neck to survey the wing flaps extension ahead of takeoff. "Without it, we would be lost in a sea of stupidity."

"Ah, but as our island of knowledge grows, so too does the shore of our ignorance."

My head swiveled around so fast, I felt a disc pop in my neck. "You know John Archibald Wheeler?"

The corner of Heath's mouth quirked up. "I do."

I stared at him, perplexed. I could hear and feel the rumble of the plane accelerating, and while my eyes itched to look out the window, I couldn't pull them away from the baffling man sitting across from me.

"What is it?" he asked, his smile wavering. "Did I say something wrong again?"

"No, it's just…" I swallowed. "I have that quote tacked to the corkboard in my lab. It's to remind me that no matter how much I think I know, the things I don't know are infinite."

"It's overwhelming, isn't it?" Heath asked softly. "It's like the more knowledge you drink in, the more parched you become."

Ironic, since his words had made my mouth go dry.

Maybe he's not a complete ignoramus after all, I thought, chewing on the inside of my cheek. The notion frightened me, and I had no idea why. "Why are you helping me?" I asked again, my voice oddly raspy. "You hardly know me."

Heath's smile appeared genuine. "In case you hadn't noticed, I've been trying to get to know you."

"But why?"

"Hmm." He tapped his lip as though considering his response. "Well, I can honestly say that of all the people I've ever met, you are by far the most interesting – and the meanest," he added with a small laugh. "Though part of me thinks there's a soft, nougat-y center beneath that rock-hard candy shell."

"There's not," I retorted, once more crossing my arms and looking out the window. My stomach suddenly felt jittery, which I attributed to the nose of the jet lifting into the air. "Don't look for something that isn't there. It's a waste of time."

Heath snorted as though I'd just told a joke. "Look, if it makes you feel better, I have a logical reason for inviting you along as well."

That vaguely sparked my attention, though I kept my gaze firmly glued to the window. "Oh?"

His reflection nodded in the glass, disrupting what was otherwise a shrinking labyrinth of vehicles and concrete that surrounded the colossal, star-shaped airport. "One of the miners found something strange at one of the Tonglushan satellite mines – something neither he nor I have ever seen before. And since you know more about mineralogy than anyone," Heath continued, "I thought you could help me figure out what exactly it is."

I frowned. "What are you saying? That you need my help identifying a mineral?"

"What I'm saying is, we may have unearthed something yet to be identified – a brand-new, undiscovered mineral."

I jerked my head in his direction, forgetting the window altogether. "An undiscovered mineral?"

Heath nodded, his expression solemn. "If you thought that chalcopyrite was spectacular, just wait 'til you see this."

Chapter 10

Three hours, twelve minutes, and thirty-eight seconds.

That's the exact amount of time Heath could have spent filling me in on this supposed "new mineral," but he chose to remain infuriatingly mum, telling me I would just have to wait and see for myself – as though I were a child wanting to know what presents were waiting for me under the Christmas tree.

"Don't you have any pictures or notes you could show me in the meantime?" I huffed as we made our way across one of the private tarmacs of Wuhan Tianhe International Airport, which was being pummeled by sheets of hot, torrential rain that fell from a heavy layer of low-hanging cumulus clouds directly above us. "I just don't understand all the secrecy!"

Heath stopped halfway between the jet we'd just disembarked and the black limo waiting to transport us to the copper mine, even though we had no rain jackets or umbrellas and his expensive suit was almost completely waterlogged. I glanced down at my own outfit – a white t-shirt and cargo pants, both of which were already soaking wet – and self-consciously crossed my arms over my chest.

Motioning for Li to go on ahead – which Topie took to mean for himself as well – Heath turned to face me, droplets of rainwater pouring down his hair and the tip of his nose. "Laney, I need you to listen to me," he said, leaning in so close I was tempted to take a step backward. "I don't need to tell you that Americans are viewed with immense scrutiny in this country, even the regular tourists who go straight to Beijing and the Great Wall." He took another step closer, dropping his mouth so that it was centimeters from my ear, and spoke so softly I could barely hear his words over the roar of the rain. "The last thing the Chinese government wants is for us to go digging around in their mines and bringing proprietary information back to the States."

I swallowed tightly. The proximity of his lips and the warmth of his breath against my neck sent an unnerving trail of goosebumps down my spine that made me want to flee in the opposite direction. Curiosity alone kept my feet planted to the asphalt. "Proprietary information like what?"

"As far as anyone knows, we're just regular tourists who came to see the ancient copper mine exhibit," he said, managing to evade my question. "But when it comes to seeing the active mine, we're going to have to sneak in."

My jaw dropped. I'd technically trespassed in private mines dozens of times. But trespassing inside one of the most prolific mines in the world, inside the sovereign lines of one of the US government's political adversaries?

I knew Heath was crazy, but I hadn't realized up until that moment that he was clinically insane.

I started to take a step backward, but he reached out and seized my arm above the elbow, rooting me to my spot. "Look"—he dropped his voice even lower—"I know you don't like breaking rules. I know you hate not knowing the answers to everything. And I know you don't trust me—"

"Because I have no reason to trust you!"

"I'm aware." He sighed, running his free hand through a tangled mess of wet hair. "But if you want to unearth what might be the greatest treasure of the last millennium, I need you to follow my lead and just go with the flow."

I jerked my head in his direction, bringing the tips of our noses just millimeters apart. "Treasure?"

A muscle in his jaw flexed. "The new mineral, that is."

I met the intensity of his gaze for a long moment – as long as I could muster – before looking away. By then, the manifold, synchronized assault on my senses was coming to a head: Heath's fingers gripping my arm, the heavy rain battering against the top of my head, soaking my clothes and dripping into my eyes... Not to mention the uncomfortably hot flush that had started in my cheeks and was slowly creeping down my chest thanks to the extreme proximity of our bodies. I rocked on my heels, the sound of my own thundering heartbeat drowning out the nearby cacophony of crashing rain and roaring airplane engines.

It was all too much.

Pulling away from him, I reached into my pocket with a trembling hand and retrieved the amethyst potion, downing the rest of it in one swig. It was bad enough that dozens – if not hundreds – of strangers had seen me with my head tucked between my knees at the airport. At that moment, I'd rather die than let Heath see that side of me. I took a deep breath, focusing on my slowing pulse.

Heath's eyes lingered on the empty glass vial, narrowing sharply. "What was that?"

I pressed my mouth into a tight line.

"Is that—Jesus!" His eyes bulged. "Do you know how dangerous it is to bring unlabeled pharmaceuticals into the PRC?"

"Almost as dangerous as breaking into a state-owned mining operation!" I shot back.

"Mister Spencer! Miss Stone!" Li called, brandishing an umbrella from the inside of the limo while gesturing us toward him. "Please, come now!"

I met Heath's piercing gaze, doing my best not to shrink away from it. "I don't like hypocrites."

His eyes closed and his shoulders rose up and down in a slow, heavy sigh. "You're right. I'm sorry."

I bit my lip, mentally calculating the time and cost required to book it all the way back to the United States. But then my thoughts trailed back to Mrs. Lautner, and the awful black stain on her lungs that was slowly killing her, and I remembered all of the rare and powerful minerals that were unique to this region – one of which might hold the key to curing her and so many others. Regardless of how I felt about Heath, if I abandoned the cause now, I might never have this opportunity again. And also, I *really* wanted to see this so-called "new mineral," as implausible as its existence may have been.

I let out the breath I'd been holding in the form of an irritable huff. "I don't trust you, Heath Spencer, and I probably never will… But I'll 'go with the flow'"—I winced at the idiotic expression – both the idiom and the one plastered on Heath's face—"for now, at least." With that, I abruptly turned away from him and made my way to the limo, where Topie was already inside, fogging up the window with his wet snout as he watched me approach.

"Laney!" Heath called after me.

I glanced over my shoulder, not bothering to stop.

He looked at me for a long moment, then said, "Thank you for being here."

"It's *De*laney. And don't bother thanking me," I replied, once more turning away from him. "I'm not here for you."

I shirked past Li's outstretched umbrella, opened the car door, and slumped against the seat, my wet clothes squelching beneath me. A moment later, Heath appeared on the other side of the car and did the same, water dripping from his nose and onto his crossed arms as he settled in the seat beside me. I kept my eyes busy, intent on looking anywhere but at him. The car wasn't actually a limo, but some sort of elongated Mercedes that boasted four reclining white leather seats in the back, with one pair of seats facing the other pair. The console had been filled with ice, two crystal flutes, and a fresh bottle of champagne.

"Overcompensating for much?" I muttered under my breath.

Still standing outside my open door, Li was peering inside the car with a grimace. "Mister Spencer, normally I do not complain, but it will make big trouble for me if I return car with damaged leather."

Heath's features softened as he uncrossed his arms to reach for the door handle. "My apologies, Li." With that, he stepped back out into the rain, circled the car to the open trunk, and began rummaging through his suitcase. "Laney, grab yourself a change of clothes, would you?" he called to me from the back.

I would have balked, but Li was staring at me expectantly. "Oh, fine!" I groused, turning around in my seat to reach for my backpack, which had my toiletries and a change of clothes inside. In truth, I was secretly relieved by Li's request, as the thought of having to sit in cold, soggy clothes for the entirety of the drive made me want to claw my epidermis off.

"Thank you!" Li's grin was borderline mischievous as he shut the car door. Once he'd climbed back in the driver's seat, he rolled up the privacy screen separating the front of the car from the back seat, ostensibly so I could change. Just as I'd started peeling my t-shirt over my head, Heath reappeared, slamming the door behind him.

"What are you doing?" I yelped, scrambling to yank my shirt back in place.

"You can't expect me to strip on the runway!" Heath groused. To my horror, he'd already removed his suit jacket and was unbuttoning his soaking-wet white shirt, which clung to his body in ways that made my heart race.

"Oh, yes I can!" I retorted, only to be thrown against my seat as Li hit the gas. "Hey, wait!" I sputtered in protest, but Li was already on the move.

Topie let out a disgruntled snort from the row of seats across from us, disdainfully shaking off the three droplets of rain I had gotten on him as though it had been an entire bucket.

I turned back to Heath, only to find he was completely naked from the belt up. He gave me a pointed look, and while my brain screamed at me to turn around, my eyes remained firmly glued to the lithe musculature of his chest and torso.

"I thought you were a gift shop salesman." The words slipped out of my mouth, breathless and accusatory.

"And I thought you were a pharmacist," he sniped, his hands reaching down to unbuckle his belt.

"I am!" I squeaked.

"And I own a gift shop."

"Gift shop owners don't have physiques like *that*." I gestured at his well-defined pectorals and abdominal muscles, which should have belonged to a Calvin Klein model, not a seller of snow globes.

"Thank you," he replied gruffly. "You're welcome to continue enjoying the show, but just know it goes both ways." He raised his eyebrows at me in a suggestive manner. "After all, you've made it abundantly clear you don't like double standards."

I stared at him for a protracted moment, brows pinched and lips pursed in consternation, then forced my shoulders into a nonchalant shrug. "Fine. Makes no difference to me. It's just skin, after all." With that, I yanked my shirt over my head and shook out my wet hair, eliciting another cranky snort from the pig – Topie, that is.

Heath, who'd been regarding me with a conceited smirk up until that moment, allowed his composure to slip into an open-mouthed stare.

Dutifully reciting the periodic table of elements in my head to keep the flush in my cheeks from creeping toward the back of my exposed neck – *Hydrogen, helium, lithium, beryllium* – I turned away from him, reached behind my back, and yanked off my sports bra. Hearing Heath's sharp intake of breath made my own lips curl into a self-satisfied smile, knowing I was causing him as much discomfort as he'd been trying to cause me. *Boron, carbon, nitrogen…* I glanced at him over my shoulder, surprised to find he was regarding me not with horror, but with the rapt expression of someone who'd just cracked open a rock and found a sparkling geode inside.

A lump appeared in my throat. *Oxygen, fluorine, neon!* I continued silently, almost frantically. *Neon, uh… magnesium… Umm…*

Halfway between magnesium and what should have been aluminum, my mind drew a complete blank. I swallowed tightly, doing everything I could not to look at Heath's newly unfastened belt buckle… or the bulge that had appeared directly below it.

Odin help me.

The unexpected sight of his erection straining against his pants sent my thoughts into such a flurry, there was no discernible thought left between my ears, only buzzing static. Heat pulsed not only in my cheeks, but deep between my thighs as Heath's fingers slowly crept toward the button atop his fly. My eyes darted up to his, which were gazing at me with such profound intensity, I couldn't bear it.

He's waiting for my permission.

That thought terrified me more than anything, because I found myself desperately wanting to give it to him.

Are you out of your mind? A shrill voice screamed in my head, drowning out the errant thought. *This man is the enemy – the ENEMY! And we don't ogle enemy penises, no matter how attractive the body they're attached to!*

"Laney," Heath whispered, the word setting fire to my loins.

Before my mouth could utter something my brain would later regret, I abruptly turned away from him, furiously berating myself. I'd made the conscious decision long ago to repress my libido, swapping out men and sex for the far more edifying – and much safer – diversion of minerals and medicine. After a while, willful repression had turned into blissful nonexistence; in fact, I barely noticed men who were conventionally good-looking, and even if I accidentally did, I'd simply avert my eyes or walk the other way. Sexually-attractive men promised nothing but distraction and distress, and I didn't miss their presence in my life one bit. I was fine without them – more than fine. I was *great*. Really, really great. The extra time and mental faculties afforded by my self-imposed celibacy allowed me to live a rich and varied life, entirely free of hardship and heartache.

Given the indisputable logic of that decision, why the *heck* was I secretly hoping he'd unbutton his fly, reach forward and pull me on top of him, and then have his way with me right there in the back seat? The very notion sent a surge of heat between my thighs that was so unexpected and intense, I had to clap a hand to my mouth to stifle a gasp.

Enough!

I shook my head, working to clear it of the nonsense. Without so much as a wayward glance in Heath's direction, I perfunctorily unbuttoned and yanked off my wet pants, hurriedly replacing them with dry ones. Damp as my skin still was, I didn't even bother putting on a new bra; I just jerked a dry shirt over my head, praying my nipples wouldn't show through the thin fabric. By then, the windows of the car had completely fogged up, so I turned my attention to the center console – pointedly avoiding Heath's side of the car in its entirety – and cranked the air conditioning to full blast to rid my body of the flush that had spread from my cheeks to my toes. I then pulled out a textbook and my noise-canceling headphones, exiling my thoughts to the complex and manifold world of minerals as a form of self-imposed solitary confinement.

It wasn't a punishment so much as a necessity, since I could no longer deny that my feelings for Heath were morphing into something wildly unfamiliar and unruly. Deep down in my core, where neither denial nor excuse could burrow deep enough to suppress the discomfiting truth, I finally recognized the undeniable source of those feelings, troubling and hard to swallow as that source may have been…

Prasiolite.

I must have inadvertently contaminated the lab with it, I mused, keeping my eyes firmly glued to my book while Heath deftly peeled away and replaced the remainder of his wet clothes on the seat beside me. *Which means I'll have to remake all of my potions from scratch,* I told myself, since they'd obviously been tainted by rogue, libido-boosting prasiolite compounds.

Rather than feeling irritated at the daunting, time-consuming prospect of having to rebrew every single tainted vial of essence in my vast collection, I felt a surge of relief. In fact, I found myself humming cheerfully as my eyes skimmed over the page, scarcely absorbing a single word as they did, so pleased was I to have found such an obvious solution to a previously-befuddling conundrum. Not to mention the welcome distraction the aforementioned solution would bring me once I arrived back in Portland. Recreating all those potions would take *weeks* of laser-focused concentration, leaving absolutely no room for daydreams or nonsensical fantasizing.

All I have to do is get through these next few days, I comforted myself, turning the page without having read it, *and then everything will be back to normal.*

The ancient copper mine of Tonglushan was located in the mountainous outskirts of Huangshi, an industrial-yet-lush mining town near the south bank of the Yangtze River. Huangshi was a young city situated in an ancient land, marked by numerous swamps and lakes and towering steel bridges – at least according to Li. It could have had purple grass and neon-pink trees for all I knew, thanks to the torrential rain and low-hanging, charcoal-gray nimbostratus clouds that obscured our view for the entirety of the drive. At least I had a backpack full of books to pass the time. Not that I wanted to interact with Heath any further, but even if I did, he kept his eyes glued to his phone the whole trip, his head pressed against the window as he mindlessly scrolled through whatever it was he was looking at. Topie, who lay between us, had also turned himself into an unblinking zombie as he watched his second favorite movie, *Babe*, on his propped-up tablet.

I shook my head at the two of them, glad that my own screen was tucked away in my suitcase.

Though I desperately wanted to – more for idle curiosity's sake than anything else – I refrained from asking Heath a single question about the "unidentified" mineral he claimed to have uncovered. I frankly didn't put much stock in the notion, given his propensity for hyperbole and lore. Still, I couldn't help but dart inquisitive glances in his direction. Not because I was secretly hoping he'd be looking back at me – definitely not – but in hopes that he might change his mind and divulge more information about the new mineral in the interim. For once, however, he remained silent, and I was left to my own devices to entertain myself.

No matter, I was used to it.

"Almost to Ancient Tonglushan Mine Museum," Li announced, rolling down the privacy screen just as the clouds began to thin, revealing a strange combination of industrial buildings and traditional Chinese pagodas in the distance.

"Museum?" I echoed, then flashed Heath an accusatory glare. "I thought we needed to get to the mine before sunset."

"The ancient mine, yes," he replied, not pulling his eyes from his phone. "I need to do some research before we sneak into the operational mine."

I opened my mouth to protest, then closed it again, remembering my earlier promise to "go with the flow."

Heath finally shifted away from Facebook or Candy Crush or whatever he'd been so engrossed in for the last two hours, turning his attention to me. "It'll all be worth it – I promise."

Topie nudged me in annoyance. He'd finally gotten to his favorite scene in the movie – the climactic sheepherding competition – and we were making far too much noise for his liking.

"Sorry," I muttered with a harrumph.

"What are you apologizing for?" Heath asked.

"Topie says we're being too loud," I replied, bringing my mineral textbook back to my nose.

For some reason, that prompted Li and Heath to exchange glances in the rearview mirror – most likely a tacit agreement to keep the noise down, I assumed.

We arrived at the ancient-mine-turned-museum ten minutes later, just before closing time, and bought three tickets. (Topie, to his dismay, wasn't allowed inside and had to wait in the car.) Even though I was extremely antsy to get to the actual, still-active mine that was just a few kilometers away, where some of the most amazing minerals I'd ever seen – including a supposedly unidentified specimen – were currently being unearthed, the museum itself was more interesting than I'd anticipated. The main hall featured a large pit, inside which was a perfectly-preserved section of the original 3,000-year-old mine that had been unearthed by Chinese archeologists in 1973.

"These ruins are part of a mining and smelting site during the Western Zhou and the Han dynasties, which were used for over a millennium, produced over 80,000 tons of copper, and covered an area of about eight square kilometers," Heath translated from the Chinese description, while I leaned on the ropes, craning my head to get a better view of the tunnels below. "It is the earliest, best-preserved, and most technologically-advanced copper mine of its time." He clicked his tongue in what I presumed to be an expression of awe. "The site was excavated between 1973 to 1985, during which eight large mining sites, fifty smelting sections, twelve smelting furnaces, two-hundred and thirty-one vertical mining shafts, more than a hundred tunnels – some of which were fifty meters deep – and thousands of mining tools were unearthed."

I let out a low whistle. "It's remarkable how advanced their operations were, given the lack of modern mining equipment and reinforced concrete." Surveying the complexity of the site below, I shook my head in disbelief. "Fifty meters deep? It's a wonder the tunnels didn't collapse on themselves."

"Ancient mine workers very smart," Li said, pointing to a nearby display case of bronze mining tools that had been recovered from the site. "They support tunnels with many pieces of strong wood that come together, like this"—he interlaced his fingers, illustrating an interlocking system of wooden logs—"and when ore veins fully finished, they pushed dug-out rocks and dirt back in finished tunnels to keep from collapse."

"They backfilled the exhausted veins to keep the tunnels from caving in," I supplemented, more for my own edification than anything else. "Incredible that they knew how to do that even back then."

"What I find most amazing is that they knew exactly where to look for copper to begin with," Heath marveled. "Especially since most of the copper they excavated was at least several meters down."

"Copperweed," I replied.

"I beg your pardon?" Heath asked.

"Copperweed," I repeated a little louder. "It's a type of Chinese flower that only grows where copper deposits are found."

"Is that true?" Heath asked, turning to Li.

I scoffed. "Of course it's true. I wouldn't say it if it weren't."

"Miss Stone very smart," Li said, nodding at me in apparent approval. "What's your Chinese zodiac sign?"

I blinked at the abrupt change of topics. "Uh…Rat?"

Li's brow furrowed as he considered that. "You sure you not Ox or Rooster?"

"According to the *Discover China* magazine tucked in the back of my seat on the flight, I was born in the year of the Rat." I waved a dismissive hand as I meandered farther down the exhibition hall. "Not that it makes any difference whatsoever, since personality traits are based on a combination of genetics, upbringing, experience, and—"

"Okay, yes, I see it now," Li interjected. "Rats very quick and intelligent—"

I smiled.

"—and also *very* stubborn and full of too many opinions."

My smile evaporated.

Heath let out a loud snort. "Got that right on the nose."

"Of course, Mr. Heath born in year of Dragon," Li continued, strolling alongside the cordoned-off pit with his hands clasped behind his back, "which is why he very smart, successful, and…*nèi ge* …" He paused in thought. "How do you say *yǒu mèilì*?"

"Charismatic?" Heath supplied, crossing his arms over his chest with a smug expression.

"*Shì de*, charismatic!" Li grinned. "That why Rat and Dragon are perfect match. Get married and stay married for a long, happy time!"

This time *I* let out a loud snort while Heath's smirk quickly turned into a grimace.

"Chinese people are very wise," I told Li as I slipped past him to get a better look at a bronze pictograph hanging on the wall, "but even the wisest among us can make terrible, *terrible* mistakes of judgment. Heath and I couldn't be more different."

Li flashed me a wide smile. "Just like Rat and Dragon."

"Uh-huh." I used that opportunity to closely examine a nearby display embedded in the floor, praying neither he nor Heath could see the fresh wave of embarrassment flaring in my cheeks

Fortunately, as Heath crouched beside my feet, he didn't pay my flushing face a second glance. His eyes were glued to his phone, where he'd zoomed in on a picture of a weathered piece of parchment covered in faded Chinese. I squinted at the screen, trying and failing to make out the symbols, which looked markedly different than the ones I'd been studying all day.

"This discovery very special," Li explained, directing my attention toward the bones, tools, and clothing that had been preserved in the dirt and protected by a panel of safety glass. He knelt beside Heath, motioning for me to do the same.

I begrudgingly did so, surprised by the contorted expression on Heath's face – as though he had a cramping foot or some equally uncomfortable affliction. When he saw me looking over at him, his features smoothed, making me wonder if it had just been a trick of the light.

"In 1973 excavation," Li was explaining, "archeologists discover miner who died in mine collapse."

"Just one miner?" I asked.

"Yes, just one. Collapse happened very fast, sending rocks and heavy mud on top of miner. The mud dry like clay blanket, protecting miner body from time and oxygen – like people in Pompeii."

"That's remarkable." I eyed the bronze tools and leather pouch that had been excavated alongside the miner's remains. "It's like a centuries-old snapshot."

"Yes." Li nodded, tapping the engraved plaque embedded in the floor beside the display. "Archeologists break mud shell and find tools and clothing, explaining much of ancient mining culture. This man is called 'Miner Without Name' – very important to China's copper history."

"That's… actually interesting," I had to admit, glancing at my watch. "Can we go to the active mine now?"

Heath's head snapped up, making me jump. "Before we go, I need to flag down the museum curator to ask him a few quick questions. Li, please stay with Miss Stone. I'll meet you back in the car in ten minutes."

I darted a quizzical look in his direction, but he either failed to notice or pretended not to as he scurried off in the opposite direction, adding to my growing list of unanswered questions.

"I really hate that guy," I muttered under my breath.

For some reason, Li let out a bark of laughter that he quickly smothered as a feigned cough.

Chapter 11

Twenty minutes later, the massive open pit that was the active, modern-day Tonglushan Mine peered up at us like a gaping maw, its dozens of horizontal, carved out layers – a.k.a. "benches" – spiraling deeper and deeper into the surrounding hills. Construction trucks and mining equipment were scattered everywhere, while several towering plumes of steam rose into the air from what I assumed to be the chimneys of a nearby smelting facility. Unlike other types of mines, which usually exist deep underground, the Tonglushan Mine is a "shallow" operation that extracts ore near the surface by continuously removing the surrounding layers of rock and soil. But that didn't make it small by any means. If I were flying a plane 30,000 feet above it on a clear day and looking down, the landmark would have easily been larger than a half-dollar.[8]

---

[8] Using the relative size equation $\theta = 2\tan^{-1}(S/2D)$, with S being the approximate diameter of the mine and D being the distance from the eye.

The storm clouds had finally dispersed and the sun had fallen well below the horizon, casting the entire operation in a long, darkening shadow. Glowing threads of truck headlights circled the wide dirt road that spiraled into the bottom of the mine, a thousand or so feet below the cliff Heath and I were standing on. Li and Topie were waiting for us in the car, which was parked a few yards away with its headlights turned off to make sure we didn't attract any unwanted attention.

"So the new mineral is down there?" I turned to Heath, doubt creeping into my voice. "How the heck are we supposed to sneak into an operation like *that?*"

"I know a few guys – miners who drive trucks in and out and can lend us uniforms and helmets to hide underneath," he replied nonchalantly. "Luckily, that's irrelevant because the mineral was found in one of the many satellite mines scattered throughout the forest." He gestured over his shoulder at the line of trees behind us.

I frowned at the thick wall of foliage. "If it's a new mineral discovery, wouldn't the mining company be actively working to extract it?"

Heath shrugged. "China's state-run mining operations aren't interested in commercially-worthless copper mining byproducts. If it can't be polished into high-priced gemstones, burned as fuel, or used in an iPhone battery, it's tossed into tailings piles with the rest of the overburden." He chuckled to himself. "Historically speaking, not even the local miners have ever cared about gangue minerals, regardless of their color and beauty. It wasn't until very recently that an entrepreneurial American convinced the locals to start selling azurite, malachite, fluorite, and the like to deep-pocketed foreign mineral collectors instead of using them for backfill or mantle decorations."

"I know all of that," I muttered, unaccustomed to being on the receiving end of a mineral lecture. "Regardless, I doubt the China Nonferrous Metal Mining Group would be comfortable with a couple of Americans digging around in the dirt, especially after the tailings dam failure that happened a few years back and made international news. The last thing they want is more negative press."

"Lucky for us, I specifically timed this visit around the Dragon Boat Festival, which is happening tomorrow. One of seven days in the Chinese calendar when no one will be working, so we'll have the entire place to ourselves." He winked, making me shift uncomfortably.

"It sounds like you put a lot of thought into this," I said, not bothering to hide the accusation in my voice. "Meanwhile, I only expressed an interest in coming to China a week ago. At what point did you decide it would be a good idea to drag me into this idiotic plan?"

Heath grinned. "About nineteen hours ago, when I saw you at the Portland Jetport and realized we were going to be in China at the exact same time."

I jutted out my chin in indignation. "Oh yeah? Then why didn't you say anything to me at the airport?"

"I shouted and even tried to chase you down, but you had your headphones on and didn't hear me… Well, that, or you were pointedly ignoring me," he added with a chuckle. "That wouldn't exactly be outside of the realm of imagination, would it?"

"No, it wouldn't," I agreed. "But how come I didn't see you on the plane? I was sitting in the second row."

"Because I flew private. I would have invited you along, but that brings us back to my aforementioned failed attempts to say hello."

I grimaced. Spending sixteen hours on a cramped jet with Heath was certainly not at the top of my list of things I wanted to do – more in the lower third, conservatively speaking – but it would have been a heck of a lot better than having to fly in an overpacked can of sardines. I opened my mouth to say so, then faltered, suspicion once more flaring in my chest. "Wait. As soon as I arrived, Li was right there, waiting for me at my gate. Airline reservations are confidential. How could you have possibly known what flight I was on or when I'd be landing?"

Heath's eyes rolled upward as he crossed his arms over his chest. "I looked at the departures board, and unless you had arrived at the airport eleven hours early, there was only one morning flight to Beijing you could have possibly been on." I opened my mouth to ask another follow-up question, but he held up a hand. "Look, unless you'd like to continue this interrogation for another few hours, there's not much more we can do tonight. I recommend getting a bite to eat and some shut-eye. Tomorrow is going to be a long day." He turned and started walking toward the car. "Where are you staying? I'll have Li drop you off in town."

"Um…" I opened my mouth then closed it again, my fingers slipping into my pocket to clasp the smooth, cool chalcopyrite ball tucked safely away in there. "Well…"

Heath raised an eyebrow. "Don't tell me you just randomly showed up in a strange country without making prior lodging plans? That doesn't sound like the Laney I know."

"You *don't* know me. And it's worked decently well in the past," I muttered, dropping my eyes to the ground. "I've just been distracted this week." *To say the least.* I cleared my throat. "Besides, I've traveled solo to forty-one countries without a single hitch. I have no concerns about number forty-two."

The corner of Heath's mouth quirked up. "Ah yes, forty-two: the answer to the ultimate question of life, the universe, and everything."

"Huh?"

"Oh, come on!" He threw up his hands in exasperation. "You can't tell me you've never read *The Hitchhiker's Guide to the Galaxy*?"

"Oh." I sniffed, folding my arms. "I don't have time for fiction."

"Right, because God forbid you allow yourself to read something for enjoyment." Heath rolled his eyes again as he continued walking.

"I—hey!" I protested, jogging to catch up. "I read for enjoyment all the time."

"Yes, textbooks and encyclopedias are simply enthralling."

I opened my mouth to say something suitably quippy and condescending – like, "science fiction is the domain of inferior minds" – but Heath was already barreling on in typical blowhard fashion.

"…anyway, the motel I'm staying at is just a few minutes from here. I'm sure they'll have an extra room for you. If not, you're always welcome to crash on my floor."

I stumbled to a halt.

He walked a few more paces before glancing back over his shoulder. "Jesus – I didn't mean that literally,

Laney." He grinned. "Worst case scenario, my bed should be plenty big enough for the both of us."

A fresh, unexpected jolt of desire surged in my core, momentarily robbing me of breath.

"I'd rather sleep on the floor," I snapped, shoving past him to get in the car, where I crossed my arms and sulked in the back seat. I didn't like feeling stupid or unprepared – or worse, being caught being either of those things, *worst of all* by Heath.

He sank into the seat beside me a moment later, chuckling to himself.

A low growl slipped from my lips.

Momentarily abandoning his movie, Topie raised an inquisitive eyebrow and a perked ear in my direction.

Grinding my bared teeth, I replied with a clipped, "Don't ask," which only seemed to amuse Heath even further. I pointedly stuck my tongue out at him, but he was too busy fumbling with his precious buzzing phone to notice.

He held it up to his ear a moment later. "Beth – hey!" A wide grin appeared on his face, which, for some reason, made a knot appear in my stomach.

I rubbed the area over my belly button, frowning. What did *I* care if some random woman's phone call had immediately brought a massive smile to Heath's face, as though she'd just told the funniest joke in the history of jokes?

"Is everything all right?" He glanced at his watch. "It's only six a.m. back home." His eyes widened. "What's wrong? Is everything okay?"

The knot tightened, making me wince. What was causing this uncomfortable pang? Hunger? Something I'd eaten on the plane? *Oh no – it's not food poisoning, is it?*

I bit my lip, my eyes darting to the trunk, where my antidiarrheal biotite potion was inconveniently stuffed under several layers of clothes.

"No!" Heath gasped, his eyes darting to me.

I froze. Was that a girlfriend on the other line? An angry, territorial girlfriend, perhaps, who didn't relish the idea of him traveling with another woman? *Has Heath ever mentioned a girlfriend…or a wife, for that matter?* I chewed on the inside of my cheek. *I mean, he'd certainly have mentioned a wife by now… Right?* My eyes darted to his ring finger, which was bare, and the knot loosened a little. I frowned at the sensation.

"You're kidding." Heath had clapped a hand over his mouth. "No, I—Yes, I know! I just…" His eyes darted to me again. "Yeah, my friend, La—er, Delaney." He sighed and rolled his eyes. "Yes, Beth, a *friend*."

Oh. My shoulders slumped as though he'd placed two heavy bags of rocks atop them. *I guess he* does *have a girlfriend.* I tried to swallow, the knot in my belly twisting so badly I pressed my fist to my mouth, briefly wondering if I was going to throw up. I tuned out the rest of his conversation after that, turning my attention to the eggplant-purple sky, which was mottled by a black stippling of Cirrocumulus clouds. My hand absentmindedly fingered the chalcopyrite ball in my pocket as I studied them, reciting the different cloud types under my breath in an attempt to distract myself from the worsening knot in my stomach – no, not a knot. A solid lead brick, more like.

When Heath set his hand on my knee some indeterminate amount of time later, I instinctively jerked away. He raised an eyebrow but didn't pull his hand away. "Sorry, did I startle you?"

"What do you want?" I snapped, my voice coarser than I'd intended it to be.

He gave me a long, level look, then said, "That was my sister—"

Just like that, the knot in my stomach unraveled, the suddenness of it rendering me nothing short of bewildered.

"—who just informed me that my nephew, Chester, has hemochromatosis."

"Er...yeah." I blinked, trying to follow his line of reasoning. "I already told you that."

"But how did you *know?*" He leaned forward, making me shrink against the back of my seat. "The kid's been seen by multiple doctors over the years – how could you have known just by looking at him?"

"I—oh." I froze, my fingers gripping the chalcopyrite ball in my pocket. Topie jerked his head in my direction, his floppy ears perking to attention. "H-He...um... Well, h-he was very pale," I eventually managed to stammer. "I-I just...um...noticed the signs."

Without warning, Heath reached forward and wrapped me in a tight hug. "Thank you," he whispered against my ear, sending goosebumps racing down my spine. "You have no idea what you've done for Chess. For our entire family."

"It was nothing." I gulped, my arms frozen at my sides. "R-Really."

He pulled away from me, letting his warm hands rest on my shoulders. "It wasn't nothing, and my sister is insisting on thanking you in person." A grin appeared on his face. "And just so you know, she's a *big* hugger."

My mouth fluttered open, then closed again. *Great.* I scrubbed my hands through my hair, grateful as ever that it was cropped short. *Just what I need – another boisterous, loud, overly-sentimental member of the Spencer family.*

And yet, for reasons entirely unbeknownst to me, my stomach did a little flip at the thought.

"It's the airline food," I muttered to myself, earning an odd look from Heath. "It *has* to be."

Shockingly true to his word, Heath's "motel" was indeed conveniently close to the mine, though it turned out to be a tiny, ramshackle, two-story complex that had perhaps ten rooms total. Li helped us carry our smaller bags inside, where a stooped-over man who looked to be older than trees was sitting at the front desk watching some sort of Chinese game show on a small black and white TV. Topie, once again, was relegated to the car, just in case the place had a no-animal policy, which it almost certainly did. I hung back as Li and Heath approached the old man with polite bows, which he absentmindedly returned. After that, the three launched into a detailed discussion in Chinese, from which I only understood the words "room," "bed," "tonight," "unfortunately," and, worst of all, "I'm very sorry."

Heath and Li turned around to look at me, the former with what appeared to be a sheepish expression, and the latter with an inexplicably toothy grin.

I scrubbed a hand down my face tiredly. "Let me guess – they don't have any extra rooms?"

"No." Heath, who looked no happier than me, was rubbing the bridge of his nose. "But he says my room has two beds in it. Now, I'm happy to have Li take you farther into town to find you a different motel, but he won't be able to pick you up in the morning since he'll be visiting his family in Yueyang for the holiday."

"How far is the nearest inn from here?" I asked Li.

"At least six miles," he replied with a barely concealed smirk that made me think he had dragons and rats on the brain. "And tomorrow the weather supposed to be very rainy. Bad thunder and strong wind."

I let out an exasperated huff. "Are there any taxis or buses that come this direction?"

The man behind the front desk shook his head. "No taxi. No bus. Dragon Boat Festival."

My hand reached into my pocket to absentmindedly roll the chalcopyrite ball between my fingers, a feeble attempt to distract myself from the dregs of hunger, sleep-deprivation, and jet lag that were fraying the already-ratty edges of my patience. "Fine! Whatever!" I leaned against my suitcase, rubbing at the growing ache in my forehead. "Just let me know how much I owe you for the room."

Heath watched me for a protracted moment, opening and closing his mouth as though he might argue, then sighed and turned back to the old man to hand him a small pile of yuan. *"Xièxiè nín."*

Extracting a large key ring from his pocket, the man ushered us outside, where he led us to the farthest door on the ground floor, removed one of the skeleton keys from the jingling brass ring, and unlocked the door for us. Then, after gesturing for us to replace our shoes with the slippers provided near the entrance, he doddered back to the front desk.

I regarded the used slippers with a grimace, opting instead to dig out the pair I'd brought from home. My bare feet would not be going inside of *anything* that had housed someone else's bare feet.

Li helped load the rest of our luggage into the foyer of the tiny room, grunting, "Mr. Spencer, if you need me come tomorrow, I happy to—"

"It's out of the question," Heath interjected, putting a hand on Li's shoulder and a large wad of cash in his palm. "Thank you for your help today. And please have a wonderful time with your family tomorrow. We'll see you in a couple of days."

Li gave him a deep bow, which Heath returned, then turned to say goodbye to me.

Even though I wanted to beg Li to take me anywhere but here and forgo the national holiday tomorrow to shuttle me around, I instead plastered what I'd hoped was a polite-looking smile on my face and nodded. "Yes, thank you. See you soon."

"My pleasure, Miss Stone," Li said with a grin and a bow. "I see you in two days."

"Unless you're planning on pig-sitting Topie during the holiday"—I gave him a pointed look—"you should probably let him out of your car. Sorry in advance if he got into the champagne."

Li's eyes widened while Heath made a noise halfway between a cough and a snort. "Oh Jesus." He palmed his forehead. "I forgot about Topie."

Topie, on the other hand, certainly hadn't forgotten about us, and came barreling into the room a few minutes later with an exuberant squeal. Without waiting for permission, he leapt onto the nearest of two twin size beds, turned in a few circles, and immediately settled in for his third nap of the day.

Heath regarded him with a tired look. "If the motel owner finds out we've smuggled a pig into this room, Topie will be turned into moo shu pork."

"Well then, we'll just make sure he doesn't find out." I hoisted my suitcase onto the bed beside Topie and began rummaging around for my toiletries.

"Your disdain for breaking rules appears to be circumstantial," Heath quipped, doing the same with his own bag on the opposite bed.

"I live by a strict internal moral code, not a frivolous societal one," I replied, eliciting a snort from him that I pointedly chose to ignore as I pulled my toiletries bag out of my suitcase. "Now, if you'll excuse me, I need to take a shower."

"Wait!" Heath called after me. "Can I at least use the restroom first?"

"I won't be long!"

"But—"

I quickly shut the door behind me, surveying the tiny, tiled bathroom with a crinkled nose. No more than six feet long and four feet wide, it had a toilet on one side and a showerhead on the other, with a single rusted drain embedded in the middle. A tiny sink and mirror were crammed directly beside the toilet.

"Wonderful," I grumbled, replacing my slippers with shower shoes before peeling off the rest of my clothes and neatly stacking them atop the toilet tank lid.

The showerhead had multiple knobs, and after a couple minutes of fiddling, I finally got the water temperature to hover somewhere between ice cold and second-degree burns. Still, as I stepped underneath the weak stream of water, a blissful sigh escaped my lips. It had been nearly thirty hours since my last shower – with germ-filled airline cabins, muggy air, and sticky leather car seats filling the interim. I generously lathered up my entire body, rinsed off the suds, then lathered up again, basking in my newfound state of cleanliness.

A loud bang on the bathroom door made me jump. "Laney, my bladder is about to explode. If you don't get out of that shower in thirty seconds, I swear to God I'm coming in!"

"I'll be out in a minute!" *Just as soon as I'm done washing my hair and brushing my teeth,* I silently amended.

What felt like barely a minute later, Heath banged on the door again. "Delaney, I am not joking!"

"I said *one minute!*"

"Which was five minutes ago! You'd better close the shower curtain, because I'm coming in!"

"No, wait—!" I sputtered.

The door burst open. "I don't know if you were an only child or what, but—" Heath froze mid-harangue, his eyes as wide as half-dollars as he took in my naked state.

"Get out!" I screamed, doing what I could to hide my body with nothing but a tiny white washcloth.

He slapped a hand over his eyes, barking, "Why the hell didn't you tell me there was no shower curtain?!"

"Because I didn't think you would actually be rude enough to burst in here!"

"I told you my bladder was about to explode!" he shouted, gesticulating wildly with his free hand. "What kind of pharmacist ignores a potential medical emergency like that?"

"The kind of pharmacist who knows that every word out of your mouth is hyperbole!"

"You are the single most insufferable person I have ever met," Heath huffed as he kicked off his slippers, then bent down to remove his pants.

"What are you doing?!" I yelped. "I said get out!"

"And I said, multiple times, that *I have to pee!*" He flung his shirt into the motel room, leaving him in nothing but boxers, one hand still clamped over his eyes. "And since you continue to be a spoiled, self-centered brat, and I don't feel like waterlogging yet *another* dry-clean-only suit on this godforsaken trip, you've left me with no other option!"

He stumbled past me blindly, slipping and skittering on the soapy tile until he'd positioned himself in front of the toilet. A split second later came the unmistakable sound of a stream of urine hitting water.

Fury feathered at my vision. After snatching the showerhead and turning the water all the way down to the blue "冷水" symbol, I aimed the freezing cascade directly at the center of Heath's back.

Emitting a shrill yelp akin to that of an injured dog's, Heath whirled around, teeth bared. "Are you out of your mind?" he barked, groping for the showerhead.

"No, but you clearly are! *Get out!*"

"*YOU* get out!" With one hand still covering his eyes, he flailed around in a blind attempt to snatch the showerhead away from me. But when his hand clamped down on the nearest thing, his fingertips didn't dig into cold metal; they squeezed warm flesh.

Heath's eyes burst open as we both regarded the foreign object he was grabbing: my left breast.

The split second that ensued did so at a physics-defying, agonizingly slow pace. Both of our jaws simultaneously fell open in slow motion, our bulging eyes rising up to meet one another's in mute horror while we each instinctively flung aside the objects we were clutching. It was at that moment that physics conveniently decided to start functioning at normal speed again, with the oppositional forces of our bodies causing us both to lose our footing on the slippery tiles. Arms flailing and naked bodies colliding, we pitched toward the bathroom floor, with Heath grabbing me at the very last second and twisting his body in such a way that he fell first, with my body landing directly on top of him.

The air rushed out of my lungs in a shocked *whoosh*, while his head hit the tiles with a *crack* that twisted my insides inside out.

"Heath!" I wheezed, shoving myself off him. "Heath, are you okay?"

He let out a pained groan, his fingers reaching for the back of his head, where a blooming cloud of crimson liquid was staining the bathroom floor.

In that moment, instinct overran thought.

"Don't move!" I shrieked.

Not bothering with slippers or a towel, I stumbled out of the bathroom and dove toward my suitcase, frantically unzipping the side pocket that contained the human-grade medicine kit I'd brewed specially for Topie. After snatching up two vials, I tossed my cell phone at Topie, who was pawing at the sheets and whinnying in agitation. "Don't panic! Just get ready to dial 120 if I tell you to!"

"Ree?"

"The number for the ambulance in China!" I shouted over my shoulder, suddenly grateful for the extra time I'd had to study my travel book on the road.

Dropping to the ground beside Heath, I hoisted his head onto my knees, and upended one of the bottles – a powerful-yet-poisonous hematite/cinnabar slurry that I kept on hand strictly for emergencies – directly into his throat. He started to sputter and protest, but I clamped a hand over his mouth. "Don't argue. Just swallow!" His eyes bulged in what was likely surprise or indignation, but I waited until the Adam's apple in his throat dipped all the way down and then all the way back up before taking my hand off his mouth.

"What was that?" he gasped, attempting to sit upright, but I pressed a firm hand against his chest, holding him down.

"Don't move!" I ordered as I peered into his eyes, checking his pupils. He let out a muffled yelp as I turned his face toward my stomach, raking my fingers through the thick, dark hair on the back of his head. It was still matted with blood, but when I parted it, I found a fully-healed, three-inch scar – the only remnant of what had moments ago been a cracked skull. I pressed the palm of my hand to my mouth, surprised to find a relieved sob welling in my chest.

"Laney...?" Heath rasped.

I started at the odd tone of his voice. When I jerked my head to look at him, afraid I'd somehow overlooked a far more serious injury, Heath was gaping up at me, his blue eyes bulging and the tips of his ears flushing as red as rubies. For a moment, I didn't understand why...until it finally dawned on me that I was still buck naked, cradling his head in my lap with my bare breasts hovering centimeters from his slack-jawed face.

Chapter 12

Topie appeared in the doorway, eyes rounded and snout dangling open at the lurid assortment of naked limbs on display in the middle of the bathroom floor.

"Um…I can explain," I started.

Except I had no idea how to explain any of it, least of all the inexplicable, overwhelming wave of relief that had flooded through me at the sight of Heath's healed injury – not pride of craftmanship or the satisfaction of having mended a complex wound, but pure, unbridled elation, as though I'd just come *this* close to losing something precious. Paired with the adrenaline coursing in my veins and the humiliation throbbing in my cheeks, my brain was as useless as a fried circuit board, leaving my unarmed body to fend for itself. And my unarmed body, at that particular moment, was completely paralyzed.

Meanwhile, Heath was gazing up at me not with fury or disgust, but with a confusing expression that I might have mistaken for longing had I not been one hundred percent certain of our mutual animosity for one another.

"Laney?" he whispered, his features softening into something that sent my heart figuratively leaping into my throat.

Okay, maybe ninety-nine percent certain.

"Y-Yes...?" I stammered.

"I..." Heath opened his mouth, faltered, licked his lips, then tried again. "Do all pharmacists administer medicine to their patients in the nude, or is today just my extraordinarily lucky day?"

Like a defibrillator to a flatlining heart, fury jolted my brain circuits back to life.

"Ugh!" I leapt to my feet, letting his head thump unceremoniously to the floor, and grabbed the closest, non-soaked items of clothing within reach: my panties and his designer suit jacket. After throwing them on, I reached down and roughly jerked Heath to his feet.

Toe-to-toe, we stared at each other for a long moment, me with my fists glued to my hips and him with a narrowed, inscrutable expression. He took a step closer, his hand hovering between us as though he might reach for me. I swallowed tightly, the proximity of our mostly-naked bodies making me uncomfortable, but stubbornness rooted me to my spot. With his face just inches from mine, Heath let his gaze rove over my body slowly and unabashedly, from my bare, wet legs to the glistening skin of my navel, fully exposed by the unbuttoned jacket I'd stolen from him, and all the way back up to my eyes. Resolve cracking, I looked away from his probing stare, taking that opportunity to reach behind him and turn off the ice-cold shower water that had been weakly pelting our ankles until that moment.

Heath cleared his throat. "Laney, I—"

"Here," I interrupted, shoving a vial of clear liquid into his hand before taking a step backward. "You'll need to take this in the next hour, preferably with food."

"I—what?" He gaped at me as he touched the back of his fully-healed scalp, then shook his head roughly as if to clear it. "Laney, what the hell just happened?"

I crossed my arms in front of my partially exposed breasts. "We slipped and fell in the bathroom after you rudely burst inside while I was showering."

"Yes, I know *that* part—"

"So, you admit you were unbelievably rude and inappropriate?" I stuck out my chin.

"Me?!" His eyes bulged. "I was having a medical emergency!"

I rolled my eyes. "Oh, please. Having to pee is not a medical emergency."

Topie trotted over and sat between us as we traded barbs, his snout pivoting back and forth as though watching a tennis match.

Heath threw up his hands in exasperation. "Regardless of who was being rude"—he gave me a pointed look, likely conceding that it was, in fact, him—"what I'm referring to is the part where I fell and cracked my skull open, only to feel completely fine less than three minutes later!" He touched the scar on the back of his head again, his cheeks paling. "Am I losing my mind?"

I opened my mouth, then closed it again, hesitating. Only a handful of people in the world knew the truth about my tonics; and even then, I'd never gone into great detail about my ability to extract the "magical" essence from minerals. Part of the reason for my secrecy was reputational preservation, since most people would understandably think I was insane. But the other, far more discomforting reason, was the deep-seated shame I carried. I was the living embodiment of my own worst fear: a fact-defying scientific anomaly with nary a hypothesis in sight. Suffice it to say, my exceptionally unique abilities weren't something I felt particularly inclined to flaunt to the world.

"Hello? Earth to Laney?" Heath waved a hand in front of my face. "Perhaps you might be kind enough to explain what just happened? Like how the hell I'm standing here talking to you instead of bleeding out on the bathroom tiles?"

I pressed my mouth into a tight line.

Several uncomfortable seconds stretched between us. Eventually, Heath sucked his teeth, knelt down, and retrieved the empty vial I had upended into his mouth. "What's this?" He squinted at the handwritten label. "Hematite? *Cinnabar?*" His eyes bulged wildly. "Did you just force-feed me *mercury?*"

"Um…"

"Delaney!"

"I—yes!" I blurted out, busying myself with a loose thread at the bottom of his jacket so I wouldn't have to look at him. "Which is why it's important you take the other vial to neutralize the toxins."

His jaw dropped as he read the label. *"Dolomite?!"* he choked out. "This stuff isn't medicine! It's poison!"

I cleared my throat awkwardly. "Actually, dolomite has highly beneficial detoxification properties—"

"I'm sorry, did you just say that *dolomite*, a.k.a. calcium magnesium carbonate, has *detoxification properties?*"

"Er…" I blinked, surprised that he knew the chemical formula.

"And you call *me* a phony?!" he exploded, making me take a startled step backward. "Why? Because I sell five-dollar quartz crystals that've been heat-treated to appear iridescent? Meanwhile, you're peddling literal poison to people and calling it homeopathic! Do you realize how dangerous that is, Delaney?"

I winced at his sudden reversion to my full name, which sounded sharp and cold and foreign coming from his mouth. "I don't give people 'toxic' potions unless it's an emergency—which this most definitely was!" I protested, nearly tripping over Topie, who had skittered out from between the two of us and was retreating toward the bed with his coiled tail tucked between his legs.

"Potions?" Heath repeated, staring at me as though I were out of my mind. "What do you think you are, some kind of witch?"

Gone were the last vestiges of warm relief from my chest, replaced instead by rib-constricting panic. My hand instinctively went to my pocket, blindly searching for my chalcopyrite, only for me to remember I was wearing Heath's jacket, not mine – beneath which, I was suddenly and acutely aware, I had no shirt. My arms tightened across my chest while I rocked back and forth on my heels.

Heath spun away from me and raked his hands through wet hair. "I can't believe you would do this, and *here* of all places! How am I supposed to find a doctor in the middle of—oh shit!" He slapped a palm against his forehead. "The Dragon Boat Festival! There won't *be* any doctors!" Muttering obscenities under his breath, he whirled away from me and strode to the toilet, where he dropped to his knees and raised two fingers to his mouth as though he was going to make himself throw up.

My brain was screaming at me to do something, but my body had locked up completely, swaying back and forth in a useless attempt to self-soothe. *There you go again, chasing away the one man who might actually be stupid enough to like you,* a voice whispered, that same hateful voice that had lurked in the back of my mind rent-free from the time I could form thoughts. *You really are a freak, Delaney.*

I pressed my forehead against the doorframe, trying to push the voice away.

You don't pretend to hate him because you think you're better than him. You pretend to hate him because you know you'll never be good enough for him.

Tears pricked at my vision as pressing turned to painful thumping.

You'll never be good enough for anyone.

My breaths were coming shallow and quick, robbing my brain and muscles of oxygen. Too weak to stand, I dropped to one knee, clutching the doorway for support as white feathered my vision.

A warm snout nudged my hip.

I glanced down to find Topie peering up at me with wide, puppy-like eyes, two vials of liquid clutched between his teeth. I reached down to take them with trembling hands, confusion, then understanding, clearing some of the fog from my mind. With a shaky breath, I took a large swig of the amethyst potion, feeling its anxiolytic properties working almost instantaneously. Then, taking another slow, deep breath that actually managed to fill my lungs, I shakily rose to my feet. At the sound of Heath's retches from inside the bathroom, Topie nudged the second potion in my hand.

"Are you sure this is a good idea?" I whispered.

He nodded.

With a sigh, I uncorked the vial and took a begrudging swig of liquefied blue apatite and sodalite – combined, a potent, cobalt-colored conductor of coercion. When I was sure the effects had fully kicked in, I stepped into the bathroom and gingerly put my hand on Heath's shoulder. "Heath, I need you to look at me."

He craned his head to look up at me with a scowl.

"Would you please get up?" I asked softly. "I have something to tell you."

His scowl deepened. "Once I clear the toxic levels of mercury from my stomach – assuming my vital organs are still functioning – I'm all yours."

"You're not poisoned," I lied, letting my newfound provisional powers take hold of my tongue, which otherwise would have been completely inept at lying on the spot.

Heath straightened away from the toilet seat. "I'm not?"

"No." I rubbed at my temples, my mind practically buzzing from sodalite-induced effects of heightened processing. Paired with the persuasive properties of blue apatite, this tonic was nothing short of a threat to national security. At that very moment, I could have phoned the Oval Office and convinced the President to launch nukes at Canada. Luckily for him (and our friendly neighbors to the north), I had my sights set on a far more myopic goal: placating Heath via blatant deceit.

I forced my eyes open, willing my mouth to work as quickly as my hyperactive brain circuits. "What you had was a cutting-edge medicine that's been used strictly by Navy SEALs up until very recently, when the military's exclusive patent expired. It causes a brief but powerful spike in the body's production of platelets, neutrophils, macrophages, and fibroblasts to induce rapid healing. The clear liquid I gave you is what counteracts that effect, since it's seldom advisable to have artificially-increased levels of cellular activity for prolonged periods of time. Both solutions are totally harmless," I added for good measure, seized by a fresh pang of guilt as I did. "Though it would be best if you drank the clear neutralizing solution sooner rather than later."

Otherwise you really will have organ failure, I added silently.

"Really?" Heath asked, eyeing the dolomite solution as he slowly rose to his bare feet. "So the name 'Cinnabar'…?"

"Is just a cutesy label I put on there as a nod to the reddish color." I smiled tightly. "I would never actually give my clients poisonous heavy metals."

Unless I accidentally cracked their skulls open first.

"Oh, thank God." Heath breathed a sigh of relief, then immediately downed the dolomite potion without so much as another suspicious glance in my direction. "I'm so sorry, Laney. I don't know what I was thinking, accusing you of something so horrible. Honestly, what you're saying makes perfect sense. I don't know how I ever could have assumed otherwise. You're always right, after all."

Beneath my tight-lipped smile I was grinding my teeth. While Heath's stubborn and contrarian nature often irritated me to no end, this compliant, agreeable version of him was somehow ten times worse.

"I hope you'll accept my apology. And, on that note," he continued, taking my hand in his, "I'm sorry for bursting in here earlier. It's my own fault I got hurt. I should have just gone outside and peed in the bushes."

A sharp zing shot through my molars as I yanked my hand away. "You don't need to apologize—"

"No, no, I *do* need to apologize. It's clear to me now that you really know your stuff and I'd be foolish to ever argue with you. Truly, Laney, I'll never doubt your word again."

"Of *course* you should doubt my word!" I shouted, rubbing at my zinging jaw. "You should doubt *everyone's* word until you have enough facts to support it!"

"You're absolutely right." Heath nodded soberly. "It's like every word you're saying is just resonating deep in my soul."

"Oh for Pete's—would you stop it?"

"Stop what?"

"Stop agreeing with me!"

His eyes widened. "Of course!" He thumped his forehead with the palm of his hand. "I should make my own opinions! Forge my own path! Manifest my own destiny!" He grabbed me by the shoulders. "Oh, Laney, I could kiss you right now!" I froze as he cocked his head, his eyes narrowing as they slowly found their way back to mine. "Do…" He licked his lips. "Do you think I should kiss you right now?"

"Y—No!" I blurted out, twisting out of his grip. "You should take a shower! Like…*right* now!"

"Yes, you're right, I should definitely take a shower right now." With that, he started to peel off his wet boxers, revealing a V-shaped indentation just above his transversus abdominis muscles that nearly made my knees buckle.

"Not *right* now!" I shrieked, covering my eyes. "After I leave!"

"Obviously!" Heath knuckled his forehead. "Why didn't I think of that?"

Without another word, I snatched my toiletries kit from the top of the toilet and spun on my heels, slamming the bathroom door behind me. After tearing off Heath's jacket and hurling it onto his bed, I ripped open my suitcase with equal zeal and dug around until I found my oversized "rock-paper-scissors-lizard-Spock" t-shirt – the only thing I ever slept in and the only sleepwear I had packed, given my previous, extremely reasonable assumption that I would be sleeping alone.

A knock sounded at the motel room door. After pulling my shirt over my head, I peeked through the window to find a young woman standing there with a tray of three covered bowls.

"Good evening," she said with a bow as I opened the door. "Here is the dinner Mr. Spencer requested. Would you like anything else before our kitchen closes for the night?"

"*Bù yòng xièxiè*," I replied automatically, gratefully taking the tray from her while mentally kicking myself. I could have been practicing Mandarin all afternoon with Li, but my mental faculties had been too sluggish and jet-lagged to even bother. Now, I could easily recall every Chinese word I'd read that day. "Maybe I should take sodalite more often," I muttered as I set down the tray in front of Topie and joined him on the bed. "Seems to work for you – when you remember to take your multivitamin,[9] at least."

---

[9] A proprietary blend of potion-filled capsules specially crafted for Topie, which aid in communication, health, intellect, and longevity.

When I lifted the lids off two of the three bowls, my mouth immediately watered at the smell. Juicy pieces of shredded chicken and chopped vegetables lay atop what appeared to be savory rice porridge that had been cooked in chicken stock. After picking out the celery, onions, and some sort of root vegetable I wasn't feeling confident about, I fumbled with the chopsticks, managing to shovel a few tiny bites of porridge into my mouth. Beside me, Topie had dunked his entire face in his bowl, sucking up his dinner like a Hoover vacuum.

"Good idea," I agreed, bringing the steaming bowl up to my face so I could dump the porridge directly into my mouth.

In my defense, it had been a really long time since I'd last eaten.

When I was finished with my dinner, I set Heath's untouched bowl and chopsticks on the foot of his bed and placed the empty bowls on the floor by the door. With the shower water still running – the only source of water in the motel room – and Heath's surprisingly good singing voice wafting from the bathroom as he belted out the theme to Rodgers and Hammerstein's *Oklahoma*, I eyed my toothbrush with a defeated sigh.

I guess brushing and flossing can wait till morning – just this once.

Grumbling, I crawled into the uncomfortably small bed Topie had insisted on sharing with me, sleep-deprivation and a full stomach luring me into the throes of slumber quicker than you could sing "The Surrey with the Fringe on Top."

Sadly, I didn't stay asleep for very long; the window curtains were too sheer to properly block out the moonlight and Topie was apparently chasing butterflies in his dreams because he kept punting me in the ribs. Of course, when I tried to shake him awake and kick him out of bed, the volume of his snores only intensified, as though he were trying to convince me he was in a deep sleep and couldn't be roused. Flashing him a glare that was obscured by darkness, I scooted as close to the edge of our tiny bed as possible, where I managed to avoid the violent flurry of hooves for a solid five minutes – at which point, he somehow managed to kick me in my left kidney for the third time that night.

My bloodshot eyes sprung open and immediately darted to Heath's side of the room, where he was peacefully curled up in the fetal position and hugging the far edge of his bed, leaving a solid eighteen inches of unmolested mattress at his back. Biting my lip, I briefly considered climbing into bed with him, then immediately thought the better of it…

That is, until the muffled sound of a bugle, followed by a blast of hot, stinky air, let me know that the rice porridge had already made its way to the rectal end of Topie's GI tract.

"You monster!" I choked out, eyes watering. Clamping a hand over my mouth and nose, I stumbled out of bed in a flatulence-induced coughing fit.

The second my feet touched the cold wooden floor, Topie maneuvered himself into the dead-center of the bed, splaying out his limbs like a capital X while using his Piglet stuffie for a pillow.

"Just you wait," I hissed, leaning in as closely as I could without suffocating in the cloud of methane unfurling from his anus. "It might not be tonight, it might not even be tomorrow night, but I *will* get my revenge."

Topie let out a well-timed snore that sounded more like a derisive snort.

Muttering swine-related obscenities, I tiptoed over to Heath's bed and carefully lifted one edge of the blanket. Then, slowly easing myself onto his mattress one ounce of body weight at a time to avoid alerting him to my uninvited presence, I climbed into bed with him. The mattress was warm from Heath's radiating body heat and smelled pleasantly of men's soap rather than stinky pig farts. I let out a contented sigh as I settled in beside him, convincing myself in my sleep-deprived delirium that I would wake up with the sun and be out of Heath's bed before he'd even realized he'd accrued a nighttime stowaway.

Alas, as is the case with so many of life's best-intended plans, mine did not come to fruition.

Chapter 13

Instead of having the courtesy to let me peacefully dream about minerals or airplanes, my brain decided to torment me with erotic, R-rated reveries, each and every one of them centering around Heath: his soft lips tenderly tracing the side of my neck as we lay side by side in a glittering crystalline cave; his arms pulling me tighter against his soaped-up body, our nakedness shrouded by the steam of the hot shower; his hands, gentle yet powerful, gripping my waist as he whispered sensual words against my ear, his rock-hard arousal pressing against my lower back—

My eyes popped open to find neither cave nor steaming shower, only darkness. But in that darkness, part of my last dream still lingered in the form of Heath's rock-hard arousal, which somehow felt like it was *still* pressing against my lower back. *Wake up!* I blinked rapidly, trying to escape this bewilderingly, excruciatingly sexy nighttime fantasy that appeared to have no end...

Except, I eventually realized, this wasn't a dream.

At some point during the night, Heath and I had subconsciously maneuvered our sleeping bodies in such a way that his frontside was lodged firmly against my backside, with his arm draped over my chest, clutching me tightly against him. His hand was wedged beneath the hollow of my waist, his thumb resting against my left breast, while his face was buried in my hair, his deep, slow breaths warming the back of my neck. Worst of all, we were all but naked, since I was clad in only an oversized t-shirt, and he appeared to be wearing nothing but boxer briefs.

My breath caught as a searing-hot pang of desire shuddered through me, quickly followed by an accompanying wave of terror. This was a man I'd hated from the very first moment we met, a man I had since done everything I could to avoid. *Everything* about him irked me, from his shop to his shoes. And yet, from the deepest part of my core, my body was aching for him, a profound, throbbing yearning that was so powerful I quite literally couldn't breathe.

Get a grip on yourself! I gulped down one shallow breath, followed by another, willing – no, *begging* – my brain to function properly. But it only continued to betray me, with my unhinged hippocampus thwarting every attempt at rationality via the steamy, wanton images it was still harboring from my dreams.

Heath let out a soft moan and shifted in his sleep, drawing me even closer against him. The heat of his body was radiating off of him in palpable waves, with the warmest, most prominent part of him wedged firmly against my ass.

With my brain and body warring against one another, I squeezed my eyes shut and started silently reciting the periodic table of elements, picking up where I'd left off before. *Aluminum, silicon, phosphorous...*

But the words were swiftly hijacked by lexical interlopers, with *sulfur, chlorine, and argon* being drowned out by *restrained, logical,* and *disciplined* – the same words that had been used to describe me in glowing reference letters from former professors and employers.

I gritted my teeth together, trying to drown out rogue adjectives with rote elements, but it was no use. Like a canister of shaving cream left in an unpressurized cargo hold, my exterior façade was succumbing to the mounting outward pressure of my own self-imposed repression. The fact of the matter was that the people who had penned those words about me were all wrong.

I wasn't restrained, logical, or disciplined.

In truth, I was restless, emotional, and impulsive – all traits that had been repeatedly deemed as negative or undesirable by others, so I'd been forced to either bury or camouflage them. Restlessness was disguised as a love of travel. Emotions were flattened and repressed. Impulsivity – namely, my proclivity to instantly succumb to fleeting desires, up to and most definitely including the carnal variety – was replaced by numerous hobbies that were so consuming, they left little room for anything else. It was a carefully-crafted system that had afforded me a lot of success in recent years, a robust suit of defensive armor with neither weakness nor chink—

"Mmm," Heath murmured in his sleep, his thumb grazing against my hardened left nipple.

Until now.

Slowly and painstakingly so as to not wake him, I swiveled around so that our hips were aligned and our noses were millimeters apart. The scent of his body was intoxicating, filling me with bizarre, errant thoughts of running my tongue down his neck to see if he tasted as good as he smelled. The notion was unfathomable, particularly coming from someone who instinctively held her breath whenever strangers passed her on the street. If this was indeed the result of a prasiolite contamination back home in my lab, then prasiolite was too potent – too dangerous – for me to keep brewing for my customers. An essence *that* powerful needed to be locked away, kept safe from myself and the world… But if it *wasn't* the result of prasiolite-tainted potions – and, if I were being honest with myself, my lab protocols were far too fastidious for that to ever happen – then I was in serious trouble.

"Laney," Heath whispered softly, still fast asleep.

Serious, *serious* trouble.

Freed from the parting clouds, a pale stripe of moonlight materialized between the curtains, illuminating Heath's face in the darkness. A lock of wavy dark hair hung in front of his forehead, reminding me of Clark Kent, minus the glasses – which I suppose would technically make him Superman. My heart raced with a foreign, forbidden desire as I watched him sleep, my eyes roving across his closed eyelids, the dark whiskers that dotted his strong jaw, and his parted lips, which looked so impossibly soft, I longed to taste them…

Before the thought had fully formed, I dropped my head, brushing my lips against his. To my surprise, Heath let out a soft moan, sliding his fingers into my hair. "Laney," he whispered against my lips.

My entire body stiffened as he pulled me deeper into the kiss, the tiny hairs on my arms and the back of my neck rising in tingling goosebumps, as though lightning were about to strike. I should have pulled away at that moment, snuck back into my own bed so this reckless error of judgment would be nothing but a hazy half-dream the next morning. But I wanted this so desperately, there was nothing I could do except surrender to the desire.

"Heath," I whimpered, my voice cracking.

His eyes popped open, then blinked several times, as though he was struggling to determine whether or not this was a dream. Then, with a soft growl that ignited my core, he abruptly wrapped both of his arms around me and pulled me against him. "You are, without a doubt, the most bewildering woman I've ever met in my life."

As I opened my mouth to stammer an apology, his lips crushed against mine, robbing me of both my voice and my breath. The logical part of my brain pleaded with me to stop hobnobbing with the enemy, but my body was having none of it. Kicking away the sheet, I hooked my left knee over the back of his right thigh to guide his arousal closer to mine, while he slid his hand beneath the small of my back, grinding himself against the buzzing junction of my thighs. We were a tangled mess of writhing limbs, kissing deeply and without restraint, our hands frantically raking over each other's bodies as though we'd both been starving and could only find the nourishment we so desperately needed in each other.

I gasped as Heath's hand twined into my hair, turning my head so he could brush his lips along the side of my neck, lingering at the erogenous spot just beneath my ear.

"How long?" he whispered, the low, raspy growl sending a thrill down my spine.

"I—" I let out a low whimper as his teeth grazed my earlobe. "I-I don't know."

Propped on his elbows, he hesitated, the warm bulge of his desire pressed against the throbbing, wet apex of mine. He was still in his boxers, and I in my t-shirt, which had been hiked up just enough to expose the underside of my left breast. I watched his Adam's apple bob up and down in the moonlight as his cupped hand slid along the narrow of my waist. As his fingers raked down my hip and across the top of my thigh, a soft whimper slipped through my lips.

His hand stopped. "Laney…" His eyes bore into mine as though searching for something. "Are you sure this is what you want?"

"Yes." I nodded fervently. In truth, I'd never wanted anyone as much as I wanted Heath at that very moment. "I want you to make love to me…" Biting my trembling lip, I added, "Please."

"Oh, God," he groaned, resting his head between my breasts. "How is it that everything you say drives me absolutely crazy?"

My breath hitched in my chest.

As if reading my mind, Heath's head popped back up. "I mean that in the best way possible." Gently cupping my face in two hands, he kissed my forehead, which somehow made all of my fears melt away like warmed wax. "Either I hit my head harder than I thought, and this is the most beautiful fever dream I've ever had, or…" He hesitated, licking his lips. "Well, let's just say, if this is a fever dream, I don't want to wake up." With that, he dropped his parted lips back to mine, kissing me tenderly. As he reached down to pull away his boxers, I let out a ragged gasp, hot desire instantly extinguished by cold horror.

"Stop!" I choked out, pushing him away.

He started as though I'd slapped him, his hand frozen on the elastic band. "What's wrong?"

I stared up at him, my chest rising and falling in short, panicked breaths. *What if I still have apatite in my system? What if he's only doing this because—*

"Oh no!" I clapped a hand over my mouth.

There was a reason I never sold blue apatite potions to anyone under *any* circumstance; the mineral's persuasive essence was so powerful, even the most well-intentioned clients could easily inflict untold damage on those around them. And in that moment, I could have manipulated Heath into chopping off his own foot – and with a smile on his face, no less.

"Butternuts!" I rolled out from underneath him, recoiling when he reached for me. Hugging my knees to my chest, with my t-shirt pulled over my knees, I stammered, "Y-You don't want to have sex with me!"

Heath sat up in bed with an expression that could only be construed as utter confusion. "Oh, I'm pretty sure I do." He reached for me.

"No, you don't!" I staggered out of his bed, hating myself for what I'd done to him, for deluding myself into thinking he'd willfully want to sleep with me.

"Laney—"

"Don't ask! Don't say anything! Just… Just trust me on this!" Shame and guilt stung at my eyes as I retreated to my own bed, where Topie was watching us through one surreptitiously-squinted eye. As if on cue, or perhaps to prove he hadn't been eavesdropping on our conversation *at all*, he let out a loud, blissful snore. "Get up!" I demanded, shaking him roughly.

He let out an overdramatic yawn, which promptly turned into an indignant yelp as I unceremoniously hoisted him out of bed and plopped him on the floor.

"You are a pig, not a person!" I shouted at him. "Act like it!"

His chin quivered as he gazed up at me in dejection, but I was already so full of guilt and shame it made little difference. Turning away from him, I crawled into the bed he'd been forced to vacate and pulled the covers over my head to hide the tears that were streaming down my face.

"Laney?" The edge of the bed sank as Heath sat beside me. "Can we talk?"

"No!" My voice was muffled by the pillow I'd clamped over my head. "Please just let me sleep. I'm exhausted!"

Heath was silent for a long moment before the distant creak of springs announced his return to his own bed. "C'mon, little guy," he murmured softly. "The floor is cold. You can sleep with me tonight."

I gritted my teeth as that four-legged traitor helped himself right into my former archnemesis's warm, cozy, delicious-smelling bed, where the two of them would probably spoon all night while I was forced to share a cold, lonely mattress with my *new* number-one nemesis: Myself.

I woke up less than three hours later to the shrieks of a nearby rooster, who was flaunting his avian virility to all the nearby hens while simultaneously ensuring no human within a five-mile radius could sleep past the first rays of dawn. Squeezing the pillow over my ears, I mentally added "roosters" to the ever-growing list of things I hated, smack-dab between tight socks and pig farts.

Try as I might to fall back to sleep, the sound of the running bathroom shower filled my head with images of Heath's naked body, which in turn triggered highly-detailed memories of our unbearably-arousing, morally-problematic midnight make-out session. The combination of horniness and humiliation made all the blood in my body fluctuate between my thighs and my cheeks, a terribly confusing and uncomfortable sensation I wouldn't wish upon my worst enemy – which, ironically[10] enough, was also me.

When the door creaked open a few minutes later, I couldn't help but peek over the edge of the sheets as Heath emerged from the bathroom wearing nothing but a white towel wrapped around his waist, low enough to display the arousing V-shaped musculature of his lower abdomen. The jolt of heat that surged between my legs was enough to make me roll over and groan into my pillow.

A moment later, a finger tapped me on my shoulder, making me yelp. I slowly turned over, using the sheet to hide the chagrin blossoming across my cheeks, and peeked over the top of the blanket to find Heath – still clothed in only a towel – casually sitting on the edge of my bed.

"Good morning," he said, casting me a side eye.

I cleared my throat roughly, extremely conscious of the fact that I hadn't brushed my teeth the night before –

---

[10] Yes, I realize that "irony" is used incorrectly here as the word is defined as "a literary technique by which the full significance of a character's words or actions are clear to the reader although unknown to the character," which is ironic in and of itself, but I'm experimenting with colloquialisms so we'll all just have to deal with it.

not that it seemed to bother Heath a few hours ago – and half-whispered, half-rasped, "Good morning."

Had I been a God-fearing woman, I might have prayed for Him to strike me dead with a divine bolt of lightning and save me from this agonizing humiliation.

If Heath was feeling remotely the same way, you'd never know it. His outward appearance seemed completely unfettered as he casually held up his fingers and began counting off as he spoke. "So...pharmacist, mineralogist, pilot, wound care specialist, *and* nighttime seductress? How ever did you find the time to excel in so many faculties, Miss Stone?"

I pulled the blanket over my head and sank into the mattress, praying to every deity I could think of to kill me right then and there.

"Every time I think you can't possibly surprise me any more than you already have," Heath continued blithely, "you somehow find a way to prove me wrong."

Please – Vishnu, Allah, Yahweh! Someone, any*one!*

"Anyway, after taking a very long, very *cold* shower, during which I pondered all sorts of theories as to what might have happened to you last night—"

"Hypotheses." The word slipped out before I could stop it.

"I—what?"

"Hypotheses," I repeated, my voice muffled by the blanket I was trying and failing to smother myself with. "A hypothesis is a tentative proposal of an observation that can be tested, whereas a theory is a more concrete explanation that can only be made *after* rigorous testing of said hypothesis."

"Right." Though barely visible through the fibers of my blanket, I was pretty sure Heath was scrubbing a hand down his face. "Anyway, as I was saying, I've just spent the better part of an hour trying to rationalize your behavior last night, and apart from sleepwalking, I've yet to come up with anything that could possibly explain why you would climb into my bed in the middle of the night, actively seduce me, and then promptly run for the hills."

I ground my teeth together, saying nothing in response. Surely if I let him continue to sit there in awkward silence, he'd eventually—

"I'm a very patient man, Delaney, and I'll gladly sit here all day if it means extracting some semblance of an explanation from you."

Butternuts, I groaned. Forcing myself into an upright position, leaving the blanket draped over my head to hide the shame broiling in my cheeks, I turned in the general direction of Heath's voice and mumbled, "I'm sorry, okay?"

"For…?" he prompted.

I squeezed my eyes shut, silently building up the courage to answer, before hastily blurting, "For coercing you into something you didn't want to do!"

Heath was silent for a long moment – long enough for me to *almost* remove the blanket and check to see if he had left the room. Eventually, he asked, "And what about my body language gave you even the faintest impression that I was being coerced into doing something I didn't want to do?"

Since I obviously couldn't tell him about the powerful manipulation tonic I'd chugged the night before, I simply said, "You hit your head and weren't in your right mind. And I-I took advantage of you… My actions were unforgivable," I added in a pitiful whisper.

Heath burst out laughing.

"What?" I asked, bewildered. "Why are you laughing?" When he didn't answer, I yanked the blanket off my head, most likely displaying a wild mop of staticky hair, only to find Heath shaking with silent laughter. *"What?"* I demanded. "Tell me!"

"Oh, Laney." Heath chuckled, wiping mirthful tears from his eyes. "I don't know what universe you think we live in that you would have to 'take advantage of me' to get me into bed with you."

I gaped at him, clutching the blanket against my chest while trying to make sense of his nonsensical words. Blue apatite was fast-acting and water soluble and therefore should have been out of my system by now – i.e., I was fairly certain I wasn't influencing his answers anymore. Furthermore, I'd seen his fully-healed head injury myself, so he couldn't have been speaking out of trauma-induced delirium. I frowned. Was it possible he was making fun of me?

As much as it physically pained me to utter the words out loud, knowing he'd most likely reject me, I *had* to know what he meant. "Are you… Are you saying you…" I looked away, forcing out the words before my courage left me altogether. "Are you saying you'd actually *want* to have sex with me?"

"Laney"—he put his hand over mine and squeezed it tightly, but not so tightly that I couldn't pull away if I wanted to—"what I'm telling you is that I wanted to make love to you so badly last night, I had to take an hour-long cold shower just to be able to function this morning."

My mouth tumbled open. Shock filled me to the brim, leaving my mind reeling and my ears buzzing. If the fate of the entire world rested on me being able to formulate a coherent sentence at that very moment, humanity would have been doomed.

I swallowed once, then twice, my eyes darting to our clasped hands. Just as my neurons had managed to reconnect to my hypoglossal nerve,[11] the front door swung open and in trounced Topie, happily chomping on a mushroom stem.

"What is *that?*" I blurted out, grateful for the excuse to turn my attention away from the burning wreckage that used to be my utter and unwavering disdain for Heath Spencer. A new emotion – one that was strange and terrifying – had started to smolder beneath those residual hot coals, and I was *not* ready for that metaphorical phoenix to rise from the ashes.

Extricating myself from Heath's grip on my hand, I practically leapt out of bed to kneel beside Topie and pry open his mouth. "Are you crazy? That might be poisonous!" I scolded him. "Did you even have the sense to check what kind of mushroom it was before blindly scarfing it down?"

Heath knelt beside me to take the stem from my hand. "I believe it's shiitake," he said, bringing it close to his nose to inspect it. "Edible *and* delicious."

"It had better be shiitake!" I shook an admonishing finger in Topie's face. "Because I barely have any dolom—er, that *military-grade detoxicant*," I quickly amended, my cheeks yet again flushing with guilt and chagrin, "left in my kit. So you'd better not go out there chomping on poisonous fungus!" I stood up in a grumpy huff, forgetting in my crankiness and haste that I wasn't wearing underwear.

---

[11] The primary nerve that connects to your tongue and enables speech.

Heath, who was still kneeling on the ground, glanced up at me before quickly turning away, the tips of his ears turning bright red.

I tugged the hem of my shirt farther down my thighs. "Oh, for Pete's—Can we all just go and look at rocks already?"

Without waiting for an answer, I grabbed my toiletries and an armful of clothes and darted into the bathroom with my proverbial tail between my legs. Besides, there was no time to sit around discussing fungi and feelings; we had a brand-new mine to explore, full of rare and possibly even undiscovered minerals to unearth and taste! It was such an exhilarating notion, one that would have normally sent me bolting out the front door without another moment's delay. However, on this particularly rousing morning there was one thing I needed to do first:

Take a long, cold shower.

Chapter 14

Ablutions finished – including an extra-long teeth cleaning session to make up for my lack of brushing the night before – I emerged from the bathroom a full thirty minutes later, lips blue and libido (mostly) tamped. I'd donned my usual spelunking outfit: leather pants to protect my legs from scrapes and falls; sturdy leather climbing boots; a tight black tank top since mines get hotter the deeper you go and baggy shirts often snag on rough edges; a utility belt slung low around my hips for easy tool and potion access; a garter-style belt around my left thigh with a dagger for cutting things loose; and a leather jacket that was currently slung over my shoulder, since the upper levels of underground mines tend to be cold and damp.

Heath had gotten dressed as well, not in his signature snooty designer suit but in cargo pants and a tight-fitting long-sleeved black shirt that clung to his torso in such a way I felt a sudden urge to turn around and march right back into the shower. He'd been sitting on his bed rummaging through a large pack that was overflowing with equipment, but when his eyes fell on me, the miniature chisel he'd been clasping between his teeth fell on the floor.

"Is that…" He swallowed, the knot in his throat bobbing, then tried again. "Is that, uh, what you'll be wearing today?"

I glanced down at my outfit, worried I'd forgotten something. "Yes. Why?"

"No reason," he replied, his voice noticeably cracking. I waited for him to explain further, but he'd gone back to examining his pack with a level of thoroughness I hadn't thought him capable of.

Bewildered, I turned to Topie, hoping he might be able to explain. But he just snorted as he tended to his own daypack, its compartments bulging with a week's worth of snacks.

"Did you take your breakfast vitamins?" I asked, nodding my approval when he proudly brandished his empty pill container. "With food?" He nudged an empty Tupperware container that used to contain four oatmeal biscuits, two of which were supposed to be for me. My hollow stomach rumbled at the thought of food. "Ugh." I poked at it in annoyance.

Heath glanced up at me, his expression creasing with what appeared to be concern. "You okay, Laney?"

"*De*laney," I answered automatically, though truth be told his stupid nickname was starting to grow on me – not that I'd ever tell him that. "And I was just thinking how hungry I am but that I don't want to waste time eating when there's a new mine to explore."

For some reason, Heath chuckled. "It's annoying when bodily necessities like food and sleep get in the way of rock-hounding, eh?"

I nodded as I shoved my jacket into my backpack, then slipped the straps over my bare arms. "It really is."

He laughed again, making my heart flutter. I normally hated it when people laughed around me, as I often failed to find the humor in the situation or worse, found myself as the unwitting subject of their laughter. But Heath's mirth no longer got under my skin quite the same way; in fact, it was almost…infectious. I forced my curling lips into a tight line to keep my teeth from showing. Sure, they might have looked normal now, but that didn't make up for more than a decade of dental-related ridicule. Wounds may heal over time, but psychological injuries seldom do.

"Well, lucky for you," Heath was saying, "a lot of street vendors will be out and about today, so we'll grab a bite on the way." Slinging his bag over his shoulder, he strode over to the front door and opened it, gesturing chivalrously. "After you."

Thinking the motion was for him, Topie trotted out the door with his backpack strapped on and his snout held high.

"Such service, eh, Topie?" I winked at Heath as we followed our guest of honor outside.

There were still some residual stratus clouds hovering just above the jagged green mountains surrounding the village, but the early morning air was already warm and humid – in other words, not a rain cloud or lightning bolt in sight.

"Thanks a lot, Li," I muttered, though I couldn't help feeling a *tiny* smidge of gratitude for the meddling man.

Taking a deep breath to fill my lungs with fresh mountain air, I fell into step behind Heath as he made his way back to the dirt road that had brought us to the tiny inn last night. The town was quiet, but in the distance, to the north, a massive floating dragon soared lazily in the sky, with fronds of red ribbons hanging from its jowls and a plume of smaller balloons rising from beneath it. Part of me wanted to see the festival, but a much bigger part of me wanted nothing to do with the crowds and the noise that accompanied it. Besides, Heath and I had a mine to break into.

We turned south, away from the festivities and toward a single plume of steam that rose from the smelting facilities on the far side of Tonglushan. The road was mostly empty, but Heath did manage to flag down an old man who was pushing a cart full of some sort of festival street food he called *zongzi*.

After giving the man a few coins, Heath unwrapped the green bamboo leaves of one of the snacks, revealing a pyramid-shaped sticky rice dumpling. "Here, buddy," he said, passing the *zongzi* to Topie. "This one has shiitake mushrooms." He turned to me, lowering his voice as he handed me mine. "This one has p-o-r-k inside, so no sharing with the p-i-g."

Though I normally tried to stay away from pork products for Topie's sake, my stomach was growling too loudly to be picky. I took a dubious nibble of my sticky rice dumpling while Topie attacked his with the urgency of a starving animal that hadn't eaten in weeks. To my surprise, the *zongzi* wasn't bad. Once you got past the unpleasant glue-like texture of the rice, the savory meat filling – which tasted a bit like barbecued pulled pork – was quite tasty. A hum of contentment slipped through my lips as we ate and walked, leisurely taking in the lush surroundings. While the city we'd driven through to get here was large and industrial, this part of town was mountainous and lush and mercifully quiet, at least during the holiday. I actually found myself enjoying the beautiful scenery. I cast a furtive glance in Heath's direction.

And, maybe, *possibly*, the company too.

I wanted to make love to you so badly last night, the memory of his husky voice slid between my ears, *I had to take an hour-long cold shower just to be able to function this morning.*

I stumbled, choking on a bite of food.

"Are you okay?" Heath asked.

"Yep," I coughed, working to dislodge the sticky rice from my windpipe. "Never better."

After pausing to make sure I was all right, he replied, "Well, I remain at your disposal should you need CPR."

I rolled my eyes. Despite his perfectly smooth, innocent expression, I was quickly acclimating to Heath's particular dialect of innuendos and implications. "You know the latest CPR guidelines advise *against* mouth-to-mouth resuscitation, right? It's just chest compressions now."

He flashed me a devious grin. "Yeah, but I still think it's the mouth-to-mouth part that's most effective."

Despite my best efforts, I burst out laughing. "Are you this much of a scoundrel around all the women you torment, or am I just lucky?"

Heath abruptly stopped in his tracks. "Delaney Stone, was that *sarcasm* that tumbled from your lips?"

I shrugged. "It's been known to happen…from time to time."

"Hmm." He glanced at me out of the corner of his eye as we resumed walking.

"What?"

"Nothing. It's just…I don't think I've ever heard you laugh before."

I crossed my arms in indignation. "I laugh!"

His eyebrow arched.

"I do!" I protested. "I just…have a different sense of humor than most people."

Heath finished his last bite, tossed the bamboo leaves on the side of the road, then wiped his mouth on his sleeve and said, "Okay. Hit me."

I regarded him warily. "Open or closed fist?"

"What? No!" He barked out a laugh. "I mean, hit me with your best joke."

"Oh." I ruminated on that for a few moments, taking my time chewing and swallowing the last of my dumpling. "When I was in pharmacology school, one of the professors – a retired pediatrician named Richard Dean – did a weekend presentation about the time he spent in Australia working with one of the local tribes. He also had an accompanying slide show that chronicled his three-year stint with Doctors Without Borders. When he was finished, he opened the floor for questions."

"Uh…okay?" Heath said, scratching his head. "I guess we've moved on from joke-telling."

I ignored the comment. "One of my classmates stood up and asked if Doctor Dean had witnessed any interesting tribal medicine in the bush. The professor answered, 'Yes, definitely. In fact, one of the shamans we worked with came up with an ingenious method of turning a rare type of palm leaf into a suppository.' Being pharmacology students, most of us had only been exposed to industry-established pharmaceutical treatments as opposed to botanical or naturopathic remedies—"

"Mm-hmm," Heath said in the same tone of voice I often used when a patient was citing WebMD to support their self-diagnosis of something wildly rare and implausible, like Achard Thiers Syndrome.[12]

"Anyway," I continued breezily, "my classmate excitedly asked the professor how well the palm leaves worked when used as suppositories – because, again, there were no naturopathic courses available at the school, and we were all eager to learn non-traditional methods."

"Uh-huh."

"And the professor replied, 'Oh, they worked quite well. In fact, with fronds like these, who needs enemas?'"

"Right," Heath started to say, then stopped. He slowly turned his head toward me, his eyebrows drawing together in consternation. Suddenly, he doubled over, clutching his stomach, and let out a peal of wheezing laughter. "Oh wow – you really got me."

I beamed proudly. "It's called a feghoot – a drawn-out story that ends in an unexpected pun or word play. I know quite a few feghoots that are much longer and 'shaggier' than that, but I figured I'd start you off gently."

"That was brilliant, truly." Still snickering, he wiped the tears from his eyes. "I await future 'feghoots' with keen anticipation."

"You don't need to cram 'keen' and 'anticipation' into the same sentence," I informed him. "It's tautological."[13]

He muttered something in response – probably thanking me for the helpful tidbit – but my attention had

---

[12] Also known as "Diabetic Bearded Woman Syndrome"
[13] The fallacy of saying the same thing twice in different words, e.g., "they arrived one after the other in succession."

already deviated to the single red balloon drifting in the air above us.

"I meant to ask you earlier. What exactly is the Dragon Boat Festival?"

"Hmm?" Heath followed my gaze to the balloon. "Ah, well, it's a little complicated. The holiday has been around in various forms for thousands of years, with its current iteration being a combination of multiple festivals and traditions that have been sort of cherry-picked from the past."

"Oh." I blinked. "Okay, well, how did it start? The end of a war, an emperor's birthday…?"

"Well, one of the most popular *theories*," he stressed the word as if to show its correct usage, even though he was still using it incorrectly, "is that the holiday is to honor Qu Yuan, a beloved Chinese poet and politician who was wrongfully accused of treason. When he drowned himself in the Miluo River on the fifth day of the fifth lunar month, his people rushed to their paddle boats and threw sticky rice in the water to keep the fish away from Qu Yuan's body."

"Huh," I remarked, making a mental note to research Qu Yuan once I was back at my computer.

"Another theory is that the Dragon Boat Festival is meant to ward off bad luck and evil spirits because the fifth lunar month was once considered to be an unlucky time. Ancient Chinese people believed the *wǔdú* would come out of their winter hiding places during that month to terrorize people."

"What are *wǔdú*?" I asked.

"The five poisonous animals: centipedes, snakes, scorpions, lizards and toads. So, to safeguard themselves during this time, China's ancient people practiced rituals such as poking pictures of the *wŭdú* with pins, which their living counterparts would feel—"

"Like voodoo?"

"Yeah." He nodded. "Though the pronunciation is just a coincidence. Still, it's kind of remarkable how these similar superstitious practices appear centuries and even hemispheres apart, huh? I've always been fascinated by the phenomenon, to the extent that I chose that very same subject for my PhD dissertation. Anyway—"

"Wait," I interrupted. "You're a doctor?"

"Well, not the kind that's sought out on airplanes for medical emergencies," he said, glancing at me out of the corner of his eye.

"Yes, but in what philosophy?" I demanded, fervently hoping – for reasons I couldn't quite understand – that his PhD was tied to a totally useless subject, like Ancient Mesopotamian Poetry or something equally silly.

"Anthropology."

Butternuts, I groaned inwardly. Anthropology was a perfectly acceptable area of science – laudable, even.

"Well, cultural anthropology," he clarified, making it even worse, "since I know you like specifics. I majored in archeology and then shifted into anthropology later on in graduate school. My primary focus was how psychological factors like cognition, motivations, and emotions impact sociocultural settings in various ancient civilizations." He cleared his throat before mercifully changing the subject. "Anyway, in addition to the threat posed by the reemergence of poisonous animals, it was believed that people were more prone to falling ill around this time. Over the years, various traditions emerged to protect people from illness and bad luck during the dreaded Double Fifth. Since the Dragon is considered a divine mystical animal, it's believed to ward off evil spirits and bestow safety to all that hold his emblem." He turned to look at me, only to realize I'd long ago stopped in my tracks and was standing motionless – immobilized, rather – a few yards behind him. "Laney? What's wrong? Did you lose something?"

Yes! I wanted to shout. *My sanity!*

The proverbial wheels in my head were spinning as though occupied by a horde[14] of hamsters. Heath Spencer, whom I had long ago categorized as smug, empty-headed, human-shaped garbage, was, well…none of those things.

"Laney?" Heath said again. He and Topie were trotting toward me, concern etched into their features.

"You were supposed to be a lummox," I whispered, not even remotely loud enough for him to hear. Topie, on the other hand, let out a loud, derisive snort. He'd been trying to convince me for *months* that Heath was a good guy. All that time, I'd brushed it aside as Heath shamelessly buying him off with truffles. But, as more and more evidence came to light, disproving my long-standing hypothesis that Heath was a vapid, self-absorbed ignoramus, I was forced to accept the mind-boggling truth: I'd been wrong…so, *so* wrong.

With that discomforting realization, my hand reached into my pocket to roll my prized chalcopyrite ball between my trembling fingers. As Heath approached me beneath a low canopy of evergreen branches, I found myself regarding him in an entirely new light, mentally stripping away the many layers of misconceptions and assumptions I'd assigned to him over the last year and a half. Bit by bit, they chipped away like dried paint,

---

[14] The literal term used to describe a group of hamsters: e.g., a horde of hamsters, a flock of geese, a murder of crows, a loveliness of ladybugs, etc.

revealing the brand-new, untarnished Heath Spencer that now stood before me.

"Are you okay?" he asked, his eyes prodding my body as though searching for injury.

Compassionate.

"I'm fine," I whispered, gazing up at him. "I just…needed to think through something."

"Oh." His features softened. "Well, if it's anything I can help you with, feel free to muse out loud."

Supportive.

I licked my lips, trying to put moisture back in my mouth. "I think I've got it, thanks. Um…should we…?" My eyes darted down the road.

He shrugged. "Probably, but the mine's not going anywhere. We can wait a little longer if you need to."

Patient.

"No." I shook my head, then thought the better of it. "Um…actually, there is one thing I wanted to say." I took in a deep, steeling breath, letting my gaze drop to the ground. "Heath, I…I'm sorry. For how I've treated you. I, um…" Inside my pocket, my hand was clenching the chalcopyrite-turned-worry-stone Heath had generously gifted me after I'd treated him so poorly. My breath rushed out in a huff, forcing the words along with it. "I thought I knew the type of person you were, but I misjudged you."

His boots inched closer to mine. "And what kind of person did you think I was?"

I swallowed hard. "The same kind of person all the other attractive, confident, flirtatious men in my life turned out to be…"

"Attractive, did you say?"

"Well, yes, obviously!" I snuck a glance up at him, surprised to find he was grinning widely at me. "Anyway, all those other men turned out to be…um…" I faltered as James' sneering face unexpectedly flashed in my memory.

Oh for fuck's sake, Stone, would you stop crying already? Why do you always have to take everything so fucking seriously? All I did was make a few harmless jokes and share some photos with the guys – which, by the way, was an attempt to defend you since none of them believed you've been hiding a tight little body underneath those stupid baggy t-shirts you always wear. You should be flattered, not pissed! I mean, Jesus! It's not like I uploaded the pictures to PornHub, which I guarantee any other guy in my shoes would have done!

I tried and failed to clear the lump in my throat. "Well, suffice it to say they hurt me…badly."

Heath inhaled sharply.

"But this entire trip," I continued, rocking back and forth on my heels, "you've treated me with kindness and patience – even when I didn't deserve it. More importantly, you've been completely honest with me. I think, having been manipulated and lied to so many times in my life, that's the part that matters to me the most. So…thank you for that." I sucked another deep breath between my teeth, gathering the courage to look Heath in the eye.

To my surprise, he was no longer smiling. On the contrary, his features had contorted into an expression that looked almost pained, like I'd just said something horribly offensive.

I froze. *What did I say?* Had I overshared? Overstepped? Over…reacted, somehow? I chewed on my lip, my brain hastily replaying everything I'd blurted out in the last minute and coming up with nothing.

It was a long time before Heath spoke again, and when he finally did, his voice sounded…off. "You don't need to thank me, Delaney. It's nothing…really." He smiled, pressing his lips into a tight line, then cleared his throat and glanced at his watch. "Shall we get going? It's only a few more minutes to the mine."

"I…" I hesitated, then nodded. "Yeah…sure."

Without another word, he turned and strode away from me.

Topie appeared at my side, a troubled crease forming between his brows as we fell into step behind Heath, whose shoulders had transformed from relaxed to rigid.

"So, I'm not just imagining it?" I muttered to Topie under my breath.

He shook his head.

"Butternuts." I sighed, biting my knuckle hard enough to make me wince from the pain. I hastily shook it out and stuffed my hand back into my pocket, where it continued worrying at the chalcopyrite. It shouldn't have mattered to me that I'd offended Heath. After all, I'd been offending him the entire trip; heck, our entire relationship had once been entirely predicated on our mutual annoyance for one another. But all those other times had been different. I'd *wanted* to annoy him then, to push him away before he'd even had the chance to get close. But now…

I swallowed tightly.

Now, I couldn't help but wonder what I'd said to upset him, wishing with all my heart that I could somehow take it back – or even better, that I'd never opened my stupid mouth in the first place.

Chapter 15

We arrived at the mine less than ten minutes later – not the massive pit that was the primary Tonglushan extraction and smelting site, but a small, cave-like opening located a few hundred meters away. Tucked out of sight and nestled deep in the surrounding forest, the entrance had been drilled into the base of a moss-covered rock outcrop and was well-hidden by vines and branches, which Heath swept away as we approached. The mine looked as though it had been abandoned for years, if not decades; the rusted cart tracks that led inside were overgrown with pink-thistled copperweed, the wooden frame of the adit was sun-bleached and splintering, and a weathered red sign that almost certainly said "Keep Out" had been tacked to the corroded bars blocking the entrance.

I looked around nervously, surveying the area for any indication of activity. Yes, I had broken into my fair share of abandoned mines over the years, but always in the middle of the night and never in a country with an active travel advisory for American citizens. Fortunately, just as

Heath had promised, there didn't appear to be any workers milling around. The flurry of mining activity we'd witnessed the night before was completely halted, and instead of gushing plumes of steam rising into the sky, a single thin coil of vapor rose from one of the nearby smelting vents.

"The night crews will most likely be back around ten o'clock tonight, which means we have about fourteen hours to explore," Heath said as he rummaged around in his pack.

I glanced at my watch. "Do we really need fourteen hours to find the mineral you were talking about?"

"No, but you never know what else we might find down there." He smiled as he pulled a pair of bolt-cutters from his bag, though the edges of his eyes didn't crinkle. "This satellite mine hasn't been active in over a century, and while it's been backfilled and ostensibly reinforced, there will almost certainly be false floors and rotting wood. And speaking of which, I don't know how far down it goes. Depending on the depth and air-tightness, there may be pockets of carbon dioxide and hydrogen sulfide, and I doubt either of us thought to pack a canary."

"No, just a pig," I agreed. "Luckily, that's what gas masks and first aid kits are for."

He chuckled, cheering me somewhat; maybe my screw-up hadn't been completely irrevocable. "Still, and this hopefully goes without saying, if you're having second thoughts about any of this—"

"I'm not," I interjected, fishing my glasses out of my bag to put them on. "We just have to be sure to—"

"Since when do you wear glasses?"

"Since I was a kid." I frowned at the smudges on the lenses, then took the glasses off and used the hem of my shirt to clean them. "My distance vision is good enough that I don't have to wear them for most activities, but navigating mines requires twenty-twenty vision." I replaced the smudge-free glasses on the bridge of my nose, surprised to find Heath staring at me intently. "What?" I demanded, my cheeks heating under his scrutiny.

"Nothing. They just…really suit you. He cleared his throat. "Anyway, what were you saying?"

"I…" My mouth momentarily fluttered open at the unexpected compliment, then clamped shut. "I don't remember."

Shrugging, he brought his bolt cutter to the lock on the bars, then stopped. "Did you say you brought a gas mask?"

"Of course." Grateful for the change of subject, I tried extra hard to keep my tone patient and non-patronizing. "I've been doing this alone for a long time – exploring old mines, that is. I've packed every possible safety precaution you've ever thought of, and probably many more you haven't."

He didn't look entirely convinced, but he didn't argue either.

"Was that lock there when you were here before?" I asked, pointing to the shiny metal padlock he was about to break open.

"Nah. I'm guessing they installed that after I got caught prowling around here the week before last."

"You were caught?"

"Yeah. And escorted off the premises by a couple of very friendly guards."

"Doubt they'll be so friendly if they catch you a second time," I muttered, rubbing the bridge of my nose.

"Definitely not." With a grunt of effort, he broke open the lock with the bolt cutters and swung the rusted metal gate open. I covered my ears against the high-pitched screech of straining hinges. "What should we do with Topie?" Heath asked. "Should we leash him up out here?"

Topie shot Heath a dark glare at his casual use of the dreaded "L" word.

"No." I rubbed at the lingering feel of metal scraping my eardrums. "Topie goes where I go. He can handle himself. Besides, there might be truffles growing inside the cave."

"Reeee!" Topie excitedly kicked his hind legs in the air.

"Take it easy, piggy." I knelt beside him so I could fasten the strap of an illuminated helmet under his chin, then did the same for myself. After putting on my leather jacket and gloves, I slung a bundle of neon-yellow paracord and steel carabiners over my shoulder, then set about unfolding and smoothing out the edges of my meticulously-written mine checklist. Heath exhaled sharply through his nose, spurring me to look up. "What?"

He just shook his head, quietly chuckling to himself.

"What is it?" I demanded. "Tell me!"

His left eyebrow arched. "Wow, you *really* don't like not knowing the immediate answer to everything, do you?"

"No." I folded my arms across my chest. "I don't."

"Fine." He let out a capitulating sigh. "If you must know, I was just thinking to myself that I never thought it was possible for someone to look so cute in mining gear. And yet…" He made an inscrutable gesture with his arm.

I looked down at Topie and uncrossed my arms. "Oh, yeah. Cute."

"Reeee!" Topie's toothy grin stretched from ear to floppy ear.

"Er, well—" Heath started.

"Yeah, yeah, just don't let it go to your head," I told Topie. "Your helmet will get too snug."

Still beaming, Topie plopped down in front of me, awaiting my customary reading of the safety checklist, which we both knew by heart, but nevertheless recited every time we entered a new mine just in case.

"Okay, here we go." I cleared my throat. "Item One: Do not go inside an abandoned mine alone." My eyes darted over to Heath, who was frozen at the entrance of the mine with one foot hovering in the air. "Check." I marked off the box with the pencil I'd tucked behind my ear. "Item Two: Research the potential structural hazards of the mine, familiarizing yourself with common dangers like gasses, flooding, and collapse." I again turned my attention to Heath, who had the wide-eyed look of a deer caught in headlights. "Tentative check, assuming our stalwart guide has already done those things." I chuckled at my own joke. "But just in case he hasn't, that brings us to Item Three: Always bring a full kit of po—er, medicine," I quickly amended, "including but not limited to—"

I retrieved a supplemental list from my pocket, which outlined a full detail of potions that I'd specifically brewed for mine exploration, and silently read over it: calcite for bone fortification, hematite and cinnabar for bone repair and rapid clotting, aquamarine for improving visual acuity in the darkness, and so on.

"—um, the usual," I conceded, very much wanting to read the entire list out loud as I'd done for every other mine. *Maybe I can recite it later, when Heath isn't listening,* I comforted myself, then continued, "Item Four: If water on the floor of an adit disappears for no reason, you may be standing on a cracked ceiling of another open space and should proceed with caution. Which is a good segway into Item Five—"

Heath cleared his throat.

I glanced at him over the top of the page. "Yes?"

"Um, just how many items are on this list, anyhow?"

"Forty-seven. Why?"

Sighing, he lowered himself onto a small rock beside Topie and rested his chin on his fists. "No reason."

I started reading the rest of Item Five—*Always make sure you have extra bulbs and batteries in case your headlamp burns out*—but stopped when I saw Heath fidgeting and glancing at his watch. "Are you…feeling impatient?" I guessed.

"A little," he admitted. "I've been looking forward to this for a very long time."

Since when is a couple of weeks a 'very long time'? I wondered, chewing on the inside of my cheek. Very much wanting to return to my checklist, I instead sighed and begrudgingly handed it to him. "Here, why don't you just give it a quick once-over – to save time since you're feeling impatient," I clarified.

"Oh—uh, thanks." He took the page and silently skimmed it, his eyes widening as he did. "Wow, this is thorough. And helpful," he added, folding and tucking the list into his back pocket. "Thank you."

"You're welcome," I replied, gesturing to the mouth of the cave. "Just be sure to keep Item Twenty-Three in mind as you head down."

Heath's hand hesitated over his back pocket. "Um...Item Twenty-Three?"

I crossed my arms. "Be wary of legal consequences, as some countries have large fines for entering abandoned mines, although often only enforced if you injure yourself," I recited from memory. "Maybe I *do* need to read the list out loud—"

"No need," Heath interjected hastily. "I got the gist of it. Really."

Not quite believing him, but equally impatient to get moving, I followed him into the cave, brushing aside spiderwebs and vines as he did. The rusted cart tracks led us down a steeply-sloping tunnel that had been carved into the rock and reinforced with concrete and wooden beams. Heath led the way, checking his various instruments for air quality, altitude, oxygen levels, and so on, while I took a surreptitious swig of a golden-yellow heliodor potion to amplify my sense of smell. Most toxic gasses are undetectable to the human nose, which is why canaries are sent into mines first; if they survive, humans follow.

Me, I prefer saving lives through my love of minerals, not sacrificing them.

While I wished I could just swallow my usual collection of mine-specific potions – like my fancy new ruby concoction that allowed me to conjure a controlled flame to indicate fluctuating oxygen levels – Heath would probably start asking questions if I chugged a potion and magically – er, 'parascientifically'– turned myself into a pyromancer.

Speaking of questions, I still had quite a few of my own.

"How far down do we need to go to find this mineral?" I asked after we'd been walking for a few minutes.

He hesitated. "I can't remember exactly. But not too far."

"I see." I glanced over at Topie, who was presently spinning in a circle as he attempted to reach over his shoulder and unzip his snack pack. "Why didn't you collect any of the mineral when you found it the first time?"

Heath cleared his throat. "Ah, well, we were pressed for time and not really in a great place to stop and admire the view—speaking of which," he continued before I could interject, "keep an eye out for emerald-green crystals."

"Is the crystal growth stalactitic, stalagmitic, or do they grow from a vertical surface, like the rock wall?"

"I'm not exactly sure," he admitted.

I frowned. *Didn't he just see this mineral a couple of weeks ago?* "Well, then, are they opaque or transparent crystals?"

"Opaque. The crystals likely form on copper schist and look almost like dioptase." Picking up the pace, he adjusted the brightness of his light as he swept it back and forth across the adit. "But we're not interested in the microcrystalline druzy formations. We're looking for clusters of prismatic, four-sided crystals with pyramidal terminations at each end, possibly up to ten inches long."

"What?" I stumbled over the back of my own foot. "Ten-inch prismatic crystals that are emerald-green and opaque? There's no such mineral!"

"I know. Watch your step, there may be unfilled tunnels underneath us."

I wanted to ask more about the mineral, but he was right; the deeper we went, the more dangerous the conditions would become. "Here," I said, looping one end of my paracord through my belt loops, then motioning for Heath to do the same. "Just in case."

He eyed the end of the rope with apparent skepticism. "The whole point of me going first is for your safety. If I fall through a shaft, I'm certainly not going to drag you with me."

Rolling my eyes, I marched up to him and wound the cord through the loops of his belt myself, not bothering to be gentle about it. After tying off the rope, effectively binding us together with less than six feet of slack, I peered up at him, startled by the proximity of his lips. As close as we were, and as heightened as my olfactory abilities were, I could smell Heath through his clothes, the intoxicating aroma of his pheromones affecting my enhanced senses in a strange and powerful way that caught me entirely off guard. I blinked, momentarily forgetting what I was about to say.

"I-I'm stronger than I look," I eventually stammered, the words barely a whisper.

Heath's lips were dangerously close to mine as he murmured, "I know you are."

My thumbs were still hooked in his belt loops, inadvertently pulling his hips against mine. Realizing that, I let go, took a hasty step back, and cleared my throat. "Anyway, if you think I'm just going to stand there and let you get hurt, you're an idiot."

Something flickered across his face. Pain? Indignation? Amusement?

How can people decipher so many subtle facial cues day after day? Grinding my teeth together, I tried to guess what he might be thinking, but it was no use. So, I switched tactics, imagining that he had said the same thing to me – that I was an idiot. A sharp knot immediately formed in my stomach. I didn't like that feeling at all…which meant he probably didn't either.

"Er—well, you're not an idiot," I backtracked, correcting myself. "Not by a long shot. But it would be idiotic for you to think I'd ever let anything bad happen to you." I chewed on my lip. *That sounded better…right?*

Heath's eyes narrowed and he cocked his head at me, the corner of his mouth pulling into what might have been a smile or a grimace. For the life of me, I couldn't tell.

"Ugh!" I threw my hands up in the air and started to walk away, but he grabbed me by the wrist, pulling me back. "Hey—!"

"Nor would I ever allow anything to happen to you," he said softly, his blue eyes boring into mine. "Which means *I* go first."

I pressed my lips together, forcing down the unexpected wave of emotion that was bubbling in my chest, and nodded feebly.

Heath's thumb rubbed a small circle against the inside of my wrist. "Good girl."

He let go of me and casually continued on his way, while I remained rooted in place. My mouth fluttered open wordlessly as a throbbing wave of heat erupted in my core. What kind of witchcraft did this man employ that those two tiny little words could figuratively set my body on fire? Truth be told, if Heath hadn't walked away at that exact moment, I might have ripped off his clothes and mounted him right then and there.

I shook my head so hard, I gave myself temporary photopsia.[15] *What the heck is wrong with me?*

"Laney, are you coming?" Heath called, tugging on the rope that connected his hips to mine.

I gulped.

Topie nudged the back of my knee, spurring me forward.

"Y-Yes!" I stuttered, forcing my feet to move. "I'm c-coming!"

I could have sworn I heard Heath groan under his breath, though I had no idea why.

It's not like he's *being driven crazy by* my *pheromones,* I thought, letting out a pitiful whimper as I fell into step behind him.

---

[15] Photopsia: seeing sparkles of light in front of one's vision that resemble glitter, sometimes referred to as "seeing stars."

Chapter 16

Old as the mine was – at least a hundred years old, judging by the broken bottles of nineteenth century "Tiger Whiskey" that had been left behind – it was in relatively good condition. Most of the branched-off tunnels we'd passed up to that point had been properly backfilled, and the vertical shafts leading to lower levels were well-marked as opposed to gaping holes randomly appearing in the ground. There were even signs, albeit weathered ones, marking our path.

Are all the mines in this country so well-maintained? I found myself wondering. *If so, I should sneak into abandoned Chinese copper mines more often.*

"We've arrived at the first of five forks," Heath announced after twenty minutes or so, when the main haul tunnel we'd been following abruptly split in two. After reaching into one of his pockets and dropping a red button on the ground, he led us down the left passageway, continuing to drop buttons every ten paces or so to mark our path; a starkly different wayfinding approach than the one I usually took, but effective nevertheless.

Hmm. I made a mental note to myself: Buying buttons would be far cheaper than traveling to Russia for electromagnetic-enhancing shungite.[16]

We continued farther and farther into the mine, though the trail of buttons remained largely unnecessary. Most of the branched-off tunnels had been backfilled, meaning the fully-tapped mineral veins had been resealed with dirt and unwanted ore to minimize tunnel collapse. As such, there was really only one direction for us to walk: forward.

Well, forward and *down*, to be precise, since the tunnel continued at a steady downward slant. Predictably, the farther we walked, the hotter it became. Temperatures increase by around eighty degrees Fahrenheit per mile of depth, mostly due to geothermal heat. Even if it's cold aboveground, underground coal mines can easily reach one hundred and twenty-five degrees. I unzipped my jacket as the cool, damp air grew increasingly warmer, wondering how far down we'd traveled. Just as I was about to pull out my altimeter to check, Heath reached into his breast pocket and retrieved what appeared to be a brass pocket watch. After popping it open, he glanced at the dials, then pulled up a photo on his phone – the same picture of the weathered, Chinese-inscribed piece of parchment he'd been looking at earlier. This time, I noticed hand-drawn scrawlings of what appeared to be large clusters of crystals.

"What's that?" I asked.

Heath jumped as I appeared at his side. "Oh, uh, it's an aneroid pocket barometer-slash-altimeter. It belonged to my great-great-great-grandfather." I'd been referring to

---

[16] The brain, of course, is surrounded by a net of electromagnetism, which assists in one's internal sense of direction.

the photo, but – for the moment, at least – this antique device was far more interesting. He turned it over, showing me the engraved initials on the back that read *H.W.S.* "His name was Heath William Spencer, just like me."

My eyes widened. "How old is it?"

"It was appraised as circa 1865. Here, take a look." He gently set it in my palm.

"Wow." I opened the lid and ran my fingers over the glass dials on the inside, marveling at the ingenuity of our ancestors. "This is amazing."

"I thought you might like that." He smiled at me as he tucked the barometer back in his pocket. "My great-great-great grandfather immigrated to the United States from Wales during the California Gold Rush. He was a miner, as was his son and his son's son. Just generation after generation of mining – until my dad came along, at least. He preferred intellectual pursuits, which is how we ended up on the East Coast—"

"When he took a job as an archeological technician at the Smithsonian. He told me." I sighed. "I wish *my* dad worked at a museum or had some sort of interesting collection to pass down. The only thing he's ever collected are seashells and stamps. You're lucky to have inherited so many interesting things from your father."

Heath's smile tightened, making me wonder if he felt as sad as I suddenly did.

I bit my lip, averting my eyes from Heath's gaze. His father, Norman, had been a friend of mine for several years, and one of the few people I'd genuinely liked spending time with. Sure, he'd stocked his store with the usual overpriced citrine and amethyst baubles that you find in every schlocky rock shop, but he also had rare minerals and fossils and even some old coins in his personal collection that he'd take out and show me from time to time. He was intense and obsessive and knew every little thing about his favorite subjects, mineralogy being chief among them. He was one of the only people in the world I could be myself around without feeling self-conscious. And he was the reason I'd established my pharmacy in the heart of Old Port. I'd been going to his shop every Sunday for the past two years by the time I graduated pharmacology school. When I casually mentioned that I'd been searching for a place to open a pharmacy, he suggested the vacant space down the alley. He even read over the commercial lease agreement and helped me with the paperwork for the small business loan.

I couldn't have done it without him.

When I asked him why he was helping me, he told me his own son and daughter didn't need his advice anymore and his wife of thirty-six years had grown bored of his stories. *"It's nice for an old man to feel needed,"* he said, clapping a warm hand on my shoulder. *"Now, wait 'til you see the mammoth tusk I just ordered from Siberia. It's bigger than your entire arm!"*

April twelfth, the day I learned Norm had died, was the same day I met Heath. I'd walked across the street during my lunch hour to show Norm my newest find – a cluster of bright blue cavansite on white stilbite that I'd just collected in India – only to find a much younger man sitting at the stool behind the front counter.

"Where's Norm?" I asked, wincing at the acrid stench of the incense that permeated the entire place. Norm never burned incense.

The young man, who was wearing a navy blue suit that looked rumpled and slept-in, glanced up from the ledger he'd been hunched over. His eyes were red-rimmed with dark circles beneath them. "Who's asking?"

I blinked at him. "Me, obviously."

His eyebrow arched. After emitting a small huff, he dropped his eyes back to the ledger and cleared his throat. "He's…gone. We lost him last night."

I let out a gasp. "Well, have you opened up a missing person's case?"

The man pulled his eyes away from the page to gape at me. "Sorry?"

I met his steely gaze, focusing on the striking blue color of his irises to keep myself from instinctively looking away. "If he's been lost since last night, you should call the police."

"I—no!" The man blustered, rising from his stool. "He's not lost. He passed away!"

"He…what?" I narrowed my eyes at him, trying to make sense of his words.

He took a slow, deep breath. "Liver failure. The man loved his drink more than anything… More than any*one*," he muttered.

"Liver failure?!" I barked out a seal-like laugh. "I just saw him last week and he looked perfectly fine!"

Didn't he?

I whirled around, waiting for Norm to pop out from behind one of the display cases and announce that this had been some sort of bizarre joke. When he didn't, I tugged at the neck of my t-shirt, which suddenly felt as though it were choking me, and turned back toward the man. "What could have possibly—"

"Hemorrhagic stroke. He was gone forty-eight hours later."

No. I pressed my hand to my mouth, my addled thoughts immediately jumping to the freshly-brewed dolomite potion sitting in my lab – my most effective detoxifying tonic to date. Cold, hollow emptiness carved me out from the inside, and I desperately clawed at the nearest emotion within reach to fill it. "Why didn't he tell me?" I snarled angrily. "I could have helped him! I could have done something, *anything!*" I spun away from the man, scrubbing my fingers through my hair. "Goddamnit, Norm!"

"Hey—" the man started, but I was already storming out the door, furious with the world, furious with Norm, and especially furious with this younger, taller, trimmer version of Norm that wasn't actually him and never would be. The Norm I knew – one of the few people in the world I not only tolerated, but actually *liked* and depended on – was gone for good and I hated him for it.

"Hey!" the man called again, this time from the doorway of what used to be Norm's shop.

I ignored him as I stomped toward the pharmacy, yanked open the door, and flipped the BACK AT 1:00 P.M. sign to CLOSED.

I didn't work for the rest of the day or the following day.

Three weeks later, the same young man came into the pharmacy, introduced himself as Heath Spencer, Norm's son, and plunked a palm-sized ammonite fossil on the glass counter in front of me. "My father left this piece of ammolite for you in his will," he said. "I'm sorry I didn't know who you were when you came by a few weeks ago. I didn't realize the two of you had been close. He…didn't have many friends, my father."

Neither did I.

An unexpected surge of anger took hold of me, which I attributed to Heath's unwelcome appearance in my shop. "Thanks," I muttered, snatching the fossil from the counter. "And it's an ammo*n*ite, the fossilized cephalopod, not ammo*l*ite, the opalized gemstone. If you're going to run a rock shop, you should learn the difference." With that, I spun on my heel and made my way to the curtain that separated my lab from the front of the shop.

To my immense surprise, Heath started *laughing.*

I turned around to gape at him. "What could possibly be funny?"

"How much you and my father are alike." He wiped a tear from his eye as he turned to go. "No wonder he liked you." Pushing the front door open, he added, "Have a nice day, Laney."

"It's *De*laney!" I shouted after him.

"Tell that to my father." He glanced over his shoulder, the corner of his mouth twisting into a smirk. "You're listed in his will as 'Dr. Laney.'"

The bell atop the door let out a loud, obnoxious *clang* as the door banged shut behind him.

"Laney?" Heath asked, waving his hand in front of my face and jerking me from the memory. "Did I lose you?"

As my eyes came back into focus, I let out a soft gasp, pressing a hand to my mouth.

Topie nudged the back of my knee, peering up at me with wide, worried eyes. When I didn't reply, he started fidgeting with his backpack – ostensibly to pull out the anxiety potion he kept readily accessible in the side pocket – but ended up spinning in a futile circle as he tried and failed to reach it.

I lowered myself to the ground beside him. "I'm okay," I reassured him, retrieving a bag of potato chips from his pack and opening it for him. "Go have a snack."

He nuzzled the side of my face in thanks before snatching the bag of chips and settling a few feet away from us to eat them.

I slowly rose to my feet, my stomach twisting with shame.

"Laney?" Heath rested his hands on my shoulders, and for once, I didn't try to pull away. "What's wrong?"

"I…" I lifted my head, forcing myself to look at him. "I was so horrible to you."

Heath blinked. "Sorry?"

"You had just lost your father…" I bit my lip hard, using the pain to keep my tears at bay. "And I was absolutely horrible to you."

"Oh." Heath ran a hand through his hair. "Yeah, well…you had just lost a close friend yourself."

Tears pricked at my eyes and my chin began to quiver. "It hadn't even occurred to me that you'd lost someone too. I was so wrapped up in my own feelings…" My head bowed. "I really am the worst."

"Hey." Heath cupped my face in his hand, gently brushing a stray tear away with his thumb. "I forgive you. Okay?"

"No." I shook my head. "I don't want you to forgive me. You shouldn't forgive me. In fact, you shouldn't even be talking to me." I tried to take a step backward, but

Heath's grip on my shoulders didn't budge. "Why?" I asked, my voice cracking. "Why do you put up with me?"

With a deep sigh, he closed his eyes and pressed his lips into a tight line, almost as though he were trying to suppress a smile – which would have been absurd, given the circumstances. "You're not a horrible person, Laney. You're just wired differently. And maybe if I hadn't been raised by a man who had also been wired so differently, I wouldn't understand how that complex brain of yours works. But for better or worse, I do. Besides"—he gently tapped the center of my forehead—"once you get past that spiky shell of yours, all that's left is a vulnerable little shell-less turtle. And what could be cuter than that?"

My mouth dropped open. "A turtle without its shell would die!"

A laugh burst from Heath's mouth, which he quickly stifled with the palm of his hand. "I was speaking metaphorically."

Frowning, I crossed my arms and grumbled, "Yeah, well, even a *metaphorical* turtle without a shell can still bite you."

He curled his finger under my chin and tilted my face toward his. "Even if she did, I wouldn't stop caring about her."

As I gazed up at him, something inside of me cracked like a fresh fault line. Here I was, holding lifelong grudges against people who dared to look at me the wrong way, while Heath was so quick to forgive even the worst parts of me again and again.

My body moved without my brain's permission. Before I knew it, my lips were crushing against Heath's and his arms were wrapping around me, pulling me close.

His fingers knotted into my hair, tilting my head back to deepen the kiss, while his other hand encircled my waist.

I let out a soft whimper – not of fear, but of bliss. In the past, this kind of intimacy had spooked me, leading me to think on more than one occasion that I might not be wired for sex and physical affection the way others were. But Heath's embrace was as warm and soothing as a weighted blanket during a storm. Instead of pushing him away, I sank into his arms. He tightened his grip around me as he cautiously explored my lower lip with the tip of his tongue. It still wasn't enough. Wanting more, I gripped him by the shirt and parted my lips to deepen the kiss.

Heath let out a small groan, pressing his forehead against mine. "Damnit."

My breath caught alongside the panic rising in my chest. Had I done something wrong? Misread the situation? I held my fingers to my parted lips, clandestinely checking my breath. It was fine…wasn't it?

He pulled away from me, increasing my mounting anxiety by three-fold.

"Heath?" My voice cracked. "Did I…" I swallowed tightly, wanting nothing more than to run while forcing my feet to stay. "What did I do?"

He held up a hand, muttering, "It's not you," only to fall silent again. After a long, agonizing minute, he finally opened his mouth to speak, uttering eight words that had been arranged in the most frightening order imaginable: "Delaney, I haven't been completely honest with you."

Chapter 17

In the brief pause between Heath's bombshell revelation and his forthcoming explanation, my brain had already manufactured the three worst follow-up statements imaginable: 1) "I'm a married man, and my wife is a heavyweight MMA fighter," 2) "I brought you into this abandoned cave so I could harvest your organs," and, worst of all, 3) "I saw an old picture of you from the fifth grade and now the mere thought of kissing you makes me want to vomit."

Rocking back and forth on my heels, I hugged myself and prepared for the worst.

From the corner of my eye, I saw Topie drop his snack and clamber to his hooves. With potato chip crumbs still whiskering his snout, he trotted over to where Heath and I were standing, wedged himself between us like a corgi-sized guard dog, and cocked his head at the man as if to say, *"Well?"*

"Um…" Heath started.

Whatever he's about to tell you, my brain warned me, kicking my amygdala into full-on fight-or-flight mode, *it's going to be bad. Really bad. As in 'run back to the main road and hitchhike all the way back to Wuhan' bad—*

"I haven't actually seen this new mineral," Heath blurted out, yanking me from my panic-induced reverie. "Not here in this mine, at least."

I stared at him, my brain still working to piece together what he'd just said.

"I lied when I told you I'd seen it first-hand." He began pacing in front of me, the light from his helmet vacillating between illuminating the damp walls on either side of us and being swallowed up by the darkness of the tunnel. "When I was in Huangshi earlier this month, one of the Tonglushan workers showed me a rock he'd found a few months ago. It was covered in a thin layer of druzy green crystals that fluoresced in the sun – a type of mineral he'd never seen in his twenty years of working in the mine. I asked him where he'd found it, and he told me he'd found it in here. He drew me a detailed map and everything. But when I came to look later that evening, I was spotted by one of the foremen and had to leave—quickly. An American man in a black suit loitering around private Chinese mines? Not a good look." Closing his eyes, he leaned his head back and scrubbed his hands through his hair. "So I don't actually know exactly where it is, or if it's even in here. It's all just…hearsay."

Rubbing at the receding goosebumps on my arms, I sucked down my first deep breath in what felt like several minutes.

"And here you are praising me about how completely honest I've been," he continued, "when I've not only been dishonest about that, but I haven't even told you the bigger thi—"

"Show me," I interjected.

He blinked. "Show you what?"

"The mineral specimen." I crossed my arms. "I assume you bought the rock off the guy. So show it to me."

"Oh—right." Muttering to himself, he rummaged around the front compartment of his pack, eventually retrieving a chunk of gray copper schist the size of an orange.

I took it from him and sat on the ground, where I pulled a loupe from my pocket to inspect the thin film of green crystals that covered the top of it like frost on a windshield. "How do you know these crystals can grow to be ten inches long?"

Heath faltered. "It's…a long story. But I have written documentation of an unnamed, fluorescent green Chinese mineral that closely fits this description."

"*Scientific* documentation?"

"Not exactly."

Ignoring his caginess – I would deal with *that* later – I focused on the mineral. "This looks almost like uvarovite," I muttered, adjusting my headlamp to see the tiny crystals better.

"I know, but—"

"I'm not talking to you," I snapped, then turned back to Topie. "Yeah, I know – I've never heard of Chinese uvarovite, either…" I nodded thoughtfully. "True, but the stuff in Finland was from volcanogenic copper-cobalt-zinc sulfide ore deposits, which have high chromium content. That's clearly not the case here."

"Are you… Are you talking to the *pig?*" Heath sputtered, scratching his head in what looked like bewilderment.

"Yes, obviously!" I rolled my eyes, tuning out his follow-up questions. "No, there's no way this is tsavorite. That has an isometric crystal system. These look more like tiny orthorhombic dipyramidal crystals, like celestine." I pulled the portable shortwave UV light out of my backpack and flicked it on. "See? At four-hundred nanometers, tsavorite turns pinkish-orange, but this stuff…" I trailed off, regarding the mineral's vivid, lime-green fluorescent light.

"It looks like kryptonite," Heath murmured.

"Yeah," I agreed, momentarily forgetting I was angry with him. "Well, if kryptonite were real, obviously. I have some Erongo hyalite that glows just like this. The color of the fluorescence could indicate the presence of trace uranium, similar to that found in hyalite. But that's doubtful, given the locality…" I bit my lip. *This would be so much easier if I could just taste it!* My eyes darted over to Heath, who was crouched a few feet away and watching me intently.

"Hey, what's that?" I pointed over his shoulder.

When he turned around to look, I broke off one of the tiny crystals and placed it under my tongue, letting out a soft hum of contentment. While this mineral no longer held any essence – it had been handled by too many people for too long – the flavor was unlike anything I'd ever tasted before: a cross between black licorice and freshly-mowed grass. I sucked on the crystal fragment a moment longer, trying to remember if I'd ever tasted anything similar. There was a strong metallic aftertaste that reminded me of galena, a lead-heavy ore mineral. I racked my brain, trying to think of green, lead-heavy, crystalline minerals. Pyromorphite was one, but I'd sneak-tasted that one at a mineral show once, and it didn't taste anything like this. And besides, that one was bright olive green with hexagonal crystals.

"I don't see anything," Heath said, turning back around.

"Never mind, must have been a shadow."

Heath's eyebrows – which had a complex language of their own that I was pleased to discover I was quickly learning – narrowed in what I was fairly certain was suspicion.

"Could it be euchroite?" I muttered to myself.

"Euchroite?" Heath echoed. "Never heard of it."

"It's an extremely rare type of hydrated arsenate that's produced from a chemical reaction rather than organically. It forms when highly acidic mine waters react with phosphates in the host rock."

"An artificial mine byproduct…" Heath murmured, touching his fingers to his lips. "If that's the case, we'd have to go where the water collects, at the bottom of mine—"

"Which would be incredibly stupid, especially given the concentrated levels of arsenic required for it to hypothetically form," I pointed out helpfully. "Besides, euchroite doesn't fluoresce, and it's only been discovered in a handful of places in the world, which are nowhere near here."

Sighing in frustration, I flicked off the UV flashlight. These strange glowing crystals were a mystery, all right – one that should have sent me racing farther into the mine to solve it as quickly as possible. But for the first time in many years, there was something else at the top of my priority list, something far more important than rocks – even undiscovered ones.

I promptly stood up, dusted off my pants, and handed Heath's mystery mineral back to him. "You told me it was just a coincidence that we ended up in China at the same time. Was that the truth or did you orchestrate this from the beginning?"

"It was the truth," he answered immediately.

"Why did you lie and tell me you'd seen the mineral first-hand?"

He faltered, then said, "Because I didn't want to get into the specifics of how I'd actually heard about it."

"You mean the miner who showed it to you?"

Heath shook his head. "The miner only confirmed the existence of something I'd already been searching for."

I crossed my arms, waiting for him to elaborate.

Sighing, he pushed himself to his feet. "Look, when I offered to help with your Chinese visa, I had no secret agenda. I did it because I could see how much you wanted to come here, and I felt badly for you."

I scoffed. "I didn't need your help, or your pity."

"Right, just like you didn't need my help when you showed up at the Beijing airport without a sponsor and would have been sent back home before even leaving the customs area."

I opened my mouth to argue, then closed it again when I realized I had no argument to that.

"Look," Heath continued, "my initial plans, as I already told you, had nothing to do with you. I'd scheduled this trip around the Dragon Boat Festival, when no one would be working in the mine. But when I saw you at the Portland airport…" He scrubbed a hand through his hair – a nervous habit of his, I'd finally pieced out. "Well, you know more about minerals than anyone

I've ever met, including my father. I'd have been an idiot not to ask you for help."

I uncrossed my arms, genuinely perplexed. "Then why not just say that? What's with all the evasiveness?"

"Because…" He hesitated, bowing his head. "Because there's more to the story, which I hadn't ever intended on telling you. I just wanted your help with finding the mineral, while keeping everything else under wraps. And since you love minerals so much, I didn't feel bad about that – at the time," he quickly added. "I figured we could, uh…"

"Forge a symbiotic relationship," I supplied, "wherein we indirectly help each other while pursuing our own end goals and gains."

"Yeah, I guess." He rubbed the back of his neck. "Which sounds extraordinarily transactional when you put it that way."

I shrugged. "There's nothing wrong with transactional relationships. You can't have a successful business without one."

"I know." Heath sighed. "But I still feel bad for acting cagey. I guess I was just…figuring out what I wanted to disclose as we went. The extent of which, if I'm being honest, fluctuated alongside your mood swings."

"That's…fair," I conceded, dropping my eyes to the ground. "I did keep telling you we weren't friends. It makes sense that you didn't trust me."

He let out his breath in a slow exhale, possibly in relief. Based on my prior, ever-so-slight overreactions, he'd probably expected me to be furious about his lie of omission, whatever that may have been. A fair assumption; I hated liars, even more than I hated steamed broccoli – but not as much as I hated hypocrites. The moment that word came to mind, a strange feeling feathered at the inside of my stomach, almost like it was hungry and gnawing on air. Having been lugging around my own secrets and fibs – which were not of omission, but rather outright, blatant lies – I had no choice but to concede to myself that I'd become one of the things I hated most in the world. And unless I was willing to rewrite my list of things I reviled – which I wasn't, because that list was perfect the way it was – it was time for me to stop being a hypocrite.

"Well…" I fingered the worry stone in my pocket to keep my resolve from slipping. "I guess it's a good thing that we're friends now…" I forced my eyes to meet his. "That way you can tell me the rest of the story and not have to worry about whether or not you can trust me."

A furrow appeared between Heath's brows, making me worried I'd upset him.

"Are…" I swallowed, then tried again. "A-Are we not friends?"

"I believe you once told me that we would *never* be friends." The corners of his mouth slowly curved into a smile. "Could it be possible that the infallible Delaney Stone was actually"—he gasped, pressing his hand to his mouth and looking both ways before whispering—*"wrong?"*

I sucked on my teeth, momentarily considering slugging him in the arm, then let out a defeated sigh. "Yes. Fine! I was wrong."

He closed his eyes.

"What are you doing?"

"Burning this moment into my memory, because I'm quite certain this is the only time in my life I'll witness such an event. This is my Stonehenge – no! My *Delaney*

Stone-henge!" He slapped his thigh, cackling at his own terrible joke.

Rolling my eyes, I patted Topie on the rump, motioning for him to continue walking down the tunnel. As the two of us sauntered away, I casually called over my shoulder, "By the way, 'Stone' isn't my birth name. I had it legally changed a few years back."

"From what?" Heath's bewildered expression abruptly morphed into shock. "Wait – were you *married?*"

"Why?" I asked innocently. "Would it be a problem if I was?"

"Of course not!" he protested, jogging to catch up with me. "It's not like I would be insanely jealous or insecure about it. Speaking of which, was your husband handsome? Successful? How big was his penis? So long as it was less than three inches, I'll be fine."

I snorted. "I've never been married. In fact, I've only ever had three boyfriends, and one of them was in kindergarten, which I'm told doesn't count."

"So long as you weren't the kindergarten teacher, it definitely counts."

"Of course I wasn't the teacher!" I scoffed. "I was the school nurse."

After a split-second beat of silence, a laugh burst from Heath's mouth, filling me with pride. Apart from Norm and the guys on the feghoot chat forums, I never made anyone laugh – not intentionally, at least. And just this morning, I'd made Heath laugh four times – on *purpose.*

Still chuckling, he asked, "So, what did your last name used to be? And why did you change it?"

"My family's last name is Isaacs. But I was never particularly fond of that surname so I had it legally changed to Stone when I got my PharmD. I still haven't told my parents, though, so just keep that in mind when y—" I coughed. "Er…*if* you ever meet them."

Heath's left eyebrow raised, as did one corner of his mouth. "I shall take your secret to the grave." he promised, solemnly crossing his finger over his heart. "Speaking of secrets, I'm ready to tell you the truth about the mystery mineral, if you'd like to hear it. But be forewarned: It's a *long* story, with a lot of details. Are you sure you're up for it?"

"Are you kidding?" I gaped at him. "Long, detailed stories are my favorite kind!"

Heath laughed. "Okay, then I'm going to tell you the story in the same manner my father would always tell me: long-winded, overly-complex, and with meandering, unnecessary tangents."

"Perfect." I grinned, not bothering to hide my teeth. "I can hear Norm's voice in my head already."

Chapter 18

Heath took a deep breath, and when he spoke, it really was like he was channeling his father, perfectly emulating Norm's deep, booming, and overly-theatrical manner of recounting stories:

"The year was 434 AD, and Attila the Hun had just inherited his father's empire, which stretched all the way from the Alps to the Caspian Sea—"

"Wait," I cut in. "This story goes all the way back to the fifth century?"

Heath gave me a sidelong glance. "I did tell you it was going to be unnecessarily long and overly-detailed."

"In that case, I'm going to need to arm myself with the proper snacks." I abruptly stopped walking to raid Topie's bulging backpack for a bag of cheddar cheese popcorn, which he regarded as an appalling, heinous act – at least until I started tossing him popped kernels, which he deftly caught mid-air.

"Reee!"

"Okay!" I announced, falling back into step beside Heath. "I'm listening."

He cleared his throat and continued.

"Despite the vastness of the land Attila's father had bestowed upon him, the young ruler set out to conquer more. Charismatic, brave, and fiercely cunning, Attila led his army from the front, earning the respect and unrelenting loyalty of his soldiers while nations toppled and kings trembled at his might. The king of the Huns was so ruthless and efficient in his conquests, the mere threat of a Hun attack was enough for the Eastern Roman Empire to offer Attila huge sums of gold in exchange for their territory to remain unmolested. This tentative "peace" lasted for several years, until the Romans foolishly reneged on the deal in 441. That spring, Attila and his army stormed the Danubian frontier, ransacking and pillaging and terrorizing their way to Constantinople, where he earned his favorite nickname, 'the scourge of God.'

"Unable to break through the fortified walls of the city, Attila begrudgingly conceded to a rekindled peace agreement in 443: he would leave Constantinople alone in exchange for an annual tribute of twenty-one hundred pounds of gold. Mountains of gold bullion, stolen treasures, and priceless antiquities of fallen nations wound up in the hands of the voracious Hun general, most never to be seen again. And as his expanse of pilfered land grew, so too did Attila's blood-soaked cache. After killing his brother to seize even more power, the unhinged autocrat continued his ferocious conquest of the continent, gaining more tributes, loot, and leverage for his empire while severely depleting his forces through his reckless disregard for human life."

"You have a serious knack for storytelling," I complimented Heath between bites of popcorn. "Whenever I try to tell someone a long story, they either nod off or walk away."

"The trick is in the execution," Heath replied after taking a large swig of water from his canteen. "Facts are important, but you also have to know when to add in a dash of 'sizzle' to keep your listeners on the edge of their seats."

"Sizzle?" I frowned. "But what you're saying is true, right? I mean, this is all fact?"

"As factual as a sixteen-hundred-year-old story can be," Heath assured me. "My father prided himself on being 'a fervent cultivator of historical accuracy.' In other words, everything I'm telling you has been rigorously fact-checked and verified through years of meticulous research."

"Yeah, well, that's what they said about the Wright brothers' biopic, and that had at least twenty-eight factual errors – several of which were completely made up," I groused, folding my arms at the unpleasant memory. "Facts are important. Without them, history is just speculative fiction—and I *hate* fiction books," I added under my breath.

"I couldn't agree more," Heath said. "Well, not about fiction books – those are great – but about factual acc—" He trailed off when the beams of our headlamps illuminated the corroded metal door at the end of the tunnel, barring us from going any farther.

"What is that?" I asked, frowning.

"If it's what I think it is," Heath said, retrieving a crowbar from his pack, "it means we're getting close. Do you have gloves?"

"On it," I replied, already digging through my pack for that very reason.

"Great – can you help me remove these screws? Be careful – they're probably pretty sharp from the corrosion."

"Sure thing." I knelt beside him. "So…you were talking about Attila and his growing stash of gold and loot?"

Heath nodded, picking up where he'd left off as the two of us set to work.

"Attila continued his conquest, increasing his enormous wealth while severely depleting his forces. After murdering his own brother in a ploy for more power, Attila's tactics became increasingly aggressive, paranoid, and belligerent. Despite his assurances to the rulers of Constantinople that he would not attack so long as they paid tribute, the king of the Huns reneged on his promise, launching a vicious assault on the fortified city that ultimately resulted in a terrible failure. Ego bruised and hands bloodied, Attila led several more campaigns in various regions, eventually setting up camp in Walachia. There, he spent his nights in a lavish tent that had been filled to the brim with the gold and riches he'd plundered along the way, while an accompaniment of thirty guards stood watch as he slept.

"One of his guards, a young man named Atakam, observed Attila's increasingly-pugnacious demeanor with unease, likening him to a 'wounded, rabid dog that had been backed into a corner.'"

"How do you know?" I interjected.

"How do I know what?"

"How do you know what Atakam said about Attila?"

"Oh. A Greek writer named Priscus conversed extensively with Attila and his men. He made a written account of his journey with the Huns, which included the very story I'm telling you now."

"Okay, good." I nodded, appeased. "Knowing the source of the information is just as important as the information itself."

"Hear, hear."

When the final screw had been removed, Heath donned a pair of gloves and goggles and traded his screwdriver for a crowbar, which he then jammed between the door and the rock. Grunting with effort, he worked to pry it open. The corroded hinges screamed in protest, eventually ripping out of the rock altogether. With a metallic clang that reverberated down the hallway, the warped metal door fell to the ground, sending up a cloud of dust and particles. The air that whooshed from the passageway was hot and stale and smelled as though it hadn't been breathed in centuries.

"Here, Topes," I said, strapping an M50 gas mask to his face. The heliodor potion I'd drunk was still active, enhancing my sense of smell, but gasses move so quickly in confined spaces, I wasn't willing to risk it.

Holding the hem of his shirt to his nose – exposing glistening, sweat-sheened abdominal muscles that momentarily robbed me of breath – Heath flicked on a lighter. When the color of the flame didn't change, he dropped the hem of his shirt and took a deep breath. "I think we're okay."

Still unable to speak, I nodded my agreement.

We peered into the tunnel we'd uncovered, the light from our headlamps swallowed up by the darkness on the other side. Unlike the main haul tunnel we'd been traipsing through up to this point, which had likely been formed via dynamite and relatively modern reinforcements like concrete, this extremely narrow passage had been mined in a starkly different fashion, with weathered chisel marks etched into the stone and dark interlocking wooden beams lining the tunnel on all sides. Some sections of the decaying wood had completely rotted away, exposing weathered rock underneath.

Motioning for me to stay back, Heath took a few tentative steps forward, pausing when the toes of his boots crested a square-shaped hole in the ground – a vertical shaft that ostensibly led to lower levels of the mine. After carefully side-stepping around it, he regarded his altimeter and compass, exhaling deeply. "According to my calculations, we're directly beneath the museum."

My eyes widened. "Wait a minute. Doesn't that mean…?"

"Yes." He nodded. "We're standing in one of the original tunnels of the ancient copper mine."

An uncharacteristic jolt of claustrophobia feathered at my insides. I hugged my body, rubbing at the goosebumps that appeared on my arms despite the sauna-like conditions of the tunnel.

"The museum only features a tiny portion of the ancient mines," Heath continued, "which are actually a sprawling underground network of tunnels and shafts that span several kilometers. The mineral pocket we're looking for is located several shafts down."

"How do you know? Did the miner who found it tell you that?"

Heath shook his head. "No. But I'm getting to that part of the story, I promise."

He stood up, his head nearly scraping the low ceiling as he did, and rapped the back of his knuckle on one of the many wooden frames reinforcing the tunnel. Old as they were, I'd expected them to be much further along in the rotting process, but the two-thousand-year-old beams appeared to be incredibly well-preserved.

"This can't be the original wood," I mused, running my fingers across the smooth grain.

"It is, if you can believe it," Heath said, inspecting the walls for any visible signs of deterioration or strain. "The ancient Chinese miners who built these tunnels used extremely dense lumber. They strengthened the wood even further by charring the beams with fire, then soaking them in tung oil."

"As a way to preserve them?"

He nodded. "Against both water and oxygen, yes. Tung oil hardens upon exposure to air via polymerization, and the resulting coating is extremely hard and durable, like plastic." He pointed to the metal door we'd just broken open, ostensibly unsealing this particular tunnel for the first time in centuries. "Paired with the low oxygen levels and minimal air circulation, I think we should be okay – at least until we hit the water table." He knelt beside the open shaft, using a laser tape measure to determine its height. "We'll need to be on high alert as we start descending vertically."

"Be careful," I warned him, eyeing the mud beneath his knee. "For all you know, there might be a rotted wood floor hiding underneath."

"It's hard to believe, I know, but both the ladder and frame seem to be in good condition." He jiggered the posts of the shaft, noting, "Did you know that archeologists found wooden furniture buried alongside ancient Egyptian Pharaohs? If kept away from the elements and free from bugs, a piece of wood can last a few thousand years."

"Let's hope that's the case. How far down does the shaft go?"

"Looks like it's about twenty feet to the bottom," he replied, tucking his tape measure back in his bag.

"Just far enough to snap both your legs if the ladder gives out." I shuddered at the painful memory of tumbling down a mineshaft a few years earlier. Sure, I'd had potions on hand to heal my ankles, but that didn't mean I'd ever forget the initial, excruciating pain of shattering them. I dubiously eyed the rope I'd wound through our belt loops, connecting us. "Do you have a belay harness? I only brought one."

"I do." He patted his bag.

I nodded my approval. "Okay, good. We'd better gear up, then."

While Heath put on his harness, I hammered a large eye bolt into the vertical stone of the wall. Once I was absolutely certain it was secure, I strapped on my own belay harness and assisted-braking device – an uncomfortably-bulky contraption in an already-narrow tunnel, but necessary given my inability to drink myself out of a potential problem. After properly hooking myself up to the rope, I turned around to check on Heath.

"Are you good?" I started to ask, only for my question to end in an abrupt squeak. In the increasing heat of the tunnel, he'd removed his long-sleeved shirt and donned his harness over a white, tight-fitting sleeveless undershirt that clung to his body in sinful ways. "Um—" My voice cracked, so I cleared my throat and tried again. "I-Is that all you're wearing down there?"

"Yeah," he said, blowing into the top of his shirt. "It's hot as hell in here. Besides, you should talk, Lara Croft." He gestured at my outfit. "You've been a major distraction ever since we left the motel."

"Is…" I bit my lip. "Is that a compliment or a complaint?"

He flashed me a wicked grin. "Both. Now come on, let's go."

Cheeks burning, I started forward, only to feel a sharp tug on the cuff of my pants. I turned around to find Topie peering up at me, his gas mask fogging with worry.

I knelt beside him to unstrap his mask. "Topes, these tunnels are over a thousand years old, so they're much more dangerous than the mines back home," I explained gently. "I need you to wait up here where it's safe and keep an eye out for us, okay?"

He looked between the square-shaped hole in the ground and me, his chin quivering.

"I know." I kissed the top of his snout. "We'll be careful, I promise. Here—" I retrieved his tablet from his daypack and pulled up *Babe: Pig in the City*. "Watch this. Heath and I will be back by the time it's over." Rummaging around in my own pack, I pulled out a large canteen, extra batteries for his headlamp, and one of two walkie-talkies. "If you need anything at all, you know which frequency to reach me on."

Topie nuzzled against my cheek, then took the radio in his teeth and set it on the ground beside his tablet before curling up on the warm stone and resting his chin on his hooves.

"Good boy." I gave him an approving pat on the head.

When I stood up, I found Heath scratching his head. "Okay, so you're really gonna have to explain how this relationship works," he said, gesturing between me and Topie.

"Right after you tell me what Attila the Hun has to do with mystery minerals and ancient Chinese copper mines."

"Deal." He sighed, tightening the knot on his belay. "Assuming I don't break my neck on the way down, I'll tell you everything."

I nodded solemnly. "I won't let you fall."

Flashing me a crooked smile, Heath carefully lowered himself into the shaft. "I know you won't."

As soon as his head was out of sight, I quickly chugged the last of my celestine potion, expense and depleted stores be darned. If Heath *did* fall, I had to make sure I was strong enough to catch him. Besides, running out of my best strength potion gave me an excuse to return to Madagascar to collect more celestine.

I wonder if Heath would be interested in coming with me? I pondered as I fed him rope slack. My stomach did a small flip at the notion. Maybe I could build up the courage to ask him later that evening—assuming he was still interested in being my friend after I told him the truth about my strange, supernatural form of pica. James was the only other person to whom I'd confessed the full extent of my rock-eating habit, and he'd made fun of me so relentlessly I'd been forced to backtrack and pretend I was joking.

I gulped at the memory, my prior resolution to tell Heath everything momentarily wavering. But then I glanced at Topie, who was forlornly watching me instead of his third favorite movie, and I felt a tug in my chest.

A friend is someone with whom you can share all of your secrets.

"I have to tell him, don't I?" I whispered, already knowing what the answer would be.

Topie nodded.

"But what if he…" I swallowed, my throat constricting at the thought. "What if he thinks I'm a liar? Or worse, a freak?"

Topie gave me a pointed look.

"Fine." I sighed. "I'll do it."

Focusing my attention back to the rope Heath was dangling from, having blindly entrusted me to safeguard both his life and his limbs, I muttered, "Life was so much easier when I hated Heath Spencer's guts."

Chapter 19

Heath's feet touched the ground with a dull thud. "It's solid," he called up to me. "Come on down – carefully, please."

After giving Topie a reassuring thumbs-up, I followed Heath into the shaft. The wooden rungs were indeed relatively stable, but I took my time climbing down. As I neared the bottom, Heath reached up and grasped me by the hips.

"I've got you," he murmured as he carefully set me on the ground, his fingers lingering at my waist and sending a thrill up my spine.

I turned around with the intention of thanking him, but as I again took in his minimal attire, which clung damply to his glistening muscles, the words stuck in my throat. What right did this rock shop owner have to be so sculpted? It was almost comical – or, at least, it would have been if his sexiness hadn't been so dang distracting. In a place like this, the man was a certifiable health risk.

With his hands still gripping my waist, Heath gazed down at me for a long moment, then abruptly cleared his throat and stepped aside to make room for me. We surveyed the narrow tunnel shoulder-to-shoulder, our beams swallowed up by the interminable darkness that stretched before us.

"Are you still feeling okay to continue?" he asked.

As much as I wanted to immediately say yes – after all, an undiscovered mineral was potentially waiting for us – I instead dropped to the ground and pressed my palm against the wet dirt, then brought a handful of it up to my nose. With my enhanced sense of smell, I didn't note anything toxic in the soil apart from a whiff of arsenic – more or less harmless in its non-aerosolized form – nor was there any trace of hydrogen sulfide or methane gas lingering in the air. It would seem the biggest threats we had to worry about were collapse or flooding, neither of which we had much control over.

I glanced over my shoulder, where the comforting glow of Topie's headlamp could still be seen through the square-shaped opening in the ceiling, then back down to the accumulating puddles on the ground. "How far are we from the water table?"

Heath checked his altimeter. "I'd say twenty to thirty feet, but we still have another shaft to go down, which will bring us even closer to it."

I considered that for a moment, absentmindedly tugging on my belay device. "Okay. Then we'll just have to tread carefully – *very* carefully."

"Agreed." He took a piece of paper from his pocket, his eyes darting across the handwritten Chinese, then regarded his phone, where he'd zoomed in on the photo of the ancient Chinese parchment to inspect what appeared to be a drawing of crystals.

"Can I see?" I asked.

Nodding, he showed me the image on the screen:

"Looks like stibnite," I murmured, squinting at the tiny, smudged picture.

"Except stibnite isn't dark green or fluorescent." Heath remarked, replacing both the paper and his phone back in his pocket. "Speaking of fluorescence, would you mind taking out your UV light and setting it to shortwave? What we're looking for is essentially a massive vug of large fluorescent crystals, which will be located next to a vertical shaft."

A tiny squeak slipped through my lips. The notion of finding a crystal-lined cavity – the giant version of the inside of a geode, essentially – made me so giddy I *almost* forgot about the stifling hot, narrow tunnel that might fill with water or collapse on our heads at any moment. Who knew what undiscovered essence might be contained within those untouched, fully-intact, naturally-growing crystals? My mouth was watering so badly at the thought I had to bite my knuckle to distract myself.

"Laney?"

I started at the sound of Heath's voice. "Oh, right – sorry." After rummaging around my crowded pack, I retrieved the hand-held UV lamp and switched it on.

Heath and I let out twin gasps of astonishment as the walls, ceiling, and floor flickered to life, thanks to the bright green speckles embedded in the exposed rock that illuminated the entire tunnel like glowing fireflies.

"We're getting close," he murmured, exhaling deeply.

I gave him a pointed look. "Then you'd better hurry up and tell me the rest of this story."

"Yes, ma'am." Heath took a swig of water from his canteen and cleared his throat.

"Atakam, one of Attila's private sentries, was becoming more and more perturbed by his leader's increasingly erratic behavior. One night, after witnessing Attila stab one of his soldiers over a heated game of Xiangqi, Atakam decided to abandon his post – but not before sneaking into Attila's tent and pilfering a bronze chest filled with enough gold to buy one thousand horses. Riding like the wind on the back of a stolen mare, Atakam fled from Walachia to the safety of Constantinople's unbreachable walls. But just as he approached the gate, breathing a sigh of relief—"

"You can't possibly know that," I interjected, rolling my eyes.

"—four Hunnic assassins, who had been sent by Attila to retrieve his stolen treasure, emerged from the darkness. Before Atakam even had the chance to cry out, one of the assassins shot an arrow through his back, killing him."

"Wait, *what?*" I stumbled to a stop. "If Atakam died, then who is this story about?"

"The story is more about a 'what' than a 'who,'" Heath explained patiently. "May I continue?"

I nodded, far less patiently.

"The assassin, a man named Dengizich, then turned on his three comrades and murdered them before robbing the stolen treasure chest from Atakam's corpse. With no witnesses – save for the soldiers guarding the gates of Constantinople – Dengizich fled the city, his sights set on Damascus. There, he used some of the gold to build a home and buy himself slaves, one of whom was a young Chinese woman named Mingxia. She quickly became his favorite servant and was often summoned to tend to him day and night. Eventually, when Mingxia and Dengizich had learned enough of one another's languages, he asked for her hand in marriage. She accepted on one condition: that he release her from servitude and return her to the land she'd been stolen from. Smitten as Dengizich was with the young woman, he agreed, and after a long, arduous journey via the Silk Road, the two of them settled in the Chinese countryside to begin anew.

"When Mingxia discovered she was pregnant, the two of them were overjoyed by the news. But several months later, when word of approaching Huns reached the village, Dengizich broke down and confessed his crimes to her. Knowing the end was drawing nigh for Dengizich, and thinking only of her unborn child, Mingxia fled during the night, taking the remaining gold with her. It's not known what became of her, though it's possible she returned to her village to be at her husband's side during his final moments. Whatever her fate may have been, her abandoned baby boy was found crying in a bale of hay beside a chest of gold and a handwritten letter naming him Jinshan."

"So you have no idea what happened to Jinshan's parents?" I interjected, surprised to feel a twinge of sadness.

"There are theories—hypotheses, that is," Heath amended. "In one version of the legend, Dengizich was killed, and Mingxia died shortly after of a broken heart. In another, both of them were brought back to Attila, where Dengizich begged forgiveness for his crimes. Upon seeing Mingxia's great beauty, Attila killed Dengizich and kept her as his concubine."

"That's awful," I said, carefully side-stepping around a hole in the ground that seemed to go on forever. When I kicked a rock in there, its splash sounded about two and a half seconds later. *Thirty meters.* I shuddered. Falling from that height would result in something far worse than shattered ankles.

Heath glanced at me over his shoulder. "Do you know how Attila the Hun died?"

"In battle?" I guessed.

"You'd think so, but no. It was the year 453, and he was preparing to attack the Eastern Roman Empire and its new emperor, Marcian. Just before launching his assault, Attila was found dead in his chambers, having choked on his own blood. Many historians, my father included, believe he died at the hands of one of his lovers. My father liked to speculate that it was Mingxia, who then fled during the chaos to live the remainder of her life in peace."

"Far-fetched, but I like it... Oh, wow," I breathed, kneeling beside the backfilled tunnel Heath had just passed. "You need to come look at this."

He crouched beside me, letting out a small gasp. Fragments of glowing green crystals were interspersed alongside the unwanted ore and dirt that had been used to fill the tunnel. Heath sifted through the detritus and picked up one of the broken crystals, which was almost as long as his pinky. "I've never seen anything like this," he murmured, turning it over in his palm.

I eyed the crystal with mounting lust, wanting nothing more than to pluck it from his hand and pop it in my mouth. Instead, I found myself gnawing on a dirty hangnail to keep the impulse at bay.

"Are you okay?" Heath asked, eyeing me with a furrowed brow. "You look pale. When was the last time you drank something?"

I started. "Oh…right." With an impatient sigh – corporal requisites like food and water were so inconvenient – I retrieved a metal canteen from my bag and took a large swig. The warm, metallic-flavored water made me gag, but I forced down a few more gulps. It was already almost impossible to stay hydrated in these conditions; the air was so hot and thick, it was stifling to breathe. "Are you sure these aren't the crystals we're looking for?" I wheezed, gesturing at the broken fragments.

Heath shook his head as he helped me to my feet. "No. These aren't them. We're looking for an entire pocket of crystals, not discarded pieces. But we're getting close," he added, glancing at the photo on his phone while I pocketed several of the mineral fragments for future scrutiny. "I'm sure of it."

Muttering a few sailor-grade obscenities, I scrubbed the sweat from my brow with the hem of my shirt, then checked the thermometer keychain dangling from my pack: one hundred and eight degrees Fahrenheit. "Look"—I crossed my arms over my sweat-stained tank top—"as much as I'm enjoying this fascinating history lesson, could we skip to the part that's actually relevant? For starters, what is that piece of parchment you're looking at? How do you know where this massive vug supposedly is? And most importantly, what *exactly* is it we're looking f—*augh!*" I shrieked as I stepped in a puddle of water that turned out to be much deeper than I'd expected. The warm, muddy liquid sloshed over the top of my boots and into my socks, which were now soaking wet and squelching. "Oh, that is just *great!*" I shouted, my voice echoing down the tunnel.

"Take it easy." Heath's eyes darted to the low ceiling.

I took a deep breath, swatting away the bead of sweat that was dangling from the tip of my nose, then scrubbed the damp strands of hair out of my eyes.

"Do you need—"

"I'm fine, okay?" I interjected.

"You don't seem fine."

I ground my teeth. "Look, I'm used to tight, dark spaces, but this place is pushing even *my* boundaries! It's hot as hell, crumbling at the seams, and the water level"—I glared at the stupid puddle, very much wanting to kick it—"is steadily rising. In addition to soaking my socks, it also significantly increases the risk of a false floor collapse. So if you could *please* hurry up and get to the point before one of us keels over from heatstroke"—I scowled, thinking of the cooling sapphire tonic in the left pouch of my backpack that I very much wanted to chug but couldn't thanks to present company—"I would *very* much appreciate it."

"You're right," Heath said, taking my hand between his. "I'm sorry."

"Er—" I eyed our conjoined hands, my tongue momentarily malfunctioning. After a few failed attempts at speech, I eventually stammered, "W-What exactly is that parchment you keep looking at on your phone?"

He hesitated briefly before answering, "It's a letter. From Mingxia's son, Jinshan, to *his* unborn son, Caishen."

My hand spasmed involuntarily, eliciting a yelp from Heath as he attempted to jerk his crushed fingers away from the makeshift iron vice of mine.

"Heath Spencer," I spat through tightly gritted teeth, flinging his hand away from me, "this story has spanned from Constantinople to Damascus and all the way to China. You have blathered on about Attila the Hun and Atakam the guard and Dengizich the assassin and Mingxia the slave and Jinshan the baby and now Caishen, the *baby's* baby—"

"Wow." Heath let out a low whistle.

"Wow *what?!*" I snarled.

"Your listening skills are top notch." He grinned. "The first few times my father tried to tell me this story, I'd fallen asleep before Dengizich had even reached Damascus. Granted, I was just an eight-year-old kid whose bedtime was being hijacked by his chatterbox father – who, by the way, subjected me to a *much* longer and more detailed story than the abridged version I've been telling you—"

I let out a low growl.

"Okay, okay!" Heath held his hands in the air. "Let's stick one more climbing piton into the wall to be safe, and by the time we're done hammering, you will have heard the entire story."

"Fine." I glared at him as I pulled out my mallet and bolts. "But no more elaborate narration or unnecessary side characters. Just tell me what I need to know."

"Okay," Heath agreed. "I'm skipping straight to the important stuff." He muttered unintelligibly under his breath for a few moments, presumably to remember where he'd left off, then continued. "Right. So, many years later, Jinshan – that's the baby Mingxia gave birth to – penned a letter to *his* unborn son—"

"And that's the photo you've been looking at?"

"Yes." Heath nodded. "The original piece of sheepskin he wrote on is back in the shop, since it's too fragile and valuable to travel with."

"How did you manage to get your hands on a sixteen-hundred-year-old piece of parchment?" I asked between mallet strikes.

Heath sighed. "I can't tell you that – not yet, at least." I opened my mouth to protest, but he continued before I could get a word in. "The letter detailed Jinshan's entire life, much of which was spent in poverty and hardship. Even though his mother had left him this stolen trunk of Roman gold, Jinshan was too frightened to touch it because of all the blood that had been spilled because of it. I mean, even his adoptive parents, who had taken some of the gold, later died of what was probably typhus fever." Heath chuckled, even though the preceding statement wasn't at all humorous. "And then his pregnant wife found it and subsequently fell sick… I mean, it's easy to understand why Jinshan thought it was cursed. The trail of blood left by this treasure was staggering. Hell, even the Romans, who had given it to Attila as part of their tribute, had likely pillaged it from the Iberian Peninsula when they won the Second Punic War—"

I shot him a dirty look as I knotted our rope through the piton.

"—which is a whole other very interesting side note, but again, I digress."

"Your father would be proud of you," I told him drily, wiping the sweat from my brow after putting my tools away. "The climbing piton is officially installed, which means it's time for you to finish this absurdly long story." I shook my head ruefully. "Now I understand what my mother meant when she said I have a habit of 'making long stories longer.' You're worse than I am."

"Blame the Spencer genes," Heath conceded. He had deftly maneuvered himself in front of me, pressing his hands to both sides of the tunnel walls as he continued walking. "I am a descendant of blabbermouths. Anyway, to make a *very* fascinating story woefully short, Jinshan wanted nothing to do with the so-called 'cursed' gold, so he kept it locked away and never told anyone about it. But when his wife fell sick during pregnancy, Jinshan panicked, thinking it was his family curse. He took the chest to a nearby abandoned copper mine, climbed deep into the lowest levels, and hid it in a backfilled tunnel located beneath to 'a forest of pine-colored gemstones that blush in the sunlight.'"

"Wait a minute..." My eyes widened. "Wait just a *dang* minute!" I stumbled to a stop, stomping in yet *another* deep puddle as I did, and rounded on him. "This whole time, you've been going on and on about this supposed undiscovered mineral when in actuality you've been traipsing across China looking for *buried treasure?"*

Chapter 20

"You're joking, right?" I gaped at Heath in disbelief. "Please tell me you're joking!"

He flashed me a grimace that could only be described as sheepish.

"But… But…that's so *stupid!*" I sputtered. "How do you know this letter you mysteriously came by is authentic? And even if it is, how can you be sure the treasure wasn't found sometime between the fifth century and today? And why am I only hearing about this *now?* Norm never mentioned anything about Huns or treasure or—"

"It was a secret he kept close to the vest."

"*What* vest?!" I demanded. "He never wore vests!"

Heath burst out laughing, which made the edges of my vision turn red.

"Heath Spencer," I growled, fists clenching as I took a menacing step in his direction.

He flashed me a devilish grin. "I love it when you say my name like that."

"STOP JOKING RIGHT N—!"

He promptly clamped a hand over my mouth, stifling what was meant to be a tirade of epic proportions. "Don't even think about biting me," he said, which was exactly what I'd been planning on doing. "Just take a few deep breaths through your nose... That's it..."

I did what I was told, glaring "daggers" at him, as my mother would say.

Heath waited until my breathing had slowed, then said, "As you know, these tunnels are literally older than dirt—"

"Figuratively," I corrected, the word muffled beneath his palm.

"*Figuratively* older than dirt, which makes them particularly susceptible to loud, shrill frequencies. Anyway," he continued merrily, keeping his hand firmly clamped to my mouth, "to answer your questions, one of my father's many compulsive, fanatical interests was in the Huns and their political conquests. Because of that, he was able to find actual historical records of the names and events Jinshan mentioned in his letter." Heath gave me a pointed look. "Now that you're no longer hyperventilating, I'm going to remove my hand from your mouth – provided you don't keep screaming at me, that is. And that's not to say you can't scream at me later, when we're no longer situated in fragile geological conditions. Just not right now... Deal?"

I shook my head.

"No deal?" he asked, eyes widening. "So, I should continue with the story...like this?"

I nodded. He'd been right about aural disturbances being a risk factor, and I wasn't completely certain I was done screaming at him yet.

He blinked a few times, then shrugged and continued, "Okay, well, while I was single-mindedly working on securing my doctorate and subsequent professorship at Boston U, I admittedly didn't pay my father's increasingly-drunken sermons about ancient buried treasure much heed... In hindsight, I wish I'd taken more of his calls."

A twinge of sympathy knotted in my chest.

"Anyway." He cleared his throat. "Inheriting the shop was a complete surprise. So much so, I'd initially planned on selling it to the first bidder. But then I found stacks upon stacks of research and hand-scrawled notebooks in the back of Dad's office, all of which had to do with this supposed treasure." He sighed, bowing his head. "And, well...I suppose my way of handling the grief was finishing what he started. Even though his obsession is probably what killed him in the end... Well, that, or his guilt," he muttered under his breath, then sighed. "So I left my entire life and career behind to sell overpriced rocks during the week and search for Attila the Hun's long-lost stolen treasure on the weekends."

I gently pulled away from his palm. "Why?"

"Why what?"

"Why do you think it killed him?"

"Oh." Heath chortled softly, and I wondered if he was a fan of gallows' humor. "For one, my dad hated not knowing the answer to things – possibly even more than you do. And the more frustrated he became at his inability to solve this puzzle, the more he drank."

I was quiet for a long moment, carefully considering my next words. "When my parents' cat died, I tried to cheer them up by getting them an identical one. But it just made them more upset."

"I'm sorry that happened." Heath cocked his head, a furrow appearing between his brows. "But…wait – why were they upset?"

I shrugged. "My mother just kept screaming, 'What the hell are we supposed to do with two dead cats?!'"

Heath's jaw dropped.

Nope. I winced, inwardly kicking myself. *Definitely not a fan of gallows' humor.* Clearing my throat, I opted for the more socially-acceptable way of making someone feel better and gave him a tight hug instead. "I'm sorry your father died," I whispered.

After a brief moment of hesitation, Heath wrapped his arms around my waist, drawing me closer. "Me too."

My heart thrummed at his touch, hot and sticky as it was. "And I'm sorry you had to abandon your career to look for the treasure that probably killed him," I added for good measure. "It's too bad we'll probably never find it, like most lost treasures of antiquity."

Heath pulled away from me, his face scrunched up in an inscrutable expression. "Has anyone ever told you that you're terrible at offering condolences?"

"Yes." I held up my black light, illuminating the narrowing passageway that stretched ahead of us. "To be clear, the only reason I came to this mine was to find an undiscovered mineral – which we've since discovered – not for some mythical buried treasure that may or may not exist. So I'm giving this expedition fifteen more minutes before I turn around. It's hot, my socks are wet, and we're getting dangerously close to the water table. Where did this 'Jinshan' fellow say he buried the chest, specifically?"

Heath chewed on his lip, and for a moment I thought he might argue with me. But then he pulled up his phone and read, *"My cherished son, Confucious says we must rise above fear and superstition, and I have tried my best. But he also says to see what is right and not do it is the worst cowardice. I see now what must be done. It seems cruel to hide such an abundance of riches and then raise you in squalor. For that, I hope you can forgive me. If they come searching for what my father took from them, do not risk further wrath by saying it is gone. Instead lead them to the depths of the old copper mine. It will be buried in the second lowest tunnel, beside a forest of pine-colored gemstones that blush in the sunlight—"*

"Hang on," I interjected. "If your father knew all of this, why didn't he come searching for the treasure himself?"

"He did," Heath answered patiently. "Many times. Every time he visited the active mine site to collect new minerals, he would comb it for days on end. He even snuck into several of the satellite mines, searching for access to the old Tonglushan ruins. But most of the original tunnels had collapsed, and the few that hadn't showed no trace of this green mineral. After Dad died, I tried to pick up where he'd left off. But with eight square kilometers of mostly-collapsed ruins, some of which go fifty meters into the ground, finding anything in them – let alone something that's been lost for centuries – isn't exactly an easy feat. It wasn't until last month, when that miner showed me the strange mineral, that I actually had a tangible lead."

"I see. Did Jinshan write anything else that might actually be useful?"

"Not particularly. He ends it with, *I hope this letter proves needless, that I may one day explain this to you myself, having broken the curse on our bloodline. If not, it is my fervent wish that my sacrifice will not be in vain."*

"So, not just treasure, but 'cursed' treasure." Flinching, I brushed aside a large centipede that had dropped from the ceiling and onto my shoulder. "Do you actually believe this nonsense?"

"I don't necessarily believe in curses, but I can understand why Jinshan might have," Heath replied, tucking his phone back into his pocket. "After all, he'd been abandoned alongside a letter saying the gold was cursed. His adoptive parents spent some of the gold, then later died. His pregnant wife discovered the chest, only to subsequently fall sick. I mean, if the woman *I* loved were terminally ill, and I thought there was even the slightest chance of saving her, I'd do whatever it took, no matter how far-fetched it might seem to someone on the outside looking in… Wouldn't you?"

"Wouldn't I what?" I balked.

Heath sighed, but his voice was patient when he spoke. "Do whatever it takes to save the person you loved most in the world, even if it was unorthodox or, God forbid, unscientific."

I'd opened my mouth to blurt out something along the lines of, *Of course not, that's absurd,* when Topie's face floated in front of my vision. If he ever got terribly sick – the thought alone made my insides twist – I wouldn't rush him to the vet's office; I'd whip out my potions kit, which was neither FDA-approved nor scientifically-supported.

Hypocrite, a voice whispered, filling me with shame. As my eyes darted back to Heath's, and my mouth opened to offer a half-hearted apology, my mind went rogue, conjuring an image of him lying sick in a hospital bed, his arms covered in IVs and his skin pallid.

Panic filled me, the unexpected force of it causing me to pitch forward. Heath's hand jerked in my direction to steady me, but I waved him away, using the tunnel wall to steady myself.

"Laney? Are you—"

"Hang on," I panted. Pressing my forehead against the uncomfortably hot rocks of the tunnel, I took several slow, deep breaths, trying to banish the terrible image from my mind.

"You're dehydrated," Heath observed, pulling the canteen from his pack to offer it to me.

I waved that away as well, desperately clawing at any emotion that might replace the raw, inexplicable terror that filled me at the thought of losing the person I'd long-convinced myself I hated most in the world. As was so often the case, the easiest – and safest – emotion to grasp was anger.

"Yes, because of this stupid wild goose chase!" Pushing away from the wall, I knocked his canteen aside. "You're telling me the ink on that parchment is still legible after sixteen hundred *years* of sunlight and humidity and general oxidation? Please!" I scoffed. "I'm not buying it!"

A muscle in Heath's jaw twitched. "The parchment was very well-preserved."

"Oh yeah?" My eyes narrowed sharply. "And where exactly did your father find it that it was so 'well-preserved?'"

"Uh…" When the Adam's apple in Heath's throat bobbed, James Ostrowski's face danced between us, *his*

Adam's apple bobbing up and down as he loosened the top button of his collar. "In a museum."

I crossed my arms. "You're lying."

"I…" Heath's mouth fluttered open as though he might refute that, then closed again.

Pain zinged through my jaw from the force of gritting my teeth so hard. My heart was racing too fast for me to count the beats, and my chest was so tight, it felt like my ribs were constricting around my lungs, preventing me from properly filling them. "If you think I'm going to continue puttering around a dilapidated ancient mine with a *liar*," I wheezed, my hand inching toward the stone in my pocket but stopping short, "then you're a bigger idiot than I thought."

Heath tilted his head back and ran his hands through his hair. "Look, everything I've told you is true, minus the part about the letter. That's not my story to tell, so I won't. I'm sorry for that – I really am. But if you could just focus on the facts I *am* able to tell you, you'll see there's enough evidence to support—"

"Evidence?" I scoffed. "You know nothing of the scientific process. You confuse hypotheses with theories and educated guesses with facts. You… You…"

Don't say it, a tiny voice warned, scarcely audible over the raging torrent of emotions flooding my brain. *It's going too far.* But I ignored it, desperate to flee this situation – this *relationship,* whatever the heck it was – that had spiraled so far out of my limited, untested comfort zone.

"I what?" Heath crossed his arms.

"You quit a prestigious, lucrative career to work at a stupid rock shop!" I blurted out. "And now you're down here putting your life at risk because of the crazy ramblings of a drunkard!"

The edges of Heath's eyes hardened. "Say what you want about me, Delaney, but don't talk about my father that way."

A twinge of guilt knotted in my chest, but it was quickly smothered by wet socks, matted clothing, stifling heat, and a growling stomach. "If you're reckless enough to keep searching for a Confucious-era urban legend, that's fine. People have devoted entire religions to stories written thousands of years ago. But I'm a scientist, and I work in facts. And the fact is, I came to verify the claims of a new mineral and nothing more."

Heath was silent for a long time, his hardened features twisted in such a way that I was expecting him to shout at me. But when he finally opened his mouth, his voice was unnervingly soft. "Because minerals are all you care about, right?"

The question brought tears to my eyes, though I had no idea why. I clenched my fists and squared my shoulders, working to keep my insides from crumbling. "Right."

We stared at each other for a long, tense moment. And then Heath took a deep breath, his features softening as he did, and opened his mouth – most likely to spew something kind, reassuring, and unbearably considerate to the last person on Earth who deserved to hear it.

I couldn't bear to listen.

Before he could utter a single sympathetic syllable, I unhooked my harness – wanting to put as much space between us as physically possible – flung it and the chalcopyrite ball he'd given me into the nearest muddy puddle, then stormed away without looking back.

Chapter 21

I stomped off in an angry huff, my boots sloshing through ankle-deep puddles as I muttered obscenities under my breath. Heath was shouting my name, but I ignored him – until he grabbed me by the wrist and spun me around.

"What the—" I started, letting out a muffled yelp as Heath's lips crushed against mine.

He pulled away for a split second, providing me with ample opportunity to either pull away or slap him. When my fist didn't immediately go flying, he again dropped his lips to mine and kissed me hard, pushing me backward. Grabbing him by the straps of his backpack, I pulled him with me as my back thumped against the wall. His hands landed on either side of my head as he kissed me forcefully, sliding his tongue between my lips.

Adrenaline jolted through my veins and heat pulsed between my thighs, while a torrent of conflicting emotions muddied my thoughts. My hands clenched fistfuls of Heath's shirt, torn between shoving him away and pulling him closer. My lips parted, simultaneously wanting to scream at him and take his tongue deeper. My thigh wedged itself between his legs, sensually grinding against his erection while my brain seriously considered kneeing him in the groin.

"Goddamnit, Laney," Heath gasped, tearing his lips from mine. "You are an infuriating, self-important brat!"

"And you're a smug, overconfident bastard!" I grabbed the back of his head, my hands fisting into his hair, and forced his mouth back to mine.

A low rumble sounded in his chest as he tilted his head to deepen the kiss, sliding his tongue across mine. I was flattened beneath the weight of his body, pressed against the wall of the tunnel, but I didn't care. I rocked my hips against his, countering his every advance with my own. The rougher he kissed me, the harder I pulled his hair. The more he pushed, the deeper I ground my thigh against the hardened bulge of his jeans. When he dug his fingers into my waist, I bit his lip – hard. Instead of letting out a curse, he moaned, making my knees buckle from the sound. His grip on my hips tightened – whether to steady me or roughhouse me, I couldn't be sure.

"Now, you listen to me—" Heath started.

I started to bark out a retort, but he clamped a hand over my mouth, bringing his nose millimeters from mine.

"I said, *listen*," he growled, silencing me. "I know I haven't been completely forthright, but neither have you."

My eyes bulged in indignation. Even if his assumption were true – and fine, maybe it was – who the heck did he think he was to make such a baseless claim, let alone declare it with such certainty? *The arrogance of this man!*

"Don't you give me that look, Delaney Stone! You have no right to demand full transparency while simultaneously being the most opaque person I've ever met!"

"Am not!" I shot back, my retort muffled by the palm of his hand.

"Please." He rolled his eyes. "Now, were you and I to become *actual* friends or something more, I would be more than happy to discuss full transparency."

I inhaled sharply through my nose. *Something more?*

"But for God's sake, Delaney, after all this time, I still can't tell if you like or loathe me! Half the time, I don't think *you* even know!"

At that, I averted my eyes.

"Now, regardless of how you may feel about me," Heath continued, his voice softening, "I have feelings for you—"

My breath caught.

"—and I would very much like to explore those feelings, *if* you can stop throwing tantrums every thirty minutes. Hell, I don't even care if you throw a tantrum! Yell and scream all you'd like, if that's what it takes. Just stop yelling at *me,* okay?"

He removed his hand from my mouth, perhaps expecting me to lash out at him, but I just stared at him wordlessly.

"Okay?" he prompted again.

I nodded.

He sighed, sounding relieved. "Thank you… Now, I don't expect you to put yourself in further danger, or to tread any deeper than you feel comfortable." He unslung my abandoned harness from his shoulder, which I hadn't noticed until now, and looped the straps over my arms.

"However, I do expect you to be safe. So if you don't want to come with me, fine. Go back up another level and wait for me so we can leave together. If you never want to speak to me after today, fine. But if you do," he said, leaning forward to brush his lips against mine, "then I'm very open to having a conversation about *this*." He gestured between us.

"This?" I asked weakly.

"Us."

"Oh." The word came out in a faint whisper.

He retrieved my abandoned rope from the ground, fed it through my belay device, then nudged me in the direction of the shaft we'd come down earlier. "Be safe as you head back up there. I'll see you soon." His mouth quirked up in a smile. "Maybe by then you'll have decided whether you like me or not."

I could barely muster a nod as I turned to walk away, my head spinning as it frantically tried to process everything that infuriating man had just yelled in my general direction.

"Oh, and Laney?"

Gritting my teeth, I slowly turned back around, only to find Heath standing directly behind me. "You dropped this," he said softly, gently taking my hand in his. After pressing the chalcopyrite in my palm and closing my fingers around it, he murmured, "I'm touched you've kept it all this time."

"I just...forgot to take it out of my pocket," I stammered.

He cocked his head at me, the left corner of his mouth curling slightly, and whispered, "Liar."

"I—ugh!" I spun around on my heels, my torturously wet socks squelching as I did, and stormed away from him.

The light from his lamp and the sound of his laughter trailed after me until I made it all the way back to the rope dangling from the vertical shaft in the ceiling. When I jumped up to climb it, easily pulling myself up with only my arms thanks to the celestine still warming my belly, Heath let out a low whistle from the other side of the tunnel.

"Delaney Stone: beguiling, vexatious, and full of endless surprises." He chuckled, the sound brushing against my ears like a soft breeze.

I jerked my head over my shoulder to shout something in response – "Be safe," perhaps – but his light had already disappeared down the narrow, winding tunnel.

Topie's face appeared in the square-shaped hole above me, his whiskers covered in cheddar-colored powder. *"Ree?"*

"He's not coming," I rasped, feeling as though a heavy stone were sitting in my belly, doubling the weight of my body. Speechless as Heath had momentarily rendered me, a strange, nervous energy was bubbling up in my chest, spurring me to fill the silence with chatter. "The idiot's gone on some wild goose chase for gold. In the meantime, I'm going to collect as many unbroken mystery crystals as I can. *That's* why I came here, so *that's* what I'm doing." I paused at the top of the rope to again glance over my shoulder, but there was no sign of Heath. With a huff, I hoisted myself out of the hole, wiped my muddy hands on my even muddier shirt, then retrieved a small chisel from my toolbelt. "Come help me."

Topie hesitated, his attention darting between me and the shaft.

"Get away from there!" I ushered him away from the hole. "Or have you forgotten Item Nineteen: 'Horizontal surfaces surrounding vertical structures are often precarious and prone to deterioration'?"

He plopped his rump in the dirt, giving me a hard look as he did.

"Oh, don't you start with me too!" I returned his glare and then some before making my way to the crystal-studded schist peeking between two decomposing beams of wood. "I'm not the one who's in the wrong here, he is! That half-brained numbskull dragged us all the way out here to dig for some made-up Hun treasure!" I began chiseling at the stone, working to loosen the crystals without breaking them. "Even if the stupid letter Norm 'mysteriously' found is authentic, there's no way the gold would still be down there after so many years! It's absolute nonsense. And even if it *is* down there"—I winced as the tiny crystal I'd been working to free cracked right down the middle—"it's probably trapped beneath two millennia's worth of rubble on the inside of a washed-out tunnel." I ground my teeth together angrily. "That stump of a man is gonna get himself killed in a subterranean cave-in before he even…" My hand slowly stopped chiseling. "Before he even…" My eyes darted to the shaft Topie had firmly planted himself beside. "Um…"

The pig's eyes narrowed at me as though *I* were the idiot sifting for gold in crumbling underground ruins.

The knot in my stomach had returned with a vengeance. I lowered my chisel, pressing my free hand to the rumbling hollow of my navel. "I…um…"

Topie cocked his head at me, waiting patiently.

"I…" I licked my lips, trying to put the moisture back in my mouth. "I really should go check on that vug he mentioned… Because if those crystals are half as big as that letter says, they'll be much more powerful than these little ones." The chisel slipped out of my hand and landed on the ground, but I didn't bother picking it up as my feet moved toward the shaft. "Topie," I whispered, swallowing tightly. "I…I need to go back and check on that vug. Would you come with me, just in case…" I trailed off, unsure how to finish the sentence.

He jumped into my arms, sending me stumbling backward, then jerked his snout toward the shaft as if to say, "Forward, *march!*"

I squeezed him tightly, burying my nose in the short hairs that grew between his floppy ears, and took a deep, steadying breath. "Starting this moment, I'm going to stop being so cranky all the time. I promise."

Topie let out a derisive snort.

"Oh, shut up!" I snapped, then winced. "Er, I mean…please be quiet."

His snort transformed into silent, pot-belly-shaking laughter as I lowered myself back down the shaft, clutching him under my left arm like an oversized football.

"Laugh it up, cheese-breath," I muttered as we dangled mid-air. When my feet hit the ground a few moments later, I plopped him in front of me and gave him a stern look. "We are officially treading into level-five danger conditions down here, got it? Flash flooding, cave-ins, dangerous methane leaks – and not just the kind from your butt."

He made an offended huff.

"The point is, we have to be extremely careful, okay? I've got my potions kit, but as you know, there's no mineral out there that can reverse death. Which reminds me, I'd better keep the level-five brews close, just in case."

Setting my bag on the ground, I rooted around the inside, swapping out most of the tools on my belt for my most powerful potions – both my regular pulverized gravel suspensions, as well as the human-grade potions I'd brewed specially for Topie. The dozen or so vials hung from my belt loops via small homemade leather pouches that clinked together like delicate bells. After hammering an extra-large climbing piton deep into the rock wall, I put on Topie's harness, tethering both of us together via a spare bundle of paracord, and gave the piton a good, sturdy tug to make sure it was anchored well.

"Okay." I adjusted our headlamps, setting the beams to high. "Time to find Hea—er, the vug," I quickly amended. "Topes, stay behind me and watch your step."

With no forks in this particular tunnel, I knew finding Heath wouldn't take long, especially with the trail of red buttons he'd left behind. Just as I'd expected, it only took me a few minutes to make my way back to the farthest spot we'd walked together. I swept my head from side to side, searching for the climbing piton he'd been tethered to when I stormed off earlier. Eventually, I caught sight of the glinting metal – sans his yellow rope.

My stomach sank.

"Why would he unhook himself?" I hissed. It was, of course, irrelevant that I had unhooked myself first.

I picked up the pace after that, my eyes anxiously scanning the ground for red buttons, yet finding none – either he'd run out, or they'd sunk into the mud. The ground angled sharply downward in this part of the tunnel, with intermittent shallow puddles quickly replaced by ankle-deep water; we were treading just above the water table. Equally if not more unnerving, this part of the main haul tunnel started branching into smaller offshoots, some of which had been backfilled, while others were dark, winding passageways that swallowed up all traces of light. I stuck my head inside each as we passed, calling Heath's name.

He didn't answer.

With eight square kilometers of mostly-collapsed ruins, some of which go fifty meters into the ground, finding something that's been lost in them isn't exactly an easy feat, Heath's voice echoed in my head, sending a jolt of panic through my stomach.

"Topie, don't!" I barked.

He jerked his head away from the nearest partially-crumbled hole in the wall, inside of which broken, rotted beams carpeted the flooded ground, and peered up at me with a quivering chin.

"I'm not angry with you," I reassured him, tightening my hand on the rope that tethered us together. "I just need you to stay behind me and not stick your nose in dangerous places, okay?"

He nodded his head obediently, staying close at my heels as we ventured deeper into the ruins.

For the first time in my life, I completely ignored the scintillating crystals and the dark veins of minerals embedded in the walls as we explored, instead double- and even triple-checking the potions dangling from my toolbelt. Compulsive or not, it was crucial to have anything and everything we could possibly need close at hand, in case we stumbled into one of the five most common mining mishaps: toxic vapors, explosives, aerosolized particles, cave-ins, and flooding. Heath, meanwhile, didn't have any potions with him. He only had himself.

I cupped my shaking hands around my mouth and shouted, "Heath!" as loudly as I dared.

No response.

Sweat was dripping into my eyes, and my heart was thumping so hard, my sternum ached. "Heath, I know you're mad at me!" I called again. "But please don't ignore me!"

Topie and I stopped to listen. Apart from the echo of my own voice ricocheting off the walls, the tunnel was completely silent. I swallowed hard, trying not to think of the literal tons of rock and soil sitting atop this very, *very* old mine, while my eyes darted to the bottoms of the interlocking wood beams. They were saturated, but not yet fully rotted – meaning this water hadn't been standing here for very long. The lump in my throat grew bigger. I took another step forward, only to immediately be tugged backward by the stopper knot at the end of my rope. We'd gone so far, I'd run out of ninety meters of slack.

"Butternuts," I muttered, breaking at least four rules in our safety checklist to abandon my harness altogether. As the equipment clattered to the ground, I turned to Topie, who had already wriggled out of his own climbing harness, and whispered, "If I asked you to stay back, would you listen?"

His responding *oink* was a firm negative.

"Shocking," I muttered, using the toe of my boot to feel around for any hidden shafts or collapsed sections of floor as we slowly ventured deeper into the tunnel. "Look, I know I've been a jerk to you," I called out as we passed yet another branched-off passageway. "But if it makes you feel better, I'm a jerk to everybody! Okay, maybe I'm a *little* meaner to you than other people," I conceded, "but it's just because you're so infuriating!"

Topie shot me a sharp look.

I winced. "Er, what I m-meant to say is, you're just so infuriatingly *nice.* And distractingly g-good-l-looking," I stammered. My teeth were chattering – not from the temperature, which was only getting hotter and hotter – but from the panic rising in my chest. "And yeah, okay, your r-rock shop might be t-tacky, but I've also n-never seen it so b-busy. Norm used to t-tell me that he n-never made any m-m-money…that he constantly w-worried about the bills he was l-leaving b-behind—" An unexpected sob slipped from my throat.

"Oh, Norm…" I whispered, stinging tears filling my eyes. How could I have been so oblivious to his suffering?

Topie let out a low grunt.

"I'm okay." Sniffling, I used the back of my hand to quickly scrub away the tears. "I'm just…angry with myself."

He made a low whinny, scraping the side of the wall with his hoof.

"But Heath's not looking for the mineral, he's looking for treasure… Oh!" I smacked my forehead, annoyed that I hadn't thought of that first. "You're absolutely right!"

Sucking down a deep breath, both for extra courage and to make sure there was no trace of toxic gas in the air, I switched off my headlamp, plunging us in darkness and eliciting a frightened shriek from Topie.

When my portable black light flickered on a moment later, the entire tunnel burst to life.

"Oh, my gosh…" I breathed, mesmerized by the splendor of thousands of glowing, neon-green crystals, which grew between every wooden beam and inside every nook and cranny of the surrounding rock. I took several steps forward, holding the UV light over my head like a lantern. "This is incredi—" My sentence ended in a sharp gasp as we turned the corner.

A massive cavity of green crystals formed the dead end of the tunnel — a geode, essentially, but on a much larger scale. Hundreds and hundreds of dazzling, pristine crystals lined the inside of the vug, all of them glowing as brightly as kryptonite while boasting perfect, pyramidal prismatic formations as long and wide as my forearm. But it wasn't the forest of glowing, emerald-green gemstones that robbed me of breath; it was the vertical shaft located directly beside the vug, which was overflowing with water and flooding the surrounding area.

There, dangling from one of the shaft's rotted wood posts, was Heath's abandoned backpack.

Chapter 22

I stared at Heath's deserted supplies, cold, sharp dread twisting in my stomach like a knife. Anchored by a metal bolt in the wall, a taut line of neon-yellow paracord led directly into the flooded shaft; it was neither moving nor vibrating. My breath caught and stuck in my throat at the sight, as though a noose had been tightened around my neck. But there was nothing to loosen – just crushing, smothering panic gripping me by the windpipe. How long ago had Heath climbed in there? Before the shaft flooded, or after?

"Topie, stay back!" I ordered. Abandoning all thought of caution or safety, I cranked the beam of my headlamp to maximum, sank to my knees beside the rotting wood posts, and peered into the pool of warm, murky water below. There was no sign of Heath – only about three feet of visible rope, which was quickly obscured by swirling mud and debris. I scrambled to my feet and gave it several hard yanks, but it didn't budge.

"That stupid idiot!" I cursed, flinging my pack off my shoulders and chucking my helmet to the flooding ground. My hands were sweaty and shaking as I removed several vials from my toolbelt, injudiciously downing one potion after another: deep green vesuvianite, shimmering gold tiger's eye, magenta-red spinel... I'd probably have a raging stomachache later, but that didn't matter.

Nothing mattered except Heath.

After giving Topie a long, emotionally-loaded look that conveyed my feelings better than words ever could, I replaced my glasses with a pair of snug-fitting prescription swim goggles, took a deep breath that filled my lungs all the way down to my diaphragm, then jumped feet-first into the shaft. The water was warm and acidic, making my skin tingle with all the minerals that had dissolved in it. I briefly closed my eyes, working to slow my galloping heart rate and conserve my oxygen. Under normal circumstances, my weak lungs wouldn't be able to support me holding my breath for more than thirty seconds. But spinel enhanced lung function, allowing me to go as long as five minutes without breathing. Past experiments showed me that anything beyond that would cause me to pass out – not a big deal in the safety of my lab. But if I passed out here, I wouldn't wake up on the floor of my pharmacy. I would drown, leaving Heath to die.

If he hasn't already.

No! I shoved the terrifying thought from my mind. Besides, that was purely conjecture, and now, more than ever, all I could afford to focus on were facts. Bolstered by the hearty dose of tiger's eye I'd just chugged for extra courage, I swam farther into the abyss, using Heath's rope to guide me. There was so much debris swirling in the turbid water, I couldn't see anything except for the tiny section of rope directly in front of me. Luckily, I had something better than sight: I had vesuvianite.

I opened my mouth, nearly choking on a mouthful of acrid, arsenic-infused mine water, and let out a series of high-pitched calls that "showed" me the surrounding area. One of my most valuable finds from the last two years, vesuvianite granted me the ability to echolocate – unbelievably useful for exploring lightless depths (and sometimes conversing with bats), though the effect was tragically short-lived. When the vibrations returned to me, I could clearly see the structure of the space, which was about the size of a two-car garage. On one side of the cavity was a small opening, too small for a human to fit inside; on the other end was a protruding pile of boulders and broken wood, with a taut rope emerging from the center of the mound.

Heath! I silently screamed, using the same rope to pull me closer.

I clung to the paracord with one hand while I shoved aside boulders and fractured pieces of wood with the other. With every dislodged stone, the rope loosened, until a small opening emerged at the top of the pile. I peered inside the hole, from which a faint light was emanating, only to immediately clamp a hand over my mouth to trap the scream in my lungs. Illuminated by his fallen headlamp, Heath's limp body lay suspended in the ceiling-high water, his legs and arms floating around him like seaweed.

Terror and desperation took hold of me, robbing me of all logic as I furiously kicked and shoved the rest of the obstructing rocks away. The second I'd made a hole big enough to swim through, I squeezed myself inside, grabbing Heath by the strap of his messenger bag. From the corner of my eye, I caught the metallic glint of something resting at the bottom of the chasm, but I paid it no mind. With one arm wrapped around Heath's middle, and the other frantically pulling on the rope, I knocked the remainder of the rocks aside with the soles of my boots and kicked as hard as I could, working to build enough upward momentum to drag him out of the collapsed tunnel. My lungs were screaming even with the spinel in my system, but all I could think about was Heath, and the fact that he'd had no spinel in his body to help him hold his breath.

Freed from the obstructing view of the tunnel, I craned my neck to locate the square hole of the shaft, where the dim light of Topie's headlamp was shining down on us from what felt like an impossibly far distance. *Just a little farther!* I tried to reassure myself. But the harder I kicked, the louder my lungs screamed. The darkness was pressing in on me from all sides, suffocating me, while gravity pulled me toward the graveyard of broken objects that had sunk to the bottom of that hole. For a moment, I seriously considered succumbing to the weight of the darkness, insurmountable and inviting as it was. But then I felt a sharp tug on the rope that was slipping through my fingers.

Topie. He was up there waiting for me, and I couldn't let him down.

That thought alone kept me kicking, even as my legs and lungs screamed in agony and the limp weight of Heath's body threatened to drag me back down. Fingers straining for the light, I released the last of the air in my lungs in a stream of bubbles and kicked with all my might, until my head burst out of the water with a wheezing gasp.

"Reeeee!" Topie squealed. The water in the tunnel had surged all the way up to his chin, and he was straining to keep his head afloat as he yanked on Heath's rope with as much force as his little body could muster.

With a surge of strength that had nothing to do with celestine, I hoisted Heath out of the shaft, then climbed up after him. At the sight of his slumped, unmoving body, Topie let out a hysterical shriek.

"Get to higher ground!" I wheezed, flinging aside my goggles and struggling to my feet. "Now!"

I nudged Topie's spotted rump with the toe of my boot to get him going. Using the dagger holstered on my thigh, I hurriedly cut Heath free of his harness, then hoisted him over my shoulder. His messenger bag was still slung around his torso, but I didn't bother grabbing his abandoned backpack or mine. At any moment, the floor of the tunnel could collapse into the flooded cavity below, taking all three of us down with it.

"Reee!"

"I'm coming!" Staggering beneath the weight of Heath's limp and surprisingly-heavy body, I stumbled through the tunnel, relying on the beam from Topie's bouncing headlamp to light our way. We didn't stop until we'd reached higher ground and the knee-deep water had ebbed to shallow puddles. Even there, the danger hadn't subsided, but too much time had already passed; Heath needed urgent medical attention *now*. As I lowered him to the ground, Topie scampered over and nudged Heath's colorless cheeks in a frantic-yet-futile attempt to wake him up.

"Move," I ordered. There was no time for niceties, not while scant, precious seconds were dwindling. After casting my potions belt to the ground, I tore off Heath's harness, ripped his shirt open, and pressed my ear to his chest.

The silence that greeted me was the worst sound I'd ever heard.

Cursing under my breath, I turned his head to the side and began doing chest compressions, wincing at the audible crack of his sternum. "Get me dolomite, spinel, morganite, amber, and silver," I instructed Topie, jerking my head toward my toolbelt. "Only the silver is for me, the rest need to come from the Topie-grade kit. Hurry!"

To his immense credit, Topie did exactly as he was told, amassing an assortment of vials between his teeth in record time. I uncorked all five of them, taking the silver for myself while setting the rest at Topie's hooves.

"Get the other four potions down his throat, starting with the amber," I grunted, diligently resuming chest compressions at a rate of one hundred per minute. "Don't let him choke. They won't do any good in his lungs."

Nodding his assent, Topie got to work while I chugged the vial of swirling, silvery liquid in one swig. An unpleasant, nauseating tingle emanated from my belly, spreading down my arms and legs until my fingers and toes were literally buzzing. I gritted my teeth, working to contain the electrical current surrounding my entire body and straining to escape. I'd never had more than a sip of silver before, out of fear the voltage might stop my heart.

Now, I could only pray it had enough power to restart one.

"Move!" I barked once Topie had emptied the vial of amber into Heath's mouth. "Now!"

He took a startled step backward as I slammed my fists onto Heath's chest. A crackling surge of electricity exploded from my hands, arcing through his body. The smell of ionized air and singed clothing filled the small space as I lowered my head to Heath's chest, once more listening for a pulse.

Nothing.

"Give him the morganite!" I shouted to Topie, my teeth buzzing with electricity. "Hurry!"

As soon as that bottle was empty, I again banged my fists against Heath's chest. The jolt of electricity made his back arc violently into the air, then slump to the ground with a stomach twisting *thud*. I pressed my ear to his chest again.

In lieu of a heartbeat, Heath's laughter filtered between my ears, as crisp and clear as if he were standing right beside me. *"Well, I remain at your disposal should you ever need CPR."*

Instead of laughing at what had clearly been meant as a joke, I'd rolled my eyes at him. *"You know the latest CPR guidelines advise against mouth-to-mouth resuscitation, right? It's just chest compressions now."*

"Yeah, but I still think it's the mouth-to-mouth part that's most effective."

At the time, Heath's accompanying expression had been so cocky and devious, I couldn't help but laugh. Now, his face was as smooth and lifeless as a mannequin's, entirely bereft of the twinkle in his eyes or charming tug on his lips.

"*Aughh!* You stupid, stupid lummox!" I shouted at him, forcing another jolt of electricity into his chest that was so strong, it nearly sent me pitching backward. "Don't you *dare* die on me!"

Topie let out a helpless wail, every hair on his body standing straight up from the ionized air.

As I gazed down at Heath's still, lifeless body, I briefly considered giving up. Any other scientist certainly would have by that point, having accepted the natural law and the limits of science. But, as it turns out, I wasn't actually a scientist; I was a potions-brewing, boundary-pushing, natural-law-breaking *para*scientist. And I still had one more trick up my proverbial sleeve.

"Elevate his head," I instructed Topie, scrubbing the sweat and tears from my eyes.

With a steadfast *oink*, Topie buried his snout under Heath's neck and crawled underneath him as a provisional pillow. After emptying the last two vials into Heath's mouth, I rubbed his throat to help the liquid go down, motioned for Topie to move to a safe distance, then pressed my free hand against Heath's chest. Bringing my face to his, I rasped, "Fine, you want mouth-to-mouth? Here's your stupid mouth-to-mouth!" With that, I crushed my lips against his, forcefully blowing air into his lungs as I slammed my electrified fist against his sternum as hard as I could.

Heath's body lurched, then spasmed, then pitched forward as he coughed up a mouthful of black water.

A strangled sob of relief tore from my throat as I rolled him over on his side, where he continued to cough up torrents of dark liquid. When there was nothing left to expel from his lungs, he curled up in the fetal position and let out an agonized groan, squeezing his eyes shut. I'd once read that getting struck by lightning is one of the most unimaginably painful experiences a human can live through; Heath, meanwhile, had just endured the equivalent of *four* lightning strikes, not to mention a cracked sternum.

"Butternuts!" I hissed, groping at my potions.

While Topie ran around us in shrieking, hysterical circles, I snatched a chalky-gray tincture of howlite from my kit – the mineral equivalent of Vicodin, minus the constipating, addictive properties – then lifted Heath's head and poured it down his throat. As soon as his groaning quieted and I was fairly certain he wasn't going to keel over and die again, I flung my arms around him, weeping like a child.

"Laney," he gasped, the sound of his voice filling me with more joy than I'd ever thought possible.

"You stupid, stupid, *stupid* man!" I sobbed, showering his face with kisses and tears. "How could you do something so reckless and idiotic? I thought I'd lost you! I thought—"

His mouth caught mine, silencing the remainder of what was meant to be a furious diatribe, while his fingers knotted into my dripping-wet hair, pulling me deeper into the kiss. "I *am* a stupid man," he wheezed, pressing a cold finger to my lips, "but not for the reason you think."

I gaped at him, stunned.

"When the wall collapsed and the tunnel began flooding, I wasn't thinking about my family, the treasure, or"—he broke off in a violent coughing fit.

I quickly passed him the last of the lung-healing amber tonic. He swallowed the last dregs of it before taking a slow, deep breath. "I wasn't even thinking about my own imminent death. I was just thinking about you."

My vision blurred with tears.

Heath gently brushed them away with his thumbs, whispering, "When I realized I was about to die, all I could think about was how much I regretted not telling you exactly how I feel." Wincing, he struggled into a sitting position, then gently cupped my face in his hands.

"You drive me crazy like no one else has ever done before. In spite of that – or maybe because of it – I'm rampantly, unequivocally, head-over-heels for you." His eyes locked on mine, and for the first time, I didn't feel the urge to look away. "Now, what do you say to that, Delaney Stone?"

I made a noise somewhere between a laugh and a sob, so overwrought with joy and gratitude and a strange, terrifying, beautiful feeling I'd never experienced before: warmer than the heaviest weighted blanket, more satisfying than the most complex of puzzles, and far more intoxicating than any mineral I'd ever tasted.

And this time, I was absolutely certain, it had nothing to do with prasiolite.

Wrapping my arms around Heath, I nuzzled my face against his neck, taking solace in the steady *thump* of his pulse, and murmured, "You can call me Laney."

Chapter 23

The two of us remained in a tight embrace for the better part of a minute, until Topie trotted over, sandwiched himself between us, and started licking Heath's face like a dog.

"Hey, c'mon!" Heath laughed, shielding his face from Topie's overly-excited kisses. "I appreciate it, bud, but I'm really okay." He turned to me, the corners of his eyes creasing from a smile. "Thanks to you."

"To be fair, Topie helped a lot," I muttered, frowning at the warm water seeping into the seat of my pants. It hadn't come from a puddle, but rather from the overflowing vertical shaft a dozen yards away, which was gradually flooding our tunnel. *Shit.*

"My pig in shining armor!" Heath enthused, giving Topie a vigorous head scratch.

"Reee!"

"We have to go. Now!" I grunted. After quickly replacing my tool belt of scant potions, I went to help Heath to his feet. But the moment I straightened, a wave of nausea caused me to double over again, this time to projectile-vomit a torrent of glittering mineral potions into the ankle-deep water.

"Laney!" Heath draped an arm over my shoulders as I violently emptied my stomach of thousands of dollars' worth of potions – heliodor, celestine, spinel, vesuvianite, tiger's eye, and silver – rendering myself defenseless.

"Well, that's just great," I muttered, wiping my mouth with the back of my hand.

Topie started fussing with the side zipper of his backpack, presumably to grab me an anti-nausea tonic, but I shook my head. The whole reason I'd gotten sick was from chugging too many potions at once; the last thing I needed at that moment was more.

"It's hot as hell down here," Heath muttered, looking around. "We've gotta get you to higher ground before you dehydrate."

"Or drown," I added drily.

He placed his palm on the small of my back to guide me. "Can you walk?"

I gave an affirmative grunt as we sloshed away from the flooding tunnel and toward the exit shaft, with the latter being at least a quarter mile away.

"I don't suppose you're hiding any extra rope or climbing equipment in those extremely tight leather pants of yours, are you?" Heath asked, giving my bottom a sideways glance.

"It's all in my pack, which I had to abandon to carry you up this tunnel. Before that, I ran out of slack and had to dump my harness."

"How did you manage that?"

"You'd wandered so far down the corridor, I hit my stopper knot!"

"No!" Heath gaped at me. "I mean, how the *hell* did you carry me so far? I'm at least forty pounds heavier than you!"

"Oh…that." I darted a glance over my shoulder at the massive surge of water bubbling up from the end of the tunnel, adding another two inches to the now calf-high stream we were presently wading through. "I'll explain once we're out of immediate danger." My eyes flitted to Heath's messenger bag. "Anything in there that could help us?"

He tightened his hands around the strap, shaking his head.

I arched an eyebrow. "What exactly happened down there, anyway?"

Heath let out a long sigh. "I found something stuck in the wall, and when I decided to yank it out, I took a significant portion of the wall with it, causing the entire thing to collapse." He winced. "Rookie mistake, I know… Anyway, that's when I discovered just how close I was to the water table, or maybe even an underground spring, because water immediately started gushing through the hole I'd created."

"That was incredibly stupid of you," I remarked, simultaneously reaching out to take his hand in mine. "I would have never forgiven you if you had died."

He squeezed my hand tightly. "Is that your way of saying you'd miss me?"

"Something like that." My free hand shifted to my potions belt as I did a mental inventory of the minerals I still had with me, racking my brain for one that might have a chance of helping us.

Flooding groundwater paired with rotting wood had made the floor conditions too tenuous to run on, so we hastily strode through the tunnel. When the water level surged to our knees, Heath reached down to pick up Topie and tucked him under his arm like a football. His other hand tightened around mine. "We need to pick up the pace."

I nodded, still silently ticking off potions. *Calcite, ruby, amethyst...* None of those would help me navigate a flooded tunnel, unless I wanted to drown with strong bones, a fiery physique, and a calm demeanor. *Hematite, peridot, shungite* – clotting, anti-nausea, and magnetic field manipulation, respectively. *All worthless!* I let out a frustrated groan, raking my fingers through my wet hair.

As my eyes fell on the tiny green crystals growing out of the ceiling, twin bricks of sadness and regret pitted in my stomach. "I never got to collect any full-sized crystals from the vug."

"I snagged you a few," Heath replied, patting his bag.

"You did?" I asked, my eyes unexpectedly blurring with tears.

"Yes. If—er, *when* we get out of here, I'll give them to you. Are you still feeling nauseous?"

"Nauseated," I corrected reflexively. "Nauseous is the thing that *causes* the nausea, like 'venomous.'"

Heath gave me a look that I was pretty sure meant, "Seriously?!"

I cleared my throat self-consciously. "Sorry. Old habit."

"Yeah, let's save the syntax lessons for *non*-life-threatening situations." He shifted Topie in his arm, using the beam from his headlamp as a flashlight. "Where the hell is the shaft?"

I had to squint, as my own headlamp was nearly dead and barely producing any light. "I think we're about halfway there."

Heath cursed under his breath.

Speeding up to a jog, we turned the corner, only to come to a stumbling halt as a wall of boulders and broken wood greeted us. By now, the water was up to our waists.

"Great," I muttered, rubbing my throbbing temples.

"Laney…" Heath started, turning toward me. "If we can clear a hole just big enough for me to hoist you and Topie through, I can stay back and refill the opening with rocks. That way you and Topie can have a running start before the water—"

"Don't be an idiot!" I snapped. "I didn't save your life just for you to die again."

He took that opportunity to launch into some speech about how it was his fault we were trapped down here, so he therefore had to do everything he possibly could to get me out alive, blah, blah, blah. I wasn't paying him an iota of attention. Having reached the end of my mental inventory of remaining potions – none of which could help us – I found myself turning in a slow circle, searching for any practical means of escape. But there was nothing except fallen rocks and rising water in our vicinity.

We were trapped.

Desperation mounting, my eyes landed once more on the strange crystals growing on the walls. It was risky – life-threatening even – since I had no idea what type of mineral it was, let alone what it'd do to me. But I was already going to die; what difference did it make if it was by drowning or, say, spontaneous combustion?

"Laney, if you would just—" Heath turned to look at me just as I was breaking off a small, green crystal from the matrix and popping it in my mouth. "Hey—*stop!* What are you doing?!"

I continued to ignore him as I sucked on the crystal, scrutinizing the odd flavor combination of black licorice and freshly-mowed grass, with a strong hint of something tangy that was reminiscent of arsenopyrite. I turned the crystal over with my tongue, drawing the essence into my tastebuds the way a wine connoisseur might enjoy a vintage merlot.

Green, crystalline, arsenic-heavy... "I think it's euchroite," I murmured, puckering my cheeks, "which shouldn't glow, so I'm guessing it's got some sort of radioactive impurity – traces of natural uranium, perhaps."

"Are you telling me you just swallowed arsenic and *uranium?!*" Heath was clutching Topie against his chest, just above the water level, and staring at me in horror. "If you're looking for a quick and painless way to die, that isn't it!"

"I'm not trying to kill myself." I closed my eyes, concentrating on any potential changes in my body, which didn't feel any different than before. "Every mineral in the world possesses its own kind of 'magic,' so to speak. By eating the euchroite, I can extract its essence and harness it. That's how I saved your life today and how I was able to heal your head injury last night." A fresh pang of guilt slithered into my warming belly. "It's also the real reason I couldn't sleep with you. I was worried you were still under the influence of the apatite potion, which is how I manipulated you into believing that I *hadn't* fed you toxic minerals, when I had." I took a deep breath, wishing

I still had tiger's eye in my tummy for bravery, and forced my eyes open to look at him.

"AUUGHHH!" I screeched, staggering backwards.

"What?!" the skeleton standing in front of me demanded, while the pig skeleton in its arms recoiled from me as though *I* were the one who had turned into talking bones. I held my hand in front of my face and let out a shrill yelp at the sight of my own, wiggling phalanges.

"What is it?" Heath grabbed my right shoulder, turning me toward him. Despite his bare-bones appearance, his hand felt solid and soft, to my immense relief. For a minute there, I was worried I'd eaten some sort of radioactive mineral and accidentally melted off our skin. "Laney, what—"

"Am I me or a skeleton?" I demanded, avoiding the hollowed-out gray cavities of his eye sockets.

"Huh?"

"Okay, so it's just me." Poking at the black, translucent skin on my palms, I took a few deep breaths, trying to get my bearings. From what I could gather, I had developed some sort of monochromatic x-ray vision, which made the hardest, densest parts of our bodies – i.e., our teeth and bones – appear pale gray and softer parts fade into varying shades of black. Blinking rapidly, I looked around the tunnel, which was no longer dimly-illuminated by my failing headlamp, but had transformed into stark black and white angles and shapes that didn't fade in brightness with distance. The rapidly rising water – which was now nearly to my shoulder – was almost invisible, nothing more than a gauzy black shadow.

Heath's increasingly agitated voice scarcely registered in my head as I held up my hand – doing my best to ignore the disconcerting sight of my own skeleton – and rested it atop a bright white section of exposed rock. When I pushed on it, it didn't budge. My hand slid across the wall, until it was hovering above a nearly-black section of rotting wood. This time, when I pushed, the wood gave away easily. Shaking Heath off of me, I shoved my entire shoulder against the crumbling black wall with all my might, falling straight through the other side. The water burst into the hole I'd created, nearly carrying me away with it, but I managed to regain my footing with the help of a nearby decaying beam.

"Laney!" Heath shouted, stumbling after me. "Are you—" He let out a ragged gasp. "What is this? Another tunnel?"

As water rushed to fill the new cavity, its depth receded to just beneath my breasts. But it wouldn't stay there for long, not with the amount of water that was rapidly gushing into the tight, narrow space. I whipped my head around, looking for more dark areas, when my gaze settled on a dark-gray spot on the ceiling about ten feet away. "Come on!" I shouted to Heath, dragging him by his exposed phalanges while his other arm still cradled a skeleton pig. When we were directly underneath the black spot, I turned to look at him, shuddering at the sight of his featureless skull.

If we died down here, that's all we would become: nameless, faceless piles of bones.

"Delaney, what are you—"

I pressed my fingertips to his lips, gently tracing the small cleft on his chin and the angular line of this jaw before cupping his warm, soft cheek... He was still here, flesh, blood, and breath.

Heath caught my hand in his, pressing his lips to my knuckles. "Laney," he whispered softly, "I just want you to know—"

"There's no time for that!" I roughly spun him around, then scrambled onto his back without waiting for his assent. "Hoist me up!"

Being the cooperative, accommodating man I had come to know, he allowed me to climb him like a tree, with nary a protest nor complaint. Narrowly avoiding kicking Topie in the face, I swung my legs over Heath's shoulders and sat atop them.

"What are you doing up there?" he grunted, wobbling precariously.

"Stand still!" Using his shoulders for leverage, I pressed my palms against the low ceiling and shoved with all my might. The loose dirt and clay showered down on us, exposing a gaping hole in the ceiling.

Heath coughed and spat clumps of dirt from his mouth. "How did you—"

"Euchroite! Now pass me Topie!"

Heath did as I asked, nearly losing his balance before steadying himself on a nearby wooden plank.

"Be careful, that beam is rotted in the middle!" I warned him. "All right, Topie," I grunted as I shoved him through the hole, "go three feet to the right, then stop!"

"Reee!" His hooves struggled against the loose dirt and rocks, but he eventually managed to get himself up and in.

I glanced down, where the mine water was now lapping against Heath's shoulders. "I need you to push me through, then I'm going to lie on my stomach and pull you up, okay?"

He let out an affirming grunt, placing his hands under my butt to push me while I groped at anything that could be used as a handhold. Finally, and with a lot of helpful shoving from Heath, I managed to hoist myself into the hole I'd created – an upper tunnel that was not yet flooded, but soon would be. I army crawled on my stomach until I made it to the portion of the floor that was light gray instead of dark gray, then shimmied myself around on scraped knees and elbows until I was peering down the hole at Heath.

"Give me your hand!" I called down to him.

Water was rushing over his shoulders and threatening to spill into his mouth as he started to reach for me, only to pull his hand away at the last second.

"What are you doing?" I shouted, thrusting my hand at him. "Take my hand!"

"Just go!" he shouted back. "That floor won't hold the weight of us both!"

"Heath Spencer!" I roared. "If you don't give me your hand *right this instant* I will jump back in there and get you!"

"Don't you da—" His retort was cut off by a series of waterlogged coughs as the gushing torrent surged above his chin.

"Shut up and give me your hand!" I screamed, thrusting my arm at him.

With a pained grimace, his hand shot out of the water and gripped mine.

"Now your other hand!" I shouted.

Heath did as he was told, locking both of his hands around my wrists. "Now what?!"

"Put your right foot on the wall directly in front of you!" I instructed him, eyeing the light gray rock. "Now, on the count of three, plant your left foot on the wall right beside it and start climbing. I'll help pull you up!"

"You'll never be able to—" He again broke off as water rushed into his mouth, eliciting a fresh series of violent, sputtering coughs.

As he loosened his grip around my wrists, I tightened mine. "Don't you *dare* let go!" I shouted down to him. "On the count of three, just shut up and climb!" I carefully shimmied into a seated position with my hands reaching between my splayed knees and braced myself. "One… Two… *Three!*"

Heath planted both of his feet against the wall, the added weight of his body nearly dragging us both down. As I pitched forward, Topie snatched the hem of my shirt and tugged as hard as he could. With his help – more emotional than physical – I pulled Heath's wrists toward me, using my shaking legs as leverage. By now, the waters in the lower tunnel weren't just rising; they were *rushing*, a raging river actively trying to carry Heath away. His left hand slipped from my grasp, nearly sending him plummeting into the frothing current.

"No!" I snatched his right hand in both of mine, holding onto him with every ounce of dwindling strength I possessed.

"Laney!" Heath groaned, his free arm fumbling at crumbling rock. "You've got to let go!"

"I promised you I wouldn't let you fall, and I won't!" I grunted, tugging on his arm as hard as I could. "Now come on! You've got this!"

With a strained groan, he swung his dangling legs for momentum and managed to catch his right foot on the edge of the hole. Seeing that, Topie let go of my shirt to grab at any accessible part of Heath's body he could.

"Ow!" he yelped as Topie "helped" lift him out of the tunnel via a mouthful of Heath's hair.

As his hand blindly fumbled for the nearest protrusion of rock, I reached out and grabbed his belt like a handle. Together, we all pulled as hard as we could, narrowly freeing Heath from the hole before tumbling backward in a somersaulting tangle of limbs.

The three of us lay on the ground for a long moment, panting and gasping and coughing, until the rising water started lapping at our boots – well, singular 'boot' in Heath's case, since he'd somehow lost his other one.

"This floor is going to collapse any minute," Heath rasped, yanking me to my feet. "We have to move!"

I looked around the tunnel anxiously, finding nothing but thin, dark rock beneath us and white, solid rock above.

"Run!" He pushed me forward.

We bolted at full speed through the upward-sloping tunnel for what felt like an hour but was probably only ten minutes. By then, my legs were desperate for celestine and my lungs were screaming for spinel. But I had neither, so my body was forced to rely on regular old Delaney, neither muscular nor athletic.

Among the many backfilled and caved-in tunnels of this three-dimensional labyrinth, we managed to find two intact shafts and continued ascending, until we reached a tiny adit with no entry nor exit – a hollow cavity, no bigger than ten feet on any side. Every surface of the hole was white or light gray, save for a tiny, dark-gray spot in the middle of the ceiling.

"Heath!" I wheezed, gesturing frantically.

He came to stand beside me while Topie literally collapsed to the ground, his legs splaying out like a starfish and his tongue lolling out of his mouth.

"Right there." I pointed at the ceiling just above my head. "It looks like shale and can't be more than a foot thick."

Instead of demanding how I could have possibly known that – as I no doubt would have, had our roles been reversed – Heath immediately began rummaging around his messenger bag for a chisel. As the euchroite essence in my system dwindled, the color of his skin was returning to normal – albeit flushed and glistening – and his bones were fading from sight. The details of the surrounding stone were coming back into focus as well, replacing the stark angles of black and white. As I shook my head, trying to clear it of the residual x-ray vision, my headlamp flickered and died, plunging us into utter blackness.

"Butternuts!" I groaned, blindly fumbling around for the nearest stone, which I then used to awkwardly thwack against the thinnest part of the ceiling, sending dirt and broken bits of rock raining down on my head.

After just a few seconds of rock-clacking, Heath gently moved me away and began hacking at the ceiling with what sounded like a metal chisel.

I gratefully slumped to the ground, too tired to stand. Hugging my knees, I leaned my head against the wall for support, enjoying the feel of cool stone on the flushed skin of my back. As dark as it was, there was no discernible difference between the darkness of the burrow and the back of my eyelids as they fluttered closed. "What I wouldn't give for a sapphire tonic," I murmured, smacking my dry, chapped lips. "Or any kind of liquid at all, for that matter."

Topie trotted over to nuzzle against my neck.

"You were so brave today," I whispered, pulling him close. "Best emotional support pig that ever lived." My eyelids fluttered closed again, too heavy to hold open as I listened to the steady *clack, clack, clack* of Heath's chisel. I dozed for some time, dreaming of deep black oceans and frightening, sharp-toothed monsters that lurked within it, their jaws snapping open and shut in the same unremitting *clack, clack, clack...*

At some point, Heath's chisel, as well as the massive angler fish chomping at my scuba fins, went silent. My eyes burst open just in time to see the ceiling crumble away and bright light pouring from the fresh hole.

"Uh, Laney?" Heath called, an odd pitch in his voice. "Would you come here please?"

Rising shakily to my feet, I held a hand in front of my squinted eyes as I approached the narrow shaft of blinding light illuminating Heath from above.

"Is that sunlight?" I asked, standing beside him.

"Er, well..."

I peered into the hole and let out a sharp gasp. It wasn't the sun shining above us, but a buzzing fluorescent light. Clapping a hand over my mouth, I turned to gape at Heath. "What the—"

A shadow crossed in front of the light, making both of us jerk our heads. An old man in a blue janitorial uniform was peering down, clutching a wet mop in two hands as though it were a weapon. *"Wa! Tiān a!"*

"Uh, *nǐ hǎo*..." Heath offered the man a polite finger wave. "How's it going?"

Chapter 24

As Heath, Topie, and I struggled to exhume ourselves from what used to be the perfectly-preserved, 2,500-year-old ruins in the heart of the Tonglushan Ancient Copper Mine Museum, the lone janitor gaped at us as though we were three of the five evil *wǔdú*. Meanwhile, the alarm we'd inadvertently set off was screeching like a piccolo forcing out a third-octave G-sharp. I winced at the noise, momentarily considering climbing back into the hole to escape it. Topie, however, couldn't wait to get out and was making his wishes known by screeching like a crazed monkey.

After plucking the squirming pig from my arms, Heath took both of my hands in his and pulled me from the hole in the floor. I collapsed against his chest with a grateful wheeze. By then, my lungs and limbs were aching so badly, I'd have given just about anything for a couple of shots of amber and howlite.

Heath held me for a brief moment before gently pulling away. "The two of you sit right here," he said, pointing to a horizontal slab of preserved wood. Then he turned to the janitor, asking, *"Wǒ kěyǐ jiè nǐ de shǒujī ma?"*

Slack-jawed and wide-eyed, the janitor handed Heath the cell phone from his pocket.

Heath thanked him, then punched in a few numbers. "Hi, Li." He spoke into the receiver. "I'm very sorry to bother you while you're visiting family, but would you mind coming down to the Tonglushan Museum? … Yes, I know they're closed for the holiday. But Miss Stone and I are about to be arrested, and I'd appreciate it a great deal if you could come and help translate. … Yes, ideally, the sooner the better. … Sorry?" he asked, rubbing his temples with his free hand. "Yes, you can definitely mark the expense at the holiday rate. See you soon. Thanks again." Heath turned toward the janitor, handing him back his phone. *"Xièxie nín."*

The janitor took it with a shaking hand, only to drop it when the doors to the museum flew open. As three Huangshi police officers burst into the museum, the janitor practically leapt out of the roped-off ruins to greet them, all the while shouting and gesticulating in our general direction. Without so much as giving the uniformed newcomers a second glance, Heath sat beside me on the calcified piece of wood I'd been using as a bench and put an arm around my shoulder.

I laid my head against him. "Think we could request a co-ed prison?"

"I can certainly inquire about it," Heath replied, kissing the top of my head. "Maybe then we can be cellmates."

"What about him?" I gestured at Topie, who – despite the cacophony of blaring alarms, chirping police radios, and yelping janitors – was fast asleep with his head in my lap.

"Hmm." Heath tapped his chin thoughtfully. "I can't imagine they'd allow pigs in a Chinese prison. Not unless they were meant to be served with fried noodles."

I grimaced.

"Which means we'd better switch to Plan B: Shameless Bribery." Heath's eyebrows waggled mischievously.

"Bribery?" I echoed. "With what? My wallet is sitting at the bottom of a flooded mine a hundred feet below us."

With a crooked smirk the old Delaney might have tried to wipe off his face, but present-day Delaney couldn't help but find endearing, Heath reached into his messenger bag. "Think ancient Hunnic treasure will be enough to whet their whistles?" he asked, withdrawing a shoebox-sized bronze chest. Despite the layer of verdigris[17] that betrayed its age, the chest was beautifully decorated with colored pieces of enamel that were shaped like two eagles and held in place by thin gold wire. The eagles' outstretched talons were reaching for a miniature golden sword in the center of the chest, which had been inserted in a jade-and-gold latch to keep the lid closed.

My mouth tumbled open in shock.

"This is what I pulled out of the tunnel wall," he explained, turning the chest over in his hands. "And seeing as it nearly killed me, I can't help but wonder if the gold might actually be cursed."

"G-Gold?" I stammered. "As in…?"

---

[17] The green patina that naturally forms on bronze. The ancient Hunnic technique for decorating metalwork objects with enamel and gold strips is known as "cloisonné."

Heath withdrew the miniature sword from its latch and cracked open the lid, displaying the tiniest sliver of glinting yellow coins. "Today seems like the perfect day to break Dengizich's family curse. Wouldn't you agree?"

I opened my mouth to answer just as the museum alarms fell silent.

Heath and I turned to see an old man in a dark suit shouldering his way through the throng of police officers that had gathered above us. When his eyes landed on the gaping hole in the center of the 2,500-year-old ruins, and the American man, woman, and pig casually lounging beside it, they nearly doubled in size.

"HEATH SPENCER!" he bellowed. *"WHAT IS THE MEANING OF THIS?"*

"Who's that?" I squeaked, clinging to Heath's arm. "And how does he know your name?"

"That's Zhao Míng, the head curator of the museum," he whispered back.

I palmed my forehead and groaned. "Oh, we are *so* going to prison."

Flashing me a wink that was probably meant to be reassuring, Heath rose to his feet, cradling the bronze chest under one arm. "Hello, Mr. Zhao! Long time no see!"

 Mr. Zhao switched to Chinese as he angrily stomped toward us, hurling a red-faced, spittle-flinging diatribe at the younger man. I didn't recognize many words because he was rapid-firing them at the top of his lungs, but I did manage to pick out "father," "America," "police," and either "clock" or "death."

I fervently hoped it was the former.

Heath, who had carefully made his way through the ancient ruins and was now climbing under the velvet ropes that were meant to keep riffraff like us out, took Mr. Zhao's rant in stride, neither arguing nor defending himself.

"Why is he always so *nice?*" I scrubbed a hand down my face, groaning. "Come on, Topes." He made an annoyed grunt as I scooped him under my arm. "Heath needs our help."

Clutching my emotional support pig against my chest while he squirmed like a toddler, I retraced Heath's steps, taking great pains not to disturb the millennia-old ruins – minus the large portion we'd already destroyed. Heath flashed me a tight smile as I ducked under the exhibit rope and came to stand beside him. Mr. Zhao, on the other hand, barely glanced in my direction as he continued his furious tirade, which seemingly had no end. It was only when the museum doors banged open again and Li rushed inside that Mr. Zhao paused for breath.

"I here, Mr. Spencer, I here!" Li shouted, adjusting his lopsided chauffeur cap and tie.

The officers reached for the batons on their hips, making my breath catch, but they relaxed as Li pulled some sort of fancy document from his breast pocket and waved it in the air. Mr. Zhao turned back to Heath, resuming his shrill invective as though he hadn't been interrupted, while the janitor and three officers remained silent, exchanging only what appeared to be bemused looks.

"Li!" I called, setting Topie on the ground to motion him over.

"Miss Stone—!" He stopped in his tracks. "What in *hell* happened to you?"

"Er…" I took a moment to take stock of myself. My mud- and blood-caked leather pants were torn at the knees, my tank top was in tatters, and an assortment of scrapes and bruises peppered both of my arms from wrist to shoulder. Poor Heath looked even worse than me, sporting a deep gash over his left eyebrow, large purple bruises on his chest and arms, and a missing boot. Topie, however, had survived the day's perils completely unscathed and had even managed to keep his backpack and beloved stuffie intact.

Li took several cautious steps in our direction, his eyes nearly doubling in size when they landed on the gaping hole in the center of the ruins. "What the—"

"We'll explain everything," I interjected, "but right now I need you to translate what Mr. Zhao is shouting at Heath!"

He glanced at the gaggle of police officers who were watching us with stern expressions and crossed arms, then let out a long sigh. "Mr. Spencer not pay me enough for this job."

"Li!"

"Okay, okay!" He listened to the old man's belligerent shouts for a few moments. "Mr. Zhao saying, 'I should have police officers make arrest right now for damage you cause museum. If your father still alive he die from shame of what you did!'"

"Hey—" I took an angry step toward Mr. Zhao, ready to jump to Heath's defense.

"Ah, ah, ah!" Li grabbed me by the arm, yanking me back. "You let Mr. Spencer talk! He dragon, very *yǒu měilì*. You rat – good heart but big mouth! If you talk, you and Mr. Spencer for sure go to jail!"

Topie nudged my hand, nodding his agreement.

"Fine," I muttered, grinding my teeth. "What's Zhao saying now?"

"*Mister* Zhao still talking about damage and money…" He paused as Heath finally managed to sneak in a few words, then translated, "Mr. Spencer asking for officer bring water for you. He very worried for you."

"He should be worrying about himself, not me!" I groused, even as a warm surge of gratitude filled my chest.

Heath continued to speak to Mr. Zhao, calmly gesturing in my direction.

Li let out a sharp gasp. "Mr. Spencer say you and he almost die! Is it true?"

"He *did* die," I muttered, gripping the chalcopyrite ball that had miraculously survived in my pocket. "His heart stopped for several minutes."

"*Āi yā!*" Li clapped a hand over his mouth. "He say you saved his life!" When he turned to look at me this time, he had a huge grin on his face.

"How is that funny?" I demanded.

Li squinted one eye and shook a finger at me. "You see? Li knows! My mother always say, 'If Li born a girl he make perfect matchmaker!'"

"We don't need a matchmaker!" I blustered, cheeks burning. "What we need is a translator!"

"No, what *you* need is *Su Nü Jing!*"

My jaw dropped. "*Why* on *Earth* would I need a book about Taoist sexual practices?!"

He gave me a pointed look, which I of course had no way of deciphering.

Mercifully, an officer came over and handed me two bottles of water just then, one and a half of which I downed within seconds. The remaining half I offered to Topie, who rolled over on his back, clutched the bottle between his front hooves, and did the same.

For some reason, the janitor and police officers seemed to get a kick out of that.

After clearing his throat, Li resumed his interpreter duties. "'Mr. Zhao, I very sorry for the damage we caused museum. I will do everything I can to make right. But first I have to tell to you something important – very more important than ancient ruins.'"

Mr. Zhao crossed his arms over his chest, looking no less displeased as Heath knelt beside the square-shaped glass panel embedded in the floor, where the remains of the nameless miner and his tools had been preserved.

Frowning, Li turned to me. "What can be more important than ruins?" His eyes widened. "Oh! Are you and Mr. Spencer having baby?"

"I—what?" I sputtered. "No!!"

Heath shot us an inscrutable look. "Would you mind?"

"Mind what?" I whispered to Li, who shrugged.

"Fifty years ago," Heath told Mr. Zhao, switching back to English, "my father invited you to the Smithsonian Museum, where you gave a lecture series on ancient Chinese mining methods. Afterward, you invited him to the Tonglushan archeological site so he could witness the excavation of the tunnels that are preserved here today."

Mr. Zhao's eyes narrowed. "Preserved *until* today."

"Oof," I muttered, pinching the bridge of my nose.

"And I again apologize for the damage we've inadvertently caused," Heath replied calmly. "But if you could just give me a few more minutes of your patience, I promise it will all be worth it."

"Worth *hundreds of thousands* of yuan's worth of damages?!" Mr. Zhao barked.

I walked over to nudge Heath in the side. "Better stick with the short version, and not the director's cut," I muttered under my breath.

"Agreed." He nodded, then cleared his throat. "Because of your kindness, Mr. Zhao, my father was able to witness a once-in-a-lifetime archeological miracle: the excavation of this ancient miner and his tools."

Mr. Zhao uncrossed his arms. "Yes, and we are very grateful for Norman's contributions to this museum, but that does not absolve you of your crime today!"

"Nor should it," Heath answered quickly.

"Then what—"

"Mr. Zhao, you gave my father the greatest experience of his life, one he would talk about for decades to come. It's one of the reasons he donated so much money to your museum, even when my family was struggling financially."

I drew in a sharp intake of breath. I'd always assumed Heath – with his fancy designer suits and lines of deep-pocketed tourists banging down the door of his mineral shop – had always been wealthy. And not once during the many hours we'd spent talking about maps and minerals, had Norm ever mentioned anything about financial problems…

Or had he? I anxiously wrung the damp, tattered hem of my shirt. Sure, he would lament about his failing business, and how it didn't make any money. But at his age, I'd just assumed the shop was a post-retirement hobby meant to entertain his love of rocks and minerals, not to put food on the table.

Clearly, I'd been wrong – *very* wrong – about many things.

"Butternuts," I whispered, knuckling my forehead. I'd spoken with Norm more than just about anybody else over the years, so eager were we to natter on at one another about all the things we loved; it only now occurred to me how few questions I'd asked during all that time.

"As much as my father was grateful to you, Mr. Zhao, I believe the reason he donated as much to you as he did was not due to gratitude, but guilt."

"Guilt?" Mr. Zhao repeated.

I frowned. *Guilt about what?* My eyes darted from Heath to the nameless miner he was crouched beside... and then everything clicked into place. For the first time ever, I knew what Heath was going to say next, and my heart broke for him.

"Hey." I put my hand on his shoulder and gave it a reassuring squeeze, something Mrs. Lautner always did when I was having a rough day. "You've got this."

Heath reached up and gripped my hand, flashing me a grateful smile. Then he took a deep breath and said, "My father was a good man. But he made a terrible mistake, something I've come here to try and rectify."

Try "to" rectify, I thought, making a mental note to correct Heath later – assuming we got sent to the same prison, that is.

"Mr. Zhao, the day you unearthed this 'nameless' miner was the same day my father robbed you of something precious"—maintaining a tight grip on my hand, Heath rose to look the older man in the eye—"a piece of parchment that had fallen from the miner's pouch."

Mr. Zhao's face turned several shades of red, the vein in his temple visibly throbbing. "I must have misunderstood you just now… Did you say *robbed?*"

"Oh, shit," Li hissed under his breath. "Now Mr. Spencer *really* go to prison."

"I did." Heath nodded. "In my defense, I knew of this letter and its contents for many years, because my father often spoke of it, but I didn't know it was stolen until the day he died."

Mr. Zhao's mouth fluttered open and shut, but no words came out. As his cheeks went from red to purple, I mentally recited the warning signs of a stroke: speech difficulty, confusion, face drooping, and arm weakness. So far, he was only displaying two out of four.

"Before you start shouting again, Mr. Zhao, please know that my father spent his entire life combing through hundreds of historical documents, tracking down the names, dates, and events contained in that letter. I'm not telling you this to excuse his behavior, but rather so you'll believe me when I tell you that this miner"—Heath gestured to the bones in the floor—"had a name… And that name was Jinshan."

Mr. Zhao, Li, the janitor, and the three police officers all let out audible gasps.

"More than a name," Heath continued, "Jinshan had a story: Abandoned by his mother as an infant, he was adopted by farmers, grew up to become a copper miner, and later died in these tunnels trying to protect his wife and unborn child."

"Protect them from what?" Mr. Zhao whispered through steepled fingers.

"From this." Heath knelt to the ground to retrieve the colorful bronze chest that had nearly killed him.

Mr. Zhao gaped at it as though he hadn't noticed it until now.

"Years before Jinshan was born, his father, Dengizich, betrayed his comrades and stole this, incurring a lifelong curse that was passed down to his son." He straightened his shoulders and lifted his chin to look Mr. Zhao in the eye. "Like Dengizich, my father betrayed and stole from you, Mr. Zhao – an unforgivable action that haunted him until his dying day. He spent the rest of his life trying to find this treasure in hopes of returning it to you and righting his wrong. Today, I hope to bring both my father and Jinshan peace by finishing what they started."

Mr. Zhao made a choking sound as Heath opened the chest, revealing a mound of glinting gold coins, a small bejeweled knife in a jade sheath, at least a dozen pieces of heavy gold jewelry, and what appeared to be a ruby-encrusted gold seal. The older man took a ginger step forward, followed by another, his fingers cautiously creeping toward the open chest. Plucking one of the coins from the top, he held it up to the light and let out a sharp gasp. "*Roman* gold? But how…?"

"This chest was stolen from Attila the Hun, who received large sums of Roman gold—"

"—as tribute for not besieging the Eastern Roman Empire," Mr. Zhao finished, his eyes growing ever wider. He took another step closer, delicately lifting what appeared to be a gold tiara from the chest. "There are six known Hunnish diadems in the world, which means this could be—wait." Replacing the diadem, he took the ruby-encrusted gold seal with two shaking hands and turned the handle over, exposing an embossed sword that had been carved into the flattened portion of the seal. It was encircled by a language I'd never seen before. A cry slipped from Mr. Zhao's lips as he sank to his knees. "*Az Isten kardja*," he mumbled, looking up at Heath with tears in his eyes. "The sword of God."

Heath pressed a hand to his mouth.

"What does that mean?" I asked, looking between the two of them.

It took Mr. Zhao a few moments to speak. "This…is the seal of Attila the Hun. The very seal he used to mark his word and send orders to his men." Closing his eyes, he brought the ruby to his trembling lips. "There has not been a more profound discovery in centuries – perhaps even millennia."

Without another word, the old man scrambled to his feet, dropping into the lowest bow I'd seen yet. "Heath Spencer, you have my gratitude…and your father has my forgiveness." He went to clasp Heath's hand, but Heath held it up to stop him.

"While I appreciate the sentiment, Mr. Zhao, I would have been dead at the bottom of a subterranean lake if it weren't for my *very* dear friend, Delaney Stone. Had she not risked her life to save mine, my father's lifelong quest for redemption would have been in vain, and Tonglushan's ancient miner would have remained nameless."

Mr. Zhao turned to face me, dropping into an even *lower* bow. "Miss Stone, as a small token of our gratitude, the Tonglushan Museum's new Hunnic treasures exhibit shall be named in your honor."

"Oh, that's really not necessary," I started, only to get elbowed in the ribs by Li.

"Say thank you," he muttered through smiling, gritted teeth.

"Uh, th-thank you," I quickly stammered. "But, there's actually something else I'd like…if that's okay."

Li shot me a look of death, but Mr. Zhao just clasped my hand in his and said, "Anything. All you have to do is name your price."

"Oh, no, I don't want your money." My hand went to my pocket to grip my favorite worry stone. "I was wondering… Would it be possible for Heath and me to get a tour of the active Tonglushan Mine? There are some minerals in there that I'd *really* like to ta—er, see."

Mr. Zhao gave me a funny look, making me wonder if I'd offended him. "Sorry, I must have misunderstood you." He shook his head and chuckled. "You nearly died while exploring a mine today, but I could have sworn you asked to go inside *another* mine—"

"She did," Heath said, standing close beside me.

"Oh." Mr. Zhao frowned. "Well, I…I suppose that would be fine… If that's really what you want?"

"It's what I want more than anything. Well…" I turned to Heath, smiling widely enough to show my teeth. "Almost anything."

"Oh?" He drew me in by the wrist, then wrapped his other arm around my waist to pull me even closer. "And what on Earth could possibly be more important than minerals, Miss Stone?"

I pressed my lips into a coy smile. "Oh, I think you know."

"Well, I have my theories. Or should I say 'hypotheses'?"

"Definitely a theory." I drew myself up on my tiptoes, brushing my lips against his. "And a sound one at that."

Chapter 25

By some stroke of luck – or, more likely, Heath's remarkable gift for charming his way out of trouble – we weren't carted off to prison. We were, however, held captive at the museum for several hours while Mr. Zhao and the police officers filled out their respective incident reports. Tired and hungry as we were, the drawn-out, simultaneous interrogations would have been unbearable had Mr. Zhao's wife not arrived with a delicious dinner of spicy braised duck and lotus root soup. She was even kind enough to bring me a spare change of clothes, though the cotton pants came up to my ankles and the t-shirt barely covered my stomach. Heath kept sneaking glances at my exposed navel and flashing me unapologetic winks whenever I caught him – not that I actually minded. Truth be told, I was eyeing his aesthetically-pleasing state of undress every chance I got, since his tattered sleeveless shirt left *very* little to the imagination.

When it came time to show the full contents of Jinshan's letter to Mr. Zhao, Heath and I were momentarily confounded. Both of our cell phones had been ruined in the flood, and local firewalls prevented Heath from logging into his email or accessing cloud storage. Fortunately, Heath was able to call in a favor from yet another of his rich and powerful friends – this time, the governor of Hubei himself – who gave the officers permission to set up a temporary VPN and allow Heath remote access to his files. Once we'd finally managed to retrieve a photo of Jinshan's letter, Mr. Zhao leaned toward the computer monitor, gasping audibly. He mumbled under his breath as he slowly worked out the weathered symbols, his eyes growing wider and shinier as he read.

"This is remarkable," he kept repeating every few minutes. "Absolutely remarkable." When he finished, he turned to Heath with tears glistening in his eyes. "You said you have the original parchment in your care back home? And you're sure it's secure?"

"Yes." Heath nodded. "It's in an airtight safe. I wouldn't feel comfortable mailing or traveling overseas with it, but I would be happy to give it to you directly, if you'd like to accompany me back to Maine."

"Of course," Mr. Zhao said fervently. "The sooner the better." His eyes darted to me. "But not before you've had a chance to tour the active mine! I've already arranged it with the Nonferrous Metal Mining Group. Their night crew is ready for you now, unless you'd prefer to clean up and get some rest first?"

"Now, please!" I chimed, ignoring my own jaw-cracking yawn. "I've been waiting my entire life to see some of these minerals!"

"Then let's not keep you waiting another moment," Mr. Zhao said with a warm smile. "If it's all right with you, I'd like to come as well. It's been quite some time since I went down there."

"It would be our pleasure," Heath replied, putting an arm around my shoulder. "Right, Laney?"

I nodded, though truth be told, I didn't care if the ghost of Attila himself accompanied us; I just wanted to hurry up and go. Thankfully, the three police officers had completed their report and were just finishing their accompanying collection of photos, several of which included peace-sign-flashing selfies of themselves and the janitor standing beside the hole we'd dug into the floor of the museum. After roping Heath, Topie, and I into joining them for a few photos, the officers finally told us we were free to go.

Li drove Mr. Zhao, Heath, Topie, and me to the reopened construction site, where the night workers were just arriving with their lunch pails in tow. After giving each of us our own set of N95 masks, hard hats, and reflective orange vests – and an extra boot for Heath – the shift boss loaded us into his truck. He then personally drove us down the long winding road to the main entrance, excitedly chattering with Li and Mr. Zhao in the front seat while Heath, Topie, and I dozed in the empty hauler. But as soon as we entered the main haul tunnel – a massive, floodlight-illuminated, steel-reinforced spectacle of modern machinery – my exhaustion was immediately replaced by excitement and adrenaline. The shift boss drove us around the entire operation, allowing us to get out of the truck every so often to examine the assortment of sparkling crystals growing alongside the copper ore. He even pretended to turn a blind eye when Heath and I wandered off to collect some of the nicest crystal specimens for ourselves. Just like Heath had said, the CNMMG didn't care about "worthless" mine byproducts like malachite, calcite, chalcopyrite, and fluorite. Fortunately, their oversight was our gain.

By the time Li dropped us off at the motel several hours later – by then, nearly one in the morning – Heath and I had each collected several buckets' worth of crystals, which Li dutifully helped us haul into the hotel.

"Thank you for your help today," Heath told him from the doorway of our motel room, after all the minerals had been carted inside. "And I'm very sorry again for cutting your vacation short."

"Oh, holiday rate more than make up for it." Li beamed at him, then turned to me, his eyes twinkling. "Miss Stone, now that Dragon Boat Festival over, buses and taxis running again. Would you like me take you to different hotel now?"

"I…er…" I glanced up at Heath, who seemed to be keeping his face carefully composed. "Well, I would, but we've still got a bunch of minerals to sort through, so…"

Li nodded. "Oh yes, mineral sorting very important." He flashed Heath a quick wink – odd, since he hadn't made an accompanying joke – then fixed me with a stern look. "You listen to me, Miss Delaney Stone. Sometime it hard for Rats to find perfect match, because they so stubborn and always complaining, like you."

"Now hang on, Li—" Heath started.

"But when they find their true person," Li continued breezily, "they become better lover than Pig, more loyal than Dog, and more passionate romancer than even Horse." He paid no mind to the broiling flush in my cheeks as he gripped me by the shoulder and looked me square in the eye. "Just remember: *ài wū jí wū*. Love the house *and* its crow." Then, radiating an air of self-importance – as though he'd just imparted some great wisdom unto me rather than idiomatic gobbledygook – he spun on his heel, whistling a jaunty tune to himself, and returned to the car.

We watched in silence as Li drove away, Heath with a crooked half-smile on his face, and me with a puzzled frown. I would have to figure out Li's bizarre Chinese riddle another time, however; right now, there were new minerals to examine.

While Heath and I carefully removed the crystals from the buckets and laid them out on the floor to marvel at, Topie went straight to bed, where he nuzzled against his Piglet stuffie and was loudly snoring less than a minute later. Tempted as I was to make him shower and brush his teeth, I instead kissed him on the snout, covered him with a blanket, and let him sleep in peace. In the larger context of having nearly died that day, teeth-brushing could wait – at least for one night.

Pig successfully wrapped in blanket, I grabbed a pair of white cotton gloves from my bag and settled on the floor to admire several of my new minerals: four clusters of perfectly spherical, interconnected chalcopyrite balls; a deep green botryoidal malachite stalactite, and a brand-new, flawless, double-terminated, rose-colored calcite crystal, to name a few.

"I might have to keep this one for my personal collection," I murmured to myself, holding the water-clear calcite crystal up to the light. "It's too nice to be turned into a potion."

"About that…" Heath started, settling in beside me. He reached into his messenger bag, retrieving a breathtaking cluster of opaque, emerald-green euchroite crystals, some of which were nearly a foot in length, and handed it to me.

My jaw dropped as he gently placed it in my gloved hands; I had never seen anything so beautiful in my entire life. "Th-This is for me?"

"It is, quite literally, the very least I can do to repay you for saving my life." He chewed on his lip, a crease appearing between his eyebrows. "And now that we finally have a quiet moment to ourselves, I was hoping you'd tell me how you did it."

"How I did it?" I parroted, my voice rising a full octave.

"Mm-hmm. For example, these so-called 'magic' potions of yours. You didn't mean that literally"—he leaned toward me, resting his chin on his fist—"did you?"

"Oh, I…uh…" I chewed on my lip, internally grappling with myself. While my intention had been to tell Heath the truth, part of me wanted to pretend it had all been another long, elaborate joke – a glorified feghoot, of sorts – lest Heath think I was a freak.

"Earlier, if you recall, we agreed that full transparency would be based on the state of our friendship. Given everything we've been through together, would you concur that we are, in fact, friends?" He leaned even closer, sending my pulse racing and my serotonin receptors into overdrive. "Perhaps even more than friends?"

I gulped. "Yes, well…it's n-not that simple."

"Well, what does your heart tell you?"

Finding myself hopelessly lost in the deep blue pools of his irises, I squeezed my eyes shut. "It's my heart that's the problem!"

And it was true; I couldn't rely on instinct or emotion, not with Heath's obnoxiously-attractive face and stupid, mouthwatering pheromones clouding my judgment. Right now, what I needed was science – cold, hard facts to help me determine a hypothesis and accompanying course of action. By that logic, and using the most basic of if/then statements, my conclusion would be simple: If Heath was truly my friend, then I would have to tell him the truth – which meant my first course of action was to prove my working theory: *A friend is someone you can be your authentic, true self around. Someone who will always be there for you and never hurt your feelings. Someone with whom you can share all of your secrets without fear of them abandoning you.*

"Laney?" Heath asked.

"Give me thirty seconds," I replied. "I need to work out a problem in my head."

"Oh, well, in that case, take your time."

"I will, thank you." I rubbed my temples, still scrunching my eyes shut.

Hypothesis 1: A friend is someone you can be your authentic, true self around.

The data to support this was overwhelming. In the entire time we'd known each other, Heath had only ever encouraged me to be myself around him: flaws, faults, and all.

Hypothesis 2: A friend is someone who will always be there for you and never hurt your feelings.

Supporting evidence: Heath never made me feel like I wasn't good enough. If anything, he made me feel better than I was, lifting me up during my lowest moments instead of leaving me to wallow in them. And during these last few days in particular, he'd seen the least attractive parts of me – overwhelmed, agitated, insecure, weepy, waterlogged, nauseated, and hysterical – and still hadn't run for the hills.

Hypothesis 3: A friend is someone with whom you can share all of your secrets without fear of them abandoning you.

And there was the rub; the singular unknown variable that threatened to derail the entire experiment. Yes, Heath had seen me at my worst, and no, he'd never made me feel bad about myself or given up on me. If anything, he'd been *too* accepting and forgiving of my past behavior. But would he have stuck around this long if he'd known the *whole* truth about me? Heck, would he have even believed me if I'd told him? *This* was the final, untested hypothesis to determine whether or not Heath was truly my friend. And in order to properly test it, I would have to conduct the most dangerous part of the experiment without first having all the facts, stumbling blindly into the unknown…

Just like trying a new mineral without having any idea of what it might do, I thought, somewhat emboldened by the realization.

Taking a deep, steeling breath, I looked Heath in the eye. "Yes." I nodded. "I meant it literally. My potions really are magic – well, 'parascientific,' as I like to call them."

He stared at me for a long moment, his smooth, unflinching expression not disclosing a single hint about his underlying thoughts. Even his eyebrows, which I'd come to rely on for valuable clues, remained motionless.

With every second of silence that ticked by, I became more and more afraid; afraid of being spurned, of being rejected…and worst of all, afraid of losing him. Having experienced a glimpse of life with Heath Spencer, the alternative suddenly seemed unbearable.

He cleared his throat, making my breath hitch in my chest. As he opened his mouth to speak, it took every ounce of courage I had to maintain eye contact.

"Would you show me?" he asked softly.

The breath I'd been holding rushed out in a heavy sigh of relief. He wasn't spurning *or* rejecting me. Like a true scientist, Heath was asking for evidence – and I loved him all the more for it.

Wordlessly setting the euchroite on the ground, I stood up, took off my gloves, and walked over to my suitcase, which still contained most of my travel potions. After a minute or two of careful consideration, I retrieved a vial of colorless, clear liquid from my kit, took a tiny sip, then turned off the bedside lamp. For a brief moment, we were shrouded in total darkness… And then – though not from any lamp or bulb – the room was once again flooded with light.

Heath's eyes grew as round as quarters as I sat beside him, my entire body lit up like a glow stick.

"Hyalite opal makes my skin glow," I told him, half-expecting him to scoot away, but he stayed perfectly still. "Celestine gives me super strength, spinel helps me hold my breath for long periods of time, and chalcopyrite, I've recently learned, allows me to see diseases in the body… like hemochromatosis, for example."

Heath sucked in a deep breath, then let it out slowly. "And euchroite?"

"A kind of x-ray vision, I think, which is what helped me find the weakest, thinnest sections of the tunnel."

Slowly, tentatively, he reached forward and took my glowing hand in his, examining it.

I chewed on the inside of my cheek, wishing I had some Inner Mongolian red fluorite to tell me what he was thinking. "The effect doesn't last very long, just a few minutes. But it does come in handy when my headlamp burns out…or when I've been asked to prove I'm not crazy." It was meant to be a joke, but my heart was thrumming too quickly for me to muster a laugh. "Do you…" I swallowed tightly, bracing myself for what was to come. "Do you think I'm a freak?"

Heath gently ran a finger across my palm, sending a thrill down my spine. "No," he murmured, lifting his gaze to mine. "I think you're absolutely remarkable."

Tears pricked at the corners of my eyes.

"I've been waiting a long time for you to come around," he said softly, "so it's going to take a lot more than glowing skin to scare me away."

A sound somewhere between a sob and a laugh escaped from my throat.

"I look forward to hearing about all the amazing things you and your magic mineral potions can do." He pressed his lips to my knuckles, sending a powerful jolt of longing straight between my thighs. "In the meantime, it's been a very long, exhausting day. Would you…" He hesitated, licking his lips. "Would you like to join me in the shower?"

I somehow managed to muster a nod.

Heath helped me to my feet, which, like the rest of me, were rapidly fading to a faint shimmer. After grabbing my toiletries bag, as well as a washcloth and a bar of soap from the foot of his bed, he led me to the bathroom. Once there, he quietly shut the door behind us, turned on the water, then faced me, his beautiful blue eyes probing mine for our next steps. Without a word, I kicked off my slippers and held my arms straight up. He gently lifted my shirt over my head, then reached behind me and removed my bra. As it fell away, my arms instinctively went to cover myself, but he gently grabbed my wrists, stopping me.

"As a purveyor of strictly beautiful things," he said, his thumbs rubbing small circles against the inside of my wrists, "please believe me when I say you have the most exquisite breasts." I bit my lip, momentarily forgetting how to speak as he dropped to one knee, his hands sensually tracing the curve of my waist as he did.

"My chalcopyrite is in the front pocket," I managed to rasp when his fingers hovered over the button of my pants. "I don't want to lose it."

He reached in there and gently fished it out, rolling it between his fingers. "Hmm. I'll have to replace this one with a nicer specimen."

"No." I shook my head, taking it from him to gently set atop my toiletries bag. "This one is perfect…" I dipped my head shyly. "It's my favorite mineral in my collection."

The corner of Heath's mouth curled into a crooked smile. Brushing a trail of kisses from my breasts to my stomach, he removed my pants, then my underwear. As his eyes roved over my naked flesh, he let out an appreciative hum. "And here I thought it would be impossible for your body to be as stunning as your mind."

I crossed my arms and clicked my tongue. "You don't have to flatter me. I'm already naked."

"Is it 'flattering' to remark on a diamond's brilliance or is it just stating a fact?"

"Er, well…" I dropped my hands to my sides. "Touché."

Still kneeling, Heath wrapped his arms around my waist and pressed his cheek against my breast. "You know," he murmured, closing his eyes and breathing deeply, "part of me wonders if I really did die back in that tunnel… But if this is Heaven, I can't complain."

"There's no empirical evidence for an afterlife," I chided him gently, running my fingers through his hair. "This is most definitely real life."

He laughed, sending my heart aflutter.

Lowering myself on trembling knees, I peeled away the remains of his shirt, noting every scratch and bruise on his shoulders and chest so I could take care of them later. Then, after glancing up at him – and receiving a fervent nod in return – I unfastened and removed his belt. He shimmied out of his pants and underwear as he stood, allowing me a front row view of his surprisingly prodigious…package. I inclined my head in disbelief, which elicited a hearty laugh from Heath as he extended a hand to help me back up.

"Gift shop owners aren't supposed to be so well-endowed," I muttered accusingly.

"I could say the same thing about pharmacists"—he smirked, openly regarding my bare breasts—"but there's really no empirical evidence to support that statement, is there?"

I sighed. "Touché again."

Still chuckling, he led me underneath the water and positioned himself behind me, pressing his hips against my back. Just as I was about to inquire about a prophylactic, he surprised me by lathering up my hair, running his fingers over my scalp luxuriously. Totally unexpected – and far from the coarse, abrupt style of intercourse I'd regrettably become accustomed to – this was the single most erotic thing a man had ever done to me. A soft moan slipped through my lips as I sank against Heath's chest. His left arm curled beneath my breasts to support me while his right hand continued massaging my scalp, lulling me into a deep state of relaxation.

"Who needs amethyst when you've got this?" I sighed.

"Is that a compliment?"

I let out a blissful moan in response.

"Compliment, then." He massaged my scalp for another few minutes, then used the showerhead to rinse the suds from my hair. From there, he lathered up my back and shoulders, running his thumbs between my shoulder blades as he kneaded the knots that had formed there. His lips caressed the side of my neck, sending a surge of goosebumps down my spine. "Is this okay?" he whispered against my ear.

"More than okay." My hands reached behind me and grabbed his hips, pulling him closer.

A low rumble vibrated in his chest. He spun me around to face him, his powerful hands gripping my arms.

I bit my lip, the intensity of Heath's gaze filling me not with unease, but with hot, pulsing desire. Even though I was ninety-nine percent sure I knew the answer, I licked my lips and asked, "Is this okay? It's…what you want?"

"More than you know," he replied, dropping his lips to mine.

I kissed him back fiercely, hungrier for this man than I'd ever been for anything or anyone in my entire life. As his arms encircled me, pulling me against his chest with tender force, the feeling appeared mutual.

Reaching behind me to grab the soap from its holder, I lathered it into my hands and massaged the suds into Heath's back, thrilled by the sounds of pleasure I was eliciting from him. We remained in that tight, feverish embrace, bathing and massaging every dip and curve of one another's torsos, our lips never straying far from one another's. When there was nothing left of Heath's upper body to wash, my fingertips dragged down the slickness of his stomach, until my hand found the hardness of his arousal.

He let out a deep, rumbling moan as his head tilted backward. "Have I mentioned how much you drive me crazy?"

"Once or twice," I replied, slowly running my hand up and down his shaft. "Hopefully, in a good way this time?"

He curled a finger beneath my chin, tilting my face toward his. "In the very best way," he whispered hoarsely. Dropping his mouth to mine, he kissed me deeply while his fingers slid between my thighs. "Do you like that?"

I nodded, too flooded by desire to speak.

Heath's fingers eased through the wetness that had gathered between my thighs, making my back arch reflexively. His other arm tightened around me, supporting my weight as pleasure shuddered through my body. Enraptured as I was, I hadn't forgotten about him. As I firmly gripped his arousal, my thumb tracing small circles around the underside of his head, his entire body stiffened. Foreheads pressed together, we relentlessly pleasured one another beneath the pounding curtains of water, rivulets of soap and water snaking down our bodies.

"Oh fuck, Delaney." Heath's mouth caught mine, his fingers sliding up and down my center even faster. I moaned into his mouth as he slipped one slick finger inside me, and then a second, fingering me from the inside.

"Curl your fingers," I gasped. "Like you're beckoning me to come."

He did exactly as I asked, vigorously massaging my g-spot while rubbing my clit with the palm of his hand. Thighs quivering, my muscles clenched tighter and tighter against his fingers, until the tension in my core was almost unbearable.

"Heath, I'm so close," I gasped.

"Me too," he whispered into my ear, his voice low and raspy.

Matching his pace, I pumped my hand up and down the entire length of his throbbing erection as he slid his fingers deeper inside me, palming the hot, tingling bundle of nerves just above my opening.

"Faster," I gasped, pressing my forehead against his shoulder as his fingers picked up speed. By then, my calves were straining and I was standing on the very tips of my toes.

He obliged me so well, my knees nearly buckled.

"Yes, just like that. Just like—*oh!*" I cut off in a ragged gasp, stars exploding in front of my vision. The muscles in my core spasmed and throbbed, producing the most powerful orgasm of my life. Crying out, I threw my head back while wave after wave of pleasure coursed through my body like seismic tremors.

As my hand tightened around Heath's erection, picking up speed and intensity, he stiffened and pressed his face against my neck, moaning. Sensing the shift in his body, my strokes became hard and vigorous. Heath's fingers dug into my back as his entire body tensed and contracted alongside mine. "Delaney," he choked out, his fingers knotting into my hair as a shudder ran through him. A deep, rumbling groan tore from his throat as he emptied himself into the palm of my hand.

The sound of his mounting pleasure intensified my own orgasm, sending a powerful spasm through my core that nearly made my knees buckle from the force of it. I abruptly sank into Heath's arms, panting for breath. Slowly sliding his dripping fingers from between my thighs, which elicited another euphoric groan from me, he wrapped his arms around me and drew me close. We stood like that, clinging to one another beneath the spray of the shower until the water ran cold. Heath turned off the faucet, draped a towel over my shoulders, and once again pulled me close. I wrapped my arms around him, swathing us both in the towel to keep him warm.

"That was the greatest shower of my life," he murmured, kissing my forehead. "Thank you."

I nuzzled beneath his chin, sighing blissfully.

"Would you sleep with me tonight?" he asked softly.

"I'll sleep with you every night," I mumbled sleepily. "If you'll let me, that is."

Heath chuckled, tightening his arms around me. "Let you? I was planning on begging you." He dropped his mouth to mine, letting his lips linger there as he whispered, "Don't be long."

"I won't," I rasped, an unexpected tendril of anxiety worming its way into my belly.

He flashed me a wink as he wrapped a fresh towel around his hips and went into the bedroom, quietly shutting the door behind him.

The moment I was alone, the icy sliver of dread turned into a frozen lead brick. "Butternuts," I cursed under my breath. Aroused and caught up in the moment as I'd been, I'd completely forgotten about this part.

Hugging the towel around my trembling body, immobilized beneath the cold, dripping faucet, I braced myself for the "ick" – the inevitable wave of remorse and revulsion that had always followed any intimate activity I'd ever engaged in. The ick had been the reason the vast majority of my past sexual exploits never progressed beyond one-night stands; the reason I'd wondered on more than one occasion if I simply wasn't wired for sex the way other people were. If the ick came now, it would be a death knell for Heath and me, dooming any chance of a potential romantic relationship between us; we would crash and burn before ever taking off.

Please don't come, I prayed to the ick. *Please. I really like him.* I anxiously gnawed on a hangnail, terrified that I might have already ruined the best thing I'd never had. *There's got to be a mineral out there that can get rid of the ick... Prasiolite, maybe? Or rose quartz?* Mentally ticking off potentially-relevant minerals, I agonized for the better part of a minute, trying to come up with a hypothetical cure for something that had plagued me my entire adult life...

But the ick never came.

In fact, the longer I lingered beneath the steady *drip, drip, drip* of the faucet, the more antsy I became – not to sneak out a back window or make up some sort of fake illness – but to just...hurry up and be with him.

A smile unfurled from my lips as the warm, comforting realization finally dawned on me: More than anything, I just wanted to be with Heath, in every sense of the word.

When I emerged from the bathroom a few minutes later, teeth brushed and sleep-shirt donned, he was already in bed, propped up on one elbow, waiting for me. Topie, meanwhile, was snoring as loudly as an electric saw, dead to the world.

"I was worried you'd gotten lost in the bathroom." Heath smiled wryly as he patted the mattress beside him.

I opened my mouth to explain how that would be impossible, given the single door in the bathroom, then thought the better of it. As I crawled under the covers and into Heath's beckoning arms, I replied, "Have I ever told you about the time I got lost in the Adirondack Mountains?"

"No." He frowned. "What happened?"

I snuggled up against his bare chest as he wrapped his arms around me. "It happened a few months ago. I was out in the middle of Mohawk Valley looking for Herkimer diamonds and somehow wandered off the trail. After a few hours of trying to find my way back—"

"A few *hours?*"

I nodded. "Yeah. I was *really* lost."

"Where was Topie?"

"Manning – well, 'pigging' – the shop. Anyway, after a few hours, I stumbled across this big evergreen tree sitting in the middle of a clearing. Something was dangling from its branches, but I couldn't figure out what. At first, I thought it was some kind of plant overgrowth, or possibly birds' nests, but as I got closer, I suddenly realized what it was."

"What?"

"Bacon."

Heath shifted his body to properly gape at me. "I'm sorry, did you say *bacon?*"

"Uh-huh. Dozens of slices of bacon, just hanging from the branches. By then, I hadn't eaten in hours and I was so hungry, I couldn't see straight. So, naturally, I start running toward the tree, thinking only of putting food in my stomach."

"But how did the bacon even get there?" Heath pressed. "Did some campers fry it up and…I don't know, hang it out to dry or something?"

"I had no idea. I was just running at full speed toward this bacon tree, my mouth watering at the sight. But as soon as I got within ten feet of it, rocks started flying at me from every direction."

"Rocks?!"

"Yep. I had no idea where the rocks were coming from, either. There were just dozens and dozens of them, pelting my body hard enough to leave bruises. As I fled in the opposite direction, trying to outrun my attackers, it suddenly occurred to me – it wasn't actually a bacon tree."

"What was it?" Heath demanded, sitting up straight.

"It was a ham-bush."

He opened his mouth, but no words came out.

"Get it?" I propped myself up on one elbow to make sure he'd comprehended the hilarity of my joke. "A *ham-bush?*"

"Delaney Stone," he groaned, scrubbing a hand down his face, "that was the *worst* joke I've ever heard in my life."

"Hey!" I half-protested, half-yawned as I reached across him to turn off the bedside lamp. "Just because *you* lack the sophistication to appreciate the complex humor of a good feghoot, doesn't mean it's a bad joke!"

"Yes, poor you," Heath agreed, pulling me close, "having to share a bed with a feghoot Philistine such as myself."

"Fortunately, your good looks mostly make up for it."

He laughed. "That might be the nicest thing you've ever said to me."

"Yeah, well, don't get used to it."

"I won't." He kissed the top of my head, still chuckling softly. "Hey, I have a question."

"Yes?"

"What would happen if someone other than you drank your hyalite potion? Would they glow as well?"

I shook my head, even though he couldn't see the gesture in the darkness. "That potion is from my personal collection, meaning it's just ground-up minerals in a neutral lipid suspension – avocado oil, usually – to preserve its essence. The potions I make for Topie and my customers have been processed for several hours or even weeks, and contain very little of the host mineral. It makes the extracted essences weaker, but still far better than any commercially-available pharmaceutical. There are exceptions, like the cinnabar tonic I keep on hand in case of emergencies…" I trailed off, biting my lip. "Sorry again about that. I really should have just let you pee first."

"Probably." He laughed, though his tone quickly became serious again. "You know, for someone who claims to not like people very much, you sure go out of your way to help them – carrying around life-saving tonics that take weeks to make, just in case someone needs them. Opening a pharmacy in a Podunk town like Old Port when you could have used your abilities to become rich and famous instead. Risking your life to save some idiot at the bottom of a mine… It's almost like, deep down, you're secretly a philanthropist."

I scoffed. "A philanthropist? Me?"

"Mm-hmm."

"Nope," I murmured, snuggling up against him. "I'm as misanthropic as it gets."

"If you say so." He pressed his lips against my forehead. "Sleep well, my magical little misanthrope."

My lips stretched into a smile as I drifted off to sleep, wrapped in the warm, comforting embrace of my archnemesis-turned-new-favorite-person.

"Goodnight, my gallant giftshop owner."

Chapter 26

~ More Than Two Weeks Later ~

The bell on the front door of the pharmacy clanged loudly against the glass, nearly making me drop the beaker of liquid I'd been painstakingly measuring. "Butternuts!" I grumbled, then shouted, "Go away, we're closed!"

"But it's ten-thirty, and your store hours on Saturday are ten to six!" a voice called from the front of the store.

"Mrs. Lautner!" I gasped.

Practically flinging the beaker aside, I darted to the front of the store, not bothering to remove my goggles or lab coat. Unbeknownst to me, I'd been working for nearly four hours, utterly focused on the new pyromorphite-infused potions I'd been developing since returning from Beijing the week before. When I burst through the curtain separating my lab from the front of the store, Mrs. Lautner was waiting for me near the entrance, her pastel-blue floral dress perfectly complimenting her blue-tinted gray hair. Topie had already beaten me out there and was circling her legs excitedly.

"Hello there, little friend!" Mrs. Lautner laughed as she reached down to pet him. "It's nice to see you too!"

"Mrs. Lautner!" I rushed forward, nearly wrapping her in a hug. Changing my mind last minute, I instead reached out and gripped her by the elbows, taking her in from head to toe. "You're okay!"

She laughed. "It's good to see you too, dear!"

I let go of her arms to give her a full once-over, circling around her as I spoke. "When your husband came by a few days ago, he said you were really sick!"

I didn't mention that I'd actually found him wandering up and down the back alley in the middle of a rainstorm because he'd forgotten which shop was mine. After giving him a very mild ruby potion to treat his hypothermia, I refilled his prescription with the new extra-strength memory formula I was working on, adding a bottle of an experimental super-charged lung tonic for Mrs. Lautner.

"I *was* really sick!" she replied, nodding her head fervently. "And Mariana had a family emergency in Belize, so it's just been Mr. Lautner and I."

Guilt and worry twinged in my chest. "I called you a few times to check in, and even drove to your house, but no one answered. I was beginning to think…" I trailed off, unable to finish the sentence.

"Oh, aren't you an angel!" Mrs. Lautner exclaimed, pressing her hand to her chest. "I'd have called you sooner, but we just got home from the hospital last night. I was so sick, the doctor had me on a ventilator and was discussing hospice care with my son. Sam rushed all the way up here from Tallahassee because Dr. Hedberg kept insisting I had two weeks to live at most. Poor Sam and Abner were just beside themselves—oh, speaking of which!" She stuck her head out the front door and shouted, "Abner!"

A moment later, Mr. Lautner doddered inside, dressed in a fedora and a sharp brown suit. "Sorry, dear"—he removed his hat to kiss her on the cheek—"I was admiring the rocks in the window across the street."

"Minerals," I muttered under my breath.

He turned to me. "Why, hello, Delaney! You're looking positively fetching today!"

I blinked in surprise. "You remember my name?"

"Indeed I do, thanks to that swell memory cocktail you whipped up!" He put an arm around Mrs. Lautner's waist, beaming widely. "And the lung tonic you made for Effie? Whew, boy! The doctor was so surprised by her improvement, he ran down to the chapel to have a word with the Big Guy!" He pointed at the ceiling.

I looked up, confused.

"He means God, dear." Mrs. Lautner winked.

"Oh." I crinkled my nose. God had nothing to do with it, but better he falsely take the credit than Pfizer come banging down my door.

"I don't know how you did it, Delaney," Mrs. Lautner said, squeezing my hands, "but Abner and I haven't felt this good since we were in our sixties!"

"Pyromorphite," I replied.

"Beg your pardon?" Mr. Lautner asked as he knelt to give Topie – who was lounging around on his back like a sunbathing turtle – some vigorous belly scritches.

"Pyromorphite," I repeated. "It's a secondary lead mineral – well, lead chloride phosphate, to be specific – found in the oxidized zones of lead deposits. When I was traveling around China, I made a pit stop at the Daoping Mine and grabbed a whole bunch of it. At first, I couldn't figure out what it did, since the effects weren't immediately apparent. But a few days later, I tried some more pyromorphite without realizing I still had magnetite in my system. Within seconds, screws were flying from my hotel room walls and I had a spoon stuck to my forehead for the better part of an hour."

Mr. and Mrs. Lautner exchanged wide-eyed glances.

Right. I sighed, reminding myself, once again, that most people prefer the simple conclusion rather than the detailed explanation. "In summary, pyromorphite amplifies the efficacy of other mineral essences, making them about thirty-five percent more effective. Because of that, I was able to 'supercharge' your usual prescriptions, making them much more potent than before. It won't cure you," I clarified. "That is to say, your cancer and dementia haven't gone away. But this should give you time and comfort…at least until I find actual cures." I felt a twinge of sadness. *1,411 minerals down; only 4,089[18] to go.*

"Time and comfort: the two greatest gifts anyone could ask for." Mrs. Lautner smiled, reaching forward to pull me into a tight hug. "Thank you, Delaney."

I patted her awkwardly on the back. "Mm-hmm."

"So"—she grinned, still clutching my elbows—"tell us all about China! You didn't happen to go with that handsome young man across the street, did you?"

"Wh-What gave you that idea?" I stammered, my cheeks heating.

"Because he's also been traveling around China, or so he was telling Abner earlier this morning."

---

[18] Now 4,091, due to the recent discovery of two new minerals: elaliite and elkinstantonite, both of which came from a 15-ton meteorite that crashed in Somalia.

"Wait..." My eyes widened. "Heath's back?" I yanked my phone out of my pocket and flipped it open, my heart sinking even further when I saw there were no missed calls.

"Er, well..." Mrs. Lautner cast a sideways glance at her husband. "I believe he told Abner he got back sometime last night."

"Oh." I chewed on the inside of my cheek. It had been more than two weeks since Heath and I had last spoken. The morning after we'd found the treasure, he and Mr. Zhao flew back to America to retrieve Jinshan's original letter while I stayed in China for another eight days. (Unlike Heath and his unlimited, ten-year visa, *my* visa was only good for one single entry). While he dealt with bureaucratic government officials – something I had no interest in dealing with – Topie and I traveled around the country, exploring some of the most famous Chinese mines in the mineral-collecting world: Daoping Mine in Guangxi, Yaogangxian Mine in Hunan, Urumqi Mine in Xinjiang, Baoshan Mine in Yunnan, and De'an Mine in Jiangxi. The only mine I didn't get to see was Huanggang Mine in Inner Mongolia – home of the octahedral, strawberry-red fluorite – because Heath and I had planned on seeing it together before returning home. But two days before our intended rendezvous, I received an email from Mrs. Lautner's son saying that she'd taken a turn for the worse. Like two ships passing in the night, I boarded a plane back to the United States just as Heath had returned to Hubei with Mr. Zhao. Thanks to wildly different time zones and terrible phone service in China, we'd hardly been in touch at all since then.

But now he was back...and he hadn't even let me know.

"What's the matter, dear?" Mrs. Lautner asked, her smile dissolving into a frown.

"I had no idea Heath was back," I replied, the flush in my cheeks deepening alongside the admission. "He probably has a bunch of things to catch up on and I'm sure he's jet-lagged, but…" My shoulders slumped. "I guess I thought…or rather, was hoping…that he would stop by. Or call, at the very least."

"Oh, sweetheart, I'm sure he will!" Mrs. Lautner said, patting my hand. "Like you said, he's probably just terribly busy and working to catch up on everything…isn't that right, dear?" She elbowed Mr. Lautner in the ribs.

"Oh, yes, that's almost certainly the case!" he quickly agreed.

"I don't think so." I shook my head despondently. "Honestly, between my mood swings and the glowing and then the spontaneous shower escapades, I think I just scared him off…" My eyes widened. "Oh, butternuts – the shower!" I turned to Topie. "Do you think Heath got the ick?"

"The *what*, dear?" Mrs. Lautner asked, her frown deepening.

"The ick!" I fretted, pacing back and forth. "You know – the icky feeling you get after being intimate with someone."

Mr. and Mrs. Lautner exchanged another loaded glance. "Poppycock!" he exclaimed. "I've never suffered from this so-called 'ick' a day in my life! What heterosexual man in his right mind would be 'icked' out by such an attractive young lady?"

"It's possible he's *not* heterosexual," Mrs. Lautner replied. "What man his age wears *cufflinks?* Besides, it's very trendy right now for young men to be gender-fluid."

"Gender fluid?" Mr. Lautner frowned. "Back in my day, we just called it jissom."

"Gender-fluid is an adjective, not a euphemism for semen." I sighed, scrubbing my hands through my hair. "Regardless, I don't think this has anything to do with sexual orientation. I'm sure I just pushed him away or scared him off somehow." I slumped against the wall. "It's kind of my modus operandi."

"That can't possibly be true," Mrs. Lautner gently admonished me. "I'm sure he has a perfectly good explanation for not calling yet."

Forcing a shaky smile to my face, I squared my shoulders and stood up straight. "It's fine. I'm fine." I cleared my throat, using that opportunity to straighten a shelf of travel-sized ibuprofen bottles. "Um, let me get you and Mr. Lautner a few more weeks' worth of medicine." Spinning on my heel so fast I nearly tripped over Topie, I rushed to the back room, where my eyes settled on the handwritten sticky note tacked to the corkboard: *"As our island of knowledge grows, so too does the shore of our ignorance – John Archibald Wheeler."*

"Oh, shut up," I muttered, snatching my newest batch of new-and-improved lung tonic off the Bunsen burner to cool and bottle it.

I never should have told him the truth, I chided myself as I furiously measured, filled, and sealed several vials of medicine. *Sure, he told me it would take "a lot more than that" to scare him off, but that was before he had two weeks to reconsider his position.* My eyes widened. *I didn't even brush my teeth before we made out in the shower! No wonder he got the ick!* I let out a humiliated groan. *Glowing skin and halitosis – not exactly a Miss-Universe-winning combination.*

When I walked back to the front of the store thirteen minutes later – having taken five minutes to prep the Lautners' order and an additional eight minutes to properly pull myself together – Mr. and Mrs. Lautner were standing by the front door, giggling.

"What's going on?" I asked, setting their prescriptions in a paper bag on the counter. I looked around the room. "Where's Topie?"

"Lured away by gourmet Chinese truffles, it would seem," Mrs. Lautner replied, trying and failing to hide her smile.

"What?"

"A certain handsome young fella stopped by asking for you," Mr. Lautner chimed in, "and when we told him you were working in the back, he kidnapped your pig."

"He *what?*" I demanded.

"To be fair, the pig needed very little persuasion," Mrs. Lautner added.

I let out a low growl. *It's not enough to simply reject me, he has to rob me of my emotional support animal too?!* After snatching their paper bag of medicine from the front counter and dropping it in Mrs. Lautner's hands with a curt "No charge!" I marched toward the door, flipped the sign to CLOSED, and impatiently motioned for Mr. and Mrs. Lautner to step outside.

"Dear, we can't just take these for free!" she protested as I nudged her out the door. "Please, let us pay you!"

"Out of the question." I shook my head roughly. "Just go home and take good care of each other."

As I raised my foot to angrily march across the street, Mrs. Lautner grabbed my wrist and pulled me back. "Wait!"

I whirled around. "What?"

Mrs. Lautner took both my hands in hers while her husband placed a hand on her shoulder. "Thank you, Delaney," she said, her eyes shining with emotion. "For everything."

"Oh." I let her squeeze my hands for a long moment, trying my best not to squirm. After about four seconds – which I assumed was more than enough time for a proper sentimental moment – I cleared my throat and gently pulled my hands away to lock the door. "You're my friend," I told her, mustering an appropriately-sized smile as I turned back around. "No thanks needed. …Now, if you'll excuse me, I need to go speak with a certain traitorous pig – and Topie as well."

I pushed open the door to Heath's shop, bracing myself for the impending violent assault on my senses… When nothing happened, I squinted one eye open, and then the other. There was no incense burning or Tibetan bowls whining. The fluorescent lights were off, and only a handful of customers were meandering about the shop, murmuring quietly to themselves.

This isn't so bad... I thought to myself, turning toward the incredible new exhibit of fine Chinese minerals. *Not bad at all…* Just as I was exhaling in relief, a finger tapped me in the middle of my back.

Whirling around, I found Heath's nephew, Chess, standing directly in front of me, his skinny arms crossed in front of his chest and a wide grin stretched across his rosy cheeks. "Hi. Have you come to eat more of my uncle's rocks?"

"Hello, *Chess.*" I folded my arms appraisingly, eyeing the assortment of anachronistic cartoon dinosaurs clustered together on the front of his t-shirt. "Didn't anybody tell you that Stegosauruses and Tyrannosauruses never actually existed together?"

"Yes," he replied matter-of-factly. "Did you know that they lived eighty million years apart, which is more than the time separating the T-Rex and homo sapiens?"

"Obviously. But did *you* know that T-Rexes evolved with tiny arms so other T-Rexes wouldn't accidentally chomp on them during feeding frenzies?"

His eyes grew wide and round behind his thick glasses. "Really?"

"Mm-hmm," I said with a note of well-earned smugness. "It's postulated that rather than sole, territorial hunters, Tyrannosaurus Rexes were actually gregarious animals that lived and hunted in groups, much like modern wolves."

"Where did you learn that?" he asked, lips pursed and eyebrow arching.

"In a 2021 study published in the *Acta Paleontologica Polonica* journal."

Chess nodded, seemingly appeased. "Are you the lady who told my uncle I have hemochromatosis?"

"Yes." I uncrossed my arms, my stomach doing a little flip at the mention of Heath. "Are you feeling better?"

"Much better!" he enthused. And indeed, his cheeks looked fuller and the dark circles under his eyes had all but disappeared. Taking a deep breath, he blurted, "They stuck an IV in my arm and took out a bunch of my blood and then donated it to the blood bank because I have Type O-negative blood which means even with Hemochromatosis I can donate blood to whoever I want—"

"Whomever."

"—*whomever* I want," he steamrolled on, "and our antigens will still match so their body won't accidentally attack the new blood cells and make them sick. What blood type are you?"

"AB-positive, the opposite of you. I can receive a blood transfusion from anyone, but I can only donate blood to other people with AB-positive blood. It's the rarest of the eight common blood types," I added with a note of pride. "Only four percent of the population has it."

"Interesting." Chess nodded thoughtfully. "I like you. You remind me of Grandpa Norm. Oh, by the way, my uncle Heath told me to get him as soon as you arrived, but then we started talking about dinosaurs so I forgot." He shoved his hands in his pockets and grinned up at me. "He's waiting for you in my grandpa's office."

My eyes darted to Norm's office door, which, to my surprise, was open. Warm light and soft classical music poured out of the room, just like it used to when he was alive. A lump appeared in my throat. I started toward the office, then abruptly stopped, remembering that Chess had just given me a compliment. "I like you too." I told him over my shoulder. "Come by my pharmacy sometime and I'll tell you why I eat rocks."

"Okay!" He flashed me an enthusiastic thumbs-up. "And I'll tell you about the tiniest dinosaur egg ever found – spoiler alert, it was smaller than a penny!"

"Deal." I smiled, my eyes lingering on Chess as he ran right up to two ladies looking at Bolivian halite crystals and started telling them all about how the Uyuni Salt flat used to be a prehistoric ocean until the earth's mantle shifted and all the water dried up.

Just like his grandpa.

Taking a deep breath, I cautiously peeked my head inside Norm's office, filled with a strange mix of joy, sadness, and nostalgia. His vintage record player, which sat between the two leather chairs we used to sit in, was quietly playing one of his favorite Benny Goodman records. I took another half step inside, breathing in the familiar scent of dusty books and old parchment. There was even a spicy note of Earl Grey, Norm's favorite kind of tea, lingering in the air. I smiled when I realized the scent was emanating from the steaming cup that rested atop Norm's massive mahogany desk, just beside Heath's elbow. He was currently poring over a leatherbound book, his signature navy blue suit jacket draped over the back of the chair, while the sleeves of his white button-up shirt had been pushed to his elbows, displaying the lithe musculature of his forearms. He was jotting down notes on a pad of lined yellow paper as he read, his left hand absentmindedly stroking Topie between his ears while he snoozed beneath the desk.

I cleared my throat softly.

"Laney!" Heath quickly rose to his feet. He crossed the room in three strides, with Topie jovially trotting beside him, to wrap me in a tight hug. "I've missed you," he murmured against the top of my head.

My knee-jerk instinct was to say something sharp and accusatory, but the warmth of his arms thawed right through my anger, leaving something softer – and far more daunting – in its place. "I…" I started, then swallowed. "I-I've missed you too…a lot." Gently pulling away, I looked up at him, my eyes unexpectedly filling with tears. "Why didn't you tell me you were back?"

"Oh!" His eyebrows arched in surprise, then furrowed, as though he hadn't expected my reaction. "I'm so sorry, Laney. I didn't get home until two in the morning and I didn't want to wake you up. As soon as Beth dropped Chess off to help watch the shop this morning, I ran over to the pharmacy to see you. But an older couple told me you were busy in the back, so I asked them to tell you I stopped by. And then this little rascal"—he reached down to scrub Topie on the head—"insisted on following me. Probably smelled the truffles in my pocket."

"Oh." I nodded, quickly scrubbing the tears from my eyes. "I thought maybe I'd done something wrong…or that you didn't want to see me, for some reason."

Heath's jaw dropped. "Are you crazy? I've thought about you every minute since we said goodbye at the hotel."

"You have?" My voice cracked.

"Oh, Laney." Heath sighed, wrapping me in another tight hug. "What part of 'I'm not going anywhere' does that brilliant little brain of yours not understand?"

A combination of a laugh and a sob tumbled from my mouth. "I'm sorry. I guess I'm just…" I took a deep, shaky breath. "I'm just not used to men like you."

"Men like me?"

"Wonderful, caring men like you," I amended.

"Ah." The corner of his mouth quirked up. "Well, get used to it, Stone. As a wise man once said: Love the house, love the crow."

Huh? I blinked. "What does that even mean?"

Heath chuckled. "It means, when you find your person, you cherish them for who they are, imperfections and all. In other words, you should love the whole house – even the noisy crow sitting on the roof."

"Oh." I pondered that for a long moment, biting my lip. "So, what you're saying is…I'm your person?"

He leaned down to brush his lips against mine. "Yes. And I'm yours."

I stood on my toes to deepen the kiss, eliciting a soft hum of pleasure from Heath and a melodramatic groan of disgust from Topie.

"Hey, if you don't like it, there's the door," I chided him.

Rolling his eyes, he loped over to one of the two leather chairs and plopped himself in it with a huff.

"I really am sorry about the last couple of weeks." Heath said as he tucked a strand of hair behind my ear. "I was looking forward to seeing Huanggang Mine with you, but in the end, it's probably better that I stayed with Mr. Zhao." He rubbed the bridge of his nose, glancing at the old picture frame sitting on the desk. "There were a *lot* of loose ends to wrap up."

I walked over to the desk and picked up the old photo of Norm and Heath – the same one I'd seen a hundred times but never paid much attention to – running my thumb along the smooth edge of the frame. Until today, it had just been a picture of Norm and his teenage son hanging out on a fishing boat. Now, when I looked at it, I noticed the damaged capillaries and pitted skin on Norm's nose, as well as the puffy bags under his eyes – both indicators of excessive alcohol use. But I also recognized the pride twinkling in his eyes as he beamed down at his son, who was holding up the trout he'd just caught. I ran my fingers across the teenaged Heath's face, filled with fondness for the wonderful, kind-hearted man he would later become.

"I'm sorry I couldn't help your father," I told him softly. "The signs were there… I just didn't see them."

Heath stood beside me to gaze at the photo in my hand. "I didn't see them either – at least, I didn't recognize their severity." He took a deep breath and turned toward me, the corner of his mouth showing the faintest hint of a smile. "My father talked about you all the time, you know."

I looked up at him in surprise. "He did?"

Heath nodded. "He liked you so much, in fact, I think he secretly wanted to make you part of the family."

"What?!"

"Anytime we spoke, he always made a point of bringing up 'Dr. Laney' – the brilliant, beautiful, slightly eccentric pharmacist across the street who could spot artificially irradiated fluorite a mile away and knew the chemical composition of every mineral by heart." Heath chuckled. "In hindsight, I'm fairly certain he was trying to finagle a meeting between the two of us, but I rarely came to visit those days and I can only imagine your reaction if he'd told you he wanted to set you up with his son. Anyway"—he shrugged one shoulder—"I'd heard so many wonderful things about you over the years, by the time I met you, I felt like I already knew you. I think that's part of the reason I was determined to get to know the 'real' Laney, the one my father knew and loved. You brightened up his life."

"I…" My mouth fluttered open, trying to find the words. Truth be told, I'd heard things about Heath too, but it never occurred to me that Norm had been trying to set us up. I just thought he was making small talk, which I've never been fond of. At the time, Norm's son was just a faceless, distant person I didn't know and had no intention of knowing, so rather than actively listening to all the praise Norm had heaped upon Heath over the years, I would just smile and nod while mentally formulating my next response – which usually involved a change of subject.

I shook my head and exhaled softly, scoffing at my past idiocy.

After gently setting the photo back in its place, I reached forward to take Heath's hands in mine. "Your father said wonderful things about you too. I just wasn't in the right place to hear them. I'm really sorry for that."

"Well, we found each other regardless." Heath smiled, squeezing my hands. "And I'd like to think my dad is up there somewhere, bragging to all of his pals that he alone orchestrated it."

"I…" I opened my mouth, then closed it again; there was a time for facts, and a time for empathy, and those times didn't always overlap. "I'd…like to think that too." I smiled. "Still, I am sorry that it took me this long to give you a chance. What can I do to make it up to you?"

"Hmm." He stroked his chin thoughtfully. "Well, I haven't had a shower in a couple of days."

A laugh burst out of my mouth. "You're incorrigible, Heath Spencer."

"Guilty as charged," Heath said with a wink. "By the way"—he let go of my hand to reach into his pocket—"I've got something for you."

My eyes widened as he pressed something cool and round into the palm of my hand. When I saw the bright yellow circle of gold glinting there, I clapped a hand over my mouth. "Is this…?"

He nodded. "It's called a solidus – a solid gold coin issued in the Late Roman Empire. It's one of the three-hundred and twelve pieces of gold you and I unearthed – er, three-hundred and *ten*, I should say, since that's the official number Mr. Zhao put in his report." Flashing me a wink, he pointed to the male profile on the front of the coin. "That's Theodosius the second, and these markings right here indicate the coin was minted in Constantinople, circa 435. Along with Attila's seal and the gold jewelry – some of which may have been stolen from the Carthaginian Empire, according to Mr. Zhao – this treasure is one of the most significant and valuable discoveries in modern history."

"That's absolutely incredible," I murmured, running my finger along the dimpled edges of the coin. "*You're* incredible."

"I couldn't have done it without you and Dad, which I've repeatedly explained to anyone with ears." He grinned. "Still, the archeology world is going nuts about it. So nuts, in fact, that Boston U is begging me to come back and teach a special course on the lost treasures of antiquity. They've offered me full tenure if I do."

"I… Oh." I blinked, taking a moment to absorb the full meaning of his words. "I see."

Heath studied me for a long moment. "Do you think I should? Go back to Boston, that is?"

Of the half dozen emotions bubbling up in my chest, anger – as usual – boiled the hottest.

Why are you asking me? Do whatever the heck you want – move to Antarctica, for all I care! The words were threatening to burst from my mouth when Topie pressed his snout against my hand. He was looking up at me with an entreating expression, and even though he hadn't yet taken his multivitamin that morning, in that moment, we understood one another perfectly.

I took a deep breath and let it out slowly. "No," I replied, forcing myself to look Heath in the eye. "I don't think you should go back to Boston. I think you should stay right here, in Old Port…" I swallowed tightly. "With me."

Heath curled one finger beneath my chin and tilted my face toward his. "That's what I was hoping you'd say." Dropping his mouth to mine, he kissed me softly yet tenderly, silently conveying all the things we hadn't yet said to each other but someday would.

Sliding my hands behind his neck, I returned his kiss with fervor, infusing it with all of my own unspoken feelings and dreams and hopes for that which was yet to come. "Thank you," I murmured, tucking the gold coin in my pocket, just beside the chalcopyrite he'd given me. "For everything."

"Thank you, Delaney, for the very same." His words were soft and full of ardor.

I kissed him again, humming softly as I savored the taste of his lips, far better than any mineral I'd ever eaten or likely ever would.

Heath pressed his forehead against mine. "Can I show you something?"

I nodded.

Taking my hand, he led me over to the desk, took a seat in the chair, and motioned for me to sit in his lap, which I readily did. After flipping through the pages of the weathered textbook he'd been reading, he pointed to a highlighted passage – beside which, Norm's handwriting was scrawled in the margins – and began reading aloud. *"Attila, the greatest of the Hun kings, ruler of a kingdom stretching from the Danube to Russia, now rests in an unmarked grave – one that has been long-sought but never found. The tomb was deliberately hidden, perhaps to prevent the desecration of his remains…or, perhaps, to protect the treasure buried beside him: a trio of coffins – one of gold, one of silver and one of iron – along with the sacred sword of Mars, the god of war, which foretold his rise to ruler of the world."*

"Wait." I jerked my head in Heath's direction. "Attila's tomb was never found?"

"Nope. The men who dug his grave were slaves who had been commanded to take him to a secret spot only they would know. After burying him, they were murdered by their Hun masters to ensure the secret location would never be discovered. Most historians believe Attila was buried in Hungary, but no one's ever found his body or his treasure."

"You know…" I mused, tapping my lip thoughtfully. "I've never been to Hungary."

Heath's mouth was unfurling in a smile. "Nor have I… But I hear Rudabanya Mine has some gorgeous mineral specimens."

I nodded slowly. "I could fly us to JFK, which has nonstop flights to Budapest… How's next weekend look for you?"

"For you, Delaney Stone, I'm free as a bird."

I threw my arms around him with an excited squeal. "I'll prep the travel potions!"

"And I'll charter the private jet, since I know a guy at JFK." He winked at me. "So long as you're not terribly worried about bending rules, I bet he'd even let you take the wheel for part of the flight."

"It's called a yoke, not a wheel," I informed him, my eyes roving the far corner of the desk, where several Chinese mineral specimens had been laid out on a white cloth, one of which was a cluster of faintly-glowing, emerald-green crystals. "Did I tell you that Mindat.org reached out to me for an interview? They're doing a special write-up on the new radioactive varietal of euchroite for their newsletter."

"Laney!" Heath wrapped his arms around my waist in a tight hug. "That's incredible!"

"I know!" I grinned widely. "They even offered to do a spotlight on…" My train of thought evaporated as my gaze settled on the rose-colored crystal clusters resting beside the euchroite on Heath's desk. "Where and when did you get that rhodochrosite?" I asked, my mouth watering.

"One of my suppliers sourced it from Wutong Mine just a few days ago and overnighted me a sample. Why?" As soon as he'd asked the question, the confusion on Heath's face morphed into understanding. "Oh! Is rhodochrosite a new mineral for you?"

I nodded, eyeing the crystals ravenously. "I've seen it in mineral shows, but never freshly-mined and with its essence intact."

"Well, in that case"—he passed me one of the smaller crystals—"it's all yours."

"Oh, Heath!" I kissed him fiercely and without warning, clutching the crystal against my breast. "Thank you!"

He chuckled. "I'll overnight rare and exotic minerals here every single day if that's going to be your reaction."

I shook my head, not bothering to pull my eyes away from the gemmy red crystals. "International shipping is too expensive. Besides, I'd much rather travel the world with you to find them."

"I'd like that very much as well," Heath said, kissing my temple. "On that note…" He leaned back in his chair, resting his hands behind his head. "Let's see it!"

With a giddy squeak, I stood up and crossed to the other side of the desk, just in case. After all, trying a new mineral is a lot like taking a blind chance at love: exhilarating, terrifying, and prone to fireworks – sometimes literally. Topie immediately took my place on Heath's lap, resting his chin in the crook of Heath's arm to watch.

"All right…" Grinning at my two favorite people in the world, I raised the rhodochrosite to my lips. "Here goes nothing."

Real-Life Photos

Old Port, Maine.
PHILLIP CAPPER, FLICKR

Chalcopyrite, Tonglushan Mine.
ARKENSTONE MINERALS

Active Tonglushan Mine, Hubei, China.
BRIAN WANG

Ancient Tonglushan Ruins.
ANCIENT TONGLUSHAN MINE MUSEUM

Red Fluorite, Inner Mongolia.
FINE MINERALS INTERNATIONAL

Bonanza A36TC.
SCOTT MACDONALD

Mineral Classifications

MINERAL NAME	REGION	COLOR	EFFECT	DURATION
Amber	Baltic Sea	Yellow-orange, transparent	Heals injuries associated with the lungs (e.g., asthma)	Lasting
Amethyst	Diamond Hill, South Carolina, USA	Light lavender to a deep purple	Anxiolytic (anti-anxiety)	Short-acting (≤ 1 hour)
Apatite (blue)	Fort Dauphin, Madagascar	Dark blue to light turquoise, semi-translucent	Facilitates persuasion / manipulation of others	Very short-acting
Aventurine	Coimbatore District, Tamil Nadu, India	Olive green, opaque	Anti-inflammatory	Dose-dependent
Biotite	Evje Mineralsti, Norway	Brown to greenish black, vitreous luster	Antidiarrheal	Short-acting (≤ 1 hour)
Calcite	Chihuahua, Mexico	Pearly/chalky white	Bolsters bone strength	Short-acting (≤ 1 hour)
Celestine	Sakoany Deposit, Boeny, Madagascar	Translucent sky blue	Bolsters muscle strength	Dose-dependent

Name	Locality	Appearance	Effect	Duration
Chalcopyrite	Tonglushan Mine, Hubei, China	Opaque navy blue, druzy, iridesces purple/gold	Shows location of various diseases in the body	Short-acting (≤ 1 hour)
Cinnabar	Almadén, Spain	Bright scarlet to brick-red, opaque	Mends fractured items at fracture point (e.g., bones)	Lasting
Dolomite	Navarra, Spain	Colorless, translucent	Detoxification	Long-acting (> 1 hour)
(atypical) Euchroite	Ancient Tonglushan Mine, Hubei, China	Deep emerald green, fluoresces bright green under UV	Modified x-ray vision	Short-acting (≤ 1 hour)
Fluorite (red)	Inner Mongolia, China	Transparent, gemmy, strawberry-red	Allows you to hear others' thoughts	Short-acting (≥ 1 hour)
Galena	Mt. Gline, Maine, USA	Metallic, lead-colored, opaque	Knowledge absorption	Dose-dependent
Hematite	Lake Superior, Wisconsin, USA	Earthy red, metallic, botryoidal	Improves clotting, coagulation	Long-acting (> 1 hour)
Heliodor	Medina, Brazil	Richly yellow, transparent	Olfactory Amplification	Short-acting (≥ 1 hour)

Howlite	New Brunswick, Canada	White or grayish-white, sometimes with darker veins	Pain management / numbing	Dose-dependent
Hyalite	Erongo Mountains, Namibia	Clear, translucent, botryoidal	Bioluminescence	Short-acting (≥ 1 hour)
Moonstone	San Lorenzo, New Mexico	Milky, white, opalescent	Tranquilizer/ sleep aid	Dose-dependent
Morganite	Minas Gerais, Brazil	Gemmy; soft pink to violet pink	Speeds up wound healing	Long-acting (> 1 hour)
Prasiolite ('Green Amethyst')	Thunder Bay, Canada.	Pale olive green, translucent	Increases libido	Long-acting (> 1 hour)
Peridot	San Carlos Apache Indian Res., Arizona, USA	Yellowish-green, transparent	Anti-nausea	Short-acting (≥ 1 hour)
Pyrite	Mt. Gline, Maine, USA	Metallic; Brassy, gold	Memory recollection	Dose-dependent
Pyromorphite	Daoping, Guangxi, China	Bright green, resinous luster, opaque	Enhances the effect of other mineral essences	Lasting
Ruby	Mogok Valley, Myanmar	Transparent, blood-red	Heat (Fire)	Short-acting (≥ 1 hour)

Name	Location	Appearance	Property	Duration
Quartz (colorless varietal)	Mt. Gline, Maine, USA	Transparent; Colorless	Antiviral (Rhinovirus a.k.a. common cold)	Long-acting (> 1 hour)
Selenite (a.k.a. gypsum)	Naica, Chihuahua, Mexico	Transparent w/ inclusions, colorless, fibrous	Antibacterial	Long-acting (> 1 hour)
Shungite	Karelia, Russia	Black, lustrous, non-crystalline, opaque	Amplifies Magnetic Fields	Short-acting (≥1 hour)
Silver	Cannington Mine, Queensland, Australia	Metallic silver luster, opaque	Electricity conductor	Very short-acting (1-4 bolts)
Sodalite	Ice River complex, British Columbia	Opaque, navy blue (also transparent crystalline form)	Increases intellectual capacity/processing	Short-acting (≥1 hour)
Spinel	Mogok, Myanmar	Magenta/ruby, transparent	Increases lung function	Dose-dependent
Tiger's Eye	Balloch Mine, Pixley ka Seme, South Africa	Chatoyant, golden to red-brown, silky luster	Courage/decreases fear	Short-acting (≥1 hour)
Vesuvianite "Idocrase"	Paraíba, Brazil	Olive green to brown, translucent	Echolocation	Very short-acting

The Gilded Blood Series

When Zayn, your smoking hot boss, tells you never to touch the cache of deluxe tattoo ink locked away in his office, you listen to him… until the day you run out of your own ink, your squirming client is on the verge of peeing his pants, and your boss is nowhere to be found. Desperate times call for desperate measures, right?

I fully expected Zayn to yell at me when he returned to the shop. What I didn't expect was the fresh cobra tattoo on my client's butt magically springing to life. Or the interdimensional filing cabinet hiding in the back of Zayn's office. And, oh, did I mention that my gorgeous, magic-ink-hoarding boss is actually an incubus?

Now – through (mostly) no fault of my own – we have to venture into a strange and distant land where a never-ending list of lethal flora, fauna, and fae await us. When you add in my Jewish mother's string of poorly-timed, hysterical phone calls, there is one thing I'm grateful for: there's no cell service in the fae realm.

The Lightning Conjurer Series

Three years ago, I woke up in an abandoned cabin without a single memory – not even my own name. Since then, I've been doing my best to stay off the grid. But this week? Well, that's proving to be a problem.

From freak tornados to exploding fireplaces, strange things are happening all around me. Aiden, my new (and irritatingly attractive) college professor, claims he knows "what" I am. A strange car is following me everywhere I go. And now an organization of people claiming to be "like me" are entreating me to join them. But the deeper I venture into this world, the more I wonder – is this organization a safe haven or a cult?

Whatever it may be, I can't turn back now. Because the only way to unearth my past, my name, and this growing power deep within me is to brave the lion's den...

Even if that means disclosing the one secret about me that will shake the very world to its core.

The Bone Whisperer Chronicles

Willow, a young and reluctant new mother, is terrified of her infant, Lilah – namely, her peculiar form of epilepsy. Every time Lilah's eyes glaze over, terrible things happen: flowers shrivel, food goes to rot, and even Willow's long, auburn hair turns stark white. Soon, it all becomes too much to bear. In the middle of the night, Willow and her mother dump the baby at the fire station two towns over – and are never heard from again.

The next morning, Chief Stanley Quinn takes Lilah home and cares for the toddler as best as he can. With medication, her epilepsy remains under control... For the most part.

But as a teenager, Lilah isn't always keen on taking her pills, and when she sneaks away to a rock concert with the cutest boy in school, something terrible happens, landing both of them in the hospital. After Stanley breaks down and confesses everything to his adopted daughter, she decides to track down the young girl who gave her up sixteen years ago; the young girl who never made it home that night...the young girl who is now presumed to be dead. Soon, Lilah's quest to find her birth mother becomes a quest to solve a sixteen-year-old missing persons case. She has everything she needs to find her – she just needs to learn how to control her peculiar 'gift' before she kills someone... Again.

The Little Morsel

Feral, a retired war hero with ancient bones and thinning scales, has been living in a dragon retirement home for several centuries. There, his daily routine is always the same: wake up with creaky joints, force down the stale protein bars from Bites of Knights, avoid the caterwauling old females on the shuffleboard court, and then return to bed to dream of flying.

But when a tiny stray human shows up at his front boulder, Feral's ho-hum world is turned upside down. Once a tentative agreement not to eat this strange little 'morsel' is forged, the two of them embark on a journey for applesauce that ends with each of them saving the other's life – in more ways than one.

THE LITTLE MORSEL is a warm, lighthearted adventure that shines a delicate light on loneliness, neglect, found family, and purpose. Multifaceted and relatable, it is a story that can be enjoyed by children and adults alike.

The Pilfered Quill

From the minds that brought you the <u>Gilded Blood</u> and <u>Hell In Haven</u> series, comes a contemporary fantasy satire like no other…

Chet Williams, a fantasy-writer extraordinaire in his own mind, has been rejected one too many times. For too long, his genius has gone unnoticed. But when Chet stumbles upon a secret that would shake the publishing world to its core, his ambitions are finally realized…for better or for worse.

Come experience the greatest romance of all time: the love which self-absorbed author Chet Williams has for himself.

Acknowledgements

Thank you so much to my editing team, Sara(h)², for your support, encouragement, and brilliant eye for detail!

Aaron, you are my best friend: ever patient, kind, understanding, and boundlessly supportive – my real-life Heath. I am forever grateful that you are my person.

To my Queen Helper Bee, Britt: I am infinitely thankful to the chaotic whims of the universe for bringing us together. Thank you for keeping me sane, organized, and best of all, writing. I can't wait for all of our future bookish adventures!

My dearest J-Squad / Shield Maidens, thank you for your love, grace, and gentle bullying. I owe much – if not all – of my sanity to the both of you.

I am boundlessly grateful to my sensitivity/alpha readers – Ryan, Andy, Janice, Travis, Rei, Trina, Mumsie `& Lauren – for your thoughtful insight and suggestions!

I'd like to extend my sincere gratitude to Rob Lavinsky at The Arkenstone, Graham Sutton at Collector's Edge Minerals, and Jan Pohunek for sharing your valuable experiences and insights on minerals and mining!

谢谢 JC Kang, for your expertise in Chinese and the time you spent assisting me. (Any errors are mine.)

Special thanks to Hudson Mineral Institute for Mindat.org, a massive online database of rocks, minerals, and meteors that's free and available to the public!

Above all, thank you from the bottom of my heart to my readers, who make all of this possible

About the Author

RACHEL RENER is a neuro-diverse, award-winning, #1 international bestselling fantasy author who loves blurring the line between science and magic. She graduated from the University of Colorado after focusing on Psychology and Neuroscience. Since then, she has lived on three continents and has traveled to nearly fifty countries.

When she's not writing or reading, Rachel enjoys art of all kinds, riding her motorcycle, going to rock shows (both musical and mineralogical), Vulcanology (the lava kind as well as the pointy-eared variety), and being the voice behind Tana the Tiefling on the popular DnD podcast, *Of Dice and Friends*.

She lives in Colorado with her husband and a feisty umbrella cockatoo named Terrance (a.k.a "Jungle Chicken") who hangs out on her shoulder as she writes – whether invited or not.

Learn more at www.RachelRener.com.

Printed in Great Britain
by Amazon